DOUBLEDAY
CELEBRATES
100 YEARS OF
EXCELLENCE

ALSO BY PETER TASKER

SILENT THUNDER

THE JAPANESE

PETER TASKER

DOUBLEDAY

New York

London

Toronto

Sydney

Auckland

BUDDHA KISS

PUBLISHED BY DOUBLEDAY
a division of Bantam Doubleday Dell Publishing Group, Inc.
1540 Broadway, New York, New York 10036

DOUBLEDAY and the portrayal of an anchor with a dolphin
are trademarks of Doubleday, a division of
Bantam Doubleday Dell Publishing Group, Inc.

BOOK DESIGN BY DANA LEIGH TREGLIA

Library of Congress Cataloging-in-Publication Data
Tasker, Peter.
    Buddha kiss: a novel / Peter Tasker. — 1st ed.
        p.   cm.
    I. Title.
    PR6070.A65B83   1997
    823'.914—DC20   96-23427
                                         CIP

ISBN 0-385-48552-2
Printed in the United States of America
September 1997

10   9   8   7   6   5   4   3   2   1

First Edition

FOR LUCY

ONE

For a moment after the earthquake jolted him awake, Tamura thought he was in hell.

The bed on which he lay naked was rattling as if a madman were shaking it. The inside of his mouth was burning, his head throbbing so hard it made his eyes water. In the red glow of the lamp swaying above his head, a devil mask was staring straight down at him. It took him a moment to recognize the grimacing face as his own, reflected in the mirrored ceiling.

The vibrations intensified. On the other side of the room, something heavy thumped to the floor. Barely aware of what he was doing, Tamura slid off the sticky sheets and crawled under the table in the center of the room. There he lay flat on his belly, heart pounding, struggling to remember where he was and why.

The lamp's swings got wilder. There was a rumbling sound, then a violent jolt that seemed to wrench the whole building off the ground. After that came the stretched seconds of perfect stillness. Tamura held his breath and put his ear to the floor. All he could hear was the thumping of his heartbeat. The pendulum swings of the lamp grew shorter and shorter. He let out his breath in a rush. It was all over.

Tamura staggered to his feet. Gradually, his head was clearing. The quake had been a long one, but not powerful enough to do serious damage. He walked over to the door, switched on the light, and slumped down in a black leather armchair, head in his hands. His stomach heaved uncontrollably.

The wave of nausea helped to clear his head. What was going on? From his surroundings, it looked as if he had woken up in a low-grade love hotel. How he had got there he had no idea. He remembered the evening meal with his clients from Matsui Heavy Industries. He remembered drinking beer, sake, then whiskey. Then there had been a small nightclub where the girls were dressed up as flight attendants and nurses. But what had happened after that? Where had everyone else gone? He racked his brains, but it was no use. The memory had gone, and the effort of trying to restore it made his head pulse like an angry wound.

Tamura hauled himself upright, and pulled on his shirt and trousers. When he picked up his watch from the bedside table, he could hardly believe his eyes. It was five o'clock in the morning! It would already be light outside! He sat down heavily on the bed, his mind racing. How was he going to get home, change his clothes, and get to work on time? What was he going to tell his wife?

His thoughts were broken by a faint splashing sound coming from the bathroom. He cocked his head and listened more carefully. The sound came and went irregularly. It was the sound of water spilling.

Tamura rushed into the bathroom, then froze in midstride. There was water overflowing, sure enough. It was pouring out of the large, circular bathtub and running in thin waves over the tiled floor. But it wasn't that which had stopped him in his tracks. It was what the bathtub contained. There, gently undulating with the wash of the water, was the prone figure of a woman, arms floating at her sides, long hair streaming out around her oval face. She was staring at the ceiling and smiling. Her head was slowly bobbing up and down as if she were approving some secret message written there.

"Excuse me," said Tamura. His voice trembled as he tried to fight away what he already knew was the truth.

The only response was another slop of water onto the bathroom floor. He edged closer and turned the heavy gold tap to the off position. The woman's eyes remained fixed on the ceiling. Scarcely knowing what he was doing, Tamura lifted a limp hand out of the water. For a moment he stared curiously at the blue veins of the wrist, the lines of the palm, the unnaturally white fingers. Then, with a jerk of revulsion, he let it splash back into the water. There could be no mistake. She was stone cold.

He backed out of the bathroom, his stomach plunging as if he were on an elevator ride to the depths of the earth. He sat down carefully on the bed and pulled on his shoes and socks.

Tamura understood one thing immediately—it would be useless to try to explain his way out of the situation. Even if the police believed him, it would still be the end of everything. He couldn't hope to keep an incident like this quiet. There would be newspaper stories, special investigations in the weekly magazines, TV crews camped outside his home. His wife, his daughter, his colleagues at the bank . . . It would be impossible to find another job at his age. . . . He would have to leave Japan! His only chance was to get away now, without being seen. There was no time to lose.

He picked up his cuff links, stuffed his tie into his jacket pocket, then hesitated at the door. What about the fingerprints? They would be everywhere! Suddenly, he was calm, his mind occupied totally with what had to be done next. He grabbed a pillowcase from the bed, went back into the bathroom, and soaked it in the sink, not even pausing to glance at the figure stretched out in the bath. Then he went over the hard surfaces—the table, the arms of the chair, the door handles—scrubbing every inch with a furious energy.

What else? For a moment, he was gripped by despair. They would find him easily! There were all sorts of new techniques these days. Blood, sweat, strands of hair—they could analyze anything. The data was probably stored on government computers, logged in by doctors and nurses when you went for a checkup. . . .

He took a deep breath and fought down his panic. It was essential to stay calm. Hurriedly, he stripped the sheets from the bed, flung them into the shower stall, and turned on the hot water. This time he did look. No, it hadn't been some freak of his imagination. She was there, all right, still gazing at the same spot on the ceiling, that strange half-smile on her face.

He could do no more. There wasn't time. He wrapped his necktie around his hand, silently eased open the door handle, and stepped out

3

into the corridor. It was deserted. The only sign of activity was a moth fluttering around a flickering neon tube. His heart still banging like a drum, Tamura tiptoed down the corridor.

The elevator stayed on the ground floor for what seemed like an eternity. Perhaps it had been put out of action by the earthquake! Perhaps everyone would have to be evacuated by the fire department! Tamura stabbed the button frantically with his forefinger. Finally the light panel indicated the elevator was rising, with painful slowness. The doors hummed open, and Tamura thrust himself inside.

The relief that welled up inside him was intense but short-lived. With a sickening sensation, Tamura realized that the elevator was slowing down as it approached the fifth floor. The doors opened again, and Tamura leaned into the wall, shielding his face with a hand. Two people entered the elevator. Tamura smelled soap and perfume, felt the heat of their bodies. When the elevator began to descend, he allowed himself a glance out of the corner of his eye. He saw two young faces, flushed and nervous; two hands squeezing each other for reassurance. For an instant, Tamura felt indignant. They couldn't be more than seventeen years old—almost the same age as his own daughter! But he knew he was lucky. They were too embarrassed to raise their eyes from the carpet.

The young couple got out on the ground floor and walked quickly, still hand in hand, through the empty lobby. Tamura took the elevator down another floor to the parking lot. He knew there would be an inconspicuous, back-street entrance used by the majority of guests who came by car or taxi.

The parking lot was dimly lit, and silent. Sticking to the shadows, Tamura worked his way toward the metal ramp that led up to street level, from which daylight was already seeping down. He was almost there when he heard the slam of a car door. At the side of the ramp was a small mountain of black plastic trash bags. He dived into it just in time to avoid the glare of the headlights.

There was the hissing sound of air escaping, and then Tamura's nostrils were assailed by the worst smell he had ever experienced—a nauseous blend of putrid fish and burned leather that had him coughing and gagging.

Thirty yards away, an engine roared into life. Eyes swimming, Tamura watched the headlights circling around toward the ramp. The glare grew brighter, and he spread himself flat on the heap of bags, pressing his face down into the plastic. As he did so, he felt something scrabbling under the weight of his belly, something lithe and muscular. It had to be a rat. Tamura closed his eyes and held his breath. The engine revved sharply and he heard the ramp buckle under the weight of the car. When he looked up, the taillights were disappearing into the street above. Faint with the power of the stench, he slid off the heap of bags. The rat scurried away and buried itself deep in the heart of the trash.

Tamura slumped against the wall, wanting to be sure that the car had really gone. He was a mess. The top two buttons of his shirt and a cuff link were missing, lost somewhere among the trash. There were dark stains on his jacket, and his hair was clotted with a cold, sticky liquid. Worse, that vile stench was everywhere—in his clothes, on his hands, in the air that he was sucking into his lungs. He turned and raced up the ramp, his heels ringing against the metal.

Outside, the pink wash of dawn was already fading. Tamura found himself in a winding street of small shops and dingy restaurants. He glanced cautiously around. To his left were a couple of parked vans and a motorbike, its silver trim flashing in the slanting rays of the sun. To his right, a huge crow with a beak like a steel spike was regarding him balefully from its perch on a beer crate. Tamura glanced at his watch. It was already six o'clock!

"Graaah!" screeched the crow, and shook a gleaming black wing. "Graaah, graaah!"

It was no good. He would never get away with it. Didn't the Japanese police have the highest arrest rate in the world? That was a fact that used to make him proud. Now it made his blood run cold.

"Graaah, graaah, graaah!"

The crow's screech had a scornful tone to it. Tamura stuffed his hands deep into his trouser pockets and started walking rapidly to the right.

Once he had put a couple of blocks between himself and the hotel, he began to feel calmer. He knew the district vaguely, a semiresidential part of Meguro ward. The back streets were still empty and would probably stay that way until the deliverymen and early schoolkids appeared. That shouldn't be for another half an hour, at least.

He stuffed his stench-ridden jacket into a trash bin out for collection, then bought a can of mineral water from a vending machine and washed his face and hair in it. That made him feel a bit more human, though the throbbing in his head was still there. A few hundred yards farther down the street, he found a rusty bicycle leaning against a boarded-up noodle stand. There was no chain or lock. He glanced around. All was quiet, except for the croaking of the crows. In an instant, he had mounted it and was pedaling hard for Shinjuku.

He abandoned the bicycle in a clump of broken bikes outside the Seikyu department store. Nearby there was a twenty-four-hour sauna patronized mainly by low-grade yakuza and hungover salarymen who had missed the last train home. He sat steaming for twenty minutes, then washed and shaved. When he left, it was six-thirty—exactly the time that the alarm clock on his bedside table went off every morning. Soon his wife would be waking too, and wondering what had happened.

He called her from a pay phone in the lobby of the sauna. Mentally, he had already rehearsed the story several times—that he had been called to a late-night strategy meeting—but it didn't come out at all smoothly. His voice quavered and he stumbled over his words. That shocked him. If he couldn't lie to his own wife, what chance would he have with the police? Luckily, she didn't ask any questions. As usual, she showed no interest in his work.

He had a "morning set" breakfast in a coffee bar, then spent forty-five minutes in a pachinko parlor, losing himself in the rush of the silver balls. He emerged into the streaming crowd of commuters feeling soothed, almost light-headed. At eight-thirty, he rang the office and informed the receptionist that he would be an hour late. That would give him time to prepare himself properly for the day ahead.

At ten o'clock, Deputy Branch Manager Tamura marched briskly into the Shinjuku branch of the Commercial Bank of Japan, one of the busiest branches of the oldest of Japan's three long-term-credit banks. Apart from the fact that he was equipped with a smart new suit and tie, there was nothing remarkable about his appearance or behavior. He grunted his usual brusque greeting to the receptionist, nodded curtly at a couple of new graduates, then sat down at his desk and started going through the day's mail.

Throughout the morning, Tamura took calls, dictated letters, and barked instructions at his subordinates in just the same way as ever. The only time that he acted at all strangely was after a comment of his secretary.

"That earthquake was scary, wasn't it!" she said. "It must have woken up the whole city."

Tamura looked up from his papers, his face suddenly pale. For a moment, he sat there staring at her as if he had just seen a ghost. His mouth moved up and down, but no sound emerged.

"That big earthquake last night. Didn't you feel it?"

"Of course," he replied finally, in a voice that was almost a whisper. "I felt it strongly."

Tamura's secretary left the room marveling at the fact that her boss, a Tokyo man born and bred, could be so fazed by a quake of magnitude five. Her respect for him, she told her friends later, had taken quite a blow.

Tamura took his lunch break twenty minutes earlier than usual, having canceled a meeting with the leader of the personnel section. He went alone to a noodle restaurant several blocks away where he knew he wouldn't be recognized. As he had expected, he was the first customer of the day. The midday tide of shirtsleeved salarymen had yet to issue forth from Shinjuku's towering office blocks.

Ignoring the welcoming shouts of the waiters, he took a seat beside the TV set and immediately switched the channel to *TV Tokyo*. That earned a frown from the cook, who had been watching a samurai drama through the steam of the noodles. Tamura didn't notice. For the next fifteen minutes, he was oblivious to everything but the news program on the TV.

He didn't know what to expect. Would they describe how she had died? Would they appeal for witnesses? Was it possible that they would name him, even? He dreaded seeing his own face on the screen, with his own name underneath it in black characters. He could almost hear the urgent tones of the newscaster: "This man is wanted by the police for inquiries." No, it wasn't possible. Not yet, anyway. There hadn't been time. Tamura sat bolt upright in his seat, eyes glued to the screen, barely tasting the noodles that he was mechanically shoveling into his mouth.

But there was nothing. Not even a brief comment among the roundup of traffic accidents and fires at the end of the program. Tamura returned to the office feeling strangely unsatisfied.

At four o'clock, he told his secretary that he had a brief unscheduled meeting with a client and left the office again. This time, he took a taxi to Shinjuku station and bought three different evening papers at a newsstand. Not daring to read in the open air, he folded them under his arm and went into a nearby coffee bar. Only after the waiter had brought him a hot face towel and taken his order did he unfold the *Nichijo Shimbun* and lay it flat on the table. Most of the accident and crime stories were on the next-to-last page. He opened the paper carefully and began to scan through the headlines.

One of them seemed to jump off the page and hit him in the eye. "Mysterious death of woman in hotel"—there it was! Tamura's heart was pounding as he read on.

"The Tokyo Police Department is today investigating the death of an unidentified woman whose body was found in a city hotel early this morning. The woman is described as being between thirty and thirty-five years of age, one hundred and fifty centimeters tall, with short hair . . ." Short hair! Impossible! Tamura's eyes raced forward. "According to the manager of the Delon Hotel in Adachi ward . . ." Adachi ward! That was on the other side of Tokyo! The incident couldn't be anything to do with him at all. Tamura felt a surge of relief, swiftly followed by irritation and then greater tension than before.

The only other incidents of the day were a couple of suicides, a helicopter crash, and a scandal over leaked exam questions. He checked the other two papers. Both of them carried the Adachi ward story in almost the same words as the *Nichijo,* but nothing else of that sort. Suddenly, it occurred to him the police might have imposed a news blackout. He had heard of such things happening when investigations were reaching a crucial stage. That could mean that the police were hot on his trail already! Tamura glanced nervously around the coffee bar. He had an urgent desire to rush out and lose himself in the crowd of shoppers.

Back at the office, Tamura glanced at the phone message on his desk and winced. That evening he had to entertain two department chiefs from Mitsutomo Real Estate. The president of Mitsutomo was an ex-CBJ man whom the bank had drafted to cement relations with the Mitsutomo group. It was impossible to cancel at this stage.

Tamura was uncharacteristically subdued for most of the evening. He ate little and seemed absentminded and listless. In fact, he didn't look at all well. The Mitsutomo people were not surprised when, at ten o'clock, Tamura left them in the hands of one of his subordinates and went home, pleading a bad cold.

Once home, Tamura went through a brief conversational ritual with his wife, both of them having lost interest in the details of the other's life long ago, then slumped in front of the TV. As usual, his wife went to bed first and read magazines. Tamura watched the news bulletins on three different channels, then tried the radio. It was the same as before. There was nothing about the incident at all.

By the time he went to bed, he was mentally and physically exhausted. The memories of all that had happened were starting to blur.

Eyes closed, he listened to the sound of the clock ticking. Here he was in the house where he had been living for twelve years, lying in bed next to the woman he had been married to for the past twenty years. Everything seemed so normal. It couldn't have happened to him. It must have been a dream, a movie, something that had happened to someone else. Nothing ever happened to him. His life was good and safe and dull. . . .

When the alarm awoke him at six-thirty, he felt totally refreshed. Over his usual breakfast of squid, banana, and miso soup, he thought through his schedule for the day ahead. Mitsutomo Real Estate—he would apologize in person and invite them out again. That relationship had to be nurtured at all costs. Out of the corner of his eye, Tamura monitored the morning news bulletin. Somehow, he knew in advance that there would be nothing. When his premonition was confirmed, he felt little surprise.

It was the same with the morning newspaper that he read on the train, and with the midday news bulletin that he watched in the noodle shop. It was the same with the evening paper, the late-night TV news, and the next day's papers. By the weekend, Tamura was following the news with only casual attention. Something had happened. He didn't know what, but there was no point in worrying about it. Much better to dismiss the whole business from his mind and concentrate on living from day to day. On Saturday, he took his daughter to a baseball game. On Sunday, he made love to his wife for the first time in six months. In the course of both events, he quite spontaneously came up with fresh ideas on how to improve business relations with Mitsutomo Real Estate.

When Tamura did glance through the papers, he scanned rapidly for the word "hotel." That was why he didn't even register a short paragraph that appeared in Monday's paper under the headline "Girl's body washed up in Tokyo Bay."

"The drowned body of a 23-year-old woman, identified as Yuriko Sano of Koto ward, was found yesterday evening by a construction crew working on the Harumi flood wall. Police estimate that the body had been in the water for about five days. Miss Sano had been out of contact with her family for the past three weeks. Her father expressed shock and great sadness at the family's loss . . ."

Tamura's eyes moved rapidly down the column, then went on to the sports page.

TWO

Funerals were events in which Mori generally tried to avoid participating in any capacity. He was attending one today only because Sano had helped him out years ago when he had been a struggling young detective. Now he was a struggling middle-aged detective, and he needed all the contacts he could lay his hands on.

He arrived ten minutes late. The old Honda banked sharply as he swerved into the parking lot, shooting a spray of gravel into a flock of portly pigeons. Dismounting before the motor had whirred to a halt, Mori pulled off his battered helmet, slapped the creases out of his raincoat, then hurried toward the temple gate.

The building on the other side was an eye-grabber. A great, bulging discus of gleaming white, it looked less like a place of devotion than a concrete UFO that had touched down in the midst of suburban Tokyo. The architect had clearly not been afraid to experiment. There was a touch of the Heian era in the long swooping eaves, a touch of neoclassicism in the fluted pillars that held them up, and plenty of *manga* cartoon in the statues of grimacing, demon-stomping deities that ringed the inner courtyard. The sect that owned the place was one of the most successful of the new religions that had grown up in the chaos of the postwar years. It was despised by the old Buddhist sects, continually attacked in the weekly magazines, and monstrously rich and influential.

Mori strode briskly across the central courtyard, scattering the pigeons as he went. Luckily, the service had not started yet. The last few guests were still filing up the huge stone staircase that led to the main hall. As Mori approached, he noticed a small puff of black smoke hanging in the air above the temple building. A tape-recorded voice was chanting sutras in a high-pitched monotone that cut through his thoughts like a saw. The air was heavy with the sweet, choking smell of incense.

At the top of the stairs, Mori took his place in the line of guests waiting to be greeted by Sano and his wife. They were all elegantly attired: the women in pleated black dresses, crepe sleeves, and odd-shaped hats; the men in silk ties and immaculate dark suits. Limbs were discreetly decorated with diamonds, pearls, and expensive European watches. Mori glanced down uneasily at his own outfit: the by now seriously off-white Burberry raincoat, the shirt with the indelible soy-sauce stain on the cuff; the ten-year-old suit that he also used for weddings and other formal occasions. It hadn't seen service since he had infiltrated a dentistry conference in Sendai two years before. The smell of mothballs was quite noticeable, even to himself.

The line shuffled forward, giving Mori his first glimpse of his old friend. It came as quite a shock. Sano's face was pinched and exhausted. He looked a good decade older than his fifty years. Mori was struck by something that he had never noticed before in all their years of acquaintance—Sano was about an inch shorter than his wife.

They were standing to the left of the altar, a gilded alcove hung with embroidered silk drapes and garlands of roses. In the middle was a trestle table on which, surrounded by bunches of incense sticks, stood a black-edged photograph of Yuriko. From the uniform that she was wearing and her solemn, doe-eyed expression, Mori guessed that it had been taken in her middle-school days.

It was Mori's turn to make the formal greeting. He stepped forward and bowed.

"My humblest condolences."

"Sincere gratitude for honoring us with your presence." Sano bowed stiffly in return, his bloodshot eyes registering not the slightest flicker of recognition. Mori took a pace forward and repeated the exchange with Mrs. Sano.

Mori was the last in line. After the greeting had been completed, he joined the other guests on the right side of the altar. The tall, baldheaded priest who was officiating led the bereaved couple to their places on the left, then squatted down on a sumptuously embroidered cushion. Eyes squeezed shut behind his steel-framed spectacles, fingers clacking through his onyx prayer beads, he began to chant in a sonorous monotone that filled the room.

Mori looked across at Sano. How long was it since he had first seen that generous, uncomplicated face, quite a bit wider than it was long? It must have been twenty years ago. He had started going to Sano's place because the noodles were red hot, just the way he liked them, because it was open all hours, and because it was phenomenally cheap. In those days, the regular customers were an interesting bunch—nightstall operators, fortune-tellers, girls from the pink salons taking a break mid-shift, karate guys from the dojo across the street. Mori would often drop in before midnight and just sit there listening to the conversation swirling around him.

Over the years, Mori did Sano a few favors, mainly relating to negotiations with the local yakuza groups. He got a few back in return. Whenever Sano heard any of his customers discussing the kind of problem that needed some discreet research, he would put in a good word for Mori, the only private investigator in Tokyo with the brains to get into one of the six great universities. That Mori had also been stupid enough to get thrown out for radical activism, thereby disqualifying himself from any conventional job for the rest of his life, was a fact that Sano chose not to stress in his recommendation. There was always a box of Mori's business cards in a drawer behind the bar, ready to be handed out with the bill.

And then the area started to change. By the early eighties, land prices were soaring, and the residents and local tradespeople were selling out. The big developers were putting up office blocks, luxury condos, weird cake-frosting buildings that were nothing but boutiques and fancy restaurants top to bottom. At first, they asked Sano nicely. Then they asked him not so nicely. Then they started telling him. It didn't matter. The more the real estate people blustered and intimidated, the more determined he became. The man was as stubborn as a stone.

Mori recalled Yuriko as she was in the memorial photograph—the quiet schoolgirl who sat behind the counter tending the steaming cauldron of noodles. Then, a few years later, as an attractive seventeen-year-old with a strong natural sexuality that she was starting to flex like a muscle. The customers liked her smile, the brush of her hair as she poured the beer into their outstretched glasses. And she enjoyed the jokes and flattering comments.

But between father and daughter, things weren't so smooth. There were quarrels about clothes, holiday jobs, staying out late—the usual stuff. Sano found out about a boyfriend in a motorbike gang and asked Mori to warn the kid off. Mori had refused: as he explained, it would have been counterproductive. Anyway, there was no chance of Yuriko turning into a hoodlum. If anything, she was too sincere, too naive. Sano had tried to handle it himself, and ended up with a split lip and a daughter who wouldn't talk to him for months.

From about that time, Mori started dropping by less often. For one thing, Sano kept raising his prices. And it may have been Mori's imagination, but the noodle broth didn't seem to have quite the same fire as it used to. For another, Mori was getting more discriminating about the kinds of jobs that he was willing to take. Scribbling down license plates in love-hotel parking lots, kneeling in the shrubbery of Shinjuku Park with an infrared camera slung around his neck, sifting credit-card slips from trash cans—the work that Sano's customers wanted done was low-margin, low-potential stuff. Mori was aiming higher.

By the late eighties, the Japanese economy was cooking like Sano's cauldron of noodles. Suddenly, lots of people had lots of new money and lots of new problems. That meant big fees, big expenses. Prewedding inquiries soon became Mori's most lucrative line of business. An early success in rooting out a grandparent with a rare blood disease, thereby stopping a wedding from going ahead in the nick of time, had established his reputation with a group of newly wealthy families. Ten years before, they would have let something like that pass, forever to remain unmentionable and unmentioned.

Missing person searches were almost as profitable. Mori's most memorable case involved tracing the young wife of an insurance company executive to a scuba-diving club in Okinawa. That job brought with it a week of fieldwork in a beachfront chalet, all expenses paid. It was a simple enough task to locate her on the first day. The diving instructor accepted a modest payoff for disappearing for the duration, and the woman was happy to spend an extra few days in Mori's company, improving her tan and sipping tropical drinks under the palm trees.

Not long after, Mori happened to be driving through Shinjuku in a Mercedes coupé that a doctor's wife had lent him. He glanced over at Sano's place as he passed, and noticed something strange: the sign was gone from the roof. He pulled in at once, letting the taxi he was following disappear out of sight—it was obvious where the guy was going anyway.

Sano looked embarrassed when he saw Mori. The way he explained it, some people from Mitsutomo Real Estate had made him an offer that he would have been an idiot to refuse. The place would be closing down in a week's time.

Mori was there on the last night. After the other customers had gone, Sano and Mori sat down together and drank the place dry. Sano said he had a confession to make. He had only been sticking out for the highest price, right from the start. That stuff about not selling because of some weird sense of pride—that had all been made up by the press. Really, he was glad to be going. The area had changed too much. He needed the rest. The words were spoken with plenty of conviction, but somehow Mori doubted them. He looked into that thickset face, red and damp with sweat. It was the face of a man who loved making food for people.

Sano got out right at the top of the real estate boom. He bought himself a German car, a few Italian suits, and stuck the rest of the money in tax-free debentures. Meanwhile the six-story building that Mitsutomo put up stayed half-empty for years. Sano had once told Mori that the secret of cooking was timing—when to take the broth up to boil, when to toss in the vegetables, when to stir in the spices. Well, in all his career as master of a noodle bar, he never showed better timing than he did in making his exit.

That was several years ago. Mori had heard nothing of Sano since then. Looking across the temple floor, he had to remind himself that it was the same man standing there, head bowed, thin gray hair neatly parted. Mori had never seen Sano wearing a suit before. In fact, he had never seen him out of his big white apron and cook's headband. It was like meeting a retired sumo wrestler, now slimmed down to normal size, topknot replaced by a normal haircut. The ghost of the familiar image was still there in his brain, struggling with the diminished reality.

After a while the priest got to his feet and disappeared through a small door behind the main altar. A voice from a loudspeaker announced that all guests should follow him down to the crematorium. Sano led the way through the door and down the narrow staircase behind.

The room at the bottom of the steps was white walled and bare, lit by painfully bright neon tubes. The air was much warmer, thick with the incense that rose in plumes from a large bronze lotus in the center of the room. The group took their places on rows of stone benches at the back.

Next to the door was an elevated platform on which stood a seat and lectern, all made of the same stone as the benches. Mori had noticed as he passed that the inset in the lectern was a small control panel, consisting of two video screens, a keyboard, and several rows of switches. Below the platform was a stone table on which stood a circular tray and a pair of ivory chopsticks.

As if in a trance, the bald priest walked slowly over to the platform, his long silk robe rustling against the tiled floor. He mounted the steps in strange jerky movements, then took his place at the seat. After a few moments of silence, he began to chant, much faster than before. It looked as if his eyes were shut, but Mori could see his fingers moving busily across the control panel.

From somewhere beyond the front wall, there was a sound like a muffled explosion, then the groan of heavy machinery. A panel in the wall opened up and there was a gust of intense heat that died away almost as soon as it was felt. At a gesture from the priest, everyone stood up. Mori noted that the area of floor in front of the panel was crisscrossed with strips of metal tape. One strip stretched farther, leading past the lotus-shaped incense blower all the way to the stone table.

There was a high-pitched electronic hum, and a strange-looking object slowly nosed through the opening in the wall. It was a small, three-wheeled vehicle, something like an unmanned golf cart. Where the seats would be on a golf cart was a square palette holding a heavy iron bowl. It edged into the room, then paused, as if uncertain what to do next. The priest's fingers flicked expertly over the keyboard. The vehicle hummed forward along the metal strip, finally coming to a halt in front of the stone table. The surface of the table was at exactly the same height as the palette, and there was barely an inch of space between them.

15

The priest's voice was racing ahead now, as if he were trying to break some kind of speed record. Sano stepped forward. He picked up the chopsticks and dipped them into the bowl. From the bed of gray ash, he lifted out what looked like a shard of white porcelain and placed it delicately on the tray on the table. He repeated this several more times, half-covering the tray with the fragments. In their varying shapes and sizes, they were scarcely recognizable for what they were—pieces of human bone.

Sano's wife was next, then the other close relatives and friends. When Mori's turn came, there was hardly anything left. After sifting through the fine flakes of ash for several seconds, at last he located something hard and white. With infinite care, he fished out a small rectangular shape and laid it on the tray. It was, he realized, the bottom section of a tooth. That broad smile of Yuriko's flashed through his mind.

When the ceremony was over, the guests congregated in the central courtyard. Everyone seemed filled with an odd sense of relief. They greeted one another in hearty tones, and swapped polite gossip in slightly louder voices than they needed. Sano seemed fairly composed as he went from group to group, thanking them all for attending. When he came to Mori, he took him by the elbow and pulled him aside.

"I need to talk," he murmured under his breath. "Can I call you this evening?"

"Talk? About what?"

"A job for you. It'll be good money, I promise."

Mori looked at Sano. From the man's tight expression, he had a fair idea what kind of job he had in mind.

"I'll be around," he answered. "You've got my number?"

"Sure," said Sano. "I've still got three boxes of your business cards in my desk at home."

Mori slapped him on the shoulder and made for the temple gate. It was bad luck to hang around this kind of event too long.

Straddling the Honda, Mori adjusted his helmet. He gunned the motor, and a group of pigeons flapped out of his way. As he eased past the temple gate, he glanced inside. The guests were still there, chatting in the courtyard. The great concrete oyster behind them was gleaming in the sunshine. And above the flowing line of its roof, a new ball of black smoke was hanging in the air.

———

Mori got back to his office at four o'clock. It was the last working day of the month, so the traffic was pretty heavy all the way through to Shin-juku, despite the recession.

He dismounted from the Honda in front of a thin, rickety-looking building of six storys. Its neighbor on the left side was a public bath-house that Mori sometimes used when he needed just to soak and think. On the other side was a cheap business hotel. This was separated from Mori's building by a six-inch gap that was highly popular with roaches, rats, and drunken salarymen who couldn't hold out until the station toilet.

Mori had recently become the building's oldest tenant. The porno emporium that used to occupy the ground floor had closed down after the old man who ran it had a heart attack. Its place was now occupied by the Suki-yaki Heaven, a restaurant where the specialty of the house involved the waitresses, mostly students from a local design college, spending the entire meal under the table.

On the floor above was an import-export company that seemed to be permanently closed for business. Mori never saw anyone going in or out. Every so often, though, the advertisements stuck to the glass panel above the door would change. Mori would read a little bit each time that he clumped past on his way to the sixth floor.

IMPROVE MALE HEALTH AND LIVE LONGER—TRY PROFESSOR TURTLE'S ESSENCE OF GIANT LEATHER-BACKED TURTLE

DID YOU KNOW THAT THE GIANT LEATHER-BACKED TURTLE CAN LIVE 120 YEARS? DID YOU KNOW THAT THE GIANT LEATHER-BACKED TURTLE CAN MAINTAIN A STATE OF SEXUAL AROUSAL FOR UP TO 8 DAYS? THE GIANT LEATHER-BACKED TURTLE IS TRULY THE MARVEL OF THE OCEANS!

PROFESSOR TURTLE HAS BEEN STUDYING THE GIANT LEATHER-BACKED TURTLE SINCE HE WAS MAROONED OFF NEW GUINEA IN THE PACIFIC WAR. HIS ESSENCE OF GIANT LEATHER-BACKED TURTLE IS AVAILABLE IN POWDER, PILL, OR LIQUID FORM. THE PRO-FESSOR GUARANTEES THAT EACH SET CONTAINS THE ESSENCE OF FIVE TURTLES.

Before the turtles, there had been a baldness cure from China, and before that a specially engineered corset that could turn a fat man into a thin man. After eight years in the building, Mori had never met the owner of the company.

On the third floor were a couple of young yakuza who used an English-language school as a front for small-time corporate extortion. And on the top floor was a metal door of battleship gray that had attached to it a plastic plate that read:

KAZUO MORI—ECONOMIC AND SOCIAL RESEARCH SERVICES.
PLEASE RING THE BELL AND SPEAK CLEARLY INTO THE INTERCOM.

It wasn't much, but it was all he could afford. Not long ago he had been planning to move out to something better. He had had visions of a large, well-furnished office with a fine view of the city. Instead of tramping up a metal staircase open to the elements, he would be smoothly transported in an elevator. Instead of having to squat down in a tiny toilet that often failed to flush, he would have a large washroom with hot water and automatic hand-driers. It would be someplace where he could receive the fussiest clients without embarrassment.

That dream had faded a couple of years ago, along with many others. When it came to managing his own personal affairs, Mori had demonstrated a sense of timing that was the exact opposite of Sano's. Fed up with the long train ride to the office, he had finally moved out of his apartment in Yokohama and bought a place in Nerima ward. That had cost him ten million yen down, pretty well all his savings, and a twenty-year loan for another thirty million. These days, according to what he read in the papers, he would be lucky to get thirty million for the place. The situation was so bad that he couldn't bear to look at the fliers that desperate real estate brokers were stuffing in mailboxes.

When the economy went off the boil, the good jobs stopped coming so frequently. There was more competition around too, and the clients were getting more difficult about the fees they were willing to pay. When you got down to it, the services of a private investigator were a luxury, not a necessity. In most cases, people could do without them if they made up their minds.

Mori sat down heavily on his battered leather sofa, drawing a groan from the springs and a hiss from a split in the cushion. He lit a Seven Stars and picked up the evening edition of the *Gendai Shimbun*. The picture on the center of the front page showed a bull-necked middle-aged man stepping out of a black limousine. He was glowering directly at the camera.

"Ogawa Establishes New Political Grouping," announced the headline in especially large characters.

Mori quickly ran his eyes down the accompanying columns of newsprint, barely taking in the main points. Ogawa, he remembered, was the ambitious lieutenant of the old Kaneshita faction of the Liberal Democratic Party. The Kaneshita faction had controlled Japanese politics since the mid-sixties, but then there had been a couple of big financial scandals and the faction had broken up into several splinter groups. What the points of difference were between them, Mori had no idea. Anyway, it seemed that Ogawa had finally decided to set up his own faction. Mori looked more closely at the face in the photograph—the small, heavy-lidded eyes, the taut muscles of the jaw, the thick lips compressed in an expression of angry defiance. It was the face of a man who knew what he wanted and would not stand for anyone getting in the way. In fact, recalled Mori, the newspaper commentators had said that it was Ogawa's disrespect for consensus that had caused the split in the LDP in the first place.

These political struggles were getting too confusing. In search of something simpler and more pleasant to follow, Mori turned to the back of the paper and ran through the baseball scores. Here was some straightforward good news. The Gendai Giants had lost again to the Porpoises in a preseason match. Mori was not a Porpoise's fan, but he had been anti-Giants for as long as he could remember.

His moment of satisfaction was ended by the ring of the phone. Mori picked up the receiver, half-expecting to hear Sano. But the voice at the other end was unfamiliar and brusquely formal.

"Mori-san, this is Kadota of the New Japan Research Bureau. I am the head of our East Shinjuku branch. Perhaps you have heard of our company?"

"I can't say I have."

"Well, I am sure that you will be hearing of us many times in the future. We opened up this branch office just last week. We are a nationwide organization, with a head office in Osaka. Our aim is to offer our clients high-quality, fully integrated investigation services using the most modern systems and techniques."

Kadota paused, waiting for a response. Mori crushed out his Seven Stars in the ashtray. He said nothing.

"I am calling you because it is our company's policy to make contact with all the small-scale local operators in each area before we commence full operations. . . ."

"Small-scale local operators!" Mori's fingers tightened around the receiver.

"We consider it a professional courtesy," Kadota went on. "We should have a meeting as soon as possible. There are several matters which I am sure that it would be to your benefit to discuss quite frankly."

"To my benefit?" Mori could not keep the edge of sarcasm out of his voice.

"Certainly, Mori-san. New Japan Research is aiming to be number one in this area. We want you to understand our strategy quite clearly. So there are no mistakes. You see?" Kadota spoke emphatically, leaving gaps between phrases as if he were talking to a child.

"If I didn't know better," said Mori, "I'd be thinking that you're trying to threaten me. But I do know better. Someone from a fine organization like yours wouldn't make a simple mistake like that, would he?"

Kadota was silent for a moment. When he spoke again, his tone was icy cold.

"First of all, we offer cooperation, Mori-san," he said. "But I can assure you that New Japan is fully competitive in all areas."

"So am I," said Mori, and slammed down the receiver with more force than he intended.

Immediately, the phone started ringing again. Mori snatched up the receiver halfway through the first ring, a good strong line of abuse ready on his lips. This time, though, it really was Sano, and he sounded in a hurry. Mori agreed to meet him two hours later at a jazz coffee bar close to Shinjuku station.

Shinjuku at eight o'clock in the evening. The gray geometry of the daytime world has dissolved. In its place is a winking, shimmering virtual city made up of hoops of color, honeycombs of light, labyrinths of signs. The neon messages twist and fizz and scroll across your retina. The noise of voices is everywhere, blurring into a single dull roar, like the roar of the traffic. The crowds are numberless, ceaseless. They flow through the streets like a thick dark liquid.

Mori sat in the window of the coffee bar listening to a funky Horace Silver piece and watching the faces stream by on the other side of the glass. This was one of the few places in Shinjuku that hadn't changed much since his student days a quarter of a century ago. They still played the same kind of music from the same gigantic hi-fi system. The walls were still decorated with the owner's favorite LP covers—Miles clutching his horn, Sonny Rollins dressed up as a cowboy, Monk hunched at his piano like a man at prayer. The place even had the same smell, a mixture of old carpet and Kilimanjaro coffee fresh from the mill.

Once upon a time, this coffee shop had been a popular meeting place for student radicals planning the next stage of the revolution. Back then, everything had seemed so new and daring and full of possibilities—the music, the girls in their miniskirts and berets, the heated debates about ideology. These days, though, the place was strictly nostalgia. The customers were mostly middle-aged salarymen, mostly on their own. They sat and smoked and gazed into their coffee cups.

To the young Mori, it had seemed that Shinjuku was the center of a great turbulence, a sudden release of energy that could never again be contained. It had its source in the hearts of the young, and it was flowing through the entire nation. All traditions and taboos and established systems would be swept away—in politics, education, and sexual morality. Especially sexual morality. In the eyes of the serious but fun-loving young law student, Shinjuku was San Francisco, Paris, and swinging London all rolled into one.

The memories were still fresh. That department store on the corner—pitched battles with the riot police had taken place just outside it. Shinjuku station, where every day hundreds of thousands of salarymen pour out of the automatic wickets like grains of rice from a threshing machine—folk-rock groups had given impromptu concerts right there in the middle of the main plaza. That bookshop across the street, where dozens of office girls in designer clothes were standing waiting for their dates—some of Mori's friends had taught themselves French and Italian just so that they could spend hours among the stacks browsing through the latest books of revolutionary theory. Unforgettable times. There had been tear gas, homemade bombs, anger, fear, and passion. When Mori looked back now, it seemed like a foreign land.

There had been no luxury hotels in those days; no thin, windowless structures that contained nothing but stacks of parked cars; no giant video screens showing ads and movie clips all day long until you see them even when you close your eyes. There hadn't been any tall buildings either. Now there was a clump of steel-and-glass towers that dwarfed

21

everything around them. And they in turn were dwarfed by the new Tokyo city hall, a Gothic monstrosity that looked like a skyscraper from a science-fiction comic book. Shinjuku had changed beyond recognition. There wasn't much left, except for the jazz and the coffee.

Mori snapped out of his reverie. Sano was standing at the side of the table, apologizing for being late. The black suit was gone, replaced by corduroy trousers and an expensive-looking sports jacket, but there was the same tension and tiredness in his face as before.

Sano sat down, wiped his forehead on the hot flannel that the waiter brought, then ordered a coffee. After a few muttered courtesies, he got straight to the point.

"It's all wrong, Mori-san," he said. "The whole thing doesn't make any sense at all."

"You have my sympathies," said Mori carefully. "It must have come as a terrible shock."

Sano shook his head. "Last time I saw her she was so contented," he said. "I'd never seen her looking so fit and relaxed."

"When was that?"

"Just three weeks ago. She didn't seem to have a care in the world. You know, we've had our problems in the past. . . ." Sano's face darkened.

"Yes," prompted Mori.

"But that's long ago now. Since she moved out, everything's been fine. She always telephoned twice a week, came to see us once a month on Sunday evening . . ."

Sano didn't finish the sentence. Mori guessed that he was thinking about what Sunday evenings were going to be like from now on.

"You said it didn't make sense. Is there anything that seems particularly strange to you?"

"Any suspicious feature, you mean? No, there's nothing like that, I'm afraid."

"What have the police said?"

"Nothing, really. There's no evidence of violence or anything. Of course, she was in the water for four days. . . ." Sano fell silent again.

"It'll be difficult for them," said Mori. "Unless they find a witness, of course. If that doesn't happen, they'll probably classify it as an accident."

"An accident?" Sano looked startled.

"It happens," said Mori in a matter-of-fact tone. "People who've drunk a bit too much can fall off bridges or boats or piers. Sometimes there's a bit of horseplay, a bet or something, and the others are too scared to come forward."

"She hardly drank at all," said Sano with some force. "And she wouldn't be involved in any stupid bet!"

"Just an example," said Mori mildly. Fathers were not usually the best people to ask about young women's tastes in fun and games.

"I don't believe it was an accident," said Sano, rapping the tabletop with his knuckles and rattling the coffee cups.

"You don't?" said Mori, glancing nervously at the other guests. No one was paying any attention. The Horace Silver number had been followed by a swooping Coltrane solo loud enough to drown out even Sano's raised voice.

"And it wasn't suicide either!"

Mori said nothing. He lit a new Seven Stars and gazed at Sano through a screen of blue smoke.

"Mori-san, I need your help. I have to know."

That last was a phrase that Mori had heard many times in his career. And very rarely had the knowledge, once secured, provided any satisfaction whatsoever.

"Fine," he said at last. "But don't get your hopes up too high. I can't promise anything. The police have probably covered most of the angles already."

"Maybe my hopes are fairly high," said Sano, "but that's because I remember what you can do."

That's pure flattery, thought Mori. And it works every time.

For the next hour, the two men sat locked in conversation. Coltrane was followed by Dave Brubeck, Brubeck by Art Blakey. The ashtray gradually filled up with stubs. Mori scribbled down Sano's responses to his questions in a brand-new notebook he had bought expressly for the purpose.

THREE

Tamura was woken by the sound of water spilling onto the floor. He wanted to put the pillow over his head and go back to sleep, but somehow he couldn't. He felt drawn toward the bathroom as if by a magnetic force. He slid off the bed, moved slowly toward the door, and pushed it open. At first he didn't dare look directly at the bath. He shot a glance in the mirror, hoping beyond hope that she wouldn't be there. But she was, just as he had known she would be, long hair floating loose, sightless eyes gazing at the ceiling, head bobbing in silent agreement.

Why didn't he turn and run, as he wanted to? He didn't know. Instead, he tiptoed across the bathroom floor and stared down into her face, so calm, so solemn. He got to his knees on the wet floor and picked her wrist out of the water, knowing as he did so that he was wasting his time. There was no pulse. Her arm fell back with a splash.

Sickened with despair, Tamura got to his feet. He

was about to hurry back to the bedroom and dress when he noticed a slight change in the shape of her mouth. Was it possible? Had the muscles of her face moved a little? He bent down again and scrutinized her face. Yes, it was true! She was trying to open her mouth! Now there was a slight noise. She was actually trying to say something!

"It wasn't me," said Tamura desperately. "I didn't do this to you. Please tell everybody that I am innocent."

Her lips parted, and there was a croaking sound. Tamura moved his head closer. What was it she was trying to say?

And then it happened. Her arm shot out of the water and wrapped itself around his neck. Suddenly Tamura couldn't hold his balance. He was falling into the bath. The girl's arm was twisting and pulling with incredible power, dragging him down . . . Water covered his eyes and filled his nose and mouth. He tried to thrash his legs, but somehow he was paralyzed. She was looking down at him now, a smile of triumph on her face. She was saying something quite clearly. She was saying, "Daddy, Daddy . . ."

Tamura sat bolt upright in his bed, heart pumping. His daughter was standing by the side of the bed, gazing at him in consternation.

25

"Papa, are you all right? Why are you making all that noise?"

"What noise?" muttered Tamura, passing a hand across his sweaty brow. Alongside, his wife was motionless, no doubt still doped up with her usual dose of sleeping pills.

"You were shouting and hitting the wall with your feet."

"Shouting what?" said Tamura, panic rising all over again. "What did I say exactly?"

"No words, just horrible noises. It must have been quite a nightmare."

"It was," said Tamura hoarsely. "But it's gone now. I can't remember anything about it."

Which wasn't true, for the dead girl's face remained engraved on his mind for the hours he lay awake, waiting for the dawn.

Richard Mitchell took his eyes off the rows of numbers on the screen in front of him and glanced at the light fixture above his head. It was swinging gently from side to side. No one else in the giant dealing room seemed to have noticed it. They were too busy jabbing at keyboards, yelling prices down telephones, or else gazing into their Reuters and Bloomberg screens as if in a zen trance. You couldn't blame them. It had been a long time since the Nikkei Index had last risen six hundred points in a single day.

The vibrations grew more intense. Cold coffee slopped from the paper cup on Mitchell's desk and splattered over a floppy disk. He grabbed the most absorbent material in reach, a copy of the Asian *Wall Street Journal*.

The whole room was shaking now, but still no one was paying the slightest attention. Mitchell got to his feet and stared nervously at the jiggling light fixture. What did that pamphlet that the personnel department had given him say? "In case of an earthquake, stay away from large windows—they might shatter at any time. Shelter from falling objects under desks and tables. Switch off all electrical machinery. Then proceed in an orderly manner to the emergency exits."

No one was doing any of this. Tanaka, the head of domestic sales, was leaning back against the window, eyes fixed on the electronic price board on the wall. He was lighting a cigarette to replace the half-smoked Mild Seven he had just stubbed into the mountain of butts in his ashtray. Darren, the chief bond trader, was standing on his chair, yelling a stream of abuse at someone on the other side of the room. Yuko, his assistant, was calling out important trades on the "squawk box." Voice racing to keep up with the frantic market action, she bent forward to the microphone, which was bobbling about with the vibrations, and steadied it between her thumb and fingertips. All of them were acting like there was no reality beyond the flickering screens and flashing numbers.

The vibrations finally subsided, and Mitchell passed a sweaty hand over a sweaty brow. It hadn't been serious, he realized with some embarrassment. Not like the one that had almost thrown him out of bed a couple of weeks back. Still, you could never be sure until it was definitely over. Any little tremor could be the prequake that signaled the Big One. According to the experts, major earthquakes in Tokyo came in cycles of sixty or seventy years, so that meant one was due any time now. It would be just Mitchell's luck if his second year in the city, which was also his second year earning serious money, coincided with the whole place being knocked flat.

"Hey, Mitch, what's happening?" Ted Shimano cuffed him on the shoulder as he passed.

"Nothing much," said Mitchell, trying to sound relaxed. "Just a small earthquake."

"Earthquake? No shit!"

Either Ted genuinely hadn't noticed, which was hard to believe, or he felt that to acknowledge it would in some obscure way be damaging to his cool. Ted's cool was easily the biggest thing in his life—much more important than his work or his numerous girlfriends.

He tossed his calfskin attaché case onto the chair next to Mitchell's and took off a long Italian raincoat, which was all folds and tucks and buckles. It hadn't rained for days and showed no signs of starting, but that didn't matter. Ted carried himself like the Great Gatsby. His father, a wealthy sake brewer, had decided to have him educated at the American school in Tokyo and the International Christian University. He had got what he had paid for—a son with a non-Japanese first name, non-Japanese self-confidence, and a thoroughly non-Japanese work ethic. At six-thirty in the evening, when his colleagues were still tapping away at their keyboards, Ted was usually cruising through the back streets of Roppongi in his BMW, a glossy assemblage of hair, lips, and legs snuggled up beside him.

"That's the second one of those things this month," said Mitchell. "Maybe those tectonic plates are getting frisky again."

"Could be. What's your favorite construction stock, anyway?"

"There's a little company in Nagoya that makes shovels. That's probably the best bet."

In the securities industry, you were supposed to joke about these things, just as you joked about AIDS, serial murder, and mass starvation. But after what had happened to Kobe, it wasn't funny anymore, if it ever had been. In just ninety seconds, a major city had shaken itself apart. Entire neighborhoods had disappeared as if they had never existed. According to what Mitchell had read, the great Kanto earthquake would be far more destructive. The images flashed through his mind like a CNN bulletin—trains toppling from bridges, huge chunks of concrete tumbling from fractured skyscrapers, hysterical crowds fleeing from curtains of fire . . .

He sat down and tried to focus on the spreadsheet on his computer screen. The rows of green numbers were oscillating gently, as if they too had been excited by the quake. He frowned and reached for what remained of the coffee. He had been working on the spreadsheet all afternoon, and he wasn't getting anywhere.

The problem was that he had been given just ten days to complete an in-depth analysis of a small company about which there was precious little information anywhere. Yazawa, the new head of research, had told him to drop everything else. He had even hinted of an upgrade to senior analyst if the report was finished in time and if the conclusions were expressed "in the appropriate way."

Mitchell knew what that last bit meant. He was being forced to put his credibility on the line by writing a buy recommendation on a company that he knew nothing about. The reason was obvious. Otaman Corporation was about to launch a one-hundred-million-dollar Eurobond issue, and Pearson Darney (Asia) Inc. was going to be the lead underwriter. It was very unusual for a non-Japanese securities house to have that very profitable responsibility, still more unusual for a minor player like Pearson. Somehow or other, Yazawa had pushed the right buttons.

The only problem was that the more Mitchell looked at the financial statements of Otaman Corporation, the less he understood them. After being a conservatively managed, medium-sized trading house for its entire history, suddenly three years ago Otaman had started to borrow vast amounts of money from the banks. Long- and short-term debt was piling up, and yet there had been no change in the company's dull performance in revenues and profits. Apart from the huge financial resources sitting there on its balance sheet, Otaman appeared to be the same sleepy, low-margin outfit it always had been.

There was nothing Mitchell could point a finger to and say that the company was in trouble. On the other hand, there was nothing that showed that it was all right. The average investor would assume that an analyst working for a reputable investment bank like Pearson wouldn't recommend a stock unless the company's fundamentals were sound and healthy. But there were several distinctive features of Pearson's Tokyo operation that the average investor didn't know about.

For example, the average investor didn't know that less than two years ago the analyst in question, one Richard Mitchell, had been gainfully employed as a motorbike dispatch rider in central London, still considering his options after scraping a lower second in Japanese Studies at Sheffield University. They didn't know that although his résumé described him as having an "in-depth understanding of the Japanese economy and financial markets," the reality was somewhat different. What he really owed his job to was his in-depth knowledge of rugby. When he had arrived for his interview at the Pearson's office in London, he had been confronted by a square-shouldered man in red suspenders whom Mitchell recognized as having played a few games for England at wing forward in the mid-eighties. Mitchell complimented him on his role in the try that had sealed a famous victory over France. After that, the rest of the interview was a formality.

Three months later, the wing forward was one of the victims of a sudden right-sizing of Pearson's London office. Mitchell, however, was safely installed in Tokyo, living proof of the firm's new strategy of, as the press releases stated, "prioritizing the development of new opportunities in the Asia-Pacific region."

If the average investor had been apprised of Mitchell's qualifications for the post of small-company analyst, he might have been concerned. If he had come face to face with Pearson's new head of research, he would have been downright scared.

Yazawa was a strange one, even by the standards of the Tokyo financial markets. He had arrived on the scene three months ago, out of the blue. No one knew much about him, apart from the fact that he had been running his own investment advisory business for the past ten years. Whom had he been advising, and why had he stopped? Again, no one seemed to have a clear idea. The branch manager had hired him as head of research quite suddenly—on the recommendation, it seemed, of a high-level contact in the Japanese business world.

The previous occupant of the job, a mild-mannered economist re-cruited from a Japanese bank, was abruptly demoted to deputy head of research. On Yazawa's first morning at work, the two men held a brief meeting, nervously observed through the glass frontage of his office by Mitchell, Ted, and the other analysts. Nothing much happened. Yazawa opened the conversation with a few words. The economist answered. Yazawa leaned back in his chair, eyes closed, totally silent for several min-utes. The economist spoke again. Yazawa rubbed his forehead and yawned, not bothering to open his eyes. The economist bowed deeply, left the room, and walked back to his desk, a fixed smile on his face. He didn't return to the office after lunch. The next day, a Friday, he phoned in sick. Over the weekend, he came in and cleared his desk.

Since then Yazawa had ruled the department like a shogun. He orig-inated most of the investment ideas himself, using Mitchell, Ted Shi-mano, Kent the Mormon, and the other analysts as glorified copywrit-ers. It shouldn't have worked, but it did. Whatever anyone said about Yazawa, it had to be admitted that his market instinct was superb. Al-though he was sparing with reasons and explanations, the stocks he picked out were almost always winners. In some cases, they would soar

20 or 30 percent in the weeks following his recommendation. It was almost as if the man had access to next month's newspaper.

So what about Otaman, his latest idea? Was that going to be another brilliant success? If so, Mitchell would get the lion's share of the credit. He would no longer be a young foreigner who had talked his way into the job through some sort of oversight. There would be a good chance of promotion to senior analyst—indeed, he would be the logical candidate for deputy head of research, a post unfilled since the economist's unheralded departure. Then again, what if it all went wrong? That didn't bear thinking about. No doubt, Yazawa would wash his hands of the whole affair. All over the world, investors in Japanese securities would remember Mitchell as the analyst who recommended Otaman without doing "due diligence." His career would be over before it had ever gotten started.

It was a dilemma that couldn't be resolved by crunching through the numbers. Any way you looked, they didn't make sense. Mitchell needed the kind of information that wasn't there in the accounts. He needed to know what was really going on.

The obvious solution was to visit Otaman and ask the top people directly the questions that needed to be asked. The only problem was that Yazawa had actively discouraged him from making contact, assuring Mitchell that he would supply all the information necessary. Which, of course, he hadn't. Mitchell had handed him a sheet of detailed queries about Otaman's business plans and financial situation. The replies that he had gotten back had been hopelessly vague.

Mitchell put the finishing touches to his spreadsheet, saved it, then walked over to the glass box that served as Yazawa's office. Inside, Yazawa was leaning forward in his swivel chair, eyes closed, a slight frown on his forehead. Standing behind him, one of the year's intake of female graduates was giving him a shoulder massage, her thumbs digging into the muscles of his neck. When Mitchell knocked, Yazawa's hyperthyroid eyes popped open and the frown deepened.

"Sorry to disturb you," said Mitchell, closing the door behind him.

"Not a big problem," said Yazawa. "Now, how is the Otaman report doing? This is a very important deal, isn't it?"

"That's what I want to talk to you about," Mitchell said carefully. "There are many things about this company that I don't understand."

Yazawa's gaze rose to fix on a spot about a yard above Mitchell's head.

The girl's hands ceased moving. There was a moment of silence, then suddenly Yazawa's shoulders convulsed and he made a harsh barking noise. At first Mitchell didn't realize that the man was laughing.

"You don't understand? Of course you don't understand! Otaman is a Japanese company which is operating on Japanese principles. This is not part of the Great British Empire here, you know!"

Yazawa laughed again. The girl standing behind him tittered gently in sympathy.

"Wait a minute," said Mitchell, reddening. "It's not a question of capability. Give me the information, and I'll do the job. That's all I ask."

Yazawa held up both hands, palms outward. "Be cool, be cool," he said soothingly. "No soccer hooligan activities here, please. This report is of great importance. It will gain you much credit, maybe a big bonus also. You will finish very quickly, please!" He had a way of pronouncing words like "please" that made them sound like obscenities.

"I'm happy to participate in the Otaman project," said Mitchell stiffly. "But in order to make it work, I need more information. The kind of information that I can only get directly from the company's management."

"Otaman people are not available to talk to foreigners," said Yazawa angrily. "I told you that before. I will provide all the information you need through my own contacts."

Mitchell shook his head. "That's not enough. This report cannot be completed without face-to-face contact with Otaman's management."

"Impossible!"

"Then the report is impossible too!"

They were both shouting now. What they were saying would have been audible in the dealing room, if it weren't for the fact that everyone out there was shouting as well.

"You want to sabotage the project!"

"Not sabotage, Yazawa-san. This is plain common sense!"

Mitchell stood there in the center of Yazawa's office, hands on hips. He was uncomfortably aware that his shirt was sticking to his sweaty back. Yazawa was red in the face, and the tendons were standing out on the sides of his neck. The girl behind him was staring at her feet, as if nothing was happening.

"Okay!" barked Yazawa finally, slapping the desk with his hand. "I understand what you're saying. As this is a foreign company, sometimes we have to do things the foreign way. I will fix for you a visit to my contact at Otaman. This is a rare favor, just for your cooperation."

At first, Mitchell couldn't believe his ears. Yazawa was backing down completely, and in the presence of a junior staff member too. This Otaman deal must be more important than he had thought!

"That's great," said Mitchell, and then, in his best Japanese: "Thank you very much for your kind consideration, department chief."

He bowed. Not as deeply as his Japanese colleagues would have—something always held him back from that—but all the same a decent lowering of the head that would communicate, he judged, a sufficient quantity of deference and humility.

He looked up to see Yazawa's mouth open wide. That strange, grating laugh emerged, louder than before. This man, thought Mitchell, is never so scary as when he's laughing.

Mitchell nodded at the girl, who had resumed her kneading of Yazawa's shoulder muscles, and turned to the door. As he opened it, Yazawa's voice rang out again.

"Mitchell-kun! Do good work! You have been chosen for this work specially. Only you are the right man! Only you!" There was another peal of laughter, accompanied by the girl's dutiful giggle.

Mitchell slowly walked back to his desk. "Only you"—what did that mean? And why was it funny? And why did Yazawa persist in calling him Mitchell-kun? "Kun" was a form of address used only to inferiors in status. Yazawa used it to the younger Japanese members of staff, but not to the other foreigners. So was the man deliberately insulting him? Or was it a kind of compliment, a sign that he was being accepted as one of the group? Mitchell shook his head in puzzlement.

Names were confusing in Japan, thought Mitchell, but also very important. Back home, he was Richard to his parents and Mitch to everyone else—pretty straightforward, really. Now he was Richard-san, Dick-san, Mitchell-kun, and Mr. Lick. If he ever made it to senior analyst, he would be known within the firm as Mitchell kacho dairi—Deputy Section Leader Mitchell. On his alien registration card, he was described as Mitchell Richard, the names inverted according to the Japanese custom. On his business card, the order was Western, but the *katakana* phonetic script represented him as "Ri-chi-yaa-do Mi-chi-ru." Once a girlfriend had shown him how to put that into *kanji* characters—six of them which together meant "Reasonable Tea Ground Tasty Wise Emeralds." That wasn't all. He knew that behind his back the office girls called him Mi-chan, which was supposed to be cute, something like Mitchie. In the street, little kids called him *gaijin-san*—"Mr. Outsider." What it came down to was that identity was a flexible concept. You simply had to get used to being whatever it was that people decided to call you. If Yazawa had chosen to call him Mitchell-kun, then he had better behave like a Mitchell-kun should.

Mitchell sat down at his desk. The Nikkei Index was now up eight hundred points, with ten minutes to go before the close of trading. The futures and options desk was in a state of pandemonium, with dealers standing up, telephones in both hands, screeching out prices. Girls clutching handfuls of order tickets rushed through the aisles between the desks, banging into elbows and knees and knocking down piles of paper.

"What the hell's going on?" said Mitchell to Ted Shimano.

"Crazy days," said Ted. "Rumors are rife. We're hearing that the ministry has instructed big banks and insurance companies to buy the market aggressively. The idea is to get share prices up as high as possible by the valuation date for their accounts."

"Interesting. Anything else?"

"The alternative story is that the remnants of the old Kaneshita faction are back in the market. The word is that they're using certain heavy capital stocks to generate funds for a new political group they're going to set up."

"Kaneshita," said Mitchell, switching on his computer screen. "I thought he was arrested for something or other a couple of years ago. Isn't he in jail?"

"In jail!" Ted looked baffled. "Of course not. The case is on appeal, which should take another decade at least. In the meantime, his people have got to keep themselves going somehow, haven't they!"

Kaneshita had once been leader of the biggest faction in the Liberal Democratic Party. He had been minister of construction in the 1970s, minister of finance in the early 1980s, then prime minister. By the late 1980s, he had gone on to an even more important role that didn't require any cabinet position at all—bankrolling the entire political establishment. When the system that had nurtured him finally collapsed under its own weight, he was one of the earliest victims. Mitchell remembered the discovery of a massive store of gold ingots in a secret room in his home; of the special interrogation in the Diet, which he had successfully mumbled and slurred his way through without giving away anything.

"But surely all that stuff is over and done with now," said Mitchell. "I mean, there's political reform on the way, isn't there? The public is demanding change."

"Nobody cares what the public is demanding," said Ted airily. "Not even the public itself really cares. I don't care. Do you care?"

"No," said Mitchell decisively.

His eyes turned to the screen in front of him: row after row of green figures that concealed more than they revealed. Half-heartedly, he ran a few "what if" tests on Otaman's financial structure. What if interest rates went up 3 percent? What if sales fell 5 percent? What if those short-term bank loans couldn't be rolled over? The answer was roughly the same in each case. Otaman would be so far under water you'd need a bathysphere to analyze its problems any further. Mitchell leaned back in his chair and let out a groan of exasperation. It was as if the company had deliberately set out to design a financial structure that contradicted all the textbooks he had ever read.

"Come on, Mitch. Things can't be that bad." Ted was standing up, pulling on his hip neo-fascist raincoat.

"This is madness," Mitchell grumbled. "I've got no idea what's going on with this company."

"You don't know when you're lucky. Yazawa has marked you down as his favorite foreigner. In your place I'd be feeling like a dog with two dicks."

"You think it's such a big deal?"

"Sure," said Ted, sliding his belt through the heavy silver buckle. "Stick with Yazawa, and you'll end up at the top of the tree. No one else can do what he does. You know that."

The top of the tree—that was an idea to conjure with. For a moment, Mitchell allowed himself a discreet peek into a forbidden paradise of wealth and success. He liked what he saw. An Italian sports car, a yacht in the Caribbean, a beautiful, sophisticated woman—not some bimbo from a Roppongi disco!—gazing at him with an adoring expression on her face. . . . It would be expensive, of course, but his investment expertise, put to work for his own benefit, not that of anonymous institutional clients, would generate more than he could ever spend in several lifetimes.

There really were people like that, plenty of them, all over the world, but they were so low-profile that only a few, select contacts even knew of their existence. They didn't spend their time crunching numbers or teasing information out of company spokesmen or getting their ugly faces on financial news bulletins. Somehow, their instincts told them what was going to happen long before anyone else had the slightest idea. They were totally at home in the currents and tides of the financial world; they frolicked through them like dolphins. Mitchell longed to be counted as one of those people. It was the height of his ambition to be a sleek, ever-buoyant financial dolphin.

A woman's voice snapped him out of his daydream. "Excuse me, Mitchell-san. Here is an urgent message for you. Department Chief Yazawa is keenly awaiting the reply."

It was the graduate who had been massaging Yazawa's shoulders a couple of minutes ago. She was holding out a folded sheet of paper. Mitchell took it and opened it, expecting to see the arrangements for the meeting he had requested with the Otaman people. Instead, there was a short message scrawled in a Japanese hand that made no concessions to the foreign reader. Mitchell's knowledge of Japanese script was barely adequate to the task.

"I will pick you up outside at seven o'clock," he read slowly. "We have many important things to discuss."

"What is your reply, Mitchell-san?"

"I'll be there."

So he was going to be spending an evening with the formidable Yazawa, genius stock-picker and all-round enigma. In Ted's parlance, that should have made him feel like a dog with three or four dicks. Instead, for some reason it gave him a queasy feeling in the pit of his stomach.

According to Sano, Yuriko had been living in a two-room apartment just north of Ikebukuro, supporting herself through work as a temporary secretary. Sano didn't know much about her private life. In fact, over the past year, she had talked less and less about her friends.

Mori decided to start with the obvious. He walked into the office of the Fuji Employment Agency wearing his best shirt, a lapel badge with a company emblem, and his sternest expression.

"Good morning," chirruped the receptionist, a pretty girl with pageboy bangs.

"Good morning," responded Mori, banging his aluminum document case down on the counter. "I would like to request a meeting with the chief of the accounting department as soon as possible."

"I'm sorry, you are . . . ?"

"My name is Mori. I work for a law firm specializing in tax matters."

He put special emphasis on the word "tax" and achieved the desired result. The girl's eyes widened and her smile vanished. "Understood," she faltered. "Please be good enough to wait for a moment."

The girl disappeared through a door behind her desk. When she returned, she was accompanied by a square-shouldered middle-aged woman who looked equally nervous.

"I am Suzuki," she said with a deep bow. "I hope that I can be of assistance. The department chief is away today, and I have responsibility for the accounting matters."

That was excellent. Looking at the woman's large, watery eyes blinking behind her glasses, Mori was confident that he would be able to bluff his way through without a problem.

"This is rather a delicate matter," he said pompously, and glanced at the receptionist.

"Yes, of course," said Suzuki. "Please come this way. By the way, can we offer you a drink, some coffee or tea?"

"Nothing, thank you," said Mori, as he followed her into the meeting room.

He made his self-introduction as formal as possible, handing out one of the fake business cards he had had printed up a few months ago. The address on it was a real one, a large building in the Otemachi business district, but the phone number was nonexistent. If anyone bothered to dial that number, he would be in big trouble. But no one ever did, at least not until it was too late. That was one of the professional principles that Mori had discovered early in his career: when you're impersonating someone, confidence beats detail every time. People check the details only when they are already suspicious.

Suzuki bowed again as she handed him her business card. Mori scrutinized it, then placed it on the table in front of him, as if he would need it to remind himself who she was. "Let me explain the situation," he began. "I'm handling the tax affairs of a certain major company. I'm afraid I can't give you the name, so let's call it X Corporation."

Suzuki nodded.

"X Corporation is planning to change the employment agency that it has been using for many years for its part-time office staff. The reason is that certain irregularities have been found in the way tax liabilities have been handled. Do you understand?"

She obviously didn't, although she nodded again.

"There is a chance, I can't say any more than that, that Fuji Employment Agency may be chosen instead. That could mean considerable business for you, stretching over many years. X Corporation is a stock-exchange–listed company, a member of a major industrial grouping which has contributed greatly to Japan's industrial development. It has dozens of subsidiaries and affiliated companies all over the country."

Suzuki smiled a smile that expressed complete subservience.

"That is where I come in. X Corporation has to ensure that there can be no repeat of those tax irregularities, no repeat . . ." Here, Mori shook his head in regretful exasperation, as if he were still offended by the memory. Suzuki pursed her lips and shook her head too.

"I know the first-class reputation of Fuji Agency," went on Mori, "so I am sure you have absolutely nothing to worry about. You should think of this as a formality, like a blood test. In fact, the whole thing shouldn't take more than forty-five minutes."

Suzuki looked gratified. "Clearly understood," she said. "We are honored to extend our cooperation. Would you require some assistance, perhaps one of our staff to help you with photocopying and so on?"

"Not necessary," said Mori with a severe air. "I need to have privacy for this task."

Nothing could have been smoother. Suzuki actually brought the ledger books and computer printouts into the room. Mori asked her to send in a cup of English tea, then got to work transcribing the details of Yuriko's work record into his notebook.

The picture was much as Sano had said. For the past few years, Yuriko had been moving around from company to company, rarely staying anywhere for long. In most places, she had worked as an executive secretary, generally attached to a board member or sometimes even the president of a company. The only point to catch Mori's attention was that her last contract had finished almost three months ago. Sano hadn't mentioned that. According to him, she had been too busy to see him in the last few weeks of her life. Mori took down the names and addresses of all the companies where Yuriko had worked, together with the dates. When he had finished, he asked the receptionist to summon Suzuki and handed back the records.

"Was everything in order?" she asked nervously.

"I'm afraid that can't be revealed yet," said Mori. "I have to make my official report first. But I think I can say that the signs are encouraging."

Suzuki came to the elevator and bowed deeply as the doors closed. She would get in trouble, of course, reflected Mori as he rode down to the ground floor. The department chief would be back tomorrow or the next day. She would tell him the story and show him the business card. He would probably be suspicious and call the number. Or they would wait and nothing would happen. At some point, it would be obvious that she had been deceived. It could happen to anyone, of course, and no real harm had been done. Mori certainly hoped the department chief would see it that way.

Mori got back to his office just before five o'clock. He spent the next quarter of an hour sorting through the pile of mail that had been building up over the past week. There were the usual bills, a couple of them in red lettering, a rare thank-you letter from a client, and a sheaf of junk pamphlets and fliers. One in particular caught Mori's attention. It was advertising low-priced burial slots in a place that was called a "Hall of Peace" but looked more like a gigantic locker room. At least, the company that owned the place considered it a low-priced deal. In fact, booking a briefcase-sized space in one of those gunmetal gray stacks of drawers would cost you what it took Mori two years to make. He tossed the pamphlet into the trash bin, along with the detritus of yesterday's takeout lunch. It was a bad omen at the start of a case.

After making himself a coffee, Mori slipped a Kenny Dorham cassette into his battered old tape player and lay down on the sofa. He contemplated his next move to the sound of Kenny's probing trumpet. According to Sano, Yuriko's latest boyfriend worked in a bookstore somewhere in Roppongi. Mori planned to pay him a visit as soon as possible. A couple of phone calls confirmed the location. First, though, Mori needed to sharpen his mental processes with a good soak.

Twenty minutes later, he was sitting up to his neck in ferociously hot water, a small white towel knotted around his forehead. One of the few advantages of working where he did was the public bath next door and a cheap, tasty Chinese restaurant on the other side of the street. That went some way toward compensating for such disadvantages as the leaky plumbing, the cockroaches, and the fact that the whole building shook like a leaf in earthquakes.

There were few people in the bath in the late afternoon, which was just the way Mori liked it. A schoolboy was sitting on a tiny plastic stool, lathering his hair with a selection of shampoos and treatment lotions. At the other end of the bath, just visible through the miasma of steam, was an elderly man whom Mori had seen many times before. According to the bathkeeper, he would stay in the bath for hours at a time, singing to himself in a strange whisper as he heated up his sticklike limbs.

Mori leaned back against the tiled wall, lifted his toes through the surface of the water, and stretched out. Soon someone else entered the bathing room and began throwing water over himself with a plastic tub. It was one of the cooks from the Chinese restaurant across the street, a fat bald man as jolly as one of the Chinese gods pictured on the restaurant wall. When he turned around, smacking his ample belly like a Sumo wrestler, he called out a greeting to Mori.

"Mori-san, our most famous customer! You've got such a touch with women. Some time I want you to tell me how you do it."

This was a running joke between them. Over the years, Mori had taken several women friends to sample the spicy Taiwanese cuisine.

"First of all, you need to lose about one third of your body weight," he answered.

"Does that mean giving up steamed dumplings, stuffed tripes, and things like that?" said the cook, lowering himself gently into the water.

"I'm afraid it does."

"Then I have to give up my job as well. For I can't cook without tasting what I'm giving the customers, can I?"

"That's a good excuse. Still, if you carry on like this, you're going to turn into a steamed dumpling!"

The cook splashed a handful of water at him. "Yaah!" He sighed facetiously. "It's a good thing not everybody's as attractive to women as you are, Mori-san. There'd be too much competition in the world. Why, that tall girl might be my mistress by now!"

"Tall girl? Which one is that?" Mori recalled the women he had taken over to the Chinese restaurant during the past few months. There hadn't been many, actually, just that hostess from Sapporo and the dentist's wife from Yokohama. Neither of them had been particularly tall.

"The girl who came in the other night. She said she was waiting for you. She really thinks a lot of you, doesn't she?"

"What do you mean?"

"All the questions she asked—she said she wanted to know as much about you as possible. No woman has ever said that about me." The cook shook his head and clicked his teeth in simulated frustration.

"That's no surprise," said Mori. "What did she look like, anyway?"

"She looked good, Mori-san. Tall, and much younger than your usual type. She was wearing a red raincoat, very fashionable, and cute little boots."

Someone's lover, wife, or daughter? A prospective client checking him out? He dismissed the subject from his mind and hauled himself out of the bath. He had quite enough mysteries on his mind already.

"You're a lucky guy, Mori-san," called out the cook, now spreading himself out in the bath like a great jellyfish. "How do you manage to do it?"

"I wish I knew that myself," grunted Mori, and pushed open the sliding door to the changing room. As he turned to say sayonara to the cook, he saw a face staring at him through the steam. It was the old guy at the other end of the bath. He was smiling to himself as he soundlessly chanted the words of his favorite song.

FOUR

At seven o'clock, Mitchell was standing on the pavement in front of the Pearson office. It was a few weeks before the cherry blossom season, and the evenings were still cool. Already a crescent moon had risen above the top of the "bubble tower," the new skyscraper that was reputed to charge the highest office rents in the world.

Despite the recession, the pavements were packed. Crowds of office workers surged across the pedestrian crossing, disappearing into the mouth of the subway entrance like iron filings drawn by an invisible magnet. Mitchell glanced up into the night sky. As usual in Tokyo, it was mauve in color, the darkness penetrated and tempered by the dense brilliance below. He became aware of something moving above his head, a large oval shape floating slowly and silently across the skyline. It was an advertising blimp, the name of a major electronics company emblazoned on its body. In the darkness, it seemed almost close enough to reach up to and touch.

"Quickly, Mitchell-san. No time for dreaming these busy days!"

A shiny black shape had pulled up to the curb. It was an Isuzu Mu, a slickly contoured four-wheel-drive vehicle. Yazawa was leaning out of the window, a frown on his face.

"Understood," responded Mitchell in his best Japanese pronunciation. The door swung open and Mitchell climbed into the bucket seat. Yazawa didn't even look at him. He just stared directly ahead, the frown having been replaced by a strange half-smile.

"Are you capable of eating Japanese food?" he asked, gunning the motor. There was no break in the line of traffic to let him in.

"Of course," said Mitchell indignantly. "Why do Japanese people always assume that foreigners can't eat Japanese food! In London, I ate Japanese almost every week. I'm very fond of Japanese food!"

That was something of an exaggeration, but Mitchell was annoyed by Yazawa's condescending tone. After all, he wasn't talking to some tourist who had just gotten off the plane.

"So you can easily eat raw things such as sushi."

"Of course!"

"Including all types?"

"Most types, I would say."

"How about living sushi with a special taste? You like that a lot, don't you?" Yazawa pushed his face disconcertingly close to Mitchell's and gave a throaty chuckle.

"Living sushi?" Mitchell glanced at him, puzzled.

"Young Japanese ladies' special sushi," said Yazawa joyfully. "Don't pretend, Mitchell-kun—I've heard all about your activities! You are a true midnight cowboy, aren't you!"

Still chuckling, he let out the clutch, and the Isuzu leapt into the line of traffic just a couple of yards ahead of an oncoming truck. Mitchell closed his eyes, uncomfortably aware that the car didn't seem to be fitted with seatbelts. The truck driver sounded his horn and flashed his headlights. Yazawa gave a yell of triumph and swerved into the outside lane.

"Good God!" said Mitchell. "Where did you learn to drive like that?"

"In Australia," said Yazawa, still chuckling to himself. "In my young days, I did some rally driving there. Have you ever engaged in rally driving?"

"No, I haven't," said Mitchell.

"An excellent sport," said Yazawa. "It trains the nerves. Every man should do something to train his nerves. It's not good for a man to spend his life just working and drinking and hunting for pussy."

"You may have a point there," said Mitchell, unable to tell whether Yazawa was being serious or not.

"Experience the night, Mitchell-kun! Learn to eat with your spirit! Not with your mouth or your stomach, but with your spirit!" As he spoke, Yazawa was glancing into the rearview mirror, ready to launch his next assault on Tokyo's usually disciplined traffic flow.

"I'll do my best," said Mitchell.

Two hours later, Mitchell was wishing he had been a little less bold and a little more honest. They were sitting at the corner table of a tiny restaurant somewhere near Ueno station. There were half a dozen other customers in the place, mainly middle-aged salarymen. The only woman present was the stoop-backed old lady who brought the food in from the kitchen. The only foreigner was Mitchell, and he had never felt so foreign before in his life.

43

The first dish had looked fairly easy, a clear soup containing a couple of blocks of tofu. Only when Mitchell peered into the copper bowl did he notice that half a dozen semitransparent fish, each no more than half an inch long, were scooting about among the strands of seaweed. The old woman lit a gas ring under the bowl and heated the soup until it was steaming vigorously. Seeking to escape the scalding temperatures, one by one the tiny fish wriggled their way deep into the quivering mass of tofu. When they had all disappeared, the old woman expertly extracted the tofu with a pair of chopsticks and served it to them in small ceramic bowls. Mitchell ate in large rapid bites, trying to keep his mind on other things. But he couldn't ignore the tickling sensation at the top of his throat as he swallowed. And he couldn't repress an unpleasant vision of the tiny fish flitting around inside his stomach, just as they had been flitting around inside the copper bowl a couple of minutes before.

What followed was worse. First came a charcoaled sparrow, beak open, wings extended, as if it had been blasted by a death ray in midflight. Mitchell started with the tail and crunched through the wings and body, until he was holding only the walnut-sized head between his finger and thumb. Realizing that Yazawa was gazing at him keenly, Mitchell took a deep draft of sake, then popped the head into his mouth, swallowing it as quickly as he could. Too quickly, as it turned out, for the beak scraped down the inside of his gullet, bringing water to his eyes and necessitating further deep drafts of sake.

Next came plates of fried grasshoppers and bee larvae. Mitchell was informed that the dark flakes in the sake they were drinking was a mashed viper's liver. Then came the eggs, small freckled ovals about the size of a plum.

"Do you guess what kind of eggs these are?" said Yazawa, peeling off the shell from one and popping it in his mouth.

Mitchell gulped down a mouthful of sake. He didn't want to guess.

"I don't know. Lark, maybe, or pigeon."

"Different," said Yazawa, chewing away with gusto. "Not a bird in this case."

A cold ripple traveled down Mitchell's stomach.

"I don't know the right English word for this one," Yazawa went on. "It's something like a snake, but it has legs. Do you know it?"

"A lizard?" said Mitchell incredulously.

"That's right, a kind of lizard. A Japanese lizard. This is the only place in Tokyo you can get them."

Mitchell drained his sake glass and reached for his chopsticks. He wasn't going to let Yazawa defeat him at this stage.

The eggs were actually not too bad, and the snake meat that followed was tender enough to be mistaken for chicken. The dark gooey shape that came next was a tougher proposition, especially after he had identified it as a duck fetus, but several refills of sake saw him through.

"You challenge well," said Yazawa, obviously impressed. "If you work as strongly as you eat, you can accomplish many things, I think."

The old lady filled his sake cup, and Mitchell knocked it back immediately, a glow of achievement spreading through his body. When he looked down again, the old lady had laid a new delicacy on the table before him. It was an object that looked like a dried-up eye, except that it was much too big.

"For a moment, I thought that bit in the middle was an eyeball," said Mitchell, poking at it with a chopstick.

"You thought!" barked Yazawa triumphantly. "You were right to think so! This is the eye of a bluefin tuna. It will certainly have many excellent effects on your brain."

"My brain," said Mitchell, pulling back his chopsticks sharply.

"Yes, indeed! The hexanoic acid in this eyeball will improve the chemical operation of your memory. As for myself, I make sure to eat this food once every week in order to prevent mental deterioration. When you are young, these things don't matter. But when a man gets older, he needs many special foods for his mind."

Mitchell stared at the tuna eyeball. The tuna eyeball stared at Mitchell.

"Eat for your brain's health," said Yazawa. "This is important for a promising analyst such as you are."

A promising analyst—that was the first professional compliment that he had heard Yazawa utter. Mitchell picked up his chopsticks and blanked out his imagination. In a matter of minutes, the plate was empty. Yazawa filled up Mitchell's sake cup.

"You eat with a strong spirit," he said. "This is unusual for a foreigner, I think. Now, one last dish and we will move to other places."

The sake was hitting Mitchell hard now, the hot numbness spreading from his throat to his cheeks and scalp. With these tiny cups, it was almost impossible to keep track of how much you were drinking. The old woman appeared from the kitchen again and laid a plate of thinly sliced raw fish on the table. She bowed almost to the waist and rasped something to Yazawa in a thick accent that Mitchell couldn't penetrate. Yazawa gave a grunt of approval, then turned to Mitchell.

45

"Do you know about Japanese fugu?" he said with exaggerated concern.

Mitchell nodded. "Fugu? That's blowfish, isn't it? Yes, I've had it a couple of times before. Tastes pretty bland, in my opinion." He remembered being disappointed by blowfish. In spite of all the fuss the Japanese made, it was about as tasteless as it was colorless.

"The organs of the fish contain a poison that can kill you instantly," Yazawa went on. "It is the bitter wine of the ovaries."

"Ovaries, eh?"

"That is correct. The door to life becomes the door to death. Have you heard of such things?"

Yazawa was smiling the stretched smile that meant he was preparing some sort of provocation. Mitchell decided that he was not going to allow himself to be intimidated. The first time he had eaten fugu, his Japanese host had made a similarly macabre allusion. It was rather pathetic, really.

"I've heard that some parts of the fish are highly poisonous. And I've also heard that it is always prepared by specially licensed chefs who know exactly what parts to remove. Sorry, Yazawa-san, you've chosen the wrong man to scare with your fugu stories."

Mitchell shook his head and chuckled. He picked up a sliver of fish from the plate, dipped it in the soy sauce, and put it in his mouth. It was excellent, rather more pungent than he remembered.

"You know many things about Japan, Mitchell-kun," said Yazawa politely. "Do you happen to know how many people have died of fugu poisoning in recent years?"

"I read something about it in the *Japan Times,*" said Mitchell casually. "Six or seven last year, weren't there?"

"You're right," said Yazawa, looking impressed at Mitchell's knowledge. "Six died last year, including a famous novelist and a high-ranking gangster. Now let me ask you another question. Do you happen to know why these six people died this death?"

Yazawa was obviously determined to persevere with his scare tactics. The man could be downright tiresome sometimes. The blowfish, though, was excellent, filling his mouth with an explosion of different taste sensations. It was almost a shame to have to swallow it.

"I don't know," replied Mitchell with a shrug. "There must have been a mistake, I suppose. Maybe the chef was new to the business."

"That's not right," said Yazawa, shaking his head in disappointment. "I was thinking that you understood Japan much better than to say something like that!"

"Well, I'm sorry, I don't," said Mitchell, beginning to lose his patience. "But I'll bet you're going to tell me the real reason." He picked up another sliver of fish with his chopsticks. Again, it was spicy enough to make his mouth tingle. However could he have thought the taste of fugu bland!

Yazawa nodded vigorously, and pointed over Mitchell's shoulder to an empty table at the corner of the room. "You see that place there—that's where the famous novelist died. Since then, it is always empty. Customers of this restaurant don't like to sit there because of bad luck."

Mitchell stopped chewing and glanced from Yazawa's manically jovial features to the table in the corner. Unlike all the others, it was completely bare—no sauce bottles, no chopsticks, no paper napkins. Was the man joking or not? As usual, it was impossible to be sure.

"Are you telling me the chef here is incompetent? If that's true, why does anyone still come here? The place should be closed down!"

Yazawa gave one of his little barks of laughter and slapped the table with his hand. "You still don't understand, do you! There is no mistake, no incompetence. The men who die of fugu poisoning have requested the fugu to be prepared with the poison left in. They are true connoisseurs!"

"That's absurd. Why would they do that?"

"Because the taste is wonderful, the best taste in the world. Don't you agree with that assessment, Mitchell-kun? After all, you are now in a position to judge."

For a moment, Mitchell stared at him in bewilderment, then he dropped his chopsticks with a clatter. A shudder passed through his body like an electric charge. "What are you telling me?" he breathed, his mouth suddenly as dry as sandpaper. "Is there something wrong with this fish I've been eating?" A stinging, burning sensation was spreading rapidly over his tongue and the inside of his lips.

"Please tell me your opinion," said Yazawa, peering at him with a serious, almost solicitous expression on his face. "Do you feel that fugu merits its high reputation or not?"

"Poison," croaked Mitchell, rising to his feet. "You've been feeding me poison!"

He put his hands to his stomach. There was an odd sensation there, heat alternating with chilly cold. Maybe he was going to die—rapidly! He had a sudden urge to call home to Sheffield and tell his mother that he loved her. But there wouldn't be time. The poison would get him before he was halfway to the door. He thought of the old novelist, falling to the floor, writhing among the tables and chairs in satiated agony. He would be the first foreigner to die in this way. It would probably make the tabloids back home!

"Sit down in your seat!" said Yazawa, pulling Mitchell down by the sleeve. "What is the matter with you—are you frightened of dying?"

Mitchell collapsed into his seat, heart pounding. The burning sensation had spread through his throat and chest into his heart. The effect was probably like a snakebite. Another couple of seconds, and boom!—it would hit his brain.

"What a ridiculous way to die," he said thickly. "Killed by fish ovaries!"

"No, a glorious way to die!" said Yazawa, reaching out with his chopsticks. "In search of one type of the perfection of the senses. I would like to die that way. Some year, I would like to be one of the six!"

"Yazawa-san, please tell me! Is this fish I have eaten poisonous?"

There was a tightness in Mitchell's throat that made his voice sound higher than usual. Yazawa gave another bark of laughter and slapped the edge of the table with his hand. "Do not worry," he chortled. "You will live many years yet! There was some touch of poisonous material that I requested specially. Not enough to satisfy a real connoisseur, but something interesting for you."

A cool tide of relief swept through Mitchell's body, and for an instant his arms and legs went limp. A feeling of intense gratitude was followed immediately by a burst of anger.

"You—you might have killed me!" he stammered. "You don't know—I might have a weak heart or a clot on the brain or something!"

The burning sensation on his tongue was abating. He reached for his sake, his hand shaking.

"It is good for a man to risk his life from time to time," said Yazawa with a dismissive wave. "A man who has never risked his life can never enjoy it fully. Now let us finish the fugu so that we can enjoy the rest of the evening in good spirits!"

"I think I've had enough," said Mitchell, pushing the plate away from him. His back and arms were slippery with sweat.

"This is a rare treat for a foreigner," said Yazawa sternly. "It can only be obtained in one or two special places like this. Come on—you must follow the words of *Hagakure.*"

"Who or what is *Hagakure?*" said Mitchell weakly.

"It is a great textbook of the period before our country opened up to foreigners. It contains the famous words "Stamp quickly and pass through a wall of iron." That is my investment philosophy, and it is also the philosophy of my life."

" 'Stamp quickly'—what on earth is that supposed to mean?" Mitchell was recovering his composure now. He gulped down his sake and wiped his mouth with the hand towel. Yazawa gazed at him intently.

"It means 'Do,' " he hissed with barely contained excitement.

"Do what, exactly?" said Mitchell, his brow furrowing. Yazawa shook his head impatiently.

"That is completely the wrong question. What to do is not important. The doing itself is the only thing. Everything can be resolved by doing!"

"Doing what?" repeated Mitchell, still mystified.

"Do!" exclaimed Yazawa, his hand suddenly crashing down on the table, rattling the plates. "Do, Mitchell-kun, do!"

Yazawa's voice was rising to a shout. Mitchell looked around in alarm, but the other customers seemed oblivious to the noise he was making. The old woman, who was carrying in another tray of atrocities, turned her head slightly, an indulgent smile on her lips.

"Do!" bellowed Yazawa, his fist pounding the table. "Not thinking, doing! Do, Mitchell-kun, DO, DO, DO!"

Mitchell stared at the plate of fugu. Examining it more closely, he could see that the clear flesh was smudged here and there by a dark paste. Without really knowing what he was doing, he seized his chopsticks, picked out the slice with the largest, darkest stain, and stuffed it into his mouth. It was as delicious as before, thrilling his taste buds with a rainbow of flavors.

Yazawa picked up his chopsticks as well, and for the next few minutes the two of them ate in silence. Soon the plate was empty. Mitchell laid down his chopsticks and finished the last of the sake. Strangely enough, the burning sensation didn't seem as strong this time, and it was limited to his lips and tongue. His throat and chest felt perfectly normal.

"This meal has been a fine experience," he said to Yazawa in Japanese. "I'm deeply thankful for having the opportunity to experience such unusual foods."

"Don't mention it," replied Yazawa in English. "This is a special restaurant which serves what we call *getemono*—that is, food only for the strong-spirited ones. Usually I come here alone because my Japanese friends refuse to accompany me. Your presence tonight is greatly valued."

Mitchell took a deep breath. His stomach twitched a few times as if it were limbering up for a larger effort. Yazawa stood up and slapped him on the shoulder.

"You fight well," he said. "For a foreigner, you have good endurance. Remember—'Stamp quickly and pass through the wall of iron!' Those words tell us everything we need for our lives, I think."

"Stamp quickly," repeated Mitchell blankly and lurched to his feet. Yazawa gestured toward the door.

"Come on, the night is just beginning. Now we must enjoy with all our spirit!"

It was a strange thing, thought Mitchell as he moved gingerly toward the entrance—Yazawa's English seemed to be getting more fluent all the time.

———

Mori got to Roppongi just after eight o'clock. The place never ceased to amaze him. Twenty-five years ago it had been nothing, just a scattering of lifeless bars and restaurants infested by fat-cat foreign businessmen. Back then Shinjuku had been the place with all the zest, the youthful energy. Now Shinjuku was middle-aged and seedy, whereas Roppongi— well, what had Roppongi become? Something high-tech, abstract, and disconnected—full of foreigners, and making foreigners out of everyone who went there.

Wandering the thronging streets, Mori felt as if he had been fast-forwarded into the future. These days, he was increasingly aware that a new century was speeding toward him. The late twentieth century, which was his home, which he understood as a son understands his parents, was almost done. The twenty-first century was just around the corner. Mori believed that it was going to be like Roppongi, and that he wasn't going to like it much.

And those smooth-faced men and women that he pushed past on his way to the bookstore—you couldn't really call them young at all. Apart from their age, there was nothing young about them. There was no fire, no impatience with the world, no readiness to commit stupid mistakes. Instead—accommodation and obedience, sexuality that was just a fashion statement, dead eyes that read you like a computer printout.

It didn't take long to find the place where Yuriko's ex-boyfriend worked. Situated in a back street between a Korean barbecue and an exotic-lingerie shop, it was one of the many bookstores that specialized in *manga* comic books. Mori liked Korean barbecue and adored exotic lingerie, but he hated comic books. In the late sixties, producing them, even reading them, had been a little act of rebellion, a demonstration that you didn't buy the traditional literary values of the Establishment. In those days, professors and critics had fulminated against this childish fad spreading among the younger generation. Naturally, as a student Mori had read comic books, without thinking much about it, in the same way he smoked cigarettes. Now, though, things were different. A new generation of professors and literary critics were celebrating *manga* as a profound form of cultural expression, superior to the written word. The artists who drew them were as rich as baseball stars, and the giant publishing companies would collapse without them. *Manga* were even used as textbooks in schools, under the authorization of the ministry of education. People of all ages and types read the things—schoolkids, office girls, salarymen, dentists, bankers, bureaucrats. Even the government and political parties produced *manga* to explain their policies. The way Mori saw it, the only problem was this—those old professors back in the late sixties had been right. *Manga* were childish. *Manga* were mental chewing gum. The reason was simple—life was not like *manga*. Life smelled and hurt. Life did things to you that you couldn't forget. Life slowly killed you.

Films, music, dance, literature—these were art forms that could fill your soul with hope and despair. Who, except for a child, would ever be moved by a comic book? Who, after tossing one into the trash can on the subway platform, would ever even think about it again?

But that was not a subject that Mori was going to broach with Arai, whom he found at the back of the shop unpacking a box of polyethylene-wrapped *manga* books. He was a tall, long-haired youth with a plump, placid face—the kind, thought Mori, who made girls feel secure. After the adventure of defying her father and going off with the wild-eyed biker, Yuriko would probably have appreciated the kind of security that Arai would offer.

Mori introduced himself as a representative of the Sano family, and handed out a business card that described his profession as "legal consultant." Arai's face fell.

"Yuriko-chan? Yes, I heard about what happened. Why are you asking me about it?"

"Unfortunately, there are some uncertainties about the incident that still need to be cleared up."

"Uncertainties? Wait a moment—are you with the police?"

"Do I look like a policeman?"

Arai gazed into Mori's face. It didn't take him long to decide. "Well—uh—no, you don't."

"I'm looking at the legal aspects of the case, insurance problems and so on."

"So you work at an insurance company?" Arai sounded quite incredulous.

"I'm a consultant," explained Mori patiently. "People pay me a fee for my expertise in investigating the problems that can arise in this kind of case."

"What—you mean like a private detective?"

"Something like that. Anyway, let's not waste time on this subject. I'm fully authorized by Yuriko-san's father to handle the whole business on his behalf. All I want is to ask you a few simple questions."

Mori asked, and Arai answered fully, without any hesitation. From the way he talked, Mori knew immediately that he was telling the truth. Arai had broken up with Yuriko about a year ago. What was the reason? Arai shrugged as if that were a strange question. No particular reason, he said. Was she upset about something? Not at all. Was there another man? Arai wasn't sure, and gave the impression of not caring much either. When had he seen her last? About a month ago, when she had dropped into the shop to browse through the *manga* books. They were still friends, you see, no regrets or bitterness. They had gone out for a coffee together and chatted about mutual friends. Was she depressed? On the contrary, she had seemed euphorically happy. Please describe.

"Well, she kept smiling. No matter what I said, no matter what the subject we were talking about. She had never done that before."

"Maybe she fell in love with someone."

Arai eyed Mori curiously. "I don't think so," he said. "She wasn't that type. Anyway, I remember that just before I left, she said something pretty weird."

"Something weird? What was that?"

Arai frowned as he tried to recall the conversation. "I asked why she was looking so happy. She said there was no reason. All that had happened was that she had learned how to dig deeply into her heart and find the happiness within."

"Dig deeply into her heart? What's that supposed to mean?"

"You see—told you it was weird."

Mori nodded. "All right, it's weird. And then?"

"And then, nothing. I had to get back to the shop."

Mori thanked Arai for his cooperation and made for the door.

"So aren't you going to buy anything, then?"

That was Arai's voice calling out as Mori turned the handle. He sounded aggrieved.

"What—you mean buy a comic book?"

"Yes, we have all types here—from the most recent to some real classics from the sixties. That was your era, wasn't it, Mori-san?"

Mori turned, hand on the door knob. "My era was no *manga*," he snapped. Arai recoiled as if he had been stung by a wasp. Mori stepped out into the bustling Roppongi night.

———

The Isuzu Mu hurtled through the traffic. Mitchell's stomach bucked and quivered and finally iced over completely. He gripped the sides of his seat and closed his eyes.

"You are famous in our company for your lady-hunting," Yazawa observed. "I will take you somewhere where you can make contact with various ladies without any problem."

"A disco?" mumbled Mitchell, his face tilted toward the roof of the car.

"Not a disco in this case. Instead a unique kind of nightclub, which is also open in the daytime. After I introduce you, it will be possible for you to go any time on your own. It is not expensive."

The unique kind of nightclub was in Shibuya, which meant a full forty minutes of swerving, accelerating, and lane-dodging through the roaring traffic. For a Japanese man verging on middle age, Yazawa was extraordinarily impatient. Mitchell wondered how he managed to stay sane.

"How about Japanese women?" Yazawa said, turning to face Mitchell as the Isuzu charged at a red light. "You have had many experiences, I think."

Many, but by no means enough. In fact, that was one of the main reasons he had come to Japan in the first place. In his twenty-five years of life in England, Mitchell had never thought of himself as an especially attractive male specimen. Not exactly ugly, but not a hunk by any means. Here in Japan, though, it was a different world. The girls that he met in bars and discos—most of them exceptionally good-looking themselves—actually liked the way he looked. They complimented him on his lank brown hair, his angular nose, his thin, rather feminine lips. They told him that he had a strong physical resemblance to various pop singers and movie actors. With that sort of encouragement, it was almost impossible to fail.

"Quite a few," said Mitchell cautiously. "But these days, I don't have so much time. I'm concentrating on studying for my analyst's exams."

That wasn't quite the whole truth, but it was, he felt, the correct answer to give the head of the research department. In fact, Friday and Saturday evenings were still dedicated to disco-crawling.

Yazawa nodded, returning his gaze to the road just in time to avoid a taxi that had slowed down in front. "I like foreign ladies," he said. "Though in many cases their necks are too large. And of course they lack self-discipline."

"You're probably right there," said Mitchell with a smile. "But so do many foreign men."

"Yes, indeed. There are many gay boys among you these days. Why is that? Is it because women have become too strong?"

"That's a very complex subject," said Mitchell, wondering what sort of response was expected of him. "I don't think anyone knows the real facts."

"Japanese women are getting stronger these days," continued Yazawa, apparently oblivious to Mitchell's comment. "And we have increasing numbers of gay boys here too. Moreover it is likely that our balls are getting weaker."

Mitchell opened his eyes. "Your balls?"

"Yes, our balls," said Yazawa gravely. "This is a very major problem, I think. Japanese sperm count has declined by forty-six percent since the war. This may be something to do with the reforms imposed on Japan under the American occupation. Phony American democracy has caused Japanese men to lose their true spirit."

"You can't be serious," said Mitchell. "You're blaming the Americans for the condition of your balls! Hiroshima I can understand, but this is ridiculous."

"Hiroshima is my hometown," said Yazawa, his gaze fixed on the road ahead. "My family lost many members in that atrocious incident."

"I'm sorry," said Mitchell, flushing at his own clumsiness. "I didn't realize . . ."

Yazawa spun the steering wheel, and the Isuzu swung across to the wrong side of the road. Mitchell flinched as they sped past a line of cars, then dodged back into a lane just ahead of the oncoming headlights.

"Bombing Hiroshima was certainly a great crime," Yazawa went on. "It was one of the great atrocious crimes of the twentieth century, don't you agree?"

"I understand the way you feel," said Mitchell carefully. "If I were Japanese, I'd feel exactly the same way myself. In the West, on the other hand, many people believe that the atomic bombing was necessary to end the war quickly."

"Necessary?" sneered Yazawa. "Pah! This is typical nonsense propaganda, I think."

Mitchell felt his self-control slipping away. "Wait a minute, Yazawa-san! The war had to be ended somehow. And it was you people who started it, after all."

"You are mistaken, I think," said Yazawa breezily. "We Japanese did not start any war."

"What!" said Mitchell, wondering whether he'd heard correctly. "You didn't start the war! What about Pearl Harbor?"

"More nonsense propaganda! The war started long before then."

"Really," said Mitchell dryly.

"The war started centuries ago, when white men first came to East Asia. And it will not end until they have packed their bags and left. This is the true meaning of modern history, isn't it? Because of this knowledge you tried to destroy us with atom bombs and democracy and imported vegetables sprayed with strange chemicals! But you will not succeed, I think!"

Yazawa gave an odd kind of snort and glanced sideways. Mitchell decided not to answer the provocation that was so obviously being offered.

"Well, what's past is past," he muttered sheepishly. "Nowadays we must learn to cooperate and learn from each other, right?"

"Wrong!" Yazawa howled. "Cooperate and learn from each other! Mitchell-kun, you sound like our stupid Japanese prime minister. What happened to the Winston Churchill spirit? What happened to James Bond?"

55

"James Bond? What's he got to do with it, for God's sake?"

"James Bond is a man of excellent British spirit," said Yazawa fiercely. "Though not Roger Moore, of course. I have no respect for him. It is Sean Connery that I like very much. No problem with his balls, I think!"

At that, he pulled in sharply to a space at the side of the road, inciting a long Klaxon blast from the car behind. Mitchell had only a vague idea of where they were. It was a garish, love-hotel-infested area at the back of Shibuya, well away from the main shopping drag. Yazawa led him through a narrow alley that smelled of cat urine, then down some garbage-strewn stone steps. At the bottom was a pink neon sign that read "Delightful Body Theater."

"This is a strip club," Mitchell said, disappointed.

"It is a good place," said Yazawa. "You can release your masculine stresses here rather easily, I think."

He pushed through the half-open door, and they entered a dank, dimly lit lobby area. On the far wall was a small ticket window behind which someone was enthusiastically slurping noodles. Yazawa rapped his knuckles against the cracked, grease-stained Perspex.

"Hoih!" he called out. "Tickets for two."

A gnarled hand snaked through a gap in the curtains to accept the proffered banknote. Yazawa grabbed Mitchell by the elbow and maneuvered him through the curtained gloom of the entrance.

The "theater" on the other side was a damp and dingy cellar about half the size of a tennis court. There were no seats. Instead, forty or fifty men were crowded around a small, semicircular stage. Loud disco music was blaring from speakers mounted on stacks of empty beer crates, the bass notes buzzing in the metal pipes that ran along the walls.

Yazawa bought a couple of cans of beer from a dispensing machine and pushed his way through the crowd. Mitchell followed in his wake, feeling more and more out of place. It wasn't just because he was a foreigner. The other members of the audience were not the kind of people he came across every day in his work. Out of the corner of his eye, he glimpsed construction workers wearing paint-splattered trousers held up by string, tough-looking men with close-cropped hair and toothpicks jutting from their lips, younger men with bandaged faces and loopy, gap-toothed grins. His nostrils caught the odor of cheap sake, garlic, sweat, paint thinner. In this crowd, Yazawa stood out almost as much as Mitchell. They both lacked something that all the others shared—the defeated look of poor men in a society that had become very rich very fast.

"You will enjoy," said Yazawa, and pulled Mitchell to the front of the crowd. There was a roll of tape-recorded drums and then, to some isolated cheers from the crowd, a large woman pushed her way through the plastic curtain at the back of the stage. She was practically naked already, wearing just a pink chiffon negligee and a pair of fluffy slippers. She had heavy, downward-pointing breasts, a four-inch scar below the navel, and thick makeup. When she turned, a green and red tattoo of a dragon was visible on one of her buttocks, its tail disappearing into the flabby crevice.

"How do you think?" said Yazawa.

"Not really my type," replied Mitchell, swigging a mouthful of beer.

"She is a veteran," said Yazawa. "She has much fighting spirit."

After the music had finished, she disappeared offstage, returning a few minutes later with a plastic shopping bag and a bedroll. The chiffon negligee was gone. Having set the bedroll in the center of the stage, she lay down on it, spread her legs like a pair of scissors, and began to enact an exaggerated parody of self-stimulation. The atmosphere around the stage had changed. Whereas during the first number there had been plenty of banter and laughter, now the men stood hushed and completely still, their faces heavy with tension. Fifty male stares converged on a few shadowy inches of female flesh.

The next part was, according to Yazawa's solemn commentary, the highlight of the show. The woman returned to her shopping bag and brought out a little plastic bottle of Yakult, a sweet, milk-based concoction that some of Mitchell's colleagues drank in midmorning. It was about the same size and shape as a salt shaker.

"Who wants a warm drink?" she called out. "Only one thousand yen a time."

"How about some?" asked Yazawa, reaching for his wallet.

"I'll stick to beer, thanks," said Mitchell. He was starting to feel quite dizzy, what with the stale air and the noise and heat of the human engines massed behind him. Why a bottle of Yakult, which normally cost one hundred yen, should be sold for one thousand was quite beyond his comprehension.

The only taker of the woman's offer was a young man with a crew cut and a rash of pimples covering one side of his face. He looked as though he might be a reject from the self-defense forces. There was an ironic cheer as he pushed his way through from the back of the crowd and mounted the stage. The woman squatted on her haunches and inserted the little plastic bottle between her thighs. She fumbled for a moment, and then it disappeared from view. "No touching," she said, and handed him a plastic straw. The crowd cheered again as she lay back on the futon. The youth crawled into position between her legs, the straw poking from his lips. The woman lay spread-eagled, gazing impassively at the ceiling.

Disco music blared from the overhead speakers—"That's the way I like it, uh-huh, uh-huh . . ." Mitchell raised his beer can and drained it. There was a sudden roar of laughter from the audience. He glanced up at the stage to see the youth flailing about with his hands, his bottom levered up ridiculously high in the air. His head was pinned fast between the woman's now tightly clamped thighs. "No hands, I said, didn't I!" she shouted, and gave a broad wink to the audience.

"He broke the rule," explained Yazawa.

"Mmmwaaw!" came the youth's muffled gurgle. The audience roared with laughter again.

"Okay!" said Yazawa, as the youth, his pimply face even redder than before, was finally released. "It's time to get ready!"

"Get ready for what?" said Mitchell.

Yazawa said nothing, but tugged him by the wrist over to the side of the stage. Several other men were waiting there expectantly. In the center of the stage, the woman got to her feet and held up the Yakult bottle to show that it was empty. There were more cheers from the audience. The music stopped, and an ingratiating male voice boomed from the speaker.

"How about another round of applause for Mari-chan, who has been making her best efforts for the enjoyment of our honored customers. Thank you for your hard work, Mari-chan! Another round of applause!"

The audience obliged, Yazawa clapping louder than anyone else.

"Now we come to the real heart of the show," continued the male voice. "What everyone has been waiting for—it's time for the real thing!"

"The real thing?" muttered Mitchell. "What does that mean?"

There was no time for an explanation. Yazawa scrambled up onto the stage, pulling Mitchell after him. Six other men who had been waiting at the edge followed.

"That's enough for now" came the voice from the speaker. "Eight honored customers with real enthusiasm and spirit!"

"You know *jun, ken, pon?*" said Yazawa hurriedly. "That is the children's game—you have to choose between rock, scissors, and paper."

"Wait a minute," said Mitchell, his dizziness mounting. "What's this all about?"

"Rock beats scissors. Scissors beats paper. Paper beats rock."

"Yes, I know all about that. What's the point, though?"

"Good luck, Mitchell-san. Do like James Bond!"

Yazawa shoved him forward to confront a man of around thirty who was wearing a pair of glasses held together with a Band-Aid. He gave a saliva-strung gape of greeting. Mitchell looked around frantically for Yazawa. He was on the other side of the stage, preparing to challenge an elderly man in blue overalls. Beyond the edge of the stage was a crowd of upturned faces. They were all staring at him. He felt the force of their gazes physically, like a beam of heat on his cheek.

"All right, altogether now," the voice from the speaker shouted gleefully. *"Jun, ken, pon!"*

Mitchell brought his hand down in the sign for scissors. From the depth of his being, he desired to lose. It was no good. The saliva-strung grin had been replaced by a wince of defeat. His opponent had chosen paper. Mitchell felt nauseous, rooted to the spot.

"Winners step forward. Hurry up now. We can't keep Mari-chan waiting much longer!"

The woman called Mari was sitting on her futon, wiping the sweat off her shoulders with a small towel. She acknowledged the comment with a smile and a short bow.

Mitchell's next opponent was a tough-looking guy with a square, heavily stubbled jaw. This time, there was no smile, just a grunt of ac- knowledgment. *"Jun, ken, pon!"* came the roar from the speaker.

Mitchell chose scissors again, on the grounds that the same sign was unlikely to win twice in a row. He was wrong. The tough guy gave another grunt, this time of frustration, and stalked off to the side of the stage.

"Only the two finalists are left. Which one will it be—the handsome foreigner or the man in the suit who looks like a company president? Who will make Mari-chan a happy lady tonight? Now comes the mo- ment of decision!"

The spotlight swung around to shine right in Mitchell's eyes. He wiped the sweat from his brow with his wrist and squinted into the fa- miliar face that confronted him.

"Okay!" whispered Yazawa excitedly. "I'll do paper. You do scissors again and you're the winner!"

Mitchell nodded dumbly.

"Jun, ken, PON!" The hidden MC's voice rose to a triumphant screech. Mitchell knew exactly what he had to do. He thrust his fist for- ward in the sign for rock, then closed his eyes, hoping to pass it off as a mistake.

"Ho!" whooped Yazawa.

Mitchell stared down blankly at Yazawa's fingers, which were poking out in the sign for scissors. "What's happening?" he mumbled weakly.

"Mari-chan," yelled Yazawa at the woman sitting on the futon like a huge cat. "This man is a real English gentleman from the Great British Empire! This man can do like James Bond."

For the second time in the evening, it occurred to Mitchell that there had been a rapid improvement in Yazawa's English. But there was no chance to consider the matter further. Yazawa was pulling him by the el- bow, and someone was pushing him from behind. "Hold on," he squawked, trying to pull himself free. "There's really no need . . ."

59

Yazawa stuck out a knee and gave his elbow a sharp twist. Suddenly, Mitchell found himself sprawling flat on the futon, with Mari's bulk looming over him. Yazawa obviously counted judo among his many accomplishments.

"Stop!" moaned Mitchell in desperation.

But it was too late. Mari had already lowered her huge buttocks onto his upper thighs and her hands were scrabbling at his belt. Mitchell tried to wriggle free, but she pushed him firmly back, her pendulous breasts slapping against his face. "Relax," she cooed in his ear, "I will give you special service." The music started up again—"Satisfaction" by the Rolling Stones. Out of the corner of his eye, Mitchell could see Yazawa sitting on the edge of the stage, trying to get the audience to clap along with the beat. He felt faint, his mind put to flight by all the heat and glare and noise. He flopped back on the futon, arms outstretched, sucking in gulps of air. Mari took his new passivity for eagerness, and swiftly reversed herself. A bunioned foot crossed his field of vision, followed by a giant knee. And then the green and red dragon was twitching its tail just a couple of inches from his face.

In this position, it was impossible to move. His trousers, he realized in a fit of panic, were sliding down to his ankles. Mick Jagger was howling. The audience was clapping rhythmically. Mitchell felt as if a metal band were tightening around his skull. From the neck downward, everything had gone numb. He closed his eyes and suddenly the music and the lights seemed very far away. Instead, his mind flickered with disconnected images—crumbling skyscrapers, hatching lizard eggs, the Otaman spreadsheet, the poached eye of a bluefish tuna slowly winking at him from the plate . . .

How long did he lie there like a man stretched out on an operating table? It seemed like hours, but at the end, when Mari lifted her haunches away and turned round to pat him on the cheek, Mick Jagger was chanting out the closing bars of the song. Mitchell sat up on the futon and pulled up his trousers. Then, cheeks stinging, he glanced around in search of the author of his humiliation. Yazawa was standing at the side of the stage, arms folded in front of his chest, a solemn expression on his face. Mari had turned away and was doing something with a small white hand towel. The audience was shouting out unintelligible words. Holding his trousers up by the belt, Mitchell stumbled toward the edge of the stage, speechless with embarrassment.

"How about that?" shouted the voice from the speaker. "Mari-chan really fell for the handsome foreigner. It's not every day that she gives such eager service as that!"

Yazawa stepped forward to help him down. "Good work," he said, slapping him on the shoulder. "No problem of frozen balls, I think. You have the true James Bond spirit. I mean, of course, Sean Connery, not Roger Moore."

Outside, Mitchell sat down heavily on a stone step, drinking in the cool evening air. Still sharp in his mind were the noise and the lights and the heavy female body looming over him.

"What's the matter?" said Yazawa. "Japanese women don't suit you well?"

"Wait a minute," gasped Mitchell. "That's not what I was expecting. I mean . . ."

There was a lot more he could have said, but there didn't seem much point. The man was obviously testing him for some bizarre purpose of his own. The best response was to let it pass, to pretend that enforced sexual congress with a middle-aged hooker in front of an audience of fifty lowlifes was something hardly worth a second thought.

Yazawa smiled broadly and slapped him on the shoulder again. "The ladies in that place are not so young, not so beautiful, but they have a strong spirit. You challenged well. That is good. Not many foreigners have the same spirit of challenge as you."

Another compliment! Mitchell wondered what kind of feat would be needed to earn the next one.

"My favorite club in the Ginza has many beautiful, elegant women, much different from Mari-san. Let me take you there. You have certainly deserved this."

"That's great, Yazawa-san," said Mitchell, fumbling with the belt of his trousers. "I'd really like to do that some time in the future."

"Not some time," snapped Yazawa. "We go now!"

"I'm hardly in the state. I mean, look at me . . ."

"No problem, I think. Zip up your zipper and comb your hair. The elegant ladies are waiting for you!"

Mitchell took a deep breath to clear his head and raised his gaze to the sky. The advertising blimp was circling the skyscrapers above his head, sedately navigating the ocean of night like a giant carp. Its presence soothed him.

"Okay," he muttered, scrambling to his feet. "Lead the way."

Again, Yazawa drove like a demon, dodging from lane to lane and taking every red light as a provocation. It took them just twenty minutes to reach the glittering Ginza back street lined with chauffeur-driven limousines. The Isuzu eased to a halt outside a four-story building with a tuxedo-clad doorman waiting outside. Yazawa tossed the man his keys and they took the elevator to the top floor. Yazawa led the way to a door marked with a single character, which Mitchell recognized as *Jun*—"pure."

The mama-san, a tall woman in a saffron kimono, greeted Yazawa like a regular customer. One arm around his shoulder, she whispered something into his ear and they both laughed. Mitchell examined her out of the corner of his eye. She could have been anywhere between thirty and fifty years of age. With her high cheekbones and porcelain complexion, she had a cool, austere beauty that was almost asexual. Women like this really did exist! After his experience in Shibuya, Mitchell felt deeply grateful for the knowledge.

The two of them stood at the entrance chatting while Mitchell looked around the interior of the nightclub. It was comfortable rather than luxurious, with rubber plants and carved wooden screens dividing the room into a number of sections, each of which contained a group of customers seated around a low table. In each group, there was a hostess sitting between the men. Next to the bar, an elderly piano player in scholarly spectacles was trilling through a Cole Porter tune. Above his bald head, a large cut-glass chandelier was gently swaying from side to side. There were, Mitchell noticed, no windows at all.

On the face of it, there was nothing special about the place. Yet Mitchell was immediately aware that it was like no other hostess bar that he had been to in Japan. The first point that struck him was the hostesses. As Yazawa had promised, they were astonishingly beautiful. It was not the stupid animal beauty of the young models who haunted the discos of Roppongi. It was something else—a knowing, controlling beauty that was beyond possession.

The second point was the customers themselves. The way they spoke and laughed, the ease of their gestures—they exuded wealth like a hidden force field. Mitchell recognized a couple of them immediately. That man in the corner with the bushy eyebrows, roaring with laughter—he had been finance minister in the last LDP administration. That man leaning back on the sofa, the one with the pouched eyes—he and his half-brother had divided up an enormous business empire between them. If you lived in certain areas of Tokyo, you probably rented your apartment from his real estate company, bought your furniture at his department store and your milk and vegetables at one of his supermarkets, traveled to work on his railway line, and watched his baseball team on TV in the evenings. The elderly man with the flowing white hair was a well-known political commentator who spoke in a rasping Osaka accent. Several others had faces that were half-familiar from TV or newspapers.

It was a different world from the dingy strip joint in Shibuya, and Yazawa was behaving like a different man. Where before he had been coarse and loud, he was now debonair, a side of him that Mitchell had never seen before. The mama-san led the way to an empty corner. As they passed in front of a table of guests, the voices there fell silent. One of the seated men nodded an acknowledgment to Yazawa. He responded with a deep bow and a smile of unaccustomed meekness.

When the girls arrived, Mitchell's fatigue immediately disappeared. The one who placed herself beside him was called Eiko. She had been educated at a posh girl's school in Surrey, where she had learned hockey and French cooking, and she spoke fluent English with a perfect home counties accent. Why had her parents sent her to England? What sort of work did her father do? Mitchell was just alert enough to note how she skillfully deflected his questions. But it didn't matter. Eiko's smile was captivating. The touch of her hand on his thigh was like electricity. Mitchell found himself swilling down glass after glass of whiskey, laughing at her sly jokes. It had been a long time since anyone had made fun of his Yorkshire accent like that. Indeed, since he had been living in Tokyo he had more or less forgotten that he had a Yorkshire accent.

After half an hour or so, he leaned across the table to Yazawa, whose arms were draped around the shoulders of a couple of sloe-eyed beauties who were taking turns feeding him strawberries and muscat grapes.

"Where's the bathroom in this place?" he muttered, trying to keep his voice down. Why was he too embarrassed to ask Eiko directly? It was something about the atmosphere of the place, something about her accent. It reminded him of his old head teacher at primary school, and she had always made the kids wait until the end of the lesson.

"The bathroom?" yelped Yazawa, a massive grin on his face. "Why is a bathroom necessary for you?"

"I wish to relieve myself," said Mitchell, flushing.

"And you need a bath for that?" said Yazawa, with a snort of laughter. "James Bond needs a bath to accommodate all his pissing!"

Mitchell was aware that all the girls were looking at him, indulgent smiles on their faces. "Don't be ridiculous," he said tightly. "I merely want to know where the toilet is, if that's not too much to ask."

Yazawa rocked back on his seat and clapped his hands together, as if he had just heard the greatest joke in the world. People in the other alcoves were turning to look at what was going on.

"Where's the bloody toilet?" said Mitchell, stumbling to his feet.

"Nothing to be angry about," said Yazawa. "Eiko-chan will guide you there. She will help you very nicely, I think. Maybe you will not have to use your hands at all!"

The girls were all giggling now. Mitchell managed to avoid Eiko's gaze as he pushed past her.

Eiko stood up, and for one alarming moment Mitchell thought that she was going to obey Yazawa's bizarre suggestion. But instead, she pointed out a small door in the corner of the room. "That's the place you're looking for," she said in her BBC accent.

Keep it cool, thought Mitchell as he passed the amused faces in the other alcoves. The man is obviously mad. Don't let him provoke you.

When he reemerged a couple of minutes later, Eiko was waiting at the door holding out a hot towel for his use. As he wiped his hands, he noticed that Yazawa had left the table and was standing by the entrance, locked in conversation with the man who had nodded to him earlier. From their expressions, it looked serious. Mitchell returned to his seat, drained his glass of whiskey, and took up where he had left off with Eiko. But she wasn't concentrating. She kept glancing over his shoulder at the two men by the entrance.

"Tell me," Mitchell muttered in her ear. "Who is that man there? The one talking to Yazawa-san?"

"That chap," said Eiko, with a dismissive flip of the wrist. "He's one of the regulars here. You wouldn't have heard of him."

She was trying to brush him off. No doubt the girls were told not to gossip about other customers. "How do you know?" said Mitchell. "I might have. What sort of business is he in?"

"Consultancy work," Eiko said, articulating the words precisely in her cut-glass accent. "I believe that he works in the political world." She poured another measure of whiskey into his glass, then used the metal tongs to lift an ice cube from the bucket.

"He's a politician, you mean," said Mitchell.

"Not exactly. Anyway, it's awfully bad manners to discuss this kind of thing. I do hate talking about other people." The ice cubes dropped into Mitchell's glass with a decisive clink.

"Of course," he said, and took another mouthful of whiskey.

The conversation resumed and flowed nowhere in particular. Eiko's hand moved onto Mitchell's knee again. Several new sets of ice cubes were lowered into his glass, and the whiskey line slipped farther down the bottle. Mitchell was losing track of time. It might have been five minutes or thirty minutes later when he looked around and noticed that the spot where the two men had been standing was now empty. Yazawa had disappeared.

"What happened to Yazawa-san?" he asked Eiko.

"Yazawa-san? Why, he's gone. He left quite a while ago."

Mitchell almost choked on his whiskey. "He left! Why didn't he say anything?"

"I've got no idea," said Eiko, wrinkling her nose. "That's exactly the kind of chap he is. But I think he left a message for you with the mama-san."

Sure enough, when Mitchell stumbled over to the entrance, the mama-san took a sheet of paper from the fold of her kimono and handed it to him. "Please," she said with an enigmatic smile.

Mitchell's eyes hurriedly glanced down the page. Fortunately, Yazawa had chosen to write the note in English.

"No time for ladies' special sushi," it read. "You have a meeting at Otaman's head office tomorrow morning at eight o'clock. Ask for Wada-san, the head of financial operations."

At eight o'clock! Otaman's head office was at least an hour and a half away by train. And he would need time to go through his notes and prepare the visit in detail. That meant he would need to be up at the crack of dawn! What time was it now? He glanced at his watch and his heart sank. It was well past midnight, and he was stuck in the middle of the Ginza, dead drunk. He stumbled toward the door.

"Wait a moment, please!"

It was Eiko's cut-glass accent. He turned, and she was walking toward him with something in her hand. For a dread moment, Mitchell had visions of being presented with a bill equivalent to a month's salary. In the Ginza, he had heard, things like that sometimes happened to unwary foreigners.

"I'd like to give you my business card," she said brightly. "Just in case you forget me."

"I could never do that," said Mitchell with a game smile. He paused for a moment while they exchanged business cards.

"It's been such good fun," said Eiko, smiling sweetly. "You will try to come again, won't you?"

"Of course," said Mitchell and headed for the elevator. It was hard to imagine any circumstances in which he would be back.

It was only when he was inside the elevator that he looked closely at Eiko's business card. It was an elegant production, with gilt characters embossed on a traditional Japanese paper, as smooth and opalescent as mother-of-pearl. But what caught Mitchell's attention was not the quality of the card; it was what was written there. Above the flowing character *Jun* was a message in neat blue ink. It read: "I'm usually at home until lunchtime on weekdays," and it was followed by a telephone number.

Mitchell put the business card carefully into his wallet. Maybe the evening hadn't been a disaster after all.

FIVE

"Graah!" shrieked the crow. "Graah, graah!"

Tamura opened his eyes and the nightmare raced away like the shadow of a cloud driven by the first spring wind. It was the same nightmare as before. Again, it had left him bathed in sweat. He shook his head and rolled away the futon cover.

"Graah! Graah!"

Sunlight was flooding into his bedroom from the gap between the curtains. The crow sounded close. It was probably perching on the rail of the tiny balcony, waiting for the housewives to bring out the plastic sacks of trash. Then it would swoop down and tear out what it could.

"Graah!"

Tamura hauled himself out of bed and stumbled toward the shower, taking care not to wake his wife. When they were first married, she had always gotten up before him and made his breakfast. When had she stopped doing that—was it ten or fifteen years ago? It didn't matter anyway. Tamura preferred to have breakfast on his own. It was better to read the paper and watch the TV news than to waste time on trivial talk about housework and shopping.

After breakfast, he peeked into his daughter's bedroom. She was still asleep, her forearm flung across her brow, a paperback book folded open on the pillow beside her head. She looked beautiful, hardly different from the child he had taken into the bath with him every night. But that, again, was long ago. Now she had a boyfriend who called for her on Sunday afternoons and took her out for drives in his parents' car. What did they get up to in Harajuku and Jiyugaoka and all those other places where young people liked to congregate? Tamura didn't like to think about it much. The important point was that she didn't get distracted from her studies. As the teachers all said, she had the brains to make it to one of the best universities. And yet on the other hand, she was a girl. He didn't want to force her too much. He wanted her to be happy.

He tiptoed back into the main bedroom and took a necktie from the rack, an expensive Italian one that he had bought at the Singapore airport. It was just right for the meeting with the finance people from the Seikyu Railway group later that morning—not flashy or insincere, but distinctive enough to show that they weren't dealing with some dull-witted city banker, but a CBJ man with taste and imagination. Seikyu had been an important client of CBJ since its first steam train trundled from Tokyo to Yokohama in the dying years of the last century. Without CBJ's support, Seikyu could never have developed into a retail, leisure, and real estate empire that practically owned western Tokyo. Today's meeting concerned the financial arrangements for the next Winter Olympic Games, which were to be held in Seikyu territory. The important decisions had already been made. All that Tamura was doing was channeling a small portion of the funds through the Shinjuku branch, a maneuver that would sidestep some tiresome finance ministry regulations.

Fifteen minutes later, after a stroll through the grounds of the local shrine and then the deserted shopping streets, Tamura arrived at the small station where he caught the train to work. Living so far away from the office had its ups and downs. Land prices were more reasonable out here, so he had been able to afford a house with a garage, a balcony, and a small garden. On the other hand, the daily journey to the office took more than ninety minutes by express train. Since his station was the last on the line, he could usually get a seat if he started early enough. The problem was that everyone else in the neighborhood had the same idea.

The station platform was already full of salarymen reading magazines and comic books, lighting Mild Sevens, swilling down canned coffee, practicing golf swings with rolled-up newspapers. Tamura pushed his way up to his usual position at the far end of the platform. Experience told him that the competition for seats was usually less there. When he removed his copy of the *Gendai Shimbun* newspaper from his briefcase, someone came and stood right next to him, exerting a fair amount of pressure against his shoulder. That in itself was not unusual, but there was a rhythmic quality to the pushing that was irritating. It was as if he was being deliberately jostled.

Tamura turned his gaze from the *Gendai's* front page. The man beside him was a young salaryman of the type that Tamura disliked instinctively. His hands were too pudgy and well manicured, his shoes too expensive, and his mustache—well, he shouldn't have had a mustache at all. Worse still, he was a head taller than Tamura, and was looking down with a supercilious grin on his face.

"Morning," he said jauntily. "Really good weather, eh! The cherry blossoms should be here soon!"

"Correct," replied Tamura curtly, and turned back to his newspaper. Really, it was too much. The man couldn't be much older than twenty-eight, yet he had addressed Tamura in a tone of complete familiarity. When Tamura came across young businessmen so lacking in common sense, he couldn't help but be worried about Japan's future prosperity. Why, the man hadn't even bothered to wear his company badge!

Before the man had time to open his mouth again, the train eased into the station. It was punctual to the half-minute—as it always was, except in case of earthquakes and other emergencies. The doors hissed open. Tamura pushed inside and secured a seat in the corner of the compartment. To his dismay, the young salaryman fought his way to the place alongside.

"That's good," he panted. "This train is so crowded these days. Don't you agree, Tamura-san?"

Tamura twitched as if he had been given an electric shock. Somehow, this impudent youngster knew his name!

"Forgive me," he said, not bothering to hide his irritation. "But I didn't realize that we had met before."

"We haven't," said the young man, his grin getting wider.

"Then how do you know who I am?"

"It's a little difficult to explain. Let's just say some friends of mine know you."

A buzzer was sounding out on the platform and the last few passengers were cramming into the train. The conductor began to recite the familiar litany of station names over the loudspeaker.

"What friends are these?"

"I'm afraid I can't tell you that, Tamura-san. But they're very keen to arrange a meeting with you."

Tamura's mouth was dry. He had a sudden desire to get up, shove his way through the press of strap-hangers, and rush out onto the platform. He wanted to be rid of the grinning young man, who, he sensed, had the power somehow to remove all the control and good order from his life and send it crashing into chaos. But it was too late for that. The train was pulling out of the station, picking up speed.

"Why should I meet your friends? I'm very busy these days."

"Busy with Seikyu Railway and Matsui Construction? Yes, we understand that perfectly. We don't want to disturb your work. We just want to suggest a very good piece of business for you."

For a moment, Tamura gazed at the smiling face in silence. It was impossible. It was as if he had never woken up from his nightmare. "What business do you mean?" he said finally.

"It's better if my friends explain everything to you themselves."

Tamura looked around the compartment. It was all right—nobody seemed to be paying any attention to them. "Are you crazy!" he hissed. "You expect me to meet people you won't name for a proposal you won't explain to me! I refuse absolutely!"

His companion gave a fatalistic sigh and opened the briefcase he was carrying. "I have something for you," he said. "Perhaps you will understand our point of view afterwards."

He took out a brown envelope and tossed it onto Tamura's lap. "Some publicity photos," he said, getting to his feet. "It's probably better to wait until you get to the office before looking at them."

"Publicity photos? Publicizing what?"

"Publicizing you, Tamura-san."

The train was slowing down for the next station. The young man turned and squeezed his way through the strap-hangers. When the train stuttered to a halt, he was the only passenger to hop out onto the platform. In an instant he was lost in the surging crowd.

Tamura looked down at the brown envelope resting on his thighs. He had an intimation that opening it would change his life forever.

————

Mori's next stop was Yuriko's apartment north of Ikebukuro. Sano had arranged for him to pick up the key from the caretaker. First of all, though, he spent an hour walking around the neighborhood, trying to get a feel for Yuriko's environment.

It was a busy, tight-packed, higgledy-piggledy kind of area, partly commercial and partly residential. No two adjacent buildings were the same shape or size. The narrow streets, not one of them straight, contained noodle bars hardly bigger than dressing rooms, bicycle shops where the repairs were done out on the pavement, rice shops and greengrocers that only three people could fit into at the same time. Above was a tangle of telegraph wires and power cables, apparently slung at random from roof to concrete pole to roof. Below was a bright, clean chaos of bustling, jostling activity.

There was no pattern to fit into, so everything fitted. As he traced Yuriko's steps to the railway station, Mori passed a 7-Eleven, a Korean barbecue, an old bathhouse with steam belching from its tiled roof, a clinic specializing in eyelid and nose jobs, and a vending machine stocked with pornographic comics. At the first corner was a pachinko parlor blaring out music of maniacal jollity. It was full of blue-suited salarymen, their faces blank as they concentrated on the flow of the silver balls. Next to that was a shop selling Buddhist relics. Then came a fish restaurant with a large tank in the window. A flotilla of tiny cuttlefish wriggled its way from one side of the tank to the other, slowly changing color from translucent pink to translucent violet.

At this time of day, the area in front of the station filled up with workers on their lunch breaks. They streamed through the labyrinth of streets and shopping arcades, swapping jokes and gossip, bumping into one another and apologizing, clustering around food vendors. The air was full of the smell of roast fish, the blare of tape-recorded announcements and advertisements. Noodle boys on bicycles swerved expertly through the confusion, their trays held steady at the shoulder, their stony faces oblivious to everything around them.

In front of the railway station, a street vendor was baking some sweet potatoes for a group of office workers, mostly female bank clerks. He shoveled charcoal into the brazier at the back of his tiny motorized cart, then took half a dozen sweet potatoes from a cardboard box, wrapped the bulging purple tubes in silver foil, and put them in to bake. A tape-recorded street cry sang out from the loudspeaker mounted on his cart: "Stone-baked sweet potatoes, hot and delicious, hot and delicious . . ."

When the potatoes were ready, the women paid their money and retreated to a bench in front of the station entrance. "Delicious," they squealed as they peeled back the silver foil and dug in.

Who says the recession's over thought Mori. When the good times were rolling, those girls would have been lunching in some pricey Italian restaurant, twirling up the spaghetti and spooning in the tiramisu. Now they were making do with the same food that their ancestors would have been snacking on a couple of hundred years ago, in the Edo period. And no doubt it would be a lot better for their complexions.

Mori bought one himself and stood eating it next to the police kiosk at the station entrance. The middle-aged policeman on duty was standing in the doorway of his tiny office, glumly inspecting the faces going by. He was clearly a house-proud kind of fellow. The windowsill of his kiosk was lined with potted plants, and there was a canary in a cage hanging from the ceiling. The bicycle parked outside had been polished to a gleaming finish. Mori had met this kind of policeman many times. They could be fussy and inflexible, but they were generally helpful, often more so than they realized.

The policeman looked bored. When a salaryman stepped up to ask directions, he was visibly gratified. All smiles, he took out a notepad and drew a map in it with his pencil, then walked with the guy to the first turning. By the time he got back, Mori had finished the baked yam and was waiting at the door of the police box.

"Excuse me," he said. "I wonder if you could help me. I'm looking for a good but cheap hotel. My budget is five thousand yen a night."

"Five thousand yen," said the policeman, scratching his ear. "Let me think. Yes, I think there is one . . ." He reached for his notebook.

"I suppose you must be pretty busy these days," said Mori casually. "What with crime rising all the time and young people being like they are."

"Crime rising?" He pondered the idea for a moment before rejecting it. "It may say so in the newspapers, but this area's not like that at all. A few bicycles get stolen from time to time. There was a hit-and-run accident at the end of last year."

"So it's totally safe, then. Even for single women at night."

The policeman didn't sense anything unusual in Mori's question. "There's no safer area in Tokyo," he affirmed proudly. "There've been one or two panty thieves at work, but nothing worse than that."

"Panty thieves?"

"I arrested one of them myself. He was using a fishing rod to pull the panties off washing lines in apartment buildings. We found more than three hundred hidden in a cupboard." The policeman chuckled appreciatively. The memory seemed to have raised his spirits. Mori decided to go one stage farther.

"It's a funny thing, though," he said. "But I remember reading in the paper about a young woman from somewhere round here being found dead in Tokyo Bay."

"A very sad business," said the policeman defensively. "But nothing to do with this area. Events of that sort just can't be helped."

"All the same, it was a strange one, wasn't it? I expect the police are investigating every possible angle."

"It was an accident," snapped the policeman. "The investigation is already complete."

Suddenly, there was irritation and suspicion in his face. Mori glanced at the page of notebook that the policeman handed him. "Five thousand a night," he mused. "Do you happen to know whether that includes breakfast or not?"

"No breakfast," said the policeman, eyeing Mori with ill-concealed hostility.

"In that case, it's over my budget," said Mori with a regretful shake of the head. Before the policeman had time to think of a reply, he had turned on his heel and was on his way back to Yuriko's place.

The caretaker wasn't much use. Closer to eighty than seventy years old and hard of hearing, he lived in a small apartment on the basement floor.

"I don't interfere with the things that go on at all," he said, shaking a bald head that was brown and mottled like an ancient tea box.

"What kind of things do you mean?" asked Mori.

"I don't know. I don't get involved, you see." It was clear that he considered not getting involved to be an important part of his job.

"What about Yuriko-san? Do you remember anything about her?"

"She was a fine girl, never caused any trouble. Except once, that is."

"Once? She caused trouble once?"

The old man paused for thought. "I think it was her," he said finally. "She lost her key somewhere and I had to open the door. . . ."

"And then what? Did something happen?"

"And then she gave me a delicious musk melon. It must have cost at least five thousand yen."

"That's all?"

"Yes, that's all."

Yuriko's apartment was on the seventh floor. There was a single small elevator and a flight of stairs. Mori, who had been worrying about his waistline, decided to take the stairs.

He waited at the door of the apartment for a couple of seconds, then slid the key into the lock and eased his way inside. Emptiness, silence, dust rising in a shaft of sunshine—he knew at a glance that no one had been there for days.

The apartment was a "1 LDK"—one small bedroom and a "living-dining-kitchen area." Everything was neat and tidy, from the plates stacked on the counter to the empty trash bins. In fact, it was too neat and tidy—almost as if Yuriko had prepared for her permanent departure. He went through the drawers of the writing desk and found nothing but pencils and empty notebooks. He went through the pockets of the coats in the closet and found nothing but rubber bands and one-yen coins. He looked in the laundry basket and, something he hated doing, checked the dirty sheets. There was nothing.

In the bedroom something caught his eye. On the window ledge was a goldfish bowl with a single inhabitant wiggling around in a drunken circle. That was strange. How long could a small fish like that survive without food or fresh water? Had someone been secretly taking care of it? Mori peered into the bowl for a moment, then intercepted the fish's path with a finger. It executed a perfect back flip and took off in the same wobbly style in the opposite direction. So it wasn't so strange at all. The fish was microprocessor controlled, probably powered by a solar panel. You didn't need to feed it or change the water, and it wouldn't smell the place up when its time came. The perfect pet for a modern Japanese girl.

Next to the bed was a half-empty bookcase containing an encyclopedia and a row of paperbacks. Mori examined it closely. From the layering of dust at the back, it looked as if the bookcase had been full until quite recently. Now half the books were gone. That was strange. His eyes lit on one of those that remained, a novel by Banana Yoshimoto. There was something a little odd about the shape of the spine. He lifted it out of the shelf and shook a couple of photos from between the pages. One showed a group of half a dozen guys on motorbikes. The other, which according to the time stamp was only eighteen months old, showed a guy holding an electric guitar.

Mori slipped the photos into his pocket, then went back to the living room. He pulled up the chair of the writing desk and sat gazing at the wall, wondering what kind of trouble Yuriko had gotten herself into. It might well be something to do with the bikers. He would certainly have to check them out.

It wasn't until several moments had passed that Mori's eyes began to focus on the wall itself. There seemed to be patterns there, a play of light and shade that he hadn't noticed before.

He got to his feet and looked more closely. There were, he discovered, a number of small holes in the wallpaper, the sort that would be made by tacks. So at one time there had been posters on the living room wall. Not just posters, either. There were also some larger holes that looked as if they had accommodated nails. That suggested a heavier kind of decoration—picture frames or perhaps some kind of souvenir. An obvious question arose in Mori's mind—why weren't they there any longer?

All of a sudden, Mori had a strong feeling that he was wasting his time. He wasn't going to find anything that might be of any use. Someone had made sure of that already.

Mori switched off the lights, locked up the apartment, and walked down the corridor to the elevator. The hum of the motor indicated that it was already rising toward the seventh floor. Mori stood back a little, curious to see who would emerge.

The doors opened to reveal a young woman in white boots and a shiny red raincoat. She was tall, pretty much the same height as Mori, with thick hair sweeping down to her shoulders. She took one look at Mori, then jabbed at the control button. "Wrong floor," she muttered, and the doors immediately closed again.

There were only two floors of apartments above the seventh. Mori raced up the stairway to the eighth, checked up and down the empty corridor, then dashed up to the ninth. The elevator was still there, doors open, but there was no one in sight. Mori walked up the corridor, making a note of the names on the doors.

The sound of the elevator doors closing made him twist around. He was just in time to catch a glimpse of white boots and a red raincoat as the doors slammed shut. For a brief moment, he thought about the staircase. Nine floors to the bottom—it might be good for his waistline, but the woman would be long gone by the time he got to the bottom. Mori cursed himself for his carelessness and waited for the elevator to come back and take him down to the basement floor.

As he had expected, the caretaker didn't know anything about the woman in the red raincoat. In fact, there were no young women resident on the ninth floor at all. Mori moved on to the next subject.

"You said that Yuriko-san once gave you a musk melon."

The caretaker's watery old eyes lit up in remembrance. "That's right, she did. It was delicious."

"Did you go into her apartment at that time?"

The caretaker wrinkled his nose as he considered the question.

"Into her apartment," he repeated dubiously. "No, I don't think I actually went into the apartment. I must have stayed outside."

"Are you sure? Try to remember."

"Well, it's difficult to say . . . It's a while ago now . . ." The old man shuffled from foot to foot. He was getting bored.

"What about the melon?" persisted Mori. "Was it a sweet one, with plenty of juice? Was it ripe?"

"Delicious," murmured the old man. "Sweet like honey." He gave a soft, almost feminine smile.

"And did you look inside the apartment? Did you see anything there?"

The old man stared at the ground. His jaw was moving up and down slightly, as if he were still chewing the melon. When he looked up again, there was a worried expression on his face. "A mask," he said slowly. "A big mask on the wall."

"What do you mean?" said Mori. "A Nō mask, or something like that?"

"Not that kind of mask," said the old man. "An ugly one made out of metal."

"What else did you see? Was there anything else that was unusual?"

"Well . . . yes . . . there was a strange hat on the table."

"A hat?" said Mori, startled.

"I never actually saw her wearing it. I've never seen anyone with a hat like that. It had all sorts of things coming out of it."

"Things coming out of it? What do you mean?"

"I don't know. Decorations, I suppose. All these fashions are beyond me. These girls dyeing their hair blond—they don't want to look like Japanese anymore, do they? It wasn't like that in the old days. Women had hair as black as a crow's wet wing, skin like the finest Kyoto silk . . ."

His voice trailed off. He was obviously remembering something, but it wasn't what Mori wanted him to remember.

"Tell me more," Mori urged. Frustration was spreading through the muscles of his face.

"There's nothing more."

"Come on. You must remember what this mask looked like."

"No, I don't," said the old man proudly. His eyes seemed cloudier now.

"The melon," said Mori urgently. "Remember the taste of the melon!"

The old man didn't seem to have heard. "I like persimmons too," he ruminated. "They're good for my bowels. Actually, my grandson brought me a box last week. Just wait there and I'll fetch you one."

"Wait—it's all right, thank you," said Mori, but it was too late. The old man had disappeared into the dark of his apartment. A couple of minutes later, he reappeared, a large persimmon clasped in his leathery hand.

"All the way from Akita Prefecture," he explained. "It'll do your bowels the world of good."

"It would have been useless to press any further. Mori accepted the fruit with thanks and made a mental note to send another box.

Mitchell's Japanese friends had warned him about sake-and-whiskey hangovers. Now he understood what they meant. When he arrived at Tokyo station, his eyes were red and puffy, his throat was dry, and his head felt as if it were being squeezed in a giant nutcracker. Bright lights, like the early morning sun slanting into his eyes, caused the pressure to tighten another notch. Loud noises, like the bellow of the loudspeaker on the platform, meant another jab of pain. Vibrations, like the rattle of the train as it pulled out of the station, made his eyes water and his stomach tremble.

Breakfast was out of the question. So was any further preparation of his notes for the meeting. Just looking at the papers bouncing about on his lap was enough to release a wave of nausea that shivered through his entire nervous system. Instead, he leaned back in his seat, loosened his collar, and watched Tokyo go flying past his window.

The formless density of urban Japan was overwhelming to contemplate. All those offices, shops, temples, warehouses, and apartment blocks baking in the sunshine; all those signs clamoring to be read; all that mighty tangle of highways, overpasses, tunnels, bridges, and railroad tracks. There was no space between the buildings, no space between the cars on the road, no space between the bodies crowding the station platforms, no space between the cities themselves. Chiba, Tokyo, Kawasaki, Yokohama—they were barely distinguishable segments of a single urban mass that seemed to stretch on to the end of the world. On that first journey in from Narita airport, the physical appearance of his new surroundings had stunned him. It was not the ugliness of economic entropy, which he understood and accepted, but a dynamic anti-beauty that upset every notion of structure and decorum. Even now, eighteen months later, he still hadn't gotten used to it.

At the last station on the line, the platform was packed with salarymen waiting to make the morning commute into Tokyo. Mitchell had to squeeze past one who bulled his way into the carriage, head down, eyes fixed on the precious empty seats. Outside the station, Mitchell stopped at a kiosk and bought a "stamina drink" that was supposed to work wonders on hangovers, and a packet of chewing gum impregnated with caffeine crystals. Then he hailed a taxi and asked to be taken to the Otaman R&D center.

The taxi driver was a friendly looking character in a peaked cap and immaculate white gloves. Once he had established that Mitchell's Japanese was comprehensible, he was eager to chat. First of all, he wanted to know what Mitchell thought of Japanese food and women. Stomach twitching with the memory of the previous evening, Mitchell replied that he liked them both. That seemed to put the driver at ease, and he began to expand on his daily routine.

"A foreigner at this time of day," he ruminated. "It's quite a surprise."

"Is that so?" said Mitchell. "I suppose foreigners are pretty rare around these parts."

"Didn't use to be, of course. Once upon a time I used to take a lot of foreigners up to Otaman—Americans, Germans, Chinese, all sorts of people. It was interesting. I could usually tell their nationality even before they got inside the car."

"Really?" said Mitchell weakly. The stamina drink didn't seem to have done much good. His head was still throbbing like a sore wound, and the taxi driver's rough treatment of the gear stick wasn't helping his stomach at all. He put a stick of chewing gum into his mouth and forced himself to move his jaws up and down.

"That was in the old days. Before all the problems cropped up."

"Problems?" said Mitchell, one hand nursing his churning stomach. "What kind of problems do you mean?"

The taxi driver peered into the mirror above his head. His red-rimmed eyes fixed on Mitchell's face. "Didn't you hear the stories?" he said. "I thought all the people who do business with Otaman had heard the stories, even the foreigners."

"What stories do you mean?" said Mitchell, now fully alert. "I haven't seen anything in the press lately."

"The press!" said the taxi driver with a dry chuckle. "No, there won't be anything there! They'll have made sure of that much."

He changed abruptly down from fourth gear to second, sending Mitchell lurching forward against the front headrest. They were turning off the main street now. That probably meant they were getting close to the Otaman headquarters. Mitchell's stomach was on the verge of a full-scale mutiny, but he was determined to get some kind of explanation.

"You must have been driving this route for a long time," he began tactfully.

"Almost twenty years," replied the taxi driver.

"With all that experience, you must know more about Otaman than the members of its staff themselves."

"You could say that."

"So what do you think their biggest mistake was? What was the real cause of their difficulties? I'll bet it's not as simple as everyone thinks."

They turned sharply again. This time Mitchell could actually see the Otaman building at the end of the street. It was just what you would expect for a minor-league trading house—an undistinguished gray block, probably several decades old.

"You're absolutely right," said the taxi driver emphatically. "It had nothing to do with that real estate venture, nothing to do with all those bad loans. The real problem was in the family."

"The family?" Mitchell clutched the seat in front. That last jerk up into second gear had set his stomach bucking like a carp in a net. He swallowed hard and gritted his teeth.

"The company's never been the same since they forced out the old man. That's when it lost its independence. His nephew's in charge now, but he doesn't know anything. He just does what they tell him."

The taxi was now cruising to a halt outside Otaman's security gate. Mitchell fought down the wave of nausea. "Does what *who* tell him?" he whispered hoarsely. "Who is actually controlling Otaman?"

The driver stopped the taxi meter, and the car's automatic door swung open. "You ask many questions," he said softly, turning around to take the money. "Sometimes, it's not good to ask too many questions."

"Who do you mean? Please tell me who!" Mitchell lifted the banknote away from the taxi driver's outstretched hand, determined to get an answer before he paid. Suddenly, there was a flash of alarm in the driver's eyes, and he turned away to face the windshield.

"Six hundred yen, please!" he said, and revved the engine.

Mitchell became aware of a presence next to the car door. It was one of the uniformed guards who manned the security gate. He bent down and looked into the interior of the taxi.

"Mitchell-san," he said. "Good morning! We welcome you to Otaman Corporation."

"Good morning," muttered Mitchell, and climbed out of the car.

He was led into a small room by the side of the security gate and given a plastic name tag and a blue cotton jacket bearing the Otaman logo on the back. The closet from which the guard took the jacket contained several others in various colors.

"I don't know if blue suits me," said Mitchell. "How about a green one?"

The guard laid down his pencil on the form that he was writing on. He didn't look amused. "Green is for customers," he said flatly. "VIP visitors like you have blue."

"I see," said Mitchell, feeling rather foolish. "And who gets to wear black?"

"Black is for senior personnel. White is for ordinary staff. This system is very helpful for security purposes."

"I'm sure it is."

It wasn't the first time that Mitchell had been through heavy security before making a company visit. Several top Japanese companies were sensitive about industrial espionage. Yet, the procedures were usually handled in a polite and friendly manner, the guards avuncular men in their late fifties who offered him green tea and complimented him on his Japanese. The Otaman guards were not like that at all. They wore white helmets and carried long staves like those used by the riot police. The three sitting around the desk in the little room were large, silent men in their early thirties. The one who had given Mitchell the jacket had returned to laboriously filling out a form recording his visit. The knuckles of his right hand were misshapen and calloused, the bones flattened into a ridge. That was what a karate man's hand looked like after years of being bashed against stone walls and wooden boards. The other two hardly took their eyes off the bank of video screens on the wall. Mitchell was surprised to see that the scenes they were monitoring so intently were not just the surroundings of the Otaman headquarters, but the interior of the offices as well—men and women sitting at desks, talking in meeting rooms, drawing up plans on blackboards.

"Now, your identification, please," said the guy with the karate knuckles.

"Identification? Will my credit card do?"

"No good. Don't you have your foreigner registration card?"

Luckily, Mitchell had brought it. He took it out of his wallet and tossed it on the desk. The guard transcribed the details onto the form, then peered into Mitchell's face like a man examining a suspicious banknote.

"What's the matter?" said Mitchell. "Didn't I shave properly this morning?"

"We'll keep this card here until your visit is complete," said the guard tersely. "Now follow me."

The guard led him across the courtyard, in through the main entrance of the building, and down a dim, low-ceilinged corridor that smelled of stale cigarettes. The atmosphere was completely different from what Mitchell had experienced in the other Japanese companies he had visited. There was no cute receptionist chirruping out greetings, no marble-tiled elevator hall, no bronze sculptures or abstract-expressionist paintings on display. Instead, everything was cramped and shabby and bare, almost as if it were no longer in use. The corridor was lined with boxes of documents that looked as if they had been there for months. The few employees that passed, all wearing the regulation white cotton jackets, didn't even acknowledge him. They seemed to shrink away, avoiding eye contact. Everything was strangely quiet.

The room in which the meeting was to take place was windowless, lit by a flickering neon tube. Mitchell took his place on a sofa that had once been green but was now mostly brown. The carpet was threadbare, the walls smudged by the outlines of long-disappeared cabinets and bookcases. The only concession to interior decor was the crystal ashtray and heavy lighter on the table in front of him, both engraved with the Otaman logo.

After a few minutes' wait, there was a knock on the door and a woman came in bearing a cup of coffee and a large envelope. Squat, with short hair and muscular calves, she looked more like a female judo champion than an employee of a listed Japanese company. The typical office lady that Mitchell was used to encountering on his company visits had a nice smile, graceful manners, and long flowing hair on which much time and money had been lavished. The woman who wordlessly put the coffee cup on the table in front of him, spilling some coffee into the saucer as she did so, wasn't like that at all. In fact, Mitchell noted with some unease, she had the same misshapen knuckles as the guard at the security gate.

"This is information for you," she said in English, and handed him the envelope. Mitchell gave a nod of acknowledgment but did not open it. For a moment, she stood there glaring at him, then turned on her heel and left the room. After she had gone, Mitchell opened the envelope and browsed through the publicity brochures that it contained. They were amateurishly put together, half in Japanese and half in fractured English, but they helped to fill in the gaps in his knowledge of the company's history.

Otaman had been founded in the 1890s by Manjiro Ota, the second son of an old samurai family. The company's original business was importing textiles from Britain for processing into Western clothes. In fact, the brochure reported proudly, Otaman played "a key role in the nation's modernization," since Japan's first business suits and overcoats were produced from cloth supplied by Otaman. Later on, the company built up a network of small cutting and stitching shops and began to produce specialty garments, such as sports outfits, tuxedos, and military uniforms. In the 1930s, Otaman expanded into China and Korea and was briefly the largest company in the Japanese textile industry. After the surrender, old Manjiro was purged by the MacArthur administration and his son Ichiro took over the helm. Through the fifties and sixties, he diversified into new businesses, such as food imports and machinery exports, gradually building up a network of branches throughout Southeast Asia.

After that, the brochure became more vague, noting only such events as the bronze medal won by an Otaman employee in the 1964 Tokyo Olympics and Ichiro's death in 1974. Here, it was what was not written that was important. Mitchell knew that Otaman had bet heavily on the real estate boom set off by Prime Minister Tanaka in the early 1970s; that it had ended up with some spectacular losses and that it had survived only thanks to a bailout organized by bureaucrats and major banks. And since then? Throughout the 1980s, profit margins had been in slow decline and the number of employees had been shrinking. More aggressive rivals were taking away market share in the food import business. The textile business was stable, but had little long-term potential. On the face of it, there was nothing about Otaman that made it an attractive investment.

The door opened again and Mitchell looked up, half-expecting the return of the muscular woman who had brought the coffee. Instead, he was confronted by an equally short and squat man wearing a black cotton jacket and carrying a folder fat with documents. He introduced himself as Wada, the deputy head of the finance department. They bowed and swapped business cards.

Wada immediately impressed Mitchell as being nervous, distracted, and keen to get the meeting over with as soon as possible. The man could hardly keep still. As he listened to Mitchell's questions, he twisted around in his seat like a man with hemorrhoids, twitched his nose, scratched his ear, and tapped his pencil impatiently against his knee. Before he answered, he flipped through his files for several minutes, clearing his throat, sucking his teeth, and generally giving the impression that to make a straight answer to a straight question would cause him physical pain.

"What I'd really like to know," probed Mitchell, "is the kind of returns you expect on the new businesses you're undertaking compared with your traditional businesses."

"Very difficult," muttered Wada, rummaging through his file. "There are many uncertainties."

"I understand that. Perhaps you could give me a best-case scenario and a worst-case scenario and then explain your assumptions."

"Worst-case scenario," said Wada uncomfortably. "I'm not sure I understand your meaning. We are very confident of success in our business."

Mitchell was speaking slow, deliberate Japanese, as he always did in these situations. It was impossible for Wada not to have understood his meaning.

"My meaning is that I'd like to know what level of profitability you are expecting from your new businesses."

"We expect a superior level of profitability. Our plans will make Otaman very healthy once again."

"Good. How superior do you mean? Can you give me some kind of target?"

"Targets are difficult. Of course, many uncertainties exist."

Once, in an expensive Japanese restaurant, Mitchell had chased a chunk of boiled tofu around and around a bowl of sukiyaki with a pair of long, pointy-ended chopsticks. When he eventually succeeded in picking it up, it immediately crumbled into two halves. When he had tried to pick up one of them, that also had crumbled in two. The other half had done exactly the same thing. His frustration had ended only when one of his amused Japanese friends had ordered a spoon for him. He was beginning to feel the same way now. Wada's answers were as slippery as that piece of tofu.

"Let's go through it again, please. What are the main uses of the money that you have raised from the banks over the past two years?"

"Diversification and rationalization."

"Can you please be more specific."

"We are aiming to restore Otaman's status as one of the top trading houses in Japan. Otaman must prepare to confront the twenty-first century boldly and creatively."

Mitchell winced at the cliché. Wada pulled a sheet of paper from his file and stared at it, brow furrowed. "We have developed a new corporate philosophy," he intoned, returning the sheet of paper to the back of the file. "We believe that Otaman can make a major contribution to human prosperity and global harmony. . . ."

It was getting worse. Mitchell put down his pen and sat back on the sofa. For a couple of minutes, he watched Wada rambling on about Otaman's newfound altruism. The man didn't even sound convinced himself. He spoke too quickly, frequently pausing to glance into the file.

"Otaman has always played an important role in Japan's economic development," he concluded hesitantly. "That's how we see our future in the next century. An era of expanded contribution and high-quality, creative diversification."

"What about the share price?" interjected Mitchell. "It has been stagnant for almost ten years now. What's going to change that?"

"Our share price will rise," Wada said calmly. "The great potential of Otaman is sure to be widely recognized."

"Management displays confidence in share price," wrote Mitchell in his notebook. But based on what? It didn't look as though he was going to find out from Wada. The man clearly viewed the meeting as a meaningless formality that had to be gone through, not an opportunity for real disclosure. Mitchell's growing impatience was heightened by a shivery sensation in the pit of his stomach, as if a pool of icy water had formed there. He thought of the fish he had consumed last night, and his throat tightened.

"Are you well, Mitchell-san? Your face is very pale." Wada had laid the file down on the desk and was peering at him attentively.

"Stomach illness," muttered Mitchell, his head throbbing harder than it had in the taxi.

"You should try our Chinese medicines," said Wada proudly. "They will strengthen your stomach immediately. We are importing a special compound of ginseng root and royal jelly."

Mitchell gulped back the saliva that was suddenly flooding his mouth and got to his feet. At that moment, he became certain that he was about to throw up. "I need to use the toilet," he said through clenched teeth.

"Certainly," said Wada with a smile. "Let me show you the way." He seemed quite relieved that the interrogation was at least temporarily over.

Mitchell hurriedly obeyed Wada's instructions, half-jogging the length of the corridor to the small, dimly lit room at the other end. There were two cubicles, both of which contained Japanese-style toilets. Mitchell had been hoping for a Western-style toilet so that he could sit down for a while and nurse his rebellious stomach back to stability. Instead, he had to kneel on the tiled floor, his head overhanging the white ceramic trench. It was an uncomfortable posture. He didn't have to wait long before his stomach heaved and strings of sour-tasting bile were hanging from his lips. After that, Mitchell began to feel better. He knelt there in silence, listening to the gurgle of the flush and the clank of the pipes.

He was just about to get to his feet and clean himself up when the outer door opened and someone entered the room. Mitchell wasn't in the mood for an exchange of courtesies. He decided to stay where he was a little longer.

The newcomer whistled softly to himself as he made lengthy and splashy use of the urinal. He had reached the last few bursts, when the door opened again and someone else came in. There was a grunt of acknowledgment from the first man, followed by a polite greeting from the newcomer.

"And how is everything on your side?" said the first man tersely. "Have the plans been finalized?"

The second man's voice was younger, his tone deferential. "Not yet," he said. "But we have been told that there is no hurry. Shipments are not expected now until next year."

"Next year!"

There was the sound of a zipper being fastened. Mitchell's knees and ankles were sore from being pressed against the tiled floor. Resisting the longing to shift position, he bit his lip and remained motionless. There was something about the conversation that intrigued him.

The second man spoke again. This time, there was a slight hesitancy in his voice. "It is said that this Kawasaki project is the most important event in our company's development since the war."

"That is correct."

"In that case, I wonder about it sometimes."

"What do you mean?" said the first man coldly. From the position of his voice, he was standing at the sink, but he had yet to turn on the tap.

"Well," said the younger man, "all this secrecy is strange. And I can't help wondering what would happen if the authorities found out. Wouldn't there be big trouble?"

"Of course there would," snapped the first man. "But there's no point in worrying about that. We are loyal employees of Otaman. Upholding the interests of Otaman should be the only thing that matters to us!"

"Yes, I understand that," said the younger man doubtfully. "But I wish we knew more about the project. Surely, that would help us work better."

"These are foolish words. Don't let anyone hear you talk like that. It might be dangerous for you."

"I am sincerely sorry. I only meant—"

"It doesn't matter what you meant. Keep your mouth shut and endure. This project must not be risked by loose talking!"

"Understood!"

The tap was turned off with a squeak. After a few moments, the door swung on its hinges and Mitchell heard the sound of footsteps disappearing down the corridor. The younger man followed soon after, allowing Mitchell finally to rise from his kneeling position. He brushed the creases out of his trousers and emerged from the cubicle. When he peered out into the corridor, he caught a glimpse of a white jacket disappearing around the corner at the other end.

When he returned to the meeting room, Mitchell found Wada as uncooperative as before. "Are you sure you are able to continue the meeting?" he asked Mitchell hopefully.

"I'm all right, thank you," said Mitchell. "It's not very serious." In fact, his stomach did feel much more settled. Perhaps it was the fact that he now had something to occupy his mind.

"That's good," said Wada. "Now let me tell you more about our new corporate philosophy."

Mitchell spent another fifteen minutes doing the equivalent of chasing the piece of tofu around a sukiyaki bowl. As he had expected, he got nowhere. Wada would give him only the vaguest idea of what the company's plans were. No specifics, no hard figures, not even an indication of when these mysterious new businesses would start to generate profit. It crossed Mitchell's mind that perhaps Wada didn't know himself. Perhaps he was just a paper-pusher who was never let into top-level business strategy. Mitchell decided to test him out.

"This is all useful information," he said casually. "But I need to have more detail. For example, investors are keen to know what the prospects are for the Kawasaki project."

The response was well beyond his expectations. Wada dropped his file onto the table with a clatter and sat there staring at Mitchell for a full minute, his mouth opening and closing like a goldfish's.

"What did you say?" he croaked finally.

"A simple question," said Mitchell, cocking his pen as if preparing to note down Wada's answer. "I would like to know how you see the Kawasaki project developing."

"Where did you learn about that?" hissed Wada. He was sitting bolt upright now, the veins standing out on his forehead.

"There were some rumors in the market," replied Mitchell coolly. "You know how investors talk."

"Rumors! Who was spreading these rumors?"

"I don't remember. There are so many stories of that sort."

The top half of Wada's face had turned sickly pale. He breathed out sharply. "The time for this meeting is over," he said, suddenly getting to his feet. "Thank you sincerely for coming here. Now let me show you to the door."

"Thank you for making time for me," said Mitchell with a bow. "It has been very useful."

Which was true. Several ideas were revolving in his mind as he followed Wada down the long corridor that led to the main entrance. Now he understood why Yazawa was so keen to recommend the stock. He obviously had inside information about what this secret project was all about. He knew that Otaman's prospects were about to be dramatically improved. If Mitchell could only dig a little deeper, he would be on to something huge, something that would make his name as an investment analyst. But how to proceed—how to find out more about this mysterious Kawasaki project without alienating Yazawa—that would require some serious thought.

Outside, Wada bade him a cold farewell. Mitchell retrieved his identification card from the security people, then walked to the bus stop at the junction with the main road. It was a fine day. The sun was glinting off the blue tiled roofs, and there was a warm breath to the boisterous southerly wind. Passing in front of a tiny wooden house with a postage stamp of a garden, Mitchell noticed some flakes of cherry blossom on a gnarled old tree. His second Japanese spring—not bad at all. He felt as if his hangover was lifting.

Mori took a shortcut back to Shinjuku, gunning the old Honda through the winding shopping streets and bustling intersections. It was a warm clear day, the sun glinting off the chrome and glass of the cars in front. On the sidewalks, this year's spring look was just starting to take shape— for women, ankle boots, flared cotton miniskirts, hair flossed out to the shoulder. It was more retro, a throwback to the styles of the mid-seventies. Mori reckoned he had some items of clothing at the back of his wardrobe that could put him right up there in the vanguard of fashion, providing the moths and damp hadn't gotten there first. But what about the future? What was there distinctive and original about the present that people would be able to get nostalgic about in twenty years' time? Probably nothing, thought Mori, sitting astride his purring Honda and watching the pedestrians come flooding over a crossing. He was living in an era that would leave no traces at all.

The lights changed; Mori shot a brief glance into his cracked rearview mirror, then let out the clutch. Twenty yards behind him, the big, heavy motorbike eased away from the curb. Mori had been half-expecting that. Its rider had kept the same distance since Mori had spotted him, at the first junction after Yuriko's apartment. With his darkened full-face helmet, shoulder pouch, and smart blue uniform, he looked like a motorbike messenger. In the way he stopped to use his walkie-talkie, he acted like a motorbike messenger too. But he didn't ride a motorbike like a motorbike messenger. He didn't lean into the corners, or thread his way between the lines of stationary cars, or use his boots to kick away from the curb. In fact, he didn't seem in a hurry at all, and that, in Mori's opinion, was good grounds for suspicion.

Mori cruised along the busy shopping street, allowing several cars to overtake him, but the messenger continued to keep the same twenty yards distance between them. Mori let his speed drop to a crawl as he approached the next set of lights. He waited until they were turning from orange to red, then suddenly opened the clutch and shot through. The messenger reacted immediately. His 750-cc engine gave an angry roar and he came squealing through the lights after Mori. On the other side, Mori slowed down again, and the messenger fell back to his previous distance.

They were approaching the edge of Shinjuku now, an area that Mori knew like the back of his hand. He took a sharp left into a busy shopping street, then immediately turned left again, this time into a warren of narrow streets containing pachinko parlors, yakitori bars, pink salons, and shops that sold fake watches and handbags. In the nighttime the area was awash with roistering salarymen. In the daytime, it was much quieter. There were some high school students milling around a porno video center, a few stray salesmen taking a break between visits, a couple of guys in white overalls and wooden sandals slopping out buckets into the gutter. No one gave Mori a second glance as he buzzed past.

Mori heard the big motorbike pause, then rumble around the corner. Not as maneuverable as the Honda, it would have difficulty in negotiating the crisscrossing alleys of the little entertainment area. Mori glanced in his mirror. The messenger was cruising down the center of the narrow street, no more than thirty yards behind him. Mori let him close the gap another ten yards, then braked sharply and twisted the Honda into a narrow passage between a pachinko parlor and a money-lending shop. It stank of urine. In fact, Mori had urinated there himself several times over the past twenty-five years.

Unable to stop in time, his bike went thundering past the entrance of the passage. Mori maneuvered the Honda past the blocks of concrete and clumps of decomposing trash. At the other end, he stopped and listened. As he had expected, the messenger had taken the next left turn and was roaring up a parallel side street. Swiftly, Mori manhandled the Honda around in a circle and shot back the way he had come. Back near the entrance, he stopped again and looked over his shoulder. The messenger had edged the big bike into the passageway, but wasn't making any attempt to follow any farther. Instead, he was sitting up in the seat, feet on the ground, reaching into his shoulder bag with his right hand. Now he had taken something out and was pointing it down the passageway. There was a sharp zinging sound, and a couple of puffs of dust from the wall next to Mori's head. Without pausing to think, he flattened himself over the handlebars and took off, lurching from side to side as the Honda revved up to an angry whine.

Mori skidded right at the pachinko parlor, roared down the narrow street for fifty yards, then took a left around the side of a Korean barbecue place. Someone had been repainting the side door. Mori squealed to a halt next to the wooden trestle table on which the tools and materials had been left. The workman was probably inside, tasting some of the fieriest kimchi in Shinjuku. Mori could hear the dull roar of the messenger's big bike a couple of hundred yards away. It would be easy enough to lose him in the tangle of alleyways, but in the end that would mean nothing. This man was a professional. The puffs of concrete dust next to Mori's head had been convincing evidence of that. He would keep coming back until the job was done.

Mori leaned across to the trestle table and took what he needed. There was no point in disturbing the family that owned the place. If they knew the circumstances, they wouldn't mind. And the next time he dropped by, Mori would be sure to order a few extra plates of tripes and salted ox tongue.

The shopping street on the other side was clogged with parked delivery vans and taxis stopping to pick up customers. Mori squeezed between the line of cars and the curb, then found a gap wide enough for him to swing the Honda across onto the other side of the road, where the traffic was lighter. A glance behind confirmed that the messenger had finally emerged from the little entertainment district and was also forcing his way through the traffic. There was a major junction ahead, where the shopping street met one of the big arteries that connected central Tokyo with the northern suburbs. The traffic lights were red, and a river of pedestrians was flowing over the crossing. Mori edged through them, drawing a number of angry glances, then banked sharply to the right, cutting across the line of oncoming traffic. Klaxons blared and headlights flashed, but in an instant he was flying along on the main artery, the Honda's engine buzzing like a boxful of hornets.

From here on, the key was going to be timing. Mori glanced in his mirror. The traffic lights were finally changing now, and the big motorbike was the first vehicle to pull out into the road behind him. Mori shifted to the inside lane, cut his speed slightly, and got ready. It didn't take long for the powerful machine to close the distance. Mori watched in the mirror as it came thundering up the section of overpass far ahead of the stream of traffic. The messenger was sitting almost upright, one hand reaching into his pouch again. He was getting closer and closer.

Mori waited for what he judged to be exactly the right moment—just over the brim of the overpass's steep, curving exit ramp. Then he braked sharply and gripped the object that had been nestling between his thighs. The messenger was some twenty yards behind, too close to take any avoiding action. He tried to brake too, but the weight of the big motorbike carried him squealing down the slope of the overpass, both hands tight on the handlebars. Almost stationary now, Mori twisted in the saddle, raised the spray can, and squirted a stream of red paint at the helmet as it came hurtling past.

His aim was good. The paint exploded onto the darkened visor in great lashes. The messenger braked harder, scrabbling frantically at the visor with one hand. But Mori had chosen his spot well. Here the overpass was curving steeply down to ground level, and the messenger was fighting blind against his own momentum.

The big bike skidded and twisted, tires screeching. The messenger rocked back in the seat as he struggled to regain control, but it was already too late. The bike was tearing away from under him and he was jackknifing over the handlebars. For one slow moment he sailed forward and upward, like a pole vaulter who has just let go of the pole. Then he rolled, dipped, and plunged to the ground. There was a loud crack as his helmet hit the tarmac. The bike went careering down the slope on its side, sparks flying from the metalwork. The messenger's body rolled over and over, his head bobbling like a football, before finally thudding against the steel barrier in the center of the road. He lay there motionless, arms and legs splayed out at a strange angle.

Was the guy dead? Probably not, thought Mori, but he wouldn't be doing any motor sports for a good long time. He glanced over his shoulder. Another wedge of traffic was appearing over the brim of the overpass. No one in any of the cars passing on the other side of the steel barrier seemed to have registered what had happened. There was nothing to be gained by waiting around. Mori heaved the Honda onto the road again, and took off like a one-eyed cat with a stolen mackerel.

SIX

In a remote and mountainous region of northwest Japan, there is a valley between two mist-wreathed peaks that contains a couple of dozen wooden houses. The village does not appear in any tourist guide and goes uncelebrated in any work of literature. To the occasional visitor who passes by in the climbing season, it is just a couple of hard-to-pronounce Chinese characters that appear faintly between the contour lines on his map. Apart from the cluster of dwellings, it contains a single store, a tiny school, and a temple half hidden in the thick pine forest that covers the rest of the valley.

The nearest highway is eighty miles away, the nearest railway line one hundred, but the village's isolation is much greater than distances can describe. Until the early years of this century, the nearest city was a week's walk away, Tokyo so distant that it might have been a foreign country. For a quarter of the year, the whole area is under heavy snow dumped by the winds that come blasting across the Japan Sea from Manchuria. In former times, the mountain passes were completely blocked for months on end. Nowadays, several of the villagers board up their houses and go and look for seasonal work in the cities of the coast. Only when the snows have melted and the gushing rivulet that bisects the village has broadened into a racing torrent do they return to their vegetable patches and fishing grounds and guns and traps.

When the spring winds are bringing the cherry blossom to the southern islands of Japan, here the snow still lies heavy on the roofs of the houses; icicles as long as swords hang from the eaves; children still sled along the single, narrow street; the few cars that make the journey from the coast road still must grind their way with chains or snow tires, taking hours to negotiate the long succession of hairpin curves that tacks up the mountainside.

Today, a few more cars than usual have arrived, and there are some unfamiliar faces at the usually quiet temple at the far end of the village. Several of the older villagers are there too. They say little, either to one another or to the priest, who is hurriedly giving some last-minute instructions to his assistants before the ceremony begins. Since the last ceremony of this type took place, over forty years ago, no one has any experience of what is to occur. The villagers were too young to be allowed to attend on that occasion, and the priest himself has only a dim memory of helping his father with the preparations. Nonetheless, when the time comes, all follow their set roles as if they were written in a script. For the ceremony that they are engaged in has been performed in the same way for many centuries—some say six, some say more. The honor of the village depends on the tradition being carried on without a false step. The villagers know this. They know that if they lose the right way it will never be recovered.

The priest, upon whom all depends, does his best to hide his nervousness. At the appointed time, he leads the others into a room at the back of the temple lit by the flickering glow of several tall candles. There are no cushions—they take the *seiza* kneeling position on the cold wooden boards. The air is heavy with the smell of incense. On the altar, behind the usual reliquary objects of bronze and gold leaf, are two stone figures so old and weather-beaten that the facial features have been reduced to smudges. Chanting a sutra in a deep, sonorous voice, the priest dips a wooden cup into a bowl of worked bronze and splashes water onto the two stony heads. Four decades of dust are washed away and the features become slightly more distinct—flat noses, long, pendulous ears, lips curled into blissful smiles.

For several hours, the only sounds apart from the voice of the priest are the creaking of the rafters and the tapping of a pine branch against the windowpane. The priest carries on chanting until the sun has slid over the mountain ridge in the west and the moon has turned silver in the darkening sky. Then he turns, bows three times in the direction of the mountain, and walks in slow, measured paces to the door, his four assistants behind, closely imitating the rhythm of his gait. One by one the others follow in an order derived from a complicated mixture of age, family status, and position of dwelling relative to the mountain. The newcomers, who are representatives of families who have moved away from the region, are the last to leave.

Outside, the temperature is already starting to drop rapidly. The priest stops, takes a large conch shell that is hanging from the belt under his cape, and raises it to his lips. A low droning sound fills the air. Two of his assistants blow into smaller conches, which produce higher-pitched drones. The other two beat a slow tom-tom on drums that they have strapped around their necks. The priest turns, makes a single bow to the small crowd behind him, then, without another backward glance, proceeds across the temple grounds, through a small gate in the back, then into the forest. The path is narrow, overhung with pine branches and ankle-deep in snow, and there is only the full moon to guide him on his way, but he doesn't hesitate or even look up to check his position. The others follow silently in his path. All that can be heard are the tramp of boots and the occasional cascade of loosened snow from the fork of a tree.

It takes just over half an hour to reach the tiny hut next to the clearing. The priest lights a match to remove the ice from the lock, then inserts a key. The door groans open, and a candle is lit. The tools are removed from the cupboard, checked for fitness, then distributed to the highest-ranking villagers. Next comes the most difficult element in the whole ceremony, one which custom does not allow the priest to rehearse at all. While the others form a circle around the clearing, he takes from his leather pouch two short sticks of polished wood and a similar length of notched bone. He delicately fits the three pieces together, lifts the strange instrument to his eye, and squints at the peak of the mountain through a tiny hole in one end of the bone. For fifteen minutes he paces backward and forward across the clearing, never once taking his eye away from the hole in the bone. Finally, he is satisfied. Using small, shuffling steps, he treads out in the snow an oblong the size of a couple of flag-stones. Within minutes, his helpers have set up metal braziers at each corner and filled them with wood, charcoal, and special mosses that have been gathered the previous autumn. Soon the braziers are crackling with flame, sending sparks shooting into the air.

After the snow has been swept from the oblong, the men start digging, using pickax and heavy spade on the frozen earth. The priest and his assistants step back into the shadows and raise a droning chorus on conch shell and drum. Even with two groups of four men alternating, it takes two hours to break up and clear away the four feet of earth that lies between the surface and the object of their search. When it first comes into sight, the priest removes the conch shell from his lips, steps forward, and bows at the gaping hole in the ground. There is a moment of silence, then he begins to chant in a ringing voice that sounds loud enough to wake up the wives and children sleeping back in the village. That is the only hint of the relief he feels. If he had identified the wrong patch of ground, if they had dug and dug but nothing had been discovered, it would have been a disaster that he would not have lived down for the rest of his life.

The most senior of the villagers, a crinkle-eyed, grizzle-cheeked man whose stooping back belies his strength and agility, lowers himself carefully into the hole. Ropes are thrown down. He fastens them in place, then climbs out again. The priest's chant rises to a new intensity as all the men present haul on the ropes. It is a hard job on the snowy ground, but finally the top of the wooden box rises over the lip of the hole. Two of the younger men rush forward and grab it by the rusty handles on the sides; some of the others use thick wooden poles to lever it upward. Finally, the box is lying by the side of the hole. The priest stops chanting and gazes at it in the light of the dancing flames in the braziers. It is not much bigger than an ordinary packing crate, but the wood is dark and knotty. It is that tough old wood that made the box so hard to lift.

The filling of the hole is left to four of the younger men. The shovels crunch and clang as they throw the earth back, tamp it down firmly, then break new earth from a nearby bank to fill the space occupied by the box. When the work is done, two long wooden poles are tied to the box and it is carried shoulder high back down the steep path that leads back to the temple. It is well past midnight now, and the silver disc of moon is floating down toward the ridge. Stars are abundant, smeared across the sky like spittle. The box sways dangerously from time to time and brushes against the snowy branches, but the ropes have been well tied. The priests blow their conch shells. No one speaks.

It takes slightly longer to make the return journey. After entering through the small gate at the rear of the temple, the priest leads them back to the candlelit room. The box is set down in front of the altar, and the men take up the same places as before, kneeling on the hard boards. The priest has resumed his chant and two of his assistants have begun unscrewing the lid of the box, when the door at the side of the room edges open and someone slips inside. The latecomer moves soundlessly, taking up a kneeling position in the backmost row. For the first time in the ceremony, the priest's composure is disturbed. There is a brief quaver in his voice, and for several seconds he stares in the latecomer's direction. Some of the others in the back row glance at him out of the corners of their eyes. The latecomer sits entirely motionless in the *seiza* position, his unblinking gaze never shifting from the wooden box. He is a big man, with a beard and long hair tied back in a ponytail. Despite the chilly air, he is wearing a thin cotton kimono and his feet are bare.

The ceremony proceeds. The screws that hold down the lid are removed, then the side panels of the box are loosened. Finally, the job is complete. The priest's chant stops. His assistants move away to the sides of the room. He takes a ladleful of water from the bronze bow and spills it onto the box. Kneeling down with his back to the altar, he lifts off the lid. The panel facing the altar requires a tug and a twist before it comes free. Next come the side panels and last of all the panel facing the rows of kneeling men. Now the box has been completely dismantled. There is a moment of complete stillness and silence while all the eyes in the room gaze at what it holds. Then the priest goes back to his position in front of the altar, takes out the conch shell, and gives a single long blast that begins as a moan as low and breathy as the wind in a chimney, then slowly builds into a dissonant roar that sounds loud enough to carry over the great mountain behind, and the next one, and on to the coast.

Even in the uncertain light of the candles, there can be no mistaking what has been revealed. Sitting on the base of the wooden box is a figure wrapped in a faded and torn orange robe. The legs are bent into the lotus position. The shape of the feet is intact, papery skin stretching from heel to toe. The blackened fingers—a couple of which have fallen off— are clasped together in a mudra mystical sign. But it is the face that seizes the attention: shrunken and mottled like an old apple, yet still imprinted with human personality. There are hanks of hair on what remains of the scalp, flaky lids above the empty eye sockets, and, most remarkable of all, two shriveled lips stretched into a beatific smile.

One by one, the men get up from the kneeling position, approach the figure squatting on the base of the box, and bow down before it, so low that their foreheads press against the floor. The latecomer is the last to pay his respects. All the eyes in the room are on him as he bends down to make his bow, his palms flat on the polished wooden boards. When he gets to his feet again, there is a moment when his eyes meet those of the priest, who immediately looks away. When he has returned to his place at the back of the room, more incense sticks are lit and the chanting begins again.

The priest and his assistants take turns in front of the altar, keeping up the chant until the first rays of dawn appear over the eastern ridge. Then he blows the conch shell one last time, a short blast that signifies to the rest of the village that the ceremony has been successfully completed. The men file out of the room and into the main hall of the temple, where the priest's wife has readied sake and rice cakes on a long table. They eat and drink a little and make brief comments to one another about what they have seen.

"He looked well!"

"Hardly different from the photographs!"

"That is because he was pure. His pure spirit kept his body whole."

"They say he carried on chanting sutras for ten days after he was buried."

But they do not stay long, because the sun is already high above the ridge and there is plenty of work to be done—breaking the ice on the lake, clearing the fallen trees from the pass, laying the first traps of the year lower down the valley. They leave in small groups, chatting about the weather and children and suchlike, ordinary men now that the mysteries of the night have passed. The priest talks with the ones who have come from afar until they too drift away, conscious of the long, arduous journey down the zigzag road to the coast. Only then does he step back to the room where the mummy squats on the base of the wooden box. As he expected, the latecomer is sitting a couple of yards in front, chanting softly under his breath as he gazes at the shrunken head with the beatific smile.

The latecomer hears the pad of the priest's stockinged feet on the floor, turns, and rises. The priest bows. The latecomer smiles and reaches out a hand to touch the sleeve of his robe. The priest seems to recoil slightly, but then he smiles too. They leave the room together, both men turning to bow at the still figure in front of the altar.

They go outside to a little garden at the side of the temple containing a frozen pond and a stone bench. It is a little warmer now. The forest behind them is already alive with birdsong, and there are children's voices coming from the village. The priest uses a bamboo broom to sweep the snow from the bench and they sit down. The priest is the first to break the silence.

"I didn't think you would come," he says. "Why did you?"

The latecomer strokes his beard. His eyes are on the huge cone of earth and rock that rises up behind the temple, its white peak gleaming in the sun. "Why not?" he says softly.

"It has been so long," says the priest. "I hardly recognize you."

"Then your brain must be softening. That is what happens if you spend your life up here in the mountains."

The priest smiles faintly. "That is what you used to say when you were a boy."

"You remember well. Of course, in those days I really used to believe it. Now I think of you with envy."

"Envy? That's a surprise."

"Is it? You asked why I came. The answer is simple. I wanted to give my little brother some support. I wanted to see him perform this ceremony in a way that would make our father proud."

"And what was the verdict?"

"Excellent. Everything was superb. The way you moved, the sense of timing—Father could not have done it any better himself."

The priest inclines his head in a modest bow. "Those are kind words. Thank you for your appreciation."

"And he looked so fine, didn't he? His face, his smile—just how I remember them. I almost expected him to get up and give me a whack on the head for not sitting properly."

They laugh in unison, then they are silent for a while. The priest takes a rice cake from his pocket, breaks it in two, and hands a piece to his brother. The two men chew slowly, listening to the sounds of the village and gazing at the massive stillness of the mountain. The sun is already warm enough to melt the snow, and clear drops are pattering down onto the path from the branches overhanging the temple wall.

"Have you ever thought about such a death?" asks the priest's brother suddenly.

"Thought about it? What do you mean?"

"I mean for yourself. It is a glorious way to die, isn't it? The men who choose it demonstrate complete mastery of the spirit over the body."

The priest frowns. "It is not done for glory, elder brother."

"But someone has to do it. Our tradition is that there should be someone every generation."

The priest's brother sounds suddenly fervent. The priest looks at him curiously, then shakes his head. "Only if there is someone whose spiritual progress has prepared him. It doesn't matter if a generation is skipped. It has happened before and will happen again."

"So you are not considering it yourself?"

"I cannot be sure at this stage of my life, but I am not confident. So far, I have not come close to what is required."

The latecomer suddenly stands up and looks down at his brother, hands on hips. "Then what about me?" he says in a quiet, urgent voice. "If I requested it, would you help me with what is necessary?"

The priest stares up at him, then turns away and smiles. "Even now I cannot understand your jokes, elder brother. Your mind works in a different way from mine."

"This is no joke," hisses the elder brother. "I mean every word. Would you help me if I requested it?"

The smile freezes on the priest's face. When he speaks, there is a note of anger in his voice. "Pardon me for speaking strongly, elder brother. What you have mentioned is a ridiculous idea. You are not even a priest, just a trainee who abandoned his studies as soon as they had begun!"

The newcomer takes a step back. "What you say is true, but there are precedents. In former times, it was possible for people other than professional priests to die this death. In the temple, there are records concerning wise men and hermits living in these mountains."

"You talk of what happened many centuries ago. Such people no longer exist."

"The principle still exists. A public ceremony is not necessary. Everything can be done in secret, as it was long ago."

The priest gives a sigh of frustration. "These are wild words, elder brother," he says. "Leaving aside spiritual questions, what about the physical preparation? Those who have fitted themselves for this death have undergone five years of rigor. They have spent the summers in a hut near the peak living on wild plants. They have let the flesh waste from their bones. They have rubbed themselves every day with special lotions and drunk special liquids every night. Without these preparations, this miracle cannot be performed. Even the holiest man would not like any ordinary corpse!"

The priest's brother is not at all discouraged. "These mysterious ingredients of yours are not too difficult to synthesize, you know. I could provide all that myself. Just say that you would help me if I ever asked you, and I will leave this mountain a contented man."

"You know that I can't say anything like that. I have responsibilities here."

"I understand your responsibilities. After all, the reason that they are yours is because I refused them—or perhaps I should say that they rejected me!"

The priest's face is gentler now. His elder brother stretches out a hand and pulls him to his feet.

"Let me ask you one last time," says the elder brother. "At least do not say that you will reject me immediately if I come to you with that request. At least say that you will reflect on it."

The priest smiles as he dusts the drops from his heavy robe. "I would never refuse you without much reflection. That is obvious, isn't it?"

The two men walk arm in arm out of the little garden and toward the temple gate. The shiny blue roof of a Toyota Land Cruiser is visible over the top of the temple wall.

"You are not staying longer?" asks the priest.

"Unfortunately, I cannot," says the elder brother. "There are many troublesome matters that need my attention."

The priest nods. "Recently, I have read many things about you," he says as they pass through the gate. "Everyone here has read many things."

"Many things are written, but little is true."

"That is what I hope."

The elder brother turns, surprised by the comment. Then he smiles and slaps the priest on the shoulder. A heavily built man with a bald head gets out of the Land Cruiser and opens the door on the passenger side.

"I meant what I said," calls out the latecomer, pausing before climbing up into the seat. "It was an excellent performance, truly. Our father would have been proud. And he would have been happy to know that the right son was taking care of him!"

The vehicle's engine roars into life and it begins to rumble down the narrow street. The priest stands in front of the temple gate, watching it go. Well before it has reached the first bend, he is taking off his straw sandals and stepping into the main hall. For him, too, there is much to attend to today.

Mitchell sat staring at the row of figures on his computer screen. What they told him was that Otaman was a zombie company. According to textbook theory, it should have been laid to rest long ago, and yet it continued to function as if nothing were wrong. Long, steady deterioration in profit margins; long, steady deterioration in asset efficiency—and now a huge buildup in bank borrowings. What Mitchell was staring at was the financial equivalent of *The Night of the Living Dead*.

"Am I missing something obvious?" he said to Ted Shimano, who was leaning back in his chair rubbing a squish of conditioning gel into the side of his head.

"Probably," said Ted, squinting into space. "It wouldn't be the first time."

"I mean, these numbers make no sense at all. How can a company—"

"Stop right there!" said Ted. "That's your explanation."

"What's that? What explanation!"

"The word 'company.' You're looking at Otaman like it's an independent enterprise, with managers trying to earn profits and workers bargaining for wages and banks checking out credit risk. That's how things are in the West."

"But Japan is different, I suppose."

"Right! Maybe you're learning something after all."

"Japan is different"—that was the standard excuse for everything that was topsy-turvy and screwed up. If Mitchell had heard it once, he had heard it a hundred times. Frowning, he wadded up a printout of Otaman's financial ratios into a ball and tossed it at a nearby trash can. It bounced off the lip and flew under the desk of one of the female research assistants. She bent down, picked it up, and threw it back at him.

"So what would you do in my position?" said Mitchell, now doubly irritated. "This report is supposed to be finished by the end of the week. The world is waiting for my considered opinion on the company."

"Your opinion doesn't matter," said Ted with a grin. "The stock price is going up, isn't it?"

Mitchell nodded. "That's what I've been given to understand, but I need more than that. I need reasons, arguments, conclusions. After all, we're supposed to be investment analysts, not astrologers."

Ted chuckled to himself. He slipped the tube of gel back into his drawer and took out a tiny grooming machine that he used for trimming the hairs inside his nose. "You know what Yazawa-san always says about the Japanese economy being like a game of Go?" he said.

"How could I forget! Don't look at the individual stones, look at the pattern. Watch how the energy flows from one part of the board to another."

"Exactly," said Ted, the tiny blades buzzing away inside his left nostril. "Doing an investment analysis of Otaman and understanding what is really going on there are two different things. If you want to understand the company, figure out who's been buying and selling the shares in the market, who's lending money that didn't use to, and who isn't that did. Identify what university the president went to—you know, stuff like that."

"What university the president went to?" Mitchell was confused. "Why on earth should that matter?"

"Check it against the personnel records of major figures in the bureaucracy or in the cabinet or in the big banks. Who knows—there might be a correlation."

He gave his nose a final rub, put the groomer back in his drawer, and took out a small bottle of mouthwash. Mitchell watched him as he tilted his head back and squirted. Ted was a toiletry manufacturer's dream. Once, when they had gone to play raquetball together, Mitchell had peeked inside the expensive Italian gym bag that Ted had brought with him. It contained a couple of dozen varieties of lotion, cream, gel, spray, paste, and foam and a set of hairdressing equipment that would have done credit to a professional coiffeur.

"Start with the simple things," continued Ted. "Run through the shareholders' register, see if there've been any big changes recently. Major shareholders have got out, new ones have come in—that sort of thing can be very revealing."

"Maybe you're right," said Mitchell doubtfully. "Anyway, I'll get my assistant to check it. Who knows—something might turn up."

Ted nodded absentmindedly and put the mouthwash back in his desk. After the nose and the mouth, next it would be the insides of the ears. For that, there were cotton swabs. Mitchell decided not to watch this part of the performance. He turned to his screen and clicked back into his Otaman spreadsheet.

Ted was a strange character—not too sharp, not too serious, yet capable of some good investment ideas from time to time. They got on well together. Somehow, he made Mitchell feel less like an Englishman abroad, more like a fellow traveler through the last years of the century. The two of them had sung video karaoke together; gone skiing on the indoor ski slope in Urayasu; gone surfing at the indoor beach in Kawasaki. It was Ted who introduced Mitchell to the best disco he had ever been to in his life, a place where models from all over the world hung around in clusters waiting to be picked up. Back in London, Mitchell would never have tried his luck with such perfect-looking women, but in fact the whole thing was amazingly easy. For them, going to bed with someone was no more of an event than going shopping or dropping into the health-food bar for a sugar-free, all-natural yogurt.

Ted's hobbies were clothes, food, and women, and he lavished much time and money on all of them. He was always relaxed, always planning his next holiday or date. And yet even Ted had his hidden depths. Mitchell had assumed that he was Ted's elder, until Kent the Mormon had mentioned that they had been in business school together ten years before. Ted looked and acted like he was fresh out of college, but in fact he was in his early thirties. The Mormon's other revelation was harder to reconcile with what Mitchell knew of his happy-go-lucky colleague. Apparently, it was during Ted's time at business school that his mother—who was not even married to his father, but had been working for decades as a private assistant—had thrown herself under an oncoming subway train. Nothing in Japan was as it seemed.

Mitchell turned his attention to the table of financial ratios quivering on his screen. Their message was hardly encouraging, but those numbers were all historical. The great investors in the world, the money masters, didn't spend their time looking backward. They concentrated on looking forward, using their gut instincts. And Mitchell's gut instincts told him that something big was developing at Otaman.

He thought back to his visit to the head office, and the conversation he had overheard. That was the key to the whole Otaman mystery. Why had Wada reacted so allergically when Mitchell had asked him about the Kawasaki project? The answer was obvious: the company was conducting some top-secret research in Kawasaki that was going to transform its prospects beyond all recognition. In all probability, at this very moment teams of Otaman scientists were working on a new high-technology product with massive market potential. No doubt Yazawa knew all the details, yet he was forcing Mitchell to write his report blind. That was unfair. Information of this sort was like gold dust to an analyst. A buy recommendation backed by solid analysis of the company's plans would change Mitchell's career trajectory for good.

Still, Yazawa was hardly a man to be trusted. The books on Japanese management that Mitchell had read talked a lot about human relations at work, about how senior staff looked after their juniors with paternalistic care. But Yazawa was unlike any other Japanese that he had ever met. This rally-driving, blowfish-guzzling embezzler—he didn't match Mitchell's conception of a middle-ranking Japanese salaryman. Somehow Mitchell doubted whether Yazawa had ever read any books on Japanese management.

The conclusion was inescapable—if he wanted to find out more about the Kawasaki project, he was going to have to do it on his own. But how to proceed? Mitchell decided to go back to the beginning. He would telephone Wada again and ask if he could visit Otaman's offices in Kawasaki. It was unlikely that the request would be granted, but Wada's response would be interesting. Would he still pretend not to understand, would he refuse outright, or would he come up with some kind of excuse? The more nervous Wada was, the keener Mitchell would be to make the visit, authorized or not.

He picked up his phone and dialed the direct number given on Wada's business card. The phone rang more than a dozen times before someone finally picked it up. The voice at the other end was female, but the tone was far from the soft, apologetic tones that office girls were trained to use when answering a phone.

"Excuse me for making a disturbance at such a busy time," said Mitchell in his best polite Japanese. "I am looking for Wada-san, your deputy head of finance."

"Who?"

The word conveyed suspicion and impatience in equal measure. Mitchell remembered the squat woman with the battered knuckles. There was no way of telling for sure, but he felt convinced that it was her voice.

"Wada-san, the deputy head of finance."

"Not that! I'm asking who you are."

"Understood! My name is Mitchell, and I am a member of the staff at a foreign securities house. I would be grateful for the opportunity to ask Wada-san—"

"Wait a moment!"

There was a crack as the receiver was unceremoniously dropped onto a hard surface, then Mitchell heard a door slam. He waited with the receiver to his ear for several minutes before the woman returned.

"You're still there, are you?" she muttered tersely. "Right—you can't talk to Wada. He has left already."

"Left already? You mean he has gone home? That's unfortunate, because I had some simple questions to ask him. Please tell Wada-san that I will call back tomorrow."

"Not gone home—gone away. He will not be coming back here at all."

Mitchell considered that statement. Could it be true? He had just been talking to the man three days before. Wada had given no indication that he was on the point of leaving. Perhaps he was just too busy to take Mitchell's calls. Perhaps he was standing there next to the phone making faces.

"Please, you could tell me where I could get in touch with him. There are some simple questions I want to ask."

"Impossible! Wada is no longer available."

There was a click and the line went dead. Thoughtfully, Mitchell replaced the receiver. Another possibility had occurred to him. Maybe Wada had been suddenly demoted, fired, even. That would explain why the woman who answered the phone sounded so uncooperative. Mitchell recalled the conversation with the taxi driver who had taken him to the Otaman head office. There were problems at the company, he had said— the new people in control were getting rid of anyone who disagreed with them. Maybe Wada had been the latest victim. Maybe he had opposed the new direction the company was taking. Mitchell pictured him on the sofa in that cramped little room, squirming unhappily on the sofa, fiddling with his papers as he dodged and blocked the questions. He tried to feel sorry for the man and failed.

Mitchell turned his attention back to the Otaman numbers. There was a new feature of the company's financial statements that had begun to attract his attention—an item on the asset side of the balance sheet called "Loans and Loan Guarantees to Group Companies." This had shown a massive increase over the past three years, and was now equivalent to almost a year's revenues. According to the brochure, Otaman controlled a network of twenty-five subsidiary and affiliated companies. However, only six of them were included in the group accounts that

Otaman submitted to the Ministry of Finance every year, and these were all small trucking and warehousing companies. So what about the other nineteen—what kinds of companies were they and why had they suddenly developed such a huge appetite for funds? There didn't seem to be any way of finding out. Ted was obviously right: conventional investment analysis was of little use when confronted by something like Otaman. You either knew what was going on or you didn't.

Mitchell took a sip of coffee from a paper cup and stared blankly at the spreadsheet of financial ratios. It was only after some seconds had passed that he became aware of the shape reflected in the glass of the computer screen—a man's head hovering behind his shoulder. He felt the physical presence, the gamma rays on his scalp and neck. Even before Mitchell swiveled around in his seat, he knew who would be standing there.

"How is your progress with the Otaman report?" said Yazawa, his heavy-lidded gaze flicking from the screen to Mitchell's face. "There is much anticipation of the results of your analysis."

How long had he been watching? There had been no sound of his approach at all. Mitchell glanced down at Yazawa's loafers, as immaculately polished as ever. Maybe he had bought those shoes especially to allow him to sneak around the office unheard.

"Things are coming along fine," he lied. "But Otaman's a complicated sort of company. There are one or two points that are still a little vague to me."

"Not a complicated company," snapped Yazawa. "Everything is simple. Your report must show that everything is beautifully simple."

"I'd like to straighten them out, all the same," said Mitchell, sounding much cockier than he felt. "Maybe I'll make another visit, talk over these issues with the management."

"No more visits!" growled Yazawa, his brow like thunder. "Anything you need, you get from me. Do you understand or not understand?"

There were a few instants of silence as they stared at each other. Yazawa's eyes were empty, two snake holes in a wall.

"I understand," said Mitchell finally, with a shrug of the shoulders. There was absolutely no point in arguing when Yazawa was in this sort of mood. Better for Mitchell to keep his mouth shut and get on with his investigations in secret.

Yazawa gave him a final soul-freezing glare, then turned on his heel and strode back to his office.

SEVEN

Deputy Branch Manager Tamura's secretary was getting worried about the disturbing change in her boss's behavior. Recently, he had canceled several important meetings, explaining that he had too much work on his hands. But from her desk outside his office, she could see that he was hardly doing anything at all, just pacing up and down or standing at the window, staring out over the city. Yesterday, when she brought him a cup of coffee, he didn't even notice her entering the room. Then when she asked him how he was feeling, he almost jumped out of his seat. She supposed that she must have surprised him when his mind was elsewhere, but even so the reaction was strange. He looked petrified. He hadn't really been himself since the day after that earthquake. He didn't drink his coffee. He didn't go out for lunch, nor did he do much more than pick at the box lunch she ordered for him. Then at five-thirty, an exceptionally early time by his usual standards, he left the office without a word to anyone.

Today was even worse. Tamura had arrived at the bank an hour late looking pallid, with dark rings under his eyes. When she greeted him, he stared at her wordlessly, as if she were a complete stranger. Then he re-treated into his office and spent the morning gazing into space. The other girls had noticed that something was wrong. They nodded at one another knowingly. Wife trouble, mistress trouble, money trouble—there were endless possibilities for enjoyable speculation. Tamura's secretary wasn't so sure. She sensed a different sort of tension about him, as if he were wait-ing for something to happen. Several times when she put phone calls through to him, she saw him snatch at the receiver, an agonized expres-sion on his face. When she told him that it was the finance director of Matsui Construction or the general affairs chief of Mitsutomo Heavy Industry, she could hear something like a sigh at the other end, though whether of relief or disappointment she could not tell.

Tamura left at five-thirty again, passing through the bustling office like a sleepwalker.

"We are grateful for your hard work," trilled the receptionist, dipping her pretty face in a bow as she uttered the formal greeting to a depart-ing superior.

"Excuse me for taking my leave before you," muttered Tamura dully.

The girl looked up in surprise. Tamura's usual farewell was a grunt and a lifted hand. Sometimes, if he were in an exceptionally jovial mood, he would offer up some mild sexual innuendo, at which she would give a well-practiced giggle of embarrassment. A formal response like this was completely unprecedented.

Tamura walked out into the early evening rush hour and allowed himself to be swept along by the crowds, not really conscious of where he was going or why. His mouth was dry, his head throbbing with the dull migraine that usually came after a sleepless night. Every so often he touched his left breast lightly with his hand, assuring himself that the en-velope was still there in his jacket pocket.

He had opened that envelope for the first time about an hour after re-ceiving it from the tall young man who had sat down beside him on the train last week. Some instinct had told Tamura to take the man's advice not to open it then and there in full view of all the commuters, so he had waited until the train pulled into Shinjuku station. Not until he was alone in the only place it was possible to be alone in that churning maelstrom of human traffic—in the cubicle of the men's toilet—did he slit the envelope open and pull out the photographs inside. The shock was immediate and physical. For an instant, Tamura felt as if he were going to throw up on the grimy tiles. He closed his eyes and waited for his heartbeat to slow down to normal again, but the images would not be banished from his mind. They were imprinted on the inside of his eyelids.

A tangle of naked limbs on a bed. A woman's face masked by her hair, under it a man's hands closing around her neck. Then the woman floating in a circular bath, her lips parted in a strange half-smile, her sightless eyes gazing up at the camera. Tamura had looked into that face for only a few brief seconds, but he recognized it instantly. There was no room for doubt. Nor could there be any doubt about the identity of the man pressing her down on the bed. That mole at the back of the neck, that square head with the protruding ears and the shiny bald spot that was growing steadily, year by year—it was exactly the same sight that had greeted Tamura a week ago when his barber had held up a mirror for his approval.

The memories came flooding back. As if it had all just happened that morning, Tamura felt the shuddering of the earthquake, saw the woman's hair waving gently in the water, smelled the overpowering stench of the trash. He wanted to cry out loud in pain and confusion; to shout that it couldn't be true, that it must all be a dreadful mistake. But at the same time he knew that there could be no mistake. That was why he felt so nauseous, why his heart was pounding like a drum.

Tamura opened his eyes, put the photos back in his inside pocket, and rejoined the crush of purposeful bodies that was Shinjuku station at eight-thirty every morning. He felt numb, almost light-headed. Nothing made sense anymore. Nothing could be analyzed or predicted. It wasn't even worth trying. All he could do was wait. For if only one thing about this whole nightmarish incident was clear, it was that the people in control, the people who were tormenting him like a schoolboy torments an insect, were not going to let him slip back into the secure, normal life he had known before.

For the next week, Tamura sat in his office in a kind of trance. The world around him, the world of secretaries and meetings and fax messages, seemed completely insubstantial. The two bodies on the bed, the hard grain of the photos, the water slopping from the circular bath—that was the reality from which he found it impossible to escape. Once or twice, he thought about going straight to Shinjuku police station and confessing everything. He would say that he wasn't responsible, that he had blacked out and remembered nothing. He would throw himself on their mercy. And what would be the response? They would ask him why he had kept quiet so long. They would ask him to explain exactly how the girl had died. And they would want to know what had happened to her body.

That was a good question. What had happened to the woman's body? Tamura assumed that the friends of the tall young man must have disposed of it. They must have planned everything meticulously in order to trap him. And of course they had succeeded. He was trapped. The more Tamura thought about the incident, the more blurred and uncertain its outlines became. Was he responsible for the girl's death, as the photos suggested? He didn't believe so, but he couldn't be absolutely sure. He couldn't be sure of anything anymore. In a sense, though, that point was irrelevant. What mattered was whether he could convince the police that he wasn't responsible. And that, he concluded, would take a miracle. Even if some kind of miracle did occur and the police let him go free, what about the scandal that would inevitably follow? It would mean the end of his marriage, the end of his career, the end of his life as a respectable member of Japanese society. The thought of it filled him with a massive emptiness.

Tamura wandered aimlessly through the back streets of Shinjuku, staring into shop windows, listening to snatches of conversation, above all trying to distract himself from the fear and despair that had suddenly come to dominate his existence. It was the last Friday of the month, and the streets were full of people out to enjoy themselves. Some of the girls were young, probably high-school students. They made him think of his daughter. What would she think if she heard what her father had done? What names would the girls in school call her? It was impossible! He could never let her know. He had to hide his secret in a dark place somewhere, make sure that it was never exposed to the light of day.

He must have been walking more quickly than he realized, for he soon found himself at the entrance of Shinjuku Park, which was several blocks from CBJ's Shinjuku branch. Inside the park, the dusk was thickening among the black boughs of the cherry trees. Looking up, Tamura saw not one sky but two. In the eastern half there was already a perfect night sky, with a fat moon and stars glinting like broken glass. Over in the west, though, the sunset was still spilling over the horizon, lighting up different bands of color—pink, copper, pale blue, indigo. In a few minutes, the last of the daylight would have gone. Tamura felt gripped by a sudden dread of the dark, like a small boy left at home by his parents. He didn't want to stay alone in the gloom of the massive park. He wanted to be back in the shopping streets, carried along by the comforting rush of busy strangers.

Tamura turned and walked swiftly back to the park entrance. He was just twenty or thirty yards away when he saw the man leaning against the heavy iron gate, hands in the pockets of his trousers. He recognized him at once. Tamura thought about turning around again and losing himself in the shadows of the trees, but then dismissed the idea. The tall young man would find him in the end anyway. If there was going to be some sort of confrontation, Tamura preferred to get it over with immediately.

"Good evening, Tamura-san! Nice evening for a walk, isn't it?"

He was just as jauntily familiar as before. Tamura gritted his teeth. "What do you want this time?" he said tersely.

"I wondered if you'd had a chance to reconsider your decision. You know, about the discussions with my friends." He was smiling pleasantly, as if he were making a perfectly normal business proposition.

"What exactly do your friends want?"

"They want to meet you, Tamura-san. They want you to give them a chance by listening to their business ideas."

"When and where?" said Tamura, his throat suddenly dry.

"Right now," said the young man brightly. "Why don't you have a seat over there. It shouldn't take them long to arrive."

Tamura nodded wearily. He had no choice but to do as he was told. He sat down on the bench and watched as the young man took a small portable phone from an inside pocket.

"Excuse me a moment," he said with an apologetic smile and stepped a couple of paces away to dial the number. When his muttered conversation was over, he turned back to Tamura and made a short bow.

"I have to leave you now," he said. "But my friends will be here soon. They are looking forward to meeting you."

The young man's tall figure disappeared through the entrance of the park. To Tamura, even the way he walked, swinging his arms vigorously from the elbow, seemed to exude insolence. For long minutes on end, Tamura sat on the bench in silence, watching and waiting. Underneath some nearby trees, a man was throwing a ball for a dog. A courting couple sauntered hand in hand across the grass. Meanwhile, the lights of the Shinjuku skyscrapers grew harder and brighter, and the inky sky above Tamura's head slid steadily westward.

What kind of people were the young man's friends? Tamura had no doubt—they had to be *chimpira*, low-grade punks on the fringes of the yakuza syndicates. Only *chimpira* would have the reckless audacity to set their aim on a senior executive of CBJ, an institution at the very heart of the Japanese financial establishment. Tamura was expecting a group of them to appear any moment. He envisaged four or five young toughs with slicked-back hair, tropical shirts, and loud, crude voices. They would drag him off to a cheap bar that they controlled and force him to sign over every last yen of his savings. But nobody fitting Tamura's mental image appeared. He scrutinized the steady trickle of people into the park. They were all obviously normal, law-abiding citizens—some more courting couples hand in hand, a college judo club out on a run, a middle-aged couple pointing out the sights of Shinjuku to each other as they enjoyed the evening air.

At first Tamura was quite irritated when the middle-aged couple, instead of passing in front of him, stopped and sat down next to him on the bench.

"I'm sorry to have kept you waiting," said the man mildly.

"Yes, we're sorry," echoed the woman. "It was rather difficult to get here in all the traffic."

Tamura stared at them incredulously. The man was quite shabbily dressed, with a wispy beard and mustache that made him look like a professor of literature at some no-name provincial university. The woman was a broad-hipped maternal type with a large, flat nose.

"What do you want?" he said finally.

"Everything has been prepared," said the woman.

The professor opened the battered leather briefcase that he had been carrying and took out a sheaf of documents. "This is the assessment of our collateral," he said. "Including works of art, real estate holdings at home and overseas, and trade notes issued by all the companies that we do business with."

Tamura scanned through the first couple of sheets. The sums of money were huge, the description of assets vague and confusing. "Who was responsible for making these valuations?" he asked, putting the papers down on his lap.

"Experts in their fields," said the professor, with a dismissive wave of the hand. "You don't need to concern yourself with who they are."

"That may be," said Tamura doubtfully. "But what exactly is the point of all this?"

"The point," exclaimed the professor. "Hasn't anyone told you yet? All we want is a loan facility from the Shinjuku branch of CBJ. As we are based in Shinjuku ourselves, we would like to consider CBJ as our local bank."

"We don't normally do business with new customers without considerable investigation," said Tamura, an icy feeling spreading in the pit of his stomach.

"I know that," said the professor softly. "But we really don't have time to waste on the formalities. That's why we are coming to you."

Tamura nodded and glanced nervously around. The colors of the sunset had drained away below the horizon, and the park was turning monochrome—gray grass, black trees, white moon caught in the twisting branches. It was getting quite cold too. "How much did you have in mind?" he asked.

"It's all set down in the final sheet. I believe the methods I have worked out will be the most convenient for all concerned."

Tamura leafed through to the final sheet and glanced through the row of figures. At first, he thought his eyes were deceiving him in the gloom. Ten loans were being requested for ten different companies. The size of each loan was huge, equivalent to what CBJ would extend to a blue-chip company such as Matsui Construction. Altogether, the amount of money that he was being asked to provide was simply absurd.

"This is impossible," he said finally, handing the documents to the professor. "I do not have the authority for something like this."

"Don't be foolish," said the professor, pushing the documents back to him.

"You are making a big mistake," said the woman, a new, hard edge to her voice. "How do you think Mika-chan is going to feel when she finds out?"

Mika-chan—they even knew his daughter's name! Tamura swallowed dryly and put the documents down on his lap again. It was going to be worse than he had thought, and there was no escape. These two people might seem mild-mannered at first sight, but they had the yakuza spirit just the same—that spirit of ruthless greed that zeros in on weakness like a shark after blood.

"I think there is no problem with authority," continued the professor. "After all, each one of our subsidiary companies has a famous stock exchange–listed company among its shareholders."

"A listed company?" said Tamura, surprised. The professor was correct. If the loans were guaranteed by a listed company, there would be no need for authorization from the head office.

"That's right," said the woman. "These companies are all joint ventures between ourselves and a certain listed company."

As the woman had indicated, a medium-ranking trading house was the majority shareholder in each one of the small ventures into which he was being asked to pour the bank's money. That was a relief. It would give him an excuse for actions that were well outside the bounds of ordinary banking practice.

"Let me think about all this," he said, leafing back through the papers. "It's going to take time."

"No time," said the professor. "The money must be made available by the end of next month."

"The end of next month! That's impossible. We have internal procedures, permissions from the head office, collateral verification—"

"You can do it. We have absolute confidence in you, Tamura-san."

"Do your best, Tamura-san. Cooperation is the only way forward!"

Tamura nodded weakly. The two stood up and made short bows before turning and walking off down the path that led around the edge of the park. Soon their figures merged into the shadows of the trees. Tamura remained sitting on the bench, lost in thought. There was a gusty wind skidding over the grass, dragging wisps of low clouds across the dirty face of the moon. From time to time, it made him shiver.

What did that business with the motorbike messenger mean? First of all, that someone somewhere thought Mori was worth killing, a compliment that he hadn't been paid for several years. At least it proved that at the age of forty-five he wasn't quite over the hill yet. But who and why? Mori didn't have any idea. There was nothing that he was working on that would justify the considerable trouble and expense of a professional hit. It was all very puzzling.

Mori left the Yuriko case alone for a few days. Personal obligation was one thing. Financial survival was another. Obeying the latter priority, he turned his attention to an inquiry that he had been working on for several weeks. The client was a middle-aged woman from Yokohama whom Mori had mentally tagged "the dragon lady." She was married to an architect but didn't want to be for any longer than she could help. Mori was supposed to come up with the evidence that would enable her to squeeze a profitable settlement. So far, there had been nothing. The dragon lady was hungry for results, but Mori couldn't manufacture them out of the thin air.

He had spent evenings following her husband around Ginza and Roppongi. He had been through the trash from his office and pieced together letters and credit card slips. At the dragon lady's insistence, Mori had even spent a night staking out the man's studio. He had borrowed a Mazda Bongo van specially for the occasion. Until four in the morning Mori had sat hunched in the back listening to Charles Mingus tapes, his 300-mm zoom poised for action. As he had expected, the whole thing was a complete waste of time. The husband arrived on his own at two, switched off the light an hour later, and no one else either came or went.

Mori spent a futile couple of hours trying to get the passenger lists from a couple of flights the architect had recently made to Shikoku, then went out and got himself a baby-octopus box lunch from the convenience store across the street. When he got back to the office, the phone was ringing. It took him a few seconds to recognize the man's voice at the other end of the phone, but when he did, his anger ignited like the gas burner at a *yaki-niku* restaurant.

"How was your evening out in Roppongi, Mori-san? I understand you're pretty careful with your money these days. That makes sense, of course—times are tough. The era of large expense claims has gone forever, hasn't it!"

"What do you want this time?" growled Mori.

"The same as before—cooperation within the industry. At New Japan Research it is our custom to arrange mutually beneficial relationships with all the small operators in our areas. It is a way of avoiding misunderstandings."

Our areas! The man was insufferable. Mori's grip tightened on the receiver, but he resolved to hold on a little longer. For one thing, he wanted to know how Kadota knew he had spent yesterday evening in Roppongi.

"The important thing is to remove excess competition. Right now, many small operators are offering unrealistically low prices, and that is damaging everyone's margins."

"You mean that guys like me are damaging New Japan Research's profits?" said Mori, jaw clenched.

"It's not impossible that you might be," came the careful reply.

"Excellent!" thundered Mori.

"That's an unhelpful remark," said Kadota, his pomposity completely unaffected. "A cooperative relationship would be much to your advantage, Mori-san. We at New Japan are in the process of setting up an umbrella organization of Shinjuku-based research companies. It's a sort of industry association, the aim being to ensure that orderly conditions are restored to the market. Given your long experience here, we were prepared to offer you an official position—perhaps even assistant secretary. That would bring many privileges, but it all depends on a more cooperative attitude from you."

"Many privileges? What kind of privileges?"

"For example, a guaranteed flow of safe, profitable work. That's very important, isn't it? After all, professional researchers such as ourselves are businessmen before anything else."

"Guaranteed by whom?" said Mori icily.

"Guaranteed by New Japan Research, of course. Since we are by far the largest of the research companies in the area, it is natural for us to take on the responsibility of industry leadership."

Mori couldn't believe what he was hearing. Kadota seemed to be assuming that he would jump at the chance of becoming one of New Japan's subcontractors!

"And what if I refuse?" he said, sounding much calmer than he felt.

"That would be a big mistake, Mori-san. You would soon find it difficult to get new business. You might even find that some of your cases started to go wrong. For example, you might find that a valuable contact became suddenly and strangely reluctant to talk to you."

"Are you threatening to sabotage my business?" said Mori in the soft, deliberate intonation he often used just before putting his fists and feet to work.

"Of course not!" said Kadota, with a little cough of a laugh. "I just wanted to make a sincere request for cooperation that will definitely be to your benefit."

"I have a sincere request for you too," said Mori. "One that will definitely work to your benefit."

"Really? What is that, Mori-san?"

"The sincere request is that you never call me again, never come within one hundred yards of my office, and never even think about interfering with my work. If you agree, it will work very much to your benefit."

"And if I don't agree?" said Kadota sharply.

"If you don't agree," said Mori, "the damage won't be just to your profit margins."

There was a moment of silence, then Kadota's voice sounded again, faster and slightly more high-pitched than before. "I'm disappointed, Mori-san. I thought you would be more—"

Mori slammed down the receiver. A lightweight cordless phone would probably have fractured with the impact. The heavy Bakelite model that Mori had been using for fifteen years just gave a loud ping of protest and stood its ground on the desk. There were some ways, he reflected, in which the old technology still couldn't be beaten.

After swallowing the last baby octopus and washing it down with a cup of cold barley tea, Mori picked up the phone again. First of all, he called Sano to see if he had come up with anything else about his daughter's recent friends and interests. He hadn't. In the last months of her life, the two of them seemed to have become complete strangers, Yuriko being polite and dutiful but giving away nothing about her personal life. Secondly, Mori called a contact at the Shinjuku police station who gave him the name of someone in the general affairs department who in turn would give him the name of someone in the pathology department who would have access to the file on Yuriko's death. It took half an hour of being bounced around the administrative labyrinth of the Tokyo law enforcement system before the female voice sounded at the other end of the phone. Mori didn't give his own name. In the unlikely event of this serious breach of police procedures being investigated, it would be simpler for both of them that way.

Mori heard the fingers tapping away on a keyboard.

"Yuriko Sano—that's right. I have it now."

She spoke in a low voice, presumably to avoid being overheard by her colleagues in the office. All the same, she sounded bright, full of life and energy. From her voice, it was obvious that she was a good-looking woman and that she knew it. She spoke with a special lightness that came from long practice in playing mental games with men. What kind of relationship did she have with the guy in the general affairs department? Mori felt obscurely jealous—but after all, how else could you break the boredom of working in a huge bureaucratic machine like that?

"Good. Now could you run over the examining doctor's report? I don't need to know about all the tests and the technical stuff—just the summary and conclusion."

"Wait a moment—yes, here it is. It's quite short, actually."

Mori listened patiently as the young woman read out the main points. The body had been in the water for four or five days. Bruising and cuts had been suffered after death, probably through contact with the concrete seawall. There was plenty of water in the lungs, and no sign of head wounds or strangulation or anything else that would indicate a struggle. Yuriko appeared to have been in good health, with no signs of disease and no alcohol found in the blood.

"Is that all?" he said finally.

"What are you expecting, exactly?"

"What about the cause of death, for a start? All you've told me so far is what didn't happen."

"Show some common sense," said the woman, more amused than angry. "This girl had been in the water for almost a week. In circumstances like that, it's quite normal not to be able to point to the exact cause of death. It happens all the time."

"So how can you be sure that this death really was an accident?"

"We can't, but we can be even less sure that it was something else. And we have to classify it as something, don't we?"

"But it might have been a murder," persisted Mori.

"Yes, it might have been," said the woman in a tone she might use to address a slow-witted but rather nice schoolboy. "But that's statistically unlikely, isn't it? After all, only a tiny proportion of all deaths are due to murder. And in the vast majority of those cases, the cause of death is absolutely clear. So when it's not clear, the only realistic choice for us at the pathology department is natural causes or accidental death. And we'd look pretty stupid classifying this one as natural causes, wouldn't we!"

"That's true," said Mori. "But you could just admit that you don't know."

"If we classified every case where there's an element of doubt as cause unknown, people would wonder what we're doing here all day. Our budget would be cut, our department chief would never get a promotion, and we would become the laughingstock of the entire ministry of justice. In the end, it would probably escalate into a big political issue."

"I understand that," said Mori. "You're doing your best for your department. No one can criticize that. But let me ask you another question. Is there anything at all that's unusual about this report, any little detail that makes it different from other so-called accident cases?"

"Not really," said the woman slowly. "I've seen dozens like this. No clear time of death or place, even . . . Hmmm . . . Here's one little point, though. It probably means nothing, of course."

"What's that?"

"Signs of small injuries to the tongue, caused by sudden clenching of the mouth. The note says that this is usually associated with epileptic seizures. But they go on to say that there was no history of epilepsy."

"So what's the explanation, then?"

"The explanation? There isn't one. There are plenty of things in this world that don't have any explanation. Why can't you just accept that?"

"There's an explanation for everything somewhere," said Mori. "The only problem is that the explanation usually leads to another question."

"Ah! You're quite a philosopher, aren't you?"

"I was in my university years," said Mori. "I read Sartre, Heidegger, Marcuse, and so on."

"What a serious guy! Do you know what I did in my college years?"

"I can probably guess," said Mori. "But maybe we could discuss it in more comfortable circumstances. Maybe, if you're free sometime this weekend, we could get together for—"

"Yaah—here comes the department chief!" The woman's voice was now a hurried whisper. "Nice to talk to you, but sorry, I've got to go."

There was a click and the line went dead. Mori sat there gazing into the black cup of the phone's earpiece. Should he wait a few seconds, then ring back and start again where he had left off? It was tempting. But if he were going to do it, now was the time. After a moment of hesitation, he rejected the idea and laid the receiver, carefully this time, back on the hook. There was a hidden force at work in these things. If they had been destined to meet and enjoy each other's company, her boss would not have interrupted their conversation at that moment. It was better to obey the flow of events than to struggle against it.

Mori left his office at five o'clock. It had been an unproductive day, with further annoyances from Kadota at New Japan, no help from Sano, and little useful information gleaned from the pathology department. To make matters worse, he now had to hurry off to one of his least favorite experiences—the regular acupuncture sessions that he was undergoing in order to cure the neuralgic pain in his upper back. Since a bad beating at the hands and feet of some Hiroshima yakuza several years ago, he had tried several types of treatment in order to put his back into shape. Bone twisting, infrared rays, thumb massage, radon baths, burial up to the neck in pits of steaming sand—so far, not one method had done more than alleviate the problem temporarily. Recently a stripper from Kyushu, who also suffered from chronic back pain, had recommended an acupuncture sensei. This was only Mori's fourth visit to the guy, but already he had the familiar feeling that he was wasting his money.

The sensei's clinic was a couple of blocks away in a building just marginally less shabby than the one that housed Mori's office. On the ground floor was a restaurant where the sushi went round and round on a conveyor belt; on the second floor a mah-jong parlor and a video rental store. The sensei's rooms were on the third floor, stuck between a couple of karaoke bars. Mori would have to lie there patiently on the couch listening to woozy renditions of "Yesterday," "North Country Spring," and "Woman from Osaka" coming through the paperboard walls while the sensei went through his routine. And it was a routine that generally encouraged Mori to focus his mind on the music.

First, it was necessary, in the words of the sensei, to use pain to defeat pain. The favored means was moxibustion—little cones of combustible material placed on key points of Mori's back and then set alight. Mori didn't like the feeling at all—it was as if tiny balls of fire had slipped under his skin and were burning through his nerve endings. Still, that was just a preparation for what came next. The sensei used just two needles, made of eighteen-carat gold and over three inches long. After inserting them deep into the muscle tissue of Mori's back, the sensei would connect them to a small machine that, he proudly claimed, he had invented himself. At the press of a button, a low-intensity electric current would flow through the needles and into Mori's back. To begin with, the sensation was quite mild, ticklish even, but then the sensei would gradually step up the current until Mori's back was clenching and twitching like a live clam on a griddle. That was when Mori would begin to croon along with the karaoke music, a habit that the sensei didn't much seem to like.

Mori's stripper friend claimed that the sensei had saved her career; that without his attentions, she would already be back in Kyushu, probably working in the same elevator-girl job in the same department store where she had started. So Mori was willing to give the guy a few more months to see if there was any improvement. The rainy season would be the real test, for that was when his back pains got so troublesome that he needed half a bottle of Suntory White before going to bed each night.

Another patient was being treated when Mori arrived, so he sat down on a canvas chair in the dingy little outer room that the sensei called his waiting area. The decoration was stark—just a few posters explaining the principles of acupuncture and an upended beer crate on which was stacked, for the benefit of bored patients, a collection of weekly magazines. Mori picked one up and casually leafed through its dog-eared, cigarette-singed pages. It was eight months old, full of sensations and rumors and scandals that had since slid into the bottomless pit of public oblivion.

Mori had flicked through the entire magazine and was on the point of tossing it back on the pile when something made him pause. There was a two-page article near the end that had somehow stuck in his mind. He went back to it and glanced over it again. At first, he couldn't work out exactly what had grabbed his attention. The subject was the young pop singer Yumi-chan. Some time back, she had disappeared for a couple of weeks. No one knew where she was—not her manager, not her family, not her friends. When she finally showed up, it was at a special press conference called by one of the weird religious cults that had been grabbing the headlines recently. Dressed in a white robe, she solemnly maintained that she wanted to spend her life as one of the cult's "Sisters of Light." According to the weekly magazine, that meant she would become one of the cult leader's dozens of mistresses. Mori skimmed through the article, unsure why he was doing so. Then his eye stopped at the heading of the final paragraph—"Happiness comes from digging in the depths of my heart." Wasn't that the phrase Yuriko had used the last time she had seen her boyfriend?

Mori reread the article from the beginning. From what he could gather, she had been recruited into this cult by another well-known young woman, a silver medalist in skating at the last Winter Olympics. After being introduced to the cult leader, she had agreed to drop out of circulation for a couple of weeks of "training" under his personal guidance. The effect had, apparently, been astonishing. From Yumi-chan's behavior, her friends and relatives could hardly recognize her as the same person. Gone was the nervous energy, the willfulness, the intense interest in clothes, men, and the activities of her rivals. Now she was passive and remote. And she couldn't stop smiling.

The cult was called Peace Technology, and its leader was a tall, bearded man called Ono. That rang a bell. About seven or eight years ago, a freelance journalist whom Mori knew vaguely had disappeared in mysterious circumstances. The guy had been staying with a girlfriend at a hot-springs resort when he was suddenly called to the telephone late in the evening. He hurried out for what he said was an urgent meeting with an important source, and that was the last that anyone saw or heard of him. The police got exactly nowhere with their inquiries, but it was known that at the time of his disappearance the journalist had been working on an investigation of the cult phenomenon.

Since then, Mori had noted the cult's frequent appearances in the mass media, though he didn't attempt to follow the subject closely. For a start, there were just too many cults around these days. They came and went like new brands of soft drink. Still, it was clear that Peace Technology had developed a good market niche. Yumi-chan was just the latest in a line of celebrities, mostly young women, whom Ono had succeeded in recruiting. Mori also remembered reading about the mass-marriage ceremonies in the Tokyo Dome and the network of temples that Ono was building across the country. The guy was also on the bestseller list almost every week—not because the public loved his writing, but because all the members of the cult were required to buy, then study closely, every one of their leader's works. Having created the demand, Ono was ready and willing to come up with the supply to satisfy it. A new collection of his philosophical ramblings was issued every two or three weeks.

Mori finished rereading the article, then examined the blurred, postage stamp–sized photo of Yumi-chan at the top of the page. She was kneeling on a small platform, staring blankly at the camera. Looking closely, Mori could see that she was wearing some strange kind of headgear, like an Arab burnoose with loops of wire attached. That and the white robe that billowed out from her shoulders had the effect of making her face look unnaturally small. She could have been a five- or six-year-old girl trying on her mother's dress. And there, just behind her shoulder, was a fuzzy shape that Mori had to squint at for several seconds before he could make it out. It was a metal mask fixed to the wall behind Yumi-chan. The features were distorted into a strange grimace that might have been either of rage or laughter, but they were still recognizable. They were the same features that were outlined in the other small photo at the bottom of the page. Yumi-chan was sitting underneath a large mask of Ono.

Yumi-chan, Yuriko, the mask, the "hat," the strange words—suddenly, everything clicked into place. Mori tore the two pages out of the weekly magazine and carefully folded them into his wallet.

"There you are. Well, come on, then—everything's prepared for you!"

Mori glanced up to see the sensei's bald head poking through the strings of wooden beads that curtained off the entrance to his treatment room. He looked like an old snake peering out of a hole in a wall.

"All ready?"

The sensei gave a gummy laugh, then abruptly retracted his head, leaving the beads swinging and rattling together. Mori tossed the magazine back onto the pile on the beer crate and went through to the treatment room, unbuttoning his shirt as he went. Two minutes later, he was lying flat on the couch while the sensei carefully positioned the little cones of moxa on the key points of his back.

"So, how has your condition been recently?" asked the sensei.

"Not much different," muttered Mori.

"It takes time," said the sensei, standing back to check that the cones were in exactly the right configuration. "But you should have confidence. This system has been proving its worth for almost two thousand years. It first came to Japan in the Heian period . . ."

The sensei liked to talk about the finer points of his trade—its Chinese and Indian origins; the necessity of using real moxa, made from the hairs on the underside of mugwort leaves, and not any modern substitute; the invisible network of therapeutic points through which energy courses in a healthy body. Mori lay there in silence, face turned to the small window in the wall, while the moxa cones burned into the flesh of his back. In the karaoke bar to his left, someone had started singing "I Left My Heart in San Francisco." From the other side came the strains of "Wakayama Blues." The sensei was still rambling on about the eighth century. The moon was visible through the grubby net curtains. Mori stared at it and thought hard about Yuriko and Yumi-chan and Ono. He had had bad feelings about this case from the start. Now they were slowly being realized.

EIGHT

Mitchell's next chance to observe Yazawa in action came a few days later. Yazawa was planning to entertain an important Scottish client in Roppongi, and for some reason he had asked Mitchell to come along.

Mitchell sat sipping a beer and listening to their conversation with detached amusement. Yazawa was at his most infuriatingly obscure. The Scotsman, who was the manager of a billion-pound pension fund, had been listening with increasing bafflement. Yet he had obviously heard of Yazawa's reputation. He knew that suffering bizarre anecdotes and sudden leaps of logic was the price you had to pay for some rare nuggets of investment advice. He kept plugging away with his questions, his granite-gray features only occasionally registering the exasperation that he had to be feeling.

Mitchell glanced down at the large sea bream lying on the plate between them. Fifteen minutes ago, one of the waiters had scooped it out of the tank in the window and chopped it up into a couple of dozen slices. Although the three of them had already eaten the tail and some of the lower body, the fish was still twitching periodically, its mouth slowly dilating and contracting in an O of astonishment. In Yazawa's company, Mitchell had often felt like that fish.

What kind of human being was Yazawa? Was he really a human being at all? Sometimes Mitchell wondered about that. For a start, there was something disconcertingly artificial about the man's appearance—the slicked-back hair, the shiny skin stretched taut over the cheekbones, the bulging, unblinking eyes. He looked like a shop-window mannequin so well made that you mistook it for one of the staff.

Then there was his inexhaustible stamina. Unusual for a Japanese salaryman, large quantities of alcohol had little noticeable effect on him, apart from making his laugh louder and his stare even more intense. Several times a week he would entertain fund managers in the Ginza until three or four in the morning. According to the few who had managed to keep pace, Yazawa's idea of recuperating for the day ahead involved an hour or so spent dozing in an all-night sauna, a sashimi breakfast at the Tsukiji fish market, and a spell in a videogame arcade "to sharpen the spirit." After that, he would stride into a seven o'clock meeting in the office looking as alert and eager to pounce as ever.

Most suspicious of all was the man's memory. Mitchell liked to think that his own memory was pretty sharp, but Yazawa's was in a different category altogether. He scattered his conversation with statistics as if he were downloading from his own private data bank. Kuwaiti oil reserves, Brazilian GNP growth, Swedish bond yields, the diffusion of TV sets in Shanghai—he could reel them off without pausing. And he wasn't limited to economic and financial subjects either. Get him onto baseball, and he would give you the starting pitchers in the 1988 World Series. Get him onto crime—one of his favorite topics—and he would give you the homicide rates of major U.S. cities. At first Mitchell had assumed that all this was the result of deliberate mental effort. But that, he now knew, couldn't be the case. The facts and figures that Yazawa came up with were too many and too various. The simple truth was that he ingested information like a vacuum cleaner ingests dust.

What about Yazawa's private life? What kind of family did he have? No one knew because no one had asked. Mitchell tried to imagine him accompanying a Mrs. Yazawa to the supermarket or playing softball with a little Taro Yazawa in a park. It was no good. Mitchell's mind just wouldn't produce the right pictures.

There was only one possible explanation for all this. Yazawa was not a human being at all, but an android—maybe an experimental model that had escaped from some secret government-funded development project. That was why people knew so little about his background. He was made not of flesh and blood but of high-performance engineering plastics, micromotors, and whirring hydraulics. Behind that shiny forehead was not a brain, but a disc drive. As Mitchell chewed his way through the bream, the idea became more compelling.

Mitchell walked into the restaurant's washroom and glimpsed Yazawa standing in front of the mirror, a screwdriver in his hand. He watched in helpless horror as Yazawa opened a panel in the side of his neck and pulled out a defective circuit board. Then Yazawa looked straight into the mirror and their eyes met. Yazawa smiled triumphantly. . . .

The Scotsman was dogged in his questions. "So it's your opinion that the market is already fully valued?" he was saying. "If I understand you rightly, you don't see much upside potential for the rest of this year."

Yazawa pursed his lips reflectively. "At the moment the market is displaying the characteristics of female anger," he said. "At such times, it is wise to prepare strong defenses against the unexpected."

The Scotsman seemed surprised. "Strong defenses? With company earnings in such good shape, I wouldn't have thought that was necessary."

That was the kind of answer Yazawa had been expecting. Tonight, he was glowing with self-confidence.

"Macpherson-san, do you understand the difference between a male anger and a female anger?"

"Uh—no. I think you've got me there, Mr. Yazawa."

"Let me explain. When a man is angry, he reacts suddenly, without thinking. The force of anger is expressed through violence, which then leaves his spirit. Do you understand my meaning?"

Yazawa turned around, his head at a lopsided angle to his shoulders. He put his hand to his eye and pulled down his lower eyelid, revealing the gleaming metal underneath. Mitchell backed out of the washroom, rushed through the restaurant and out onto the street. Yazawa charged after him, tossing aside tables and chairs with superhuman strength.

"Well, sort of, I suppose," answered the Scotsman dubiously.

"As for female anger, it is much different, I think. There is nothing so terrible as the smile of an angry woman. Behind her quiet words, she is already enjoying her revenge. She will wait until you are totally unprepared—and then!"

"And then, what?" said the Scotsman, reaching for another piece of fish.

"And then, she will strike like a cobra. She will bring you humiliation, disgrace, ruin. And from this, her satisfaction will be intense, the deepest satisfaction that a woman can experience. Macpherson-san, I hope you never have to satisfy a woman in this way."

"I'll certainly do my best not to," said the Scotsman in his dry Edinburgh accent.

"In my thinking, the market is now in the same mental condition as the angry smiling woman. It ignores our insults now, just as it will ignore our apologies and cries for mercy later."

"So you actually see downside potential from these levels? Do you believe that earnings are going to come in below expectations, or what?"

"I see the face of a smiling woman, Macpherson-san. The longer she waits, the more savage the satisfaction she will demand."

The Scotsman was looking confused. "So what sort of portfolio structure would you suggest? A reasonable concentration on defensive stocks, I assume."

"That would be sensible indeed. But in order to defend successfully, it is necessary to maintain the capacity of surprise."

"How do you mean? The capacity to surprise who, exactly?"

"First of all, surprise yourself. That is the important point. If you yourself are surprised, then, of course, all others will be surprised, too. Dare to do, Macpherson-san! Dare to do!"

"Do," repeated the Scotsman blankly. "Do what?"

"That is not the important question. Do what is nothing. Do how is everything."

"All right. In that case, do how?"

"As a British man, do like James Bond. That would be a good way, I think."

"James Bond! What has he got to do with it!"

"Everything and nothing," said Yazawa smugly. "All things are connected, but in ways that are invisible. Have you ever played our Japanese board game called Go, Macpherson-san?"

"I have not," said Macpherson, reaching for a piece of bream with his chopsticks. The fish's eyes were mistier now, but the tail fin was still twitching from time to time.

"An excellent game," said Yazawa. "There are many complex patterns to connect the stones on the board. But the good player does not understand them by analyzing the relations of individual stones. Instead, he must feel the flow of energy. This is the same as the skilled investor in the stock market, I think."

"How do you work that one out?" said the Scotsman, dabbing at a fleck of soy sauce that had landed on the cuff of his jacket.

Yazawa nodded at Mitchell. "Perhaps you can understand this idea," he said.

"Yes, I think so," said Mitchell, recalling Yazawa's monologue at the previous week's strategy meeting. "The Japanese economy is like a vast and never-ending game of Go. Many companies that seem to have no connection actually have strong lines of power flowing between them. And some companies that are positioned closely together have no connection at all. If you can read the patterns correctly, you can understand many events in the stock market that otherwise may seem inexplicable."

"Excellent," purred Yazawa. "That is exactly the necessary point."

"I see," said the Scotsman, staring strangely at Mitchell. "And do these marvelous patterns of yours tell you anything interesting at this moment or not?"

Without warning, Yazawa suddenly leaned forward, pushing his face right up to the Scotsman's. Startled, Macpherson dropped his chopsticks and jerked backward, his head rapping against the screen on the wall behind. Yazawa followed, going so close that for one mad moment it looked as if he were going to kiss the man on the lips.

"I have an idea that may interest you extremely," he breathed in a melodramatic whisper. "Depending, course, on your strength of spirit."

"What kind of idea?" said the Scotsman, an edge of panic to his voice.

"The name," said Yazawa, staring straight into the man's eyes from the distance of six inches, "is Otaman."

"Otaman," said the Scotsman, puzzled. "You mean that little trading house? What's so special there?"

"So much is so special," said Yazawa exultantly. "Mitchell-kun is here tonight to explain the story to you in the very fullest details."

That was the first Mitchell had heard of it. He looked up from the table, where the bream's mouth was still dilating weakly, and stared at the smirking Yazawa.

"Very well!" said Macpherson, shifting sideways in his seat. "I would be most interested to hear your presentation. Wait a moment, though."

He reached into his jacket pocket and took out a small notebook and fountain pen. "Right!" he said, his pen poised above the paper. "Fire away!"

Mitchell licked his lips. What he knew about Otaman could be summed up in a few brief sentences. First, the company's balance sheet made no sense at all. Second, there was a special project going on that not even the staff at the research center knew much about. Third, and from Mitchell's point of view, most important of all, Yazawa was maximum bullish on the stock.

"Well," he said nervously. "It's a complex story. Yazawa-san would be the ideal person to give you—"

"You are a well-paid and promising analyst of this company," Yazawa interrupted angrily. "So it is for you to highlight the merits of the stock. Do, Mitchell-kun! Do now!" He banged the table for emphasis, sending another fleck of soy sauce flying onto the Scotsman's sleeve.

Mitchell managed to string out his explanation for about five minutes. He spoke of the company's stable earnings profile, of its patient exploitation of niche markets, of the management's dedication to enhancing profit margins. All through, he was unhappily aware that he was convincing no one, not even himself.

"Is that all?" said the Scotsman when he had finally stuttered to a finish. "That doesn't sound at all interesting to me."

Exasperated, he slammed down his pen, which had remained hovering above the virgin white of the paper. Yazawa thrust his face forward again.

"His talk is not interesting!" he breathed. "It is very tedious indeed, I think. What Mitchell-kun has just explained to you is the knowledge of Otaman that is common to all investors. What I will explain to you now is something else. I will explain to you the reason that you must dare to buy this stock now, without delay. If you do not, you will hate your own face in the morning for many years to come. Your cowardice will disgust you like a bad smell from your body!"

Mitchell's pique at being used as a tactical diversion was rapidly succeeded by admiration. Yazawa had got the Scotsman right where he wanted him. The craggy gray face was heavy with curiosity.

"Go on," he said slowly.

"No writing, please," Yazawa hissed, seizing the Scotsman's wrist as he reached for the pen. "This is not information that should live on paper and ink. Drink it with your ears, then forget we have spoken on this matter. Be sure that I will never mention it to you again."

The Scotsman was almost salivating now. All his caution had evaporated like dew on the sunlit heather.

Yazawa drained his beer glass, held a thirty-second pause as he wiped his lips carefully with a napkin, then began speaking in a murmur so low that both Mitchell and the Scotsman had to crane forward to make out what he was saying.

"To understand clearly this unique situation, you need to know of the rivalry between the two main factions of the Choshu clan which began in the late eighteenth century . . ."

Mitchell listened with mounting disbelief. Yazawa didn't make any reference at all to the company's profitability or its diversification program. Instead, he talked about the historical dispute between two branches of the founding family, about shifting alliances with different zaibatsu industrial groups in the first years of the century, about wartime relations with the bureaucratic controllers of Manchukuo, Japan's puppet state in northern China. The way Yazawa told it, Otaman's future prospects depended not on new products or increasing market share but on the company regaining its place in a complex network of connections among bankers, bureaucrats, and politicians.

"Remember what we said of the game Go," he concluded. "Do not concentrate on the position of any stone in relation to the neighboring stones. Instead, attempt to feel the movement of energy around the whole board. If you understand this principle correctly, you will know that the potential of Otaman is truly exceptional."

Mitchell observed the Scotsman's reaction with surprise. There wasn't a hint of scepticism or impatience. He appeared to have swallowed Yazawa's story in its entirety. He wanted to ask questions, to know more, but Yazawa held up his hand.

"I will say no more of this subject. Forget everything I have told you, and then, when the time is right—do!"

"Do?" said the Scotsman, still not getting it.

"Not do what," said Mitchell helpfully. "Do how. That's what is important."

"Ah," said the Scotsman, trying to hide his confusion.

Yazawa stood up abruptly, causing the table leg to squeak across the tiled floor. "Now it is time to enjoy the life of the city," he announced, loud enough for the entire restaurant to hear. "Let us go find music and ladies to relax our spirits!"

"Fascinating chap," the Scotsman murmured to Mitchell as they followed in his wake. "Quite an asset to your firm, I'd say. What's his background, exactly?"

"He doesn't have one," said Mitchell, picturing white-coated scientists busily at work over the android's prone body.

He stopped to pay at the cashier's counter. Without turning around, Yazawa marched out into the street like a general leading his troops into battle.

The last week in the month, and the neon-splattered streets of Roppongi were seething with bodies. The citizens of the new electronic Edo were out in force, swarming through their digital floating world: young salarymen with jackets slung over their shoulders; slinky women in shiny stockings and tight miniskirts trotting in and out of nightclubs; office girls with glee in their eyes; students with ponytails and bandanas and ripped jeans, all meticulously tidy and clean. Music melded in the air—samba, bluegrass, heavy metal, Dixieland, chanson. The signs shimmered and fizzed and invited.

The next few hours passed in a blur. Everywhere Yazawa went, the hostesses greeted him like a long-lost friend. He drank heavily—whiskey, beer, wine, sake, brandy—and he insisted that Mitchell and the Scotsman drank in equal quantities. The only effect seemed to be that as the night wore on, he grew louder and more restless. Half an hour seemed to be the maximum he was willing to stay in any one place before abruptly getting to his feet and leading them out into the night again.

"Looks like you know the Tokyo nightlife like the back of your hand," said the Scotsman at one point.

"That would be impossible," replied Yazawa, sounding offended by the thought. "You see, Macpherson-san, there are over three thousand bars and clubs in the central area of Tokyo, and several of these are going out of business every week. That means if I start purposely to visit every place, by the time I finish everything would be changed. I would need to start from the beginning again."

"It sounds a bit like painting the Firth of Forth Bridge," said the Scotsman.

"There is always more to be discovered," said Yazawa sternly. "A man's lifetime would be insufficient for full knowledge of the night in Tokyo."

At the time, they were sitting in a small bar called Marilyn's, which was staffed by blond Australian girls with collagen pouts and strategically placed moles. When they passed over certain areas of the floor, a jet of warm air would send their billowy skirts flying around their elbows, revealing healthy golden haunches adorned with just garter belts and stockings. The Scotsman liked the place a lot. He sat slumped in the chair cradling his whiskey, a glassy smile on his face. Mitchell was feeling pretty jaded too. Everything around looked remote and slightly out of focus, as if he were viewing it through a thick windowpane. Only Yazawa was as full of energy as ever.

"Music is coming," he crowed as a three-piece group set up their equipment on a tiny stage in the corner. "Macpherson-san, are you a man of musical moods?"

"Can't say I am that," said the Scotsman, his voice starting to slur. Since sitting down, he hadn't take his eyes off the waitresses crossing and recrossing the room.

"You like Scottish songs, I think," Yazawa went on. "I also enjoy sometimes, especially in the environment of karaoke singing. Old, traditional songs have a good effect on us, don't they! They remind us of our hometowns and the spirits of our ancestors."

There were three members of the band—a drummer built like a small sumo wrestler, a bass player with tattooed biceps and dyed red hair that reached down to his waist, and a lead guitarist wearing a fringed-leather jacket and skintight bicycle pants. They spent a couple of minutes tuning their instruments before they were ready. The guitarist gave a short bow and a few sheepish words of introduction. Then came a flailing on the drums, a crashing power chord, and a bloodcurdling whoop from the bass player.

Mitchell glanced at the Scotsman. He seemed oblivious to the surge of decibels, his attention still totally occupied by the expanses of well-tanned flesh that were flashing before his eyes at regular intervals. Yazawa, on the other hand, was staring at the band and frowning darkly. Mitchell had some sympathy with his boss. He had wanted to hear ballads about hometowns and ancestors, and instead he was confronted by the bass player shaking his hennaed mane and screeching like a banshee.

"Get your motor runnin'
Head out on the highway."

Without warning, Yazawa suddenly shot to his feet, almost knocking the table over. He started waving his hands about and yelling something that was lost in the sea of noise. Too loud for him, thought Mitchell. There were shouts to sit down from the tables behind, but Yazawa ignored them. What was he trying to do? Surely, he wasn't going to start a fight? With mounting nervousness, Mitchell watched him push his chair aside and march toward the band, who were now reaching a full, arm-thrashing, grimacing frenzy.

"Like a true nature's child
We were born, born to be wild . . .
We're gonna fly so high
Gonna touch the sky."

Yazawa stood at the front of the stage shouting and wagging his finger at the guitarist while the band did their best to ignore him. Suddenly, he reached over to the amplifier and yanked out a couple of plugs. The roar of the guitars faded to nothingness, leaving just the thump of the drums and the bass player's wailing voice floating in space. The group continued their movements for several seconds, apparently unable to register what had happened.

"Good Lord," said the Scotsman. "What does the man think he's doing?"

Mitchell didn't bother to answer. Everyone was staring at them, including the waitresses. He had a sudden desire to slide under the table and stay there.

"I am making serious criticisms of this music," Yazawa said, turning around. "Yet they try to ignore me. That is not possible, I think!"

Too true, thought Mitchell with a sinking feeling. There was going to be a fight, he felt certain. He reached for the comfort of his whiskey glass.

The shouting began. There was a strange fascination in the sight of the forty-five-year-old salaryman arguing with the tattooed biceps and the skintight bicycle pants. The Japanese was too fast and slangy for

Mitchell to understand what was being said, but incredibly it sounded as if the musicians were gradually wilting under Yazawa's onslaught. There was a defensive tone to the bass player's remarks, and finally he gave a little bow of apology. At that, the lead guitarist pulled off his guitar and left the stage muttering something to himself. Typically, Yazawa had got his own way.

"Can you explain all this nonsense?" said the Scotsman, his good humor fading fast.

"Yazawa-san's quite a character," said Mitchell, aware of the absurdity of the understatement. "It seems that he disapproves of the band."

"Disapproves? Why, for God's sake! No one comes here for the music, I presume."

Yazawa had now mounted the stage himself. To Mitchell's amazement, he took off his jacket, hung it carefully over a speaker cabinet, and picked up the discarded guitar. For a few moments, he fiddled with the knobs, then leaned over and muttered something to the bass player, who gave an apprehensive nod.

"What on earth," said Macpherson. "I mean . . ."

His voice was lost as the first chords of "Crossroads" came booming out of the speakers. For a moment, Mitchell thought he was dreaming. Yazawa's fingers were dancing over the frets of the guitar as if he had been playing every night for years. When he stepped up to the microphone, his singing voice was husky and warm, his pronunciation perfect. He sounded like a different person. In the guitar solo, he squeezed and bent the notes in a perfect imitation of Eric Clapton. It was an astonishing performance. The band's original guitarist appeared at the side of the stage and stood, arms crossed, staring up at Yazawa's imperturbable features. Yazawa finished the number with a series of lightning runs up and down the fretboard, a whine of feedback, and a heavy-metal crash. Then immediately, without looking up to acknowledge the applause, he broke into the opening riff of "Hoochie Coochie Man," using his foot to stamp out a slow, bluesy beat.

"Remarkable," said the Scotsman, when Yazawa finally rejoined them at the table. "I would never have guessed you had it in you."

"Neither would I," said Mitchell.

"That guitarist was intolerable," said Yazawa, wiping his face with a handkerchief. "He was a weak-spirited man, with no respect for the music he played. No respect and no sincerity, I think."

"But where did you learn to play like that?" persisted Mitchell.

"I began this in my university days. Many girls were captured by my playing of the guitar. In my second year, I put a little star on the back of my guitar for each girl. By the time of my graduation, it was completely covered with stars!"

Yazawa gave one of his short, barking laughs. The Scotsman looked impressed.

"This was Hiroshima University, wasn't it?" said Mitchell casually.

"Not Hiroshima," said Yazawa with a glare. "Anyway, that's a long time ago, I think. No time for serious stories now! Let us drink to many profit opportunities in the big board game of Go that we must play with all the strength in our spirit. Drink to the bottom of your glasses! Let us enjoy! Let us do!"

"Let us do!" echoed Macpherson, and raised his glass.

Not do what, but do how. The thought flashed into Mitchell's mind an hour later, after he had left the other two merrily dancing the conga in another of Yazawa's favorite bars. Here, the "hostesses" were all trans-sexuals, a fact which seemed to amuse Yazawa greatly, but filled Mitchell with a deep discomfort. The Scotsman manifested little reaction for the simple reason that he hadn't been told.

Standing on the pavement outside, Mitchell felt exhausted, disoriented, and more than a little drunk. The sensible thing would be to take a taxi straight home and collapse into bed. And yet never in his life had he felt less ready for a peaceful night's sleep. His brain was buzzing with hopes, confusions, and wild hypotheses. What was going on at Otaman? What sort of man was Yazawa, this genius stock-picker who liked to eat lizard eggs, worried about the national sperm count, and treated sixties rock music like a martial art? Could he be trusted or not? The more Mitchell considered the problem, the more his uncertainties multiplied.

He glanced at his watch. Surprisingly, it was only eleven o'clock. Plenty of time left to do. To do what? To do like James Bond.

Fifteen minutes later, a taxi deposited Mitchell in the Otemachi business district a block away from the Pearson office. He walked the rest of the way, wanting to make his late-night return to the office look as casual as possible. In fact, he needn't have worried, for the streets were deserted and most of the office windows already dark. The only exception was the Matsui Corporation head office, which had a line of empty taxis waiting outside. The lights were blazing on the top floor, where the employees of the giant trading house processed information from its worldwide network of subsidiaries twenty-four hours a day.

Mitchell paused for a moment outside the skyscraper that contained the office where he had been working going on two years. As he had expected, all the lights were off on the fifteenth floor, home of the Pearson Darney branch. He stepped into the giant atrium with its wall of falling water and a huge bronze sculpture on a plinth in the middle. What was it supposed to represent, this object described on the plaque beneath as *Opus 15—Conditionality?* Sometimes, it looked to Mitchell like a headless, limbless body; sometimes like a deformed potato; sometimes like a huge golden turd that had been dropped from on high. Depending on his mood, it could symbolize despair or triumph or wonder or anything else. Tonight, it evoked effort, the kind of indefatigible effort that would be required for a constipated god to deposit something like that on the world below.

The building was alive, even though the human beings who inhabited it in the daytime were no longer there. The speckled carp still nosed through the pool at the bottom of the waterfall; the empty elevators continued to hum up and down to the commands of the central computer, the toilets still hissed and whooshed at preordained intervals. When Mitchell stepped out of the elevator on the fifteenth floor, an electronic eye blinked redly at him and a security camera dipped obediently. When he passed his magnetic card through the reader in the door, the machine chattered out a greeting.

The lights were off in the dealing room, but there was a blue-green glow from several high-resolution computer terminals. They had to be left on all night, every night, flickering with screenful after screenful of unheeded information—Swedish housing starts, consumer prices in New Zealand, the activities of the Brazilian central bank. For a moment, as he peered around the room, Mitchell thought that he could make out a human figure squatting behind one of these terminals, head sunk deep on its chest. Only after his eyes had accustomed themselves to the gloom did he recognize the pile of books stacked on a chair.

That reminded him of a story that he had heard from a Japanese bond trader. Apparently, the district had been haunted for decades by the ghost of a samurai warrior whose grave had been disturbed during the construction of an office building. It had last been sighted five years ago in the Matsui Corporation headquarters. After that, the company had suffered a number of misfortunes, including the bombing of its chemical plant in Iraq, the kidnapping of its branch manager in the Philippines, and the prosecution of a senior executive for bribery. Finally, the chairman of Matsui decided enough was enough. He brought the top exorcist in Kyushu up to Tokyo and, after months of regular salt-sprinkling and chanting, the ghost was induced to leave. The only problem was that no one knew where it had gone. The bond trader claimed that late one evening he had heard a strange moaning in the air-conditioning vents, as if the samurai was pleading to be let into the Pearson office, and then some tapping and scratching sounds at the window. He had immediately hurried out of the office, for just to lay eyes on the ghost was to guarantee yourself ten years of bad luck.

Mitchell had smiled at the story then, and he smiled again at it now. But he couldn't help peering from side to side as he walked through the dealing room to the personnel department. There was something about the deserted office—the whirring of the fax and the restless blinking of the screens—that made him uneasy.

He sat down at the desk of the head of the personnel department, a mah-jong fanatic called Makino, and switched on his computer. Theoretically, it should have been impossible for Mitchell to access any of Makino's files, but Mitchell had been standing behind him when he logged on in the mornings. He had noticed that the password that Makino had chosen for himself was less than imaginative, consisting of the first four letters of his own name.

Makino had set up numerous libraries, with dozens of files in each one. They covered training courses, bonus schedules, overtime hours, and the like. It took Mitchell several minutes to find what he was looking for—the personal records that all employees had to submit when they joined the company. He ran down the list of names, stopping at the final one. With a triumphant tap of the enter key, he called up on the screen a brief summary of Yazawa's life history.

The very first line was intriguing—"Birth 3.6.49, Saitama Prefecture." So Yazawa was born near Tokyo! The story about Hiroshima had been a complete fabrication. For some reason, Mitchell wasn't all that surprised. Since he had been working with Yazawa, his capacity for surprise was being eroded by the day. There were other details that gave him plenty of food for thought. According to the record, Yazawa had studied economics at Keio University and taken a master's degree in finance at Columbia University. After that, he had joined Mitsutomo Bank, spending a year in Geneva and then two in Los Angeles. Yazawa sometimes dropped references to experiences in Europe or the States into his conversation, but from his general demeanor you would never guess that he had spent six years overseas. When Yazawa spoke English, the heavy accent and screwed-up words suggested a man who had never been farther than Narita airport.

Mitchell read on. Yazawa had left Mitsutomo in 1985, shortly after returning to Japan. For the next two years, he had been research manager of Maruhachi Securities, a firm that Mitchell hadn't come across before. Then from 1987 until the previous autumn, he had worked for his own company, Yazawa Investment Services. Altogether, it made for an unusual career path, one that prompted a single obvious question: What could make an elite employee of a major city bank quit in midcareer and join a third-string securities house? Not surprisingly, there was nothing in the personnel file that provided any sort of answer.

Mitchell exited from Makino's files and switched off the computer, taking care to leave the keyboard propped against the side of the monitor exactly as he had found it. Was there anything else that could help him? On the spur of the moment, Mitchell padded into the research department and switched on the data-retrieval terminal that Pearson Darney had recently installed. Theoretically, this gave him access to all the most important Japanese newspapers and periodicals. Would the financial press have noted Yazawa's departure from the bank or commented on the activities of his investment advisory company? It was a long shot, but worth trying. Mitchell keyed in the name of his head of research and waited for the machine to complete its search of the archives.

After a couple of minutes a message appeared on the screen informing Mitchell that the upcoming list of headlines was several hundred long. Mitchell gazed at it with disappointment. Evidently there were more Yazawas in the world than he had expected. One, for example, had been a champion speed skater in the early sixties. Could that be the Yazawa that Mitchell knew? No, the age didn't fit. Another had received a prize for his work on ancient Chinese ceramics. With a man like Yazawa, anything was possible, but that wasn't really his style.

There was a way to narrow the field by adding an extra search item. Mitchell keyed in "Mitsutomo" and waited for the machine to run through its procedures. He wasn't really expecting anything to come up. There was no real reason for the press to pick up on someone like Yazawa.

But he was there, nonetheless. There were four references, all from the autumn of 1981. This had to be the story of the man's departure from the bank! With mounting excitement, Mitchell called up the headlines on his screen. It took a few seconds for the wobbly green script to appear out of the void, another few seconds for Mitchell to absorb what the Japanese characters meant.

"Whoa!" he said faintly, and leaned back in his chair.

Could it be a mistake? Was it possible that there were two men called Terumasa Yazawa working at Mitsutomo Bank? If so they would have been the same age and both working at the Los Angeles branch at the same time. That was hardly likely. The man in the headlines had to be Pearson's new head of research. Mitchell ran through the headlines again, making sure that he had not misread anything. No, there was no ambiguity. It said what he thought it said.

FBI PROBE OF JAPANESE BANK—33-YEAR-OLD EMPLOYEE AT CENTER OF FRAUD SUSPICIONS

Then, the next day:

MITSUTOMO SCANDAL IN LOS ANGELES—YAZAWA EMBEZZLED TO FUND FINANCIAL SPECULATION AND HIGH LIVING

Three days later:

MITSUTOMO IN CONFLICT WITH FBI—REFUSES COOPERATION WITH PROBE. YAZAWA ALREADY REPATRIATED?

And finally, a headline for an opinion column:

TEMPTATION OF THE ELITE—REFLECTIONS ON THE LOOSE MORALS AND LACK OF COMMON SENSE OF JAPANESE WORKING OVERSEAS

Mitchell called up the main body of the articles and slowly read through them, mentally checking and rechecking every word. The story was just as the headlines indicated. An elite credit officer in the Los Angeles branch of Mitsutomo had been caught in an elaborate fraud. He had authorized loans made to a number of dummy companies set up in the Southern California area. The money had been immediately siphoned off to a Cayman Islands bank account, then shifted to accounts in the names of other dummy companies at domestic American banks.

The FBI had had Yazawa under observation for six months. The details of the scandal were chronicled in careful detail—the holidays in the Caribbean, the trips to Las Vegas, the wild parties, the cars and the women. For Mitchell, there was one element in particular that convinced him there was no possibility of a mistake. That was the explanation of what the fraudster had done with his ill-gotten gains. According to the FBI, Yazawa had set up accounts with a number of brokerage firms and invested aggressively in commodity futures, stock options, and junk bonds. The reason that Mitsutomo Bank gave for breaking off cooperation with the FBI investigation was a good one—in the end, no money had been stolen. The money discovered in Yazawa's various accounts exceeded the amount that had been channeled in by almost 50 percent. In other words, instead of the fraud costing Mitsutomo money, the bank had actually made a fat profit. That, thought Mitchell, was the unmistakable mark of Yazawa. Even in those days, the man's investment skills had been phenomenal.

Mitchell took a deep breath and logged out. Now he knew why Yazawa had given up his career with the biggest bank in the world and moved to a tiny regional brokerage house. It made perfect sense that he should then set up his own investment advisory business, no doubt managing money for a discreet group of clients. What he didn't know, however, was what the man was doing at Pearson Darney. And what about Otaman—where did that fit in with Yazawa's plans?

Mitchell closed his eyes and rubbed them. A dull pain was tightening around his skull like a headband. He was going to have to examine every possibility. Nobody and nothing could be trusted.

Next morning, Mori arranged a meeting with the man who was going to help him with the next stage of his research. It took him three quarters of an hour on his Honda to get over to the building in Shinagawa that contained the new offices of Tsutomu Togo.

Mori had first come across Togo more than a dozen years ago when they had found themselves working together on a missing person case. At that time, Togo was busily acquiring a reputation as a radical young lawyer unafraid to take on the might of the Establishment in controversial human rights and pollution cases. What was even more unusual was that he actually won some of them. He successfully defended a student radical accused of a fire bombing that was actually committed by his brother, a member of a rival faction. Following that, he represented a whole fishing village that had suffered from diseases and birth defects caused by the dumping of chemical waste. That case had already been dragging on for a decade when Togo took it over, but within a year he had pressured the government into admitting supervisory negligence, a new legal concept at the time.

Since then, Togo had gone on to defend the rights of political refugees from China, pornographers, and the families of men who had died from the stress of overwork. Over the years, though, he had mellowed both personally and politically. The hot-tempered young moralist who saw a conspiracy in every injustice had grown into a fatalistic, rather paunchy middle-aged man. These days, Togo no longer focused his attention on headline-grabbing anti-government issues. Instead, he acted as an advisor for a number of small citizens' movements—for stricter product-liability regulations, against the building of an environmentally destructive dam, and so on. It was during this phase of his career that he had taken up a couple of cases involving religious cults, in one preventing a cult from being unfairly expelled from the land it was renting, in another helping a father to win the return of his missing daughter. As a result of what he had learned in these legal tussles, Togo had set up the New Religious Movement Information Center, which offered to mediate in any dispute involving the cults. Nobody in Japan knew more about the way they operated than he did.

When Mori arrived at Togo's office, he was greeted with a slap on the shoulder and a comment about his waistline. Togo was in no position to talk. That lean, hawklike face that had stared out of news photos and TV screens in the mid-1970s had softened and widened considerably. He led Mori into a comfortable office. A full suit of samurai armor stood in the corner behind his desk.

"Don't worry about him," said Togo, noticing Mori's curious stare. "That's my great-great-grandfather, who was a masterless samurai at the time of the Meiji Restoration. He's not in there now, of course, but I like to think that some of his spirit remains. It gives me confidence in my own little struggles."

"He must have been quite a fighter," said Mori, noting the dents on the dull metal of the breastplate.

"He fought for the Satsuma clan against the Choshu clan, then he fought for the emperor against the shogun's armies. Ten years later, he took up his sword again and joined the rebellion against the Meiji government. Fighting was his life."

"But not his death?"

"No. After that, he was put in charge of a tea-growing cooperative. He lived until he was eighty-five years old."

"Maybe it runs in the family," said Mori, sitting down in an armchair. "What does?"

"The ability to fight as fiercely as you can and still manage to survive."

"I don't fight so fiercely anymore," said Togo with a quiet smile. "Nobody does these days—except you, of course."

"I do it because there isn't any alternative. Still, maybe someone is going to present me with a tea-growing business someday. Or even a jazz coffee bar would do, actually."

They both laughed without really knowing the reason why. Then Togo sat down at his desk and listened, chin propped on his hand, while Mori sketched out what he needed to know. Mori didn't explain the background to his sudden interest in Ono and Peace Technology, and Togo knew better than to ask. The unspoken agreement between them was that Mori would pass on all the information he had gathered when the case was finally closed.

When Mori had finished, Togo swiveled his seat around and jerked open a drawer of the tall filing cabinet that stood next to the samurai warrior.

"This is the information center," he said, rapping a knuckle against the gray metal. "It doesn't look like much, but I doubt whether the police have got anything better. The only way to find out about these organizations is to talk to the people who run them. No one else knows anything."

"You've talked to Ono?" said Mori, surprised.

"No, I haven't, but I've talked to plenty of his competitors. It's an industry, you see, Mori-san, just like any other. If you want an objective appraisal of what's going on at Mitsutomo Electric Industries, don't ask the managers there. Go and talk to the people at Sanwa Electric or Sumikawa. The same thing goes with the religious cults. They watch each other closely, swap gossip, copy marketing methods, even try to lure away each other's customers."

"So what is the industry's view of these Peace Technology people?"

Togo pulled a slim cardboard file out of the cabinet and tossed it onto the desk. "Here's everything that's come up over the past few years. Compared to what I've got on the other cults, it's not much. Ono's information control is pretty tight."

Mori opened the file and flicked through the pages inside. There were some copies of newspaper articles, several typed-up interviews with people identified just by their initials, and a dozen pages of notes tightly written in Togo's own hand. Mori skimmed through the summary on the first page, which gave Togo's assessment of the cult.

" 'Expanding aggressively . . . apocalyptic and nihilistic teachings . . . profound personality changes observable among members . . . repeated intimidation of defectors . . . potentially the most dangerous and antisocial of the new breed of cults . . .' You don't paint a very attractive picture here. In fact, I'd say you don't like them at all."

Togo drummed his fingers on the desktop. "I try to collect information, not make value judgments, but these Peace Technology people worry me. Over the years, they've accumulated a huge amount of assets, mainly real estate. They're much better organized than the usual cults, much smarter in their methods. Of course, that's not surprising given the leader's background."

"His background? Is there something special there?"

"Ono's an interesting guy. He comes from a family of Buddhist priests—they have this temple in north Japan that they've been running for several hundred years or so. It's one of these minor esoteric sects, pretty traditional from what I understand. Anyway, Ono was the eldest son in the family, the one you'd expect to take over the temple. But he didn't. It turned out that he was a brilliant student at school, and he went on to study biochemistry at Tokyo University."

143

"Is that so?" said Mori. "From Buddhism to biochemistry—maybe it's not so far as it sounds."

"Wait—there's more to come. After graduation, he went to work in the laboratories of Sumikawa Foods, which was diversifying into pharmaceuticals at that time. He was considered such a promising researcher that he was sent to the United States for another two years of study."

"Then what happened?"

"It's unclear. I'm guessing that he saw how fringe religions had become a big money-making business over there and decided to try the same thing here in Japan. Anyway, he dropped out of circulation for a couple of years and then he turned up in Tokyo again wearing a white robe and a beard, ranting on about earthquakes and divine lights."

"So Ono was once an ordinary company employee?"

"That's right. He used to put on his suit in the mornings and go to work on the train, just like everyone else. Now, of course, he's a living god."

"And his followers are willing to swallow that?"

Togo chuckled. "Peace Technology people are willing to swallow many things. Let me give you some idea of what kind of organization we're talking about here."

He opened one of the drawers of his desk, took out three Perspex vials, and placed them carefully in front of him. They were about the same size and shape as small perfume bottles. Each was filled with a different kind of liquid—one pale yellow, one red, and one gray and cloudy.

"Is that what it looks like?" said Mori.

Togo nodded and tapped the yellow bottle with his finger. "A sample of the living god's urine," he said. "Medium-ranking disciples have the privilege of consuming one every week of their lives—at ten thousand yen a shot. The blood, on the other hand, is for higher ranks only. Being rarer, you can get it only once every two months—at eighty thousand yen a shot."

"How are you supposed to take it?" said Mori. "Straight or mixed with Suntory White?"

Togo smiled and pointed at the vial of cloudy liquid. "And this, of course, is the rarest of all. A quarter of a million yen, and only available twice a year to specially favored disciples. I got the whole lot from one of the few high-ranking disciples ever to break with the cult. He's now living in Australia under an assumed identity."

"I get the picture," said Mori. "Is there anything else I need to know?"

"There may be something," said Togo, leaning back in his chair. "As a lawyer, I like to deal in facts, not rumors or ungrounded suspicions. Still, there are some features of the whole Peace Technology setup that raise questions in my mind."

"Go on," said Mori.

"It's just an idea of mine," said Togo, looking up at the ceiling, his hands clasped behind the back of his neck. "But recently many yakuza groups have been transforming themselves into smaller, less visible entities—religious foundations, charities, educational institutes, things like that. Actually, religious foundations are special favorites because of their tax-exempt status. The problem is that the yakuza can't get a license if what they're doing is too obvious. So ideally, what they need to do is merge themselves into an existing organization, one that everyone recognizes as legitimate. Once they've done that, a screen goes up. The authorities can't investigate without due cause. No one can lay a finger on them."

"You're saying Ono is yakuza-backed? Is there any evidence for that?"

"No evidence at all," said Togo, still staring into space. "That's why there's nothing mentioned in the file. But the real question is how the guy gets his money."

"From books and donations, I suppose," said Mori.

"That's not enough. He says he's got two million followers, but my sources tell me that the real figure is just a third of that. Yet he's got real estate holdings in central Tokyo, branch offices all over the country, and runs a fleet of helicopters. Why, the network of temples they're building—have you seen the pictures? It must be costing tens of billions of yen."

"Maybe he's got some rich backers, like that singer Yumi-chan."

"Yumi-chan doesn't have any money. Her production company takes ninety yen out of every hundred she earns, and her manager gets most of the rest. That's the way it is in her line of business. As far as Ono is concerned, she's just bait for neurotic teenagers. A pretty successful strategy too, from what I hear. Since all the publicity started, new recruits have been pouring into the cult."

"So Ono's market share is still growing. It's a strange business, isn't it? I'll never understand what makes people give up their homes and families and follow someone like that."

145

"It's happened before," said Togo, with a little shrug of the shoulders. "Look at Jesus Christ, Buddha, Confucius. People probably thought exactly the same thing about them."

"But they weren't backed by the yakuza."

"That's true," said Togo. "But if the yakuza had been around in those days, who knows what would have happened!"

They both laughed.

"Anyway," Togo continued, "the rise of the cults is a complex phenomenon. You probably need to be a psychologist to understand it fully. Basically, the need to belong is very strong among young people today, but the modern family unit isn't strong enough to satisfy it. The fathers are away at work all the time and use the home as a kind of dormitory, and these days the mothers have their own work and interests, too. In our time, there were political and social movements to commit yourself to, but no one is interested in them anymore. Music, fashion, sports—they're also losing their ability to engage people fully. Why, even the Gendai Giants aren't as popular as they used to be!"

"They lost the Japan Series again last year," said Mori with satisfaction.

"That's not the point," said Togo, who had a soft spot for the Giants. "In the old days, it didn't matter whether the Giants won or lost—they were popular just for existing! That's not the case anymore. Young people today can't find their identity in mass entertainment. They want something more powerful—not something to sip at, but something to drown themselves in. That's where Ono and the other cults come in."

"You make it sound perfectly normal, Togo-san." said Mori, shaking his head.

"This is just background," said Togo. "In fact, each cult becomes a closed world, with its own rules and inner politics and psychological structure. Outsiders can never understand the mentality fully. For that, it's necessary actually to become a member."

Nodding thoughtfully, Mori placed the Peace Technology file back on the desk. "Become a member, you say. Yes—maybe that's not such a bad idea."

Togo gave a little snuffle of laughter. "You—a cult member! I don't think you're the right kind of person, Mori-san."

"Why not?" said Mori.

"These cults prefer to find people with many deep, insoluble problems."

"Problems! I've got plenty of deep, insoluble problems," exploded Mori. "I'm on a big losing streak at the bicycle track, my best girlfriend has gone to Kyushu to become a pro wrestler, and a guy on a motorbike just tried to kill me. How can you say I don't have deep, insoluble problems?"

"No good," said Togo, still smiling. "You need to be unhappy. The trouble with you is that you're happy with your problems. You couldn't live without them."

"Well, let's see," said Mori, getting up from his chair. "Maybe Ono's people will make some miraculous change in my life. That's what they promise, isn't it?"

"Wait a minute," said Togo, as Mori headed for the door. "If you're really determined to join up, you might as well take this with you. You can put it in your coffee sometime."

He picked up the vial of cloudy liquid and tossed it across the room, not very accurately. Mori had to stretch to catch it one-handed. He put it down carefully on the bookshelf next to the door. "No thanks," he said. "I always take my coffee black."

———

Mori got back to his office just after one. He parked his Honda next to the trash cans and empty beer crates that were permanent features of the pavement in front of the Suki-yaki Heaven restaurant. At lunchtimes, it operated a conventional service, with the lights on bright and a couple of middle-aged waitresses in attendance. The only indication that the evening menu was richer was the polyethylene sack of crumpled, discolored hand towels that leaned against one of the beer crates. Mori stamped up the metal staircase that the anonymous architect had tacked to the side of the concrete box that he had designed. The offices of the import-export business were as dark and silent as ever. Mori glanced at the Professor Turtle posters as he passed the door. There was one in particular that drew his attention. A big-bellied man in spectacles and a white coat was standing in some kind of laboratory. On the table in front of him were a rack of test tubes and the upended shell of a giant turtle, completely empty. The man, presumably the famous Professor Turtle himself, was beaming at the camera, his chubby face redolent of health and vigor.

"Learn the secret of long life and male stamina from the marvel of the oceans!" read the headline. "Giant Leather-backed Turtles live for 120 years!"

Except for the ones who meet up with the professor, thought Mori as he trudged up the stairs.

On the third floor, one of the two junior yakuza who ran the English-language school was just emerging from his office. There was a woman with him—skimpy leopard skin–print dress and a cloud of cheap perfume, obviously just sprayed on.

"Going out for lunch?" remarked Mori in passing. He knew the guy vaguely, and they usually exchanged greetings.

"Yes, that's right," mumbled the yakuza sheepishly, bobbing his head forward in a miniature bow. The woman gave Mori a long, slow, head-to-toe appraisal, which she ended with a loud pop of the bubble gum she was chewing.

"You didn't notice anyone looking around for me this morning?"

The yakuza shook his head. He was a simple kind of guy who had only two basic modes of address—deferential or violently hostile. He seemed to view Mori as a senior figure in an allied trade, and showed him the kind of respect that age commanded in the rigidly conservative world he inhabited. It was, thought Mori, a dubious compliment.

"But I did," said the woman, fluttering her mauve-tinted eyelids up at

Mori. "There was this girl looking for you. A tall one, with hair down to her tits."

Mori felt a tickling sensation under his scalp. "Is that right?" he said quietly. "Where did you see her, exactly?"

The woman fiddled with the black strap of her bra, which was showing beneath the thin shoulder piece of her dress. She had a throaty Osaka accent that reminded Mori of women he had known in the clubs of Namba and Kita.

"She was downstairs when I arrived. I asked what she was doing, hanging around like that. She asked me if I knew anything about a detective called Mori. That's you, isn't it?"

"Wait a moment," growled the yakuza, his good manners disappearing fast. "I don't remember you telling me any of this!"

"I don't have to tell you everything, you big bear. You're not my husband, you know. If you were, I'd jump in the river." She squealed with laughter and gave a broad wink in Mori's direction.

"So what did you say?" said Mori.

The woman pulled at her lower lip like a little girl. "Let me see. I think I told her to get out of here before I called my boyfriend. Was that wrong, Mori-san? Is she your lover, or maybe one of your sex friends? I should think a man like you has a lot of sex friends."

The woman leaned in close, placing a hand lightly on Mori's forearm. Under the perfume was a strong smell of whiskey.

"Enough to cause me all the trouble I need," said Mori, aware of the yakuza's darkening features. "Thanks for your information."

"No problem," giggled the woman, squeezing his arm. "I'd be happy to help you any time."

She raised a hand to his cheek and stroked it lightly with her long red fingernails. Mori looked across at the yakuza and read in his face exactly what was going to happen next.

It was all over in a couple of seconds. The yakuza's movements were fast and smooth, using just minimum effort. The woman's head jerked back, twisted around, then there was a dull smack and she collapsed against the stairway, blood oozing from her mashed lip and nose. For a moment, she sprawled there blinking and frowning, as if trying to remember what they had been talking about. Then she screwed up her face and gave out a wordless wail of shock and pain.

The yakuza turned to Mori, rubbing the knuckles of his right hand.

The little finger was just a stub, and it gave the whole hand a thick, bulbous appearance. Mori gazed back at him quizzically.

"Please accept my sincere regrets," muttered the yakuza gruffly. "This woman who has caused you inconvenience is my responsibility." He put his arms straight down at his sides and made a formal bow of apology, revealing a shiny disc of scalp at the crown of his frizzy "punch perm."

"Don't mind," said Mori. "Women are getting pretty hard to handle these days."

"I will make stronger efforts to control her in the future. This is my promise."

Mori made a short bow in return. It was important not to let the guy feel that he had lost face. A yakuza who had lost face was a dangerously combustible quantity, like a box of fireworks left near an open fire. There was always a chance that nothing would happen, but it wasn't a good idea to wait around and make sure.

The woman lay curled up on the ground, her body heaving with the deep sobbing sounds she was making. A bubble of blood had formed at the bottom of her nose. It was the same color as her lipstick.

"Stop those noises," growled the yakuza, obviously embarrassed. "People around here are trying to do work!"

He grabbed her by the shoulder and shook her hard, till blood and saliva flew from her mouth. She gazed up at them dizzily. "I'm sorry," she said, gulping in air. "I didn't mean to cause anyone any trouble."

"Apologize to Mori-san! He is the senior resident in this building. Apologize to him properly!"

She nodded wearily, having been through all this, Mori guessed, numerous times before. With her eyes puffed and her makeup smeared, she suddenly looked a lot older. Panting with the effort, she rolled onto all fours and pressed her forehead down to the metal floor. The yakuza was gazing at him expectantly. Mori paused for a moment and glanced down at the woman's bent back and heaving shoulders.

"Enough," he grunted finally. "Your apologies are accepted."

"It will not happen twice," said the yakuza. "This I can promise."

"What you say is good. I value your consideration for our building's users. Such a sense of responsibility is rare these days."

The yakuza made another deep bow, his face flushing slightly. Mori stepped over the woman's prone body and carried on up the stairs.

———

Mitchell spent most of the afternoon brooding about Yazawa, Ota-man, Tokyo, his own future, and the state of the world in general. What had he accomplished so far in his life? Not much, really. Not enough. He had to move fast, before it was too late.

The day that he heard he had got the job at Pearson's, Mitchell had mapped out the next phase of his life on his personal computer, assigning probability weightings to the different courses ahead. On the reasonable assumptions that had been fed in, the computer worked out that Mitchell had a 20 percent chance of making a million pounds by the age of thirty, and a 60 percent chance by the age of forty. What he hadn't realized at the time, but had soon become painfully obvious to him as soon as he arrived in Japan, was that making a million pounds counted for nothing anymore. In central Tokyo, a million pounds wouldn't even buy you a two-story house with a postage stamp of a garden.

Mitchell had heard that Japan was expensive, but he had assumed that meant expensive according to a Western scale of cheapness and expensiveness. What he found was something that didn't appear on the Western scale at all. His most serious problem was that the contract the rugby player in the London office had offered him was denominated in American dollars. Since Mitchell had signed up, the dollar had been in free fall. Apparently, the U.S. administration had adopted a deliberate policy of talking up the yen in order to exert leverage on the Japanese government on trade issues. Well, they had been so successful that his salary had fallen by a quarter in yen terms. Even though he was now earning more than the British prime minister, he was still poor. The bills at sushi shops made him wince. He never took taxis when the trains were running. He thought about money all the time. He had to, otherwise he would soon have none left.

Mitchell's contract would be up for renewal in a year's time. What happened then depended entirely on Yazawa. If Mitchell weren't careful, he would soon be back at the dispatch company, living off takeout food in a mangy Hackney bed-sit. But there was nothing genetically determined about any of that. He didn't have to stay poor. If he played his cards right, he could make himself indispensable. After a few years, he could be out there frolicking with the select flock of financial dolphins.

Mitchell's instincts told him that events were leading him to a critical point in his life, more important than any that he had worked through on his old personal computer. Until he had come to Tokyo, nothing out of the ordinary had ever happened to him. Now, suddenly, he was the right man in the right place at the right time. Yazawa wanted his help. Nothing like this would ever happen to him again. So there was no choice, really. He had to grab the opportunities that were waiting to be grabbed. He had to take risks.

"Don't go pissing on his fireworks," said Ted Shimano, patting him on the shoulder as he walked past. "That would be a mistake."

"What's that?" said Mitchell, his mind slow to return to focus.

"I'm talking about Yazawa. When he's made up his mind about something, nothing is going to change it."

"That's for sure," said Mitchell, with a nervous glance over his shoulder. To his relief, Yazawa was clearly visible in his office on the other side of the dealing room. He was sitting bolt upright in his chair, the female graduate standing behind him massaging his neck.

"Incidentally," he continued as Ted sat down and switched on his computer, "I've been meaning to ask you a question. What do you know about *Hagakure?*"

"What's that you say?" said Ted absently.

"*Hagakure*—I just wanted to know what you thought of it."

Ted turned away from his screen, a puzzled expression on his face. "I'm not familiar with that one. Does it trade on the over-the-counter market?"

Mitchell examined Ted's expression closely for any trace of humor. There was nothing. Ted was a bright guy conversationally, but there were huge gaps in his store of knowledge. Basically, he was ignorant about anything that had happened before 1986, whether in Japan or anywhere else in the world. Asking him about a work of seventeenth-century literature was like ordering a bottle of good wine at the fast-food joint across the street.

"Never mind," said Mitchell. He got up from his seat, walked over to the giant filing cabinet that covered one wall of the research room, and flipped through the Otaman file. There wasn't much inside—no research notes or memos of meetings, just a few old annual reports and product brochures. As Mitchell knew only too well, the company had been in the doldrums for so long that no analyst had bothered to look at it for years. He took the documents back to his desk and began leafing through them, scrutinizing the small print under photos and the lists of addresses.

The process of searching took a long time. Even after three years of study, Mitchell found Japanese place names difficult to read correctly. They weren't formed in a logical way. There were so many complicated characters, so many combinations, so many different ways of pronouncing them. Nelson's Dictionary, to which he made frequent reference as he pored over the Otaman documents, listed more than five thousand Japanese characters. After over two years of study, Mitchell estimated that he knew about eight hundred, and they were the easy ones. At that rate, it would take twelve years to get the rest. Twelve years—by that time he would be almost forty years old!

When he had finished, Mitchell put an elastic band around the documents and dropped them into a desk drawer. As far as he could see, there had been no mention anywhere of an Otaman factory, branch, or sales office in Kawasaki City. That was a surprise, since Mitchell had assumed that the Kawasaki project, whatever it was, would be housed in facilities of reasonable scale. Now he had to examine some other possibilities. The Otaman people seemed to be obsessed with secrecy. Perhaps they were shielding their project in Kawasaki under some other name, in which case it would be difficult for Mitchell to investigate further.

On the spur of the moment, Mitchell picked up the phone and dialed the number for directory inquiries. "I would like the number for Otaman in Kawasaki City, please," he said in his slow, deliberate Japanese. Speaking on the phone always made him realize how foreign he sounded.

"Understood! Please wait for a moment."

He heard the woman's fingers tapping away on a computer keyboard, then she spoke again, her bright tone announcing her success. "Is it possible that this is what you are searching for? Otaman Distribution Center—Matsuoka five, nine, twenty-two."

"That's it, without any mistake," said Mitchell. So it was really as simple as that. He hadn't needed to labor through those Otaman documents after all. A distribution center—that certainly wouldn't be worth mentioning in the publicity materials. But it might be large enough to contain a top-secret project that the company was anxious to keep under wraps.

Mitchell put the phone down and went to get a map of Kawasaki City from the office library. His mind was made up. Enough of the spreadsheets and balance-sheet ratios. From now on, his research methods were going to be much more direct.

NINE

At seven-thirty in the evening, Mitchell was wandering through the back streets of Kawasaki, trying to match the photocopied map in his hand with the glittering, disorienting reality all around him. After nearly an hour of searching, he wasn't exactly lost, but he didn't exactly know where he was either. The streets and signs and crossroads all looked the same, and he had failed to locate any of the buildings marked on the map. That might be because the map was nearly ten years old and they had all been knocked down, or it might be because Mitchell's sense of direction was completely scrambled.

Already groups of salarymen were reeling in tipsy merriment from pink cabaret to massage parlor to strip club. Several of Pearson's sales people did their expense account entertaining in the back streets of Kawasaki; it was much cheaper than the Ginza and more popular with the clients in these nervy, stress-ridden times. For in

Kawasaki, there was no need to pretend, no need for smart conversation or elegant manners; just the fulfillment of basic human appetites. Looking around, Mitchell could see nothing that resembled a distribution center. But it had to be around here somewhere. He used the mauve glow of a massage parlor entrance to peer at his map again. Which direction was Yokohama? Was he facing north or south? It was impossible to tell.

"Hey, Joe, what you think you're doing here? This is not right place for you!"

It was a rasping male voice, speaking English with a scrambled, half-Texan, half-Japanese accent. Mitchell wheeled around to face a man sitting on a chair just inside the entrance. He was wearing shiny white shoes, a white suit over a black shirt, and an outrageous polka-dot tie. Despite the gloom inside, his eyes were concealed behind a pair of metal-framed sunglasses. Mitchell nodded a nervous acknowledgment. This man looked like a parody of a yakuza, down to the ugly scar on his cheek. And the downward twist of his mouth suggested that he wasn't exactly overjoyed with Mitchell's presence.

"Are you white-boy American shithead?"

This time the tone was unmistakably hostile. Mitchell edged away from the entrance, keen not to attract attention to himself. Just as he was about to turn and head off down the steet, the yakuza leapt up from the chair and grabbed him by the shoulder. The sunglasses clattered to the ground, revealing a pair of furious bloodshot eyes.

"Wait, let go of me!" panted Mitchell, trying in vain to twist away from the yakuza's powerful grip.

"Big horse-prick foreigner, huh! You try to bring deadly diseases to Kawasaki City, don't you!"

The yakuza swung him around, and suddenly their faces were just inches apart and Mitchell's nostrils were taking in a powerful mixture of garlic and whiskey.

"What are you talking about?" protested Mitchell, his palms raised in front of his chest. "I don't have any diseases. I'm perfectly healthy!"

"I know you," snarled the yakuza, twisting Mitchell's shirt collar in his stubby fingers. "Gay-boy sailor spreading diseases around Japan! You try to kill our women, kill our business."

Mitchell was pinned against the wall, forced up on his tiptoes. He could see curious faces over the yakuza's shoulder. On the other side of the road, small crowds of salarymen had stopped to watch.

"You've got me wrong," jabbered Mitchell. "I'm not a sailor. And I always practice safe sex, honest to God."

"God!" The yakuza made a noisy pretense of spitting. "You white shithead gay boy! You spread foreign virus around Kawasaki City with your big horse prick!"

"Listen, I have no infections or illnesses!" Mitchell said desperately.

"All foreigners have foreign virus," bellowed the yakuza, loud enough to turn heads at the other end of the street. "Enough foreigners! Foreigners kill our business in Kawasaki City."

The sex industry was going through hard times, just like every other industry that depended on consumer spending. But that was hardly Mitchell's fault. According to Pearson's economic research, insufficient demand was the result of mistakes in fiscal policy. The yakuza, though, didn't seem in the mood to analyze the situation logically. He had turned his head away and was making loud snorting noises while twisting Mitchell's collar so hard that he thought it might tear away from his shirt.

"Smell like animal," the yakuza yelled between snorts. "Eat too much pig meat and you gonna smell like pig!"

The crowd on the other side of the street had grown larger, and the cars were passing more slowly now as people gazed out the windows to see what the fuss was about. Mitchell examined his options. He could stay there pinned to the wall while the yakuza got increasingly aggressive. Or he could do something about it. The yakuza was heavily built, but also looked drunk and out of condition. If only Mitchell could get him off balance for a moment, he would probably be able to break free.

The yakuza shifted his stance slightly, and Mitchell seized the opportunity, stomping with all his strength on one of the shiny white shoes. There was a grunt of pain, and the yakuza hopped backward. Mitchell ducked and twisted, but the yakuza's grip on his collar did not loosen. Instead, Mitchell was tugged off balance as well.

"Big mistake for you, shithead Joe," roared the yakuza, gazing down at his feet. "You make my good shoes dirty!"

There was indeed a large black smudge across the toe of his left foot. Mitchell steadied himself. The yakuza reached under his jacket. What did he have there—a knife, a gun, or just a blackjack? Mitchell froze with panic. He was in a fight, a dangerous one. What was he going to do? What were the choices?

The yakuza was fumbling in his inside pocket with one hand, hanging on to Mitchell's collar with the other. Suddenly, Mitchell found himself behaving according to some deep instinct. Without making any conscious decision to defend himself, he was twisting backward, balling his right hand into a fist, then swinging it as hard as he could against the side of the yakuza's head.

There was a sound like an orange hitting a wall and a jarring sensation in his hand that traveled all the way up to his shoulder. The yakuza took a step backward and gazed at Mitchell thoughtfully, eyebrows curling upward. His right hand seemed to be stuck under his jacket. Mitchell's blood froze. This was it. He could see the report in the *Japan Times,* a small headline near the bottom of the second page—"Foreign Investment Analyst Killed Outside Bordello." His mother would be so ashamed. No doubt Yazawa would laugh like a drain.

"Don't do anything stupid," he croaked, conscious of the wall pressing against his back. "There are witnesses everywhere."

The yakuza's left hand dropped from Mitchell's collar. He lifted his gaze to a place well above Mitchell's head, then, suddenly, without a sound, his knees buckled and he slumped to the pavement, where he rolled over and lay on his side like a man trying to sleep. Mitchell stared at him in amazement, then glanced around. It seemed as if the whole street were watching him—salarymen, working girls, even the taxi drivers peering from their cabs.

"Not my fault," he said in Japanese to no one in particular. "He was very drunk. It couldn't be helped."

The silent eyes didn't budge. It was as if a spotlight were on him. Mitchell edged away from the yakuza's inert body, then wheeled around and made rapidly for the next street, his stiff-legged walk soon breaking into a trot.

Swerving around the corner, he found himself in a narrow side street, dimmer and less crowded than the busy thoroughfare he had just left. The small groups of salarymen glanced at him curiously as he jogged by, one or two of them making ribald comments. Mitchell kept going. He turned left at the next side street, then right, then left again. The lights and faces passed by in a blur as he pounded down the ever darker, ever quieter streets, never staying on any one for longer than necessary. After twenty minutes or so, he found himself in a different type of area—full of winding bicycle lanes, darkened sheds, and empty lots that claimed to be car parks. He glanced over his shoulder to reassure himself that no one was following, then ducked into an arched gateway and sank to his knees. He was out of breath and his hands were shaking with the shock, yet he felt strangely exhilarated. The yakuza had chosen to mess with him. Mitchell had responded. Stamp once—on those shiny white shoes—and pass through a wall of iron! Yazawa couldn't have failed to be impressed with that piece of work!

As his pulse rate returned to normal, Mitchell considered what to do next. He had dropped the map somewhere along the way. He had no idea where he was, no idea which direction would lead him back to the entertainment district—which was probably now being scoured by a posse of the yakuza's pals. He clambered to his feet and looked around. The arched gateway opened on a child's playground, deserted except for a couple of mangy cats scavenging in a nearby trash can. Their heads jerked up at his approach, eyes glittering orange in the light of a street lamp.

Mitchell examined the area on the other side of the playground, hoping to find a shortcut back to the station. Immediately behind was a wall of corrugated iron that hid everything beyond it. Next to that was a fenced-off space empty except for a couple of vans in the far corner. Mitchell was about to return to the gateway of the playground when his eye caught the inscription on the side of one of the vans, just visible in the dim light. "One hundred years of history," it read. That was a familiar slogan. Mitchell's pulse began to pick up speed again. Peering through the wire netting of the fence, he was just able to make out the darker characters—"Otaman Company Limited." This had to be the mysterious distribution center. At last, he had found it!

The next problem was to find out what was going on inside. Pressing his face against the wire netting, Mitchell was able to get a full view of the building. There were lights on in the entrance hall, but no sign of movement. On the upper two levels, the windows were all dark. Straining his ears, he couldn't make out any sounds at all. From the looks of the place, no work on the Kawasaki project went on at nighttime. That was good. It would give him a chance to investigate the facilities at close range.

The fence was about ten feet high, with a single strand of barbed wire at the top. Mitchell hooked his fingers into the netting and pulled himself up. Dropping to the other side, he stumbled and fell noisily to the ground. He was half-expecting searchlights, sirens, men shouting through bullhorns, but there was nothing. The only movement was the flicker of neon in the deserted entrance hall, the only sound the drone of an electric generator somewhere around the back. Mitchell edged along the side of the building, sticking to the shadows and ducking under the empty windows.

At the next corner, he paused to get his bearings. He was now at the back of the building, invisible from both the entrance hall and the car park. Mitchell glanced up, and something surprising caught his eye. One of the windows on the second floor had been left ajar. Furthermore, it was within easy reach of the drainpipe that led up to the plastic guttering on the roof. The security at the Kawasaki project was certainly a good deal laxer than he had expected. What did that mean? Had all the secret work been completed already? Or perhaps the Otaman people were even subtler than he had thought—they were feigning carelessness to convince the rest of the neighborhood that the distribution center was of no importance. That would be a master stroke!

He tested the drainpipe and found that it was firm. Using hands, elbows, knees, and feet, he managed to scramble up to the second floor, where he reached inside, freed the catch, and pulled the window open. Next, he took a deep breath and swung his legs up onto the ledge, wriggling until his lower body was inside the room. Gingerly, he let go of the drainpipe, and for a moment he pivoted on the window ledge like a human seesaw, his head pitching down into the darkness below. Then he grabbed the ledge with one hand, gave a final kick with his legs, and slid backward into the room, hitting the floor with a thud.

Mitchell rolled over and sat leaning against a wooden crate while his eyes got used to the dim light. The second floor was a single giant room with blocks of storage shelves divided by narrow aisles. He got to his feet and padded toward the stairwell, inspecting the boxes and crates on the shelves as he went. There were several different sizes, each marked with big black characters giving the lot number and the weight in kilograms. The light was stronger at the other end of the room, near the stairwell. Mitchell used it to pull one of the crates off the shelf for inspection.

It wasn't heavy, nor was it difficult to open. Mitchell used a coin to pry out the tacks that held the lid in place, then dumped the contents onto the floor. There were half a dozen items, each wrapped in a thick polystyrene casing. What could they be, pondered Mitchell—next-generation optical memory devices, wafers of newly developed superconductor material, flat electrodes for generating cold fusion reactions? Mitchell's mind raced with the possibilities as his fingers scrabbled at the tough polystyrene. At last, he was on the verge of solving the mystery of the Kawasaki project.

After finally tearing off the casing, he stood staring at the contents, unable to believe his eyes. What he was now holding in his hands was a plate of curried prawns of the type that he had ordered and consumed in dozens of cheap restaurants and coffee bars. Except that there was no smell of curry, and when Mitchell turned the plate upside down, its contents did not immediately splatter to the ground. Being made of molded plastic, they stuck to their positions on the plate. Mitchell picked up another of the packages and tore away its wrapping. This one contained a highly realistic representation of a ham-and-cheese omelette, gleaming with grease and streaked with ketchup. The next one contained a plastic club sandwich topped with a sprig of plastic parsley and held together by a plastic cocktail stick. Mitchell didn't bother with the rest. He stuffed them all back into the crate, tacked down the lid, and shoved it back onto the shelf. It was a frustrating moment, but at least he had discovered something new about Otaman. Among the thousands of products that the company traded were the plastic models used in restaurant windows to display the contents of the menu. In order to attract customers, these models needed to look as good as or preferably better than the food itself. Mitchell had often wondered what kind of company was involved in that business. Now he knew.

Mitchell spent the next hour searching through the lower two floors, selecting crates at random, checking their contents, then putting them back on the shelves. The range of products that Otaman dealt in was impressive, their technological sophistication less so. There were jeans, T-shirts bearing slogans in surreal English, plastic sandals, curtains, futon covers, towels, wooden dolls, and dozens of different types of fluffy animals. Mitchell went through an unlocked door near the entrance and switched on the light. He found himself in a small, shabbily furnished room containing a row of filing cabinets. He rifled through them but there was nothing. He checked the basement, even the loading bays. Nowhere did he find anything that even hinted at the existence of a secret project.

Mitchell sat down heavily on one of the crates and stared blankly into the gloom. Was it possible that he had gotten it all wrong—that he had somehow misunderstood what he had heard in the Otaman toilet? His Japanese was far from perfect, but the conversation between the two men had seemed so straightforward. Mitchell clearly remembered the urgency in the elder man's voice as he had reprimanded the other. Surely that warning had more behind it than ridiculous T-shirts and plastic models of omelettes. There had to be something that he was missing.

He was just about to return to the second floor when he heard noises outside—the purr of an approaching engine, the slamming of a vehicle's door, then the clang of the gate being opened. He froze and listened. The engine started up again and came closer, stopping no more than twenty yards from where he stood. With a rising sense of panic, Mitchell heard the vehicle's doors opening again and the sound of voices. He glanced around. There were no obvious traces of his presence. He turned and raced up the staircase just as the side door swung open.

Peering down from his vantage point on the floor above, Mitchell watched a group of dark shapes cross the area in which he had just been standing seconds earlier. One of them switched on the main lights. Before pulling his head out of sight, Mitchell registered that there were three men in their early twenties, all wearing the white cotton jackets that were the uniform of junior personnel at Otaman. From the raucous tone of their voices, he judged that they had stopped somewhere for refreshments on their way to the distribution center.

"So where is this stuff supposed to go? Second floor?"

"Different! Ground floor at the back, with the rest of the women's clothing."

That was good. They wouldn't be coming up the staircase to disturb him. Mitchell breathed a silent sigh of relief.

"And this one here?"

"Blankets and towels? That goes on the third floor somewhere."

They were coming after all! Mitchell's relief turned to panic. Once the lights were on, almost every nook of the giant room would be visible. Nerves jangling, he stared around for somewhere to hide. It was immediately apparent that there was only one suitable place—the small area behind the staircase, which was cluttered with empty crates. If he bent down, they would just about hide him from view. The voices were almost at the foot of the staircase now. He had to move fast. Noiselessly, Mitchell crept around to the other side of the staircase and crouched down behind a pile of three crates in the farthermost corner.

The men's boots clattered on the metal stairs. They were moving slowly and deliberately, suggesting that their loads were fairly heavy. Mitchell peered over the top of the pile of crates and saw the first dark shape emerging at the top of the staircase. The man was carrying a stack of three crates, his head and shoulders bent back with the effort.

"Where is the light switch?" he called down to the others.

"Just behind the staircase" came the answer from below.

The boxes dropped to the ground with a thud and the footsteps came closer. Mitchell shrank farther into the corner, his knees and elbows sticking out awkwardly. His six-foot-two-inch, two-hundred-pound frame was no better suited for games of hide-and-seek than it was for blending into the crowds of salarymen in downtown Kawasaki.

"It is difficult to see. Where behind the staircase?"

The man had stopped just two or three yards from where Mitchell was squatting. His hands were patting the wall as he searched for the switch.

"Right in the corner. Wait, I will show you." The second man dropped his load and followed the first into the area behind the staircase.

"Hurry up, will you!" The third man was waiting at the top of the stairs. He sounded impatient. Mitchell tried to breathe softly through his mouth. His knees were stiff and he had pins and needles in his feet, but he didn't dare budge an inch. The second man was reaching into the corner just above Mitchell's head now. Neck muscles rigid with tension, Mitchell kept his eyes fixed on the ground. The outline of the toe section of a rubber boot was clearly visible at the side of the crate.

"Here it is—just where I said!"

161

There was a click, and suddenly the whole room was flooded with light. Mitchell shut his eyes and held his breath. For a second he was aware of nothing but the thumping of his own pulse.

"Good," grunted the first man with satisfaction. "Come on, let's hurry up and put everything into place. There are many more deliveries to be done tonight."

"The fact that we have so many deliveries shows that the economy is truly recovering, doesn't it?"

"The economy is always strong when the Gendai Giants are the strongest baseball team. This is a historical fact."

The first man grunted his agreement and the footsteps moved away. Mitchell shifted on his haunches, easing the blood flow to his rapidly numbing feet. That proved to be a costly mistake, for he lost his balance leaning into the pile of crates and pushed the middle one a critical few inches forward. There was a creaking sound, and the whole structure started to topple over. Mitchell watched in horror-struck fascination as the topmost crate slid back toward him. He held up a hand to shove it back into place, but it was too late. The crate fell sideways, hitting the floor with a loud smack.

"What's that noise?"

"The crates—there is someone behind them!"

"Who is there? Come out and show yourself!"

Mitchell squeezed himself behind the remaining two crates, but there was not enough cover. His knees were protruding from one side, and his left shoulder was jutting over the top. His mind worked quickly. There was clearly no point in staying where he was. He could make a dash for the staircase, but with the three Otaman men just twenty yards away, he would be unlikely to make it. He needed to play for time.

"This is a thief!"

"Come on, let's get him!"

What to do? What would distract them most? A strange thought flashed into Mitchell's mind. There was one foreigner at Pearson's office who had a powerful effect on ordinary Japanese people. When he approached them in the street, they would hurry away from him as if he had the plague. He intimidated and disoriented them without even trying. That man was Kent the Mormon. Suddenly, Mitchell knew what he was going to do. It was risky, but he had nothing to lose.

162 Mitchell got to his feet and stepped out into full view. He moved slowly, his eyes fixed on the three astonished faces in front of him.

"A foreign thief!"

"Let's seize him!"

They were fit-looking men, square-shouldered and square-faced. But their ruddy complexions suggested that they had consumed enough alcohol to make a difference. They seemed nervous too, glancing at one another as they moved warily toward him. The largest of them unclipped a hammer from his workbelt and waved it in Mitchell's face. The other two dropped into karate stances, spreading out as they circled around him.

Mitchell halted within ten yards of the big man and stared at each of them in turn. He then gave a short bow and clasped his hands together. "Do you believe in the Lord Jesus Christ?" he enunciated in slow, clear English.

The man with the hammer stopped in his tracks, his eyes wide with surprise. The other two dropped their hands to their sides. "He's a missionary," muttered the man with the hammer. "What is a missionary doing in our warehouse?"

"Have no fear," boomed Mitchell, advancing toward the man. "The Lord moveth in mysterious ways. Now tell me, children—how many times a week do you study the Bible?"

"B-bible," stammered the man in uncomfortable English. "No bible, no sankyu!"

"And what of you?" said Mitchell sternly to the other two. "Are you ready to be born again into our flock? Will you turn your heathen ears to the holy words of the Latter-Day Saints?"

They were staring at him as if he had two heads. That was good. The Kent effect was working better than he had hoped. "Repent your sins!" roared Mitchell, pressing home his advantage. "Get down on your knees and pray!"

All three of them backed away, their faces betraying varying degrees of dismay and confusion. This, Mitchell decided, was the right moment to make his move. He turned and walked briskly toward the staircase. It took them a few crucial seconds to react.

"Stop!" called one of them finally.

Mitchell had never been expecting them to let him walk out of the place unmolested. He broke into a sprint and clattered down the staircase, taking the steps four at a time. The Otaman men were obviously taken by surprise, for it was some moments before he heard them come thundering after him. Mitchell leapt the last half-dozen steps and raced across the hard concrete floor, his feet tingling with the impact. Judging from the noises behind, he had a good thirty yards' lead.

"Seize him!" bellowed one of them. "Seize the foreign thief missionary!"

The side door had been left half-open. As he charged through it Mitchell caught sight of a padlock hanging off the outside hasp. He swung around, slammed the door, and fumbled with the bolt, but his fingers were stiff and clumsy. One of his pursuers bashed against the inside of the door, forcing it open several inches. Mitchell countered with a massive thump of the shoulder. Pressing against the door with all his might, he finally managed to click the padlock shut.

There was no time to lose. It wouldn't take long for the three of them to get to the main entrance and come chasing after him again. Hardly pausing to catch his breath, Mitchell raced through the parking lot to the gate and out into the street.

The scenery here was different from the shabby lanes and disused lots at the back of the warehouse. The street was wider and better lit, with rows of parked cars on either side. Mitchell kept going, well aware that the Otaman people would soon be following. Twisting around as he ran, he noticed a taxi cruising up the street behind him. The red light showed that it was empty. Mitchell stopped and flapped his arm up and down, but the cab suddenly accelerated and zoomed past him, the driver staring blankly ahead. Mitchell spat out a stream of obscenities. He was used to taxi drivers ignoring him on rainy nights in Roppongi, but this was too much to bear.

There was still no sign of his pursuers. Mitchell put his hands on his knees and took a couple of deep breaths before continuing up the street. His legs were feeling like lead now, and he had a sharp pain in the side of his stomach. When another taxi appeared two minutes later, Mitchell decided to take no chances. He walked out into the middle of the road and stood there, feet wide apart, arms held straight out at each side. The taxi squealed to a halt and the driver rolled down the window.

"This is crazy behavior." He scowled at Mitchell. He was a young unshaven guy, the type who only works the night routes around the entertainment districts.

Mitchell glanced over the top of the taxi. The three Otaman workers had just run out into the street in front of the warehouse. They were a good three hundred yards away, but he could hear the shouts as they spotted the taxi. Hurriedly, Mitchell thrust his hand in through the driver's open window and flipped the catch that locked the back door.

"That's not allowed!" protested the taxi driver. "That's the wrong door! The regulations say you've got to use the left door!"

Out of the corner of his eye, Mitchell could see the Otaman workers in their white jackets racing up the street behind him. He yanked open the back door on the driver's side. The taxi driver revved the engine and lifted off the clutch. The taxi leapt forward just as Mitchell swung himself inside. The driver glanced in his mirror, then slammed the brakes on hard, causing Mitchell to jerk forward, thumping his forehead against the headrest. They had gone no more than twenty yards.

"You've broken the regulations," yelled the taxi driver, his sweaty face pale with anger. "Get out of my cab or I'll call the police!"

"Listen to me," panted Mitchell desperately. "I'll give you twenty thousand yen to take me to central Tokyo."

"Twenty thousand yen? Show me!"

Mitchell pulled the notes from his wallet and threw them onto the front seat. The taxi driver stared at him disbelievingly. The rearview mirror showed that the Otaman workers were less than a hundred yards behind now. Mitchell could make out the square shape of their crew-cut heads as they came jogging up the middle of the road.

"What are you waiting for?" he exploded at the driver. "I have urgent business!"

"Understood!" He revved the engine again and the taxi roared up the street. Mitchell glanced behind. The Otaman workers had stopped running now. They were standing at the side of the road with their hands on their hips.

"I'm sincerely grateful for your patronage," said the taxi driver, fitting the notes into a grubby wallet of red plastic.

Mitchell gave a grunt of acknowledgment and eased back in his seat. Behind him, the white jackets were diminishing to tiny dots. The money had obviously done the trick. Twenty thousand yen—back home, that would be enough to rent a car for a couple of days! For once, though, Mitchell wasn't in the mood to complain about Japanese prices.

It took just over an hour for the taxi to weave through the traffic into central Tokyo. Mitchell gazed out the window at the crowds that covered the pavements like a restless sea; the crystal towers, cold and perfect against the night sky; the bullet train twisting its way between the buildings like a great electric worm. Sometimes Japan made him feel as if he were trapped in an alternative universe, where everything looked hauntingly familiar, yet nothing made sense as it should.

The taxi halted at a traffic light. Mitchell again glanced nervously in the mirror, half-expecting to see the three Otaman men jogging up the pavement behind him, their faces set in masks of steely determination. But they were thirty miles behind in Kawasaki, probably relaxing in a pink salon by now. It had been a narrow escape, and what exactly had Mitchell achieved? The whole Otaman business was as mysterious as ever. Despite the risks he had taken, he was hardly any better informed about the company than when Yazawa had first given him the job.

As the taxi neared the turn that led to his apartment block, Mitchell realized that he wasn't in the mood to go straight home. He had too much adrenaline in his blood, too much frustration in his mind. What he needed now was sympathetic company. On the spur of the moment, an idea occurred to him. He took a business card out of his wallet and handed it to the taxi driver.

"Take me to this address," he said.

The taxi driver held the business card up to the light and squinted at it. "What—you mean this place in Ginza?"

Mitchell caught the man's eye in the mirror, staring at him incredulously. That didn't improve his mood at all. "Only one address is written there, isn't it!" he snapped, and took the card back.

The taxi driver shrugged his shoulders and swung the car into the Ginza lane of the expressway.

Mitchell thought back to the drunken evening he had spent in the nightclub with Yazawa. The owner of that business card was unforgettable. Her face and voice had been stuck in the back of his mind ever since, challenging him to act. Eiko had been just as elegant as the other hostesses, but there was a willful intelligence about her that set her apart. Maybe it was that oddly disturbing accent. Maybe it was the playful, half-mocking way she had listened to Mitchell's words. Whatever the reason, she was fascinating. Ginza hostesses were supposed to be gold diggers and cold-hearted mercenaries, but this one was different. She was genuinely interested in him. She had even given him her private phone number. Since then he had often thought about calling her up and asking for a date, but that would be too dull, too predictable. Much better to surprise her with some spontaneous, masterful gesture to demonstrate that he wasn't just another foreigner lost in Tokyo.

Mitchell paid the taxi driver, who shook his head and sucked air through his teeth in bemusement. It was true that Mitchell wasn't exactly dressed in the orthodox style for an expensive Ginza nightclub. The jeans that he had put on for his exploration of Kawasaki were torn at the knee and he had lost a couple of buttons from his shirt. Still, he wasn't planning to go inside. It was already eleven-thirty. At some point in the next half-hour or so, Eiko would appear on the street to bow farewell to important guests. That was when Mitchell would step out of the shadows and attract her attention.

The street was quiet. A few salarymen was standing at the corner, sharing a joke. A startlingly attractive woman, probably a hostess who had finished work early, was walking quickly toward them, high heels rapping the sidewalk, face as blank as a switched-off TV. As a result of the cutbacks in corporate expense accounts, the Ginza was going through hard times these days. The lower tier of customer had defected en masse to the coarser pleasures of Shinjuku and Kawasaki.

It didn't take Mitchell long to find the place. There it was on the other side of the street, a smudge of mauve neon reading *Jun*—which meant "pure," he reminded himself. Waiting outside was a black Mercedes with lace curtains covering the back windows. The chauffeur sat bolt upright, the peak of his cap low over his eyes, his white gloves motionless on the steering wheel. The purr of the engine was barely audible. So an important guest was just about to leave. That was good. It meant Eiko might appear at any time. Mitchell stepped into the entrance of the building across the street and sat down on the staircase inside.

He waited for ten minutes, listening to the sound of karaoke floating down from one of the floors above. It was a female voice, strong and clear enough for him to catch the words of the sentimental song.

"Alone again, the tears are flowing
It's a ballad of strife
A woman's life, a woman's life . . ."

She sang well, wobbling the high notes with easy control. Mitchell sat and thought about women's lives, focusing on one in particular. Why on earth had Eiko chosen to work in a Ginza club? As an intelligent and well-educated woman, she was hardly fulfilling her potential by stroking the egos and thighs of middle-aged executives night after night. Maybe there was a secret there somewhere, a broken love affair that had caused her to turn her back on society. Or maybe it was just impatience with the discrimination that Japanese women faced in the ordinary business world. Mitchell felt a wave of sympathetic indignation. There were so few opportunities for a girl like Eiko. Back home, a woman with her talents would be a lawyer or an investment banker.

The sound of voices switched Mitchell's attention back to the street outside. The chauffeur had got out of the Mercedes and was holding the back door open, as silent and expressionless as before. Two men were standing with their faces turned away from Mitchell. The taller one was wearing a cashmere coat draped over his shoulders, the sleeves hanging empty at his sides. Slightly closer to the car stood a woman in a crimson and rust kimono, her hair piled high on her head. She bowed low, revealing a jeweled hair clip that sparkled brilliantly in the streetlight.

"Many thanks for your repeated patronage," she trilled. "Please honor us with your presence again."

That was the first shock. The voice was definitely Eiko's. But what had she done to her appearance? It wasn't just her hairstyle and clothing that were different. She seemed to have changed the shape of her face, even the contours of her body. Her cheeks were rounder and flatter, her nose and eyes smaller. She stooped slightly as she walked, and the pert breasts that had occupied Mitchell's thoughts several times in the past week seemed to have disappeared entirely. She looked like a different person.

The two men continued talking, barely paying any attention to Eiko. Then the one in the cashmere coat draped an arm over her shoulder and whispered something in her ear. She put her hand to her mouth and shrilled with laughter, a completely different type of laugh from the teasing giggle that Mitchell remembered. When she bowed again, the man in the coat put out a hand and slapped her lightly on the half-apple of her buttocks, allowing his hand to linger there for what seemed to Mitchell like an eternity. What was Eiko going to do about that? Would she raise her voice in anger, perhaps even try to slap the man's face? To Mitchell's dismay, she did neither. She just gave a little skip backward and another high-pitched giggle. He tensed with indignation. He felt like charging across the street and hauling the man to the ground by the neck of his expensive coat.

The man in the cashmere coat got into the car. Mitchell didn't get a clear view of his features, but something about him was vaguely familiar. The other man, whose back was still turned to Mitchell, leaned close to Eiko and quickly muttered something in her ear. She nodded in response like a dutiful pupil. Then he turned to get into the car, and for a moment his face was caught fully in the streetlight. Mitchell recognized him at once and instinctively ducked out of sight. It was Yazawa's mysterious friend, the one Eiko had pretended to know so little about that evening at Jun. He was wearing a dark suit with a white handkerchief peeking from the breast pocket and a self-satisfied smile that set Mitchell's teeth on edge. How had Eiko described him—as some kind of politician? Well, he would never get Mitchell's vote. It was too bad that Eiko's job required her to consort with men like that.

Yazawa's friend got into the car and the chauffeur shut the door softly behind him. A few seconds later, the Mercedes was purring down the street toward the junction with the main Ginza thoroughfare. Eiko stood on the pavement, still waving as the car turned at the lights. Probably, the two men were sitting back comfortably behind those lace curtains sharing a joke about her. To them, Eiko was just a toy to provide a couple of hours' amusement. It was wrong for her to allow herself to be treated like that. Mitchell felt the insult hotly, personally.

The Mercedes had pulled out of sight now. Eiko went back into the building and pressed the elevator button. The door opened and she stepped inside. Mitchell emerged from his shadowy hiding place and sprinted across the road after her.

"Eiko," he called out. "Remember me? It's Richard Mitchell—from the other night."

She stopped the elevator door with her hand and stood there staring at him as if he were a ghost. For a moment, there was silence.

"What are you doing here?" she said, rather harshly.

"I just wanted to see how you're getting on, have a chat, maybe . . ." Mitchell's words trailed into silence. Her stare was unsettling.

"So you've been hanging around out here, spying on me!"

This time her tone was very harsh, accusing. That cut-glass accent didn't help. In the dark of the nightclub, it had been strangely sexy, reminding Mitchell of the secretary with the spectacles in the James Bond movies. Now she sounded like the queen after she'd been bitten by one of her corgis.

"Absolutely not. I just happened to be passing close by here on my way home. I saw you on the street, so I thought I'd come over and say hello."

Eiko frowned, obviously wondering whether to believe him.

"I wanted to see you again after what happened the other night. I think you're a very special girl, you know . . ."

That usually worked, and indeed Eiko nodded graciously. She still looked beautiful, thought Mitchell, but in a different way—harder, much more remote.

"What on earth are you talking about, you silly man?" She was almost smiling now. That was good.

"This hostess work must be awfully tedious. Why don't you meet me after you finish here tonight? We can have a quiet drink in Roppongi."

"Out of the question, I'm afraid. I've arranged to meet a girlfriend after work."

Mitchell nodded glumly. This was the brush-off. He had failed completely. He should have stuck to the conventional approach. "How about sometime next week?" he said hopelessly.

She stopped and stared at him again. "You're very persistent, aren't you!"

She was shifting. He could feel it instinctively. It was time to press home his advantage. "I mean it. This is very important to me. That's why

I rushed all the way here." In these circumstances, what did pride matter anyway? If he failed, they would never set eyes on each other again.

"All right, then," she said brightly. "If you insist. I'll call you at your office next week."

Miss Moneypenny—wasn't that the name of M's secretary? Eiko was sounding just like Miss Moneypenny again. She jabbed the elevator button. Mitchell heaved a sigh of relief. It had worked.

"I work at Pearson Darney," he called out jubilantly as the doors closed. "It's an American securities company, remember. Wait, let me give you the phone number—"

"I know the number, thank you," said Eiko through the last few inches of space, and then she was gone. The lights on the panel above the elevator door ascended slowly to "5."

Mitchell walked back into the street and glanced up at the orange glow from the curtained window. Maybe it really had been the brush-off and she would never call. No, he didn't believe that. There was something in her face, something in her voice that told him she was serious. Just when it had seemed that his plan had backfired, she had suggested exactly what he was hoping for. Somehow, he must have gotten through to her after all.

The Ginza glittered like a tray of gems. Above, the moon was a silver medallion on a dark velvet cushion. Mitchell walked rapidly toward the station, oblivious to everything but the promise of next week's date. He felt certain that it was going to be memorable.

About five miles from the Ginza stands a slim, trim building of thirty-eight stories containing a hotel that, while not of international class, is as comfortable and smooth-running and anonymous as a top-of-the-line Toyota. The location is excellent, overlooking the rhomboid bulk of the National Diet building on one side and on the other the Akasaka entertainment district, playground of real estate developers and politicians. In the Tokyo night, its clean concrete surfaces reflect the ambient light of the city, giving it the appearance of a newly chiseled gravestone.

The man who sat at the window on the thirty-eighth floor, his fingers poised over the keyboard of a laptop computer, had been occupying his room for almost a month. There were several features of the hotel that attracted his favor, such as the good communications facilities, including a fax and modem link in every room, the efficiency of the room service, and the discretion of the management. Most of all, however, he valued the view in the early morning, when he could sweep the curtains aside and see Mount Fuji rising above the distant horizon, its jagged crown gleaming white. That was a rare sight at this time of year, only obtainable at an hour before the sky had thickened into its usual blur of photochemical smog. It gave him an obscure but palpable sense of advantage over the people he had to deal with later in the day.

In the nights there was a different kind of view, hardly as classical but also inspiring in its own way. He liked to sit in the easy chair by the window contemplating the forests of neon, the rivers of headlights, the escarpments and valleys of concrete and glass. Then, when the moment was right, he would take up his laptop computer and add another section to the sequence of linked haiku verses that he had begun earlier in the year.

He glanced down at the words that were softly pulsing in the liquid crystal display. They did not satisfy him by any means. Still, the spring winds, the arrival of the cherry blossom—these were challenging subjects. After all that had been said about them over the centuries, it was so difficult to make something that was fresh and yet at the same time natural and sincere.

He stood up and went to the drawer of his desk, catching a glimpse of his reflection in the mirror as he passed: dark glasses, a shock of white hair, skin like paper, mouth like a wound. He had ceased to be concerned about his appearance long ago, but he still felt twinges when he glimpsed the discomfort in other's faces. It reminded him of the hard days at school: the taunts, the dead rabbits in his locker . . . his mother's tearful efforts to explain. There was nothing to worry about, she had said, it was just a difference. But her face had told another story, a story of shame and fear.

As he stooped to the desk drawer, he forced himself to look straight in the mirror and smiled, revealing tiny jagged teeth and gums the color of fresh blood. The editors and readers of his poems had never seen that smile, indeed, never looked into that face. And, naturally, they didn't know his real name or how he earned his living. If they did, would they still praise his work as "rich and harmonious" and "delicately balanced"?

He took a bundle of poetry magazines from the desk drawer and went back to his chair by the window. Stockinged feet stretched out on the window ledge, he leafed through a well-known publication containing work by recognized masters and a range of accomplished amateurs, from brilliant young students to senior businessmen and bureaucrats. There was even a section contributed by an ex-prime minister who had been toppled in a major financial scandal. Insufferable, thought the reader as he quickly turned the page. The man's self-satisfaction and ostentation dripped from every line! Finally, he turned to a short sequence of linked haiku attributed to a poet who went under the pseudonym "Snowbird." He read carefully, allowing each image to spread slowly across his consciousness like oil across the surface of a pond.

After ten minutes of contemplation, he placed the magazine beside him on the floor. Was there something a little strained about the flow of the words? An obtrusion of intellect that spoiled the naturalness of the original perception? He had to admit that there was that tendency. His first sensei had once said he would never achieve his true potential until he had mastered the most important quality of all—simplicity. But what did that mean? For a long time, he had assumed that simplicity meant reducing complexity to its essence—in other words, stripping a landscape of emotion down to a single, core image. Now he wasn't so sure. Perhaps the simplicity he was searching for didn't come from stripping things down at all. Perhaps simplicity actually contained everything else, just as the first raindrop that exploded on the pavement contained the following storm. "Learn how to look with the eye of a child"—that was what his sensei used to tell him. "Look with the eye of a child, and understand with the mind of a child." His gashlike mouth extended into an ironic smile. His sensei had been dead for twenty years now. He would never have guessed what his star pupil had become.

The chime of the doorbell cut through Snowbird's reveries.

"What is it?" he called out, without shifting his gaze from the window. Akasaka was stretched out below him like a labyrinth of light.

"This is Takenaka," said a man's voice, gruff yet respectful. "Their car has just arrived, so they should be here in three or four minutes."

"Good," said Snowbird. "Tell Sato to meet them at the elevator, then have Kato arrange the food and drink as I specified."

"Understood! I will undertake these matters at once."

Snowbird put the bundle of poetry magazines back in his desk drawer and took out a smooth black object about the same size and shape as a Go pebble. He tossed it into the air and caught it, then approached the table next to the window, on which lay a slim Samsonite briefcase. It took him only a moment to pry open a small panel in the case's spine and click the object into the gap underneath. After sliding the panel back into place, he inspected the case from close up, then from a couple of steps back. He gave a small grunt of satisfaction. As far as the eye could tell, it was the same case he had been handed a week before. Even the manufacturer would have had difficulty in spotting the difference.

"Is there anything else we should do?"

"Make sure that there is no one in the corridor. I don't want anyone to see them coming out of the elevator on this floor."

"Understood!"

"And one more thing, Takenaka—make sure you search them both when they enter this room."

"Search them for weapons!" The man outside the door seemed shocked by the idea.

"Certainly," replied Snowbird sharply. "It is important to cover all possibilities, however remote. When you have as many people wanting you dead as I do, perhaps you will understand that!"

"Of course! I apologize for such thoughtlessness." Takenaka still sounded dubious. That was natural. It wasn't every day that he was asked to make a body search of an ex-cabinet minister.

173

A few minutes later the door opened and Takenaka ushered in two men. "Humble apologies for this lack of courtesy," he muttered, and swiftly patted down the chest and legs of the first of the visitors, a tall man who wore his cashmere coat over his shoulders like a cape.

"Now wait a minute," protested the other, a sallow-faced individual with a silk handkerchief peeking from the breast pocket of his dark jacket. "Is this really necessary? We are not common pimps that you are used to dealing with!"

The tall man held up his hand. "It is not a problem," he said calmly. "I like to work with men who recognize the importance of checking details. Prudence is a virtue in all spheres of human activity."

"Thank you for your understanding," said Snowbird with a small bow.

"So please be thorough with the search," continued the tall man. "You have checked the obvious places, but what about my groin? You should check there too. After all, I might have a weapon hidden somewhere between my legs!"

He signaled the joke with a grunt. His companion followed up with a nervous snicker, expressed mostly with the nose and shoulders.

"You might," agreed Snowbird, also smiling. "But there wouldn't be much point."

"Why not?"

"Because you would be dead before you could get your hand out of your underpants. Takenaka here would see to that."

Takenaka was bending down to check the ankles of the man with the mustache. He swiveled around on his haunches and nodded.

"I have supervised Takenaka's training myself," Snowbird continued. "His social graces may be lacking in some degree, but you need have no worries about his professional skills. They are complete in all aspects."

Takenaka stood up very fast, as if his knees were spring-loaded. The man with a mustache took an involuntary step backward, clumping an elbow against the wall. Snowbird made another bow, this time a deeper one of formal welcome, and motioned his two visitors to the circular table in the middle of the room.

Forty minutes later, the impassive chauffeur was guiding the Mercedes with the lace-curtained windows through the backstreets of the Akasaka entertainment district. It was well past midnight, and the neon empire was quiet. On one corner, a couple of *chimpira* were squatting on their haunches, discussing the evening's business over bowls of steaming noodles. On the next, a middle-aged salaryman with a heavily made-up blond woman on his arm was waiting for a taxi. They were both so drunk that it was hard to tell which one was holding up the other. As the black limousine glided past them, a nearby fortune-teller snuffed his candle and folded his chair. The district's hostesses, masseuses, and salon girls, the keenest users of his services, had already finished work and gone. All that was left were the signs—orange, purple, and green on the gleaming hood of the Mercedes.

"That guy is a strange one," muttered the man with the mustache to his companion.

"He is a professional in his business," replied the man in the cashmere coat, gazing through the car's lacy curtains at an empty pachinko parlor. It was still lit with a glaring white light. Inside, an old man wearing wooden sandals and long underpants was wiping down the game machines.

"They say he has killed many men. They say he killed his own brother when he was a high school student."

The Mercedes rounded a corner and nosed into a narrow lane barely wide enough to accommodate its bulk. The headlights raked across the startled face of a lone salaryman standing with his back arched as he urinated against a wall.

"It is difficult to look into his eyes when he talks," continued the first man. "He is an unnatural creature, like a two-headed frog."

Both men laughed at the idea.

"I understand your opinion," said the man in the cashmere coat. "But we are working in the world of politics, not the world of art. Aesthetic considerations cannot be relevant to our plans."

The Mercedes eased to a halt outside a sprawling wooden building with a row of paper lanterns hanging from the eave of the porch. The young chauffeur stepped out of the car and held the back door open, the peak of his cap angled down to his shoes. At the sound of voices, a middle-aged woman in a flowery kimono appeared at the door and gave a low bow.

"Welcome," she trilled.

"Has everyone arrived?" asked the man in the cashmere coat.

The man with the mustache glanced at his watch. "They should certainly be here by now," he said.

"Good," grunted the other, and reached back into the car for the Samsonite briefcase. He thrust it at the man with the mustache. "You should be more careful," he snorted. "It wouldn't do to leave this behind."

175

The man with the mustache gave an embarrassed simper and cradled the briefcase to his chest.

The two men marched into the lobby of the building, the woman in the kimono ushering them in with another perfect bow. The chauffeur returned to the driver's seat of the Mercedes and sat there like a statue, his white gloves resting on the wheel. The paper lanterns wobbled and twisted in the wind.

On the thirty-eighth floor of the anonymous modern hotel, Snowbird sat in his armchair by the window. In his lap lay an earphone, which he had just removed from his ear. He stared out over the lights of Akasaka, his rubbery lips twisted into a bitter smile. These people who needed his help—they had slandered and mocked him without a moment's hesitation. But in so doing, they had revealed a profound unease that comes from fear. One day, he would use that against them.

Snowbird took a thoughtful sip from his glass of milk. "Two-headed frog"—that was a strange insult. It made him think of Bashō's most famous haiku:

The ancient pond
The frog jumps in
The sound of the water

What kind of sound would a two-headed frog make? Just an ordinary *plop* probably, but that didn't matter. A two-headed frog would spoil the zen of the moment completely. In Bashō's poem, the frog was transformed into an absence, a ripple spreading outward across the surface of the pond. But a two-headed frog could not be transformed like that. It would dive to the bottom, its four eyes bulging as it darted among the weeds. Even a great genius like Bashō would have had difficulty in dealing with a two-headed frog. The thing would just hop out of any poem it was put into.

And so Snowbird would hop out of any plans that the politicians were devising. If they thought that they could use him like a tool and then discard him, they were making a big mistake. No one had ever done that successfully. Indeed, the few who had tried had soon regretted their actions.

Snowbird picked up the earphone again and fitted it to his ear. There was much important information still to be gathered tonight.

Some three miles away, inside an unmarked wooden building at the end of a narrow cul-de-sac that was dark and shadowy even in daylight, the tall man handed his cashmere coat to the woman in the kimono. Behind them, a younger woman closed the heavy shutters. The tall man strode down a long, creaking corridor. The man with the mustache hurried after him, the briefcase still clutched to his chest.

Back in the hotel room, Snowbird took another sip from his glass of milk and rested his chin in the palm of his hand. With the help of the earphone, it wasn't difficult to imagine the scene that was unfolding. *There—the footsteps stop. That is the sound of the tall man clearing his throat.* Then came the squeak of a sliding door being opened. Snowbird tilted his head back and closed his eyes. It was almost as if he were gliding down the corridor behind them.

TEN

Every once in a while, the earth goes mad. Every once in a while the catfish thrashes its tail.

According to Japanese legend, the world rests on the back of a giant catfish, whose occasional squirmings cause the surface of the earth to tremble and shake. In a small shrine north of Tokyo, there is a wedge of rock driven into the ground in order, it is said, to hold the creature in place. Sometimes, however, it manages to work its way loose.

There is a rumbling, a grinding, a shuddering that quickly gathers to a head. The material world is coming alive.

It doesn't take long. The quake that destroyed the center of Kobe, collapsing bridges and burying thousands in the debris of their homes, lasted just ninety seconds. No time to follow the disaster drills, no time to collect your valuables, no time to think at all.

The walls are disintegrating. The ceiling comes crashing to the floor.

In the Tokyo region, tremors occur almost every

day, most too weak to be sensed by humans. Large-scale quakes, strong enough to flatten whole neighborhoods, have occurred at an average interval of seventy-five years. The last such quake occurred in September 1923. Two thirds of all dwellings were destroyed, and the loss of life was similar to that caused by the bombing of Hiroshima.

The giant city is an idiot. Instructions cannot flow through its scrambled nerves.

Tokyo is different now, bigger and denser. Under the concrete the systems have proliferated, carrying people, water, energy, money, data. Tall buildings have gone up on land reclaimed from the sea. Everywhere the air hums with the noise of machines.

The city breaks like an egg.

A few days later, there was another medium-scale quake, the third inside a month. Ono sensed it hours in advance, the accumulation of energy straining to be released. And then, just before it arrived, he felt the familiar tingling in his fingers and the soles of his feet. A wave of electromagnetic activity was surging toward him, racing through the earth's crust like a wave. But he didn't pay it much attention. He could feel the energy dissipating well before it shook the platform beneath his feet.

It passed, and he looked out over the sea of people. There were uncountable heads staring back at him, uncountable arms waving in the air, uncountable voices chanting the blissful words that he had created for them. It was satisfying to look down on them, like Napoleon or the Great Khan on the hordes of fighting men willing to risk everything for their leader. He raised his hands high above his head. Immediately, there was a roar of response from the huge crowd that echoed in his ears like the roar of the sea.

"Let us give thanks to the sensei."

One of the senior disciples on the platform next to him was bellowing into a microphone, his voice hoarse with emotion, his eyes bulging. "Banzai!" he yelled. "Banzai for the sensei."

The response filled the huge stadium, rebounding off the curved panels of the roof.

Ono bowed deeply, then the dry ice started to pour around his feet, the music welled from the loudspeakers, and the laser beams crisscrossed in geometric patterns above his head. For a split second the stadium lights went off and the panel beneath Ono's feet engaged. When the lights came on again, slightly dimmer than before, Ono was lying flat in the compartment under the platform, motionless, while two senior disciples strapped on the harness. Above, he could hear the hoarse disciple bellowing out words of celebration, the crowd roaring out its responses. It sounded as if the look-alike who had taken his place was making the right gestures at exactly the right moments. His sense of timing was getting better.

The two disciples gave the harness a last tug to confirm that it was tight, then they moved him onto the trolley and rushed him through the curtain at the back of the little compartment. They ran the thirty yards to the elevator and handed him over to the disciple waiting there, who pulled him off the trolley by the wrist. As the elevator shot upward, Ono glanced at his watch. It was just twenty seconds since he had been standing on the platform, arms stretched above his head.

The elevator came to a sudden stop and the doors slid open. They were up among the struts that held up the huge curving roof, more than one hundred feet from ground level. As the disciple behind him fiddled with the harness, Ono gazed down on the mass of human beings. What he saw was a carpet of small black shapes. They were insects—no, not even insects. They were bubbles, froth on a polluted lake.

Almost immediately below him was the platform. On it he could make out the tiny figure of the look-alike, standing out from the rest in the long white robe. Ono knew exactly when the figure was going to raise its hands in a gesture of triumph, when it was going to bow, when it was going to walk across to the disciple at the microphone and clasp him around the shoulders. Ono himself had followed exactly the same routine dozens of times before. As he watched, he could sense what was happening almost as vividly as if he were experiencing it himself. The heat and noise of the crowd; the feel of the metal platform under his bare feet; the flapping of his robe as he walked across to the disciple; the tang of sweat as they embraced. It was a strange thing, being there and not being there, acting and watching himself act.

The disciple behind him in the elevator raised an intercom to his ear. "Ten seconds, sensei," he muttered.

Ono nodded and wriggled his shoulder. No problem—the harness was tight.

"Eight, seven, six . . ."

The look-alike was back in his place on the platform. He would be tensing his calf muscles now, preparing to drop down into the hidden compartment.

"Five, four, three . . ."

Here the lights suddenly dimmed again. Down below there was a puff of smoke and a bolt of laser lightning that flashed above the platform.

"Two, one—GO!"

There was a shove in Ono's back, and suddenly he was hanging in space, his feet kicking free, while the laser beams swept around him in arcs. The disciple with the hoarse voice was bellowing even louder than before.

"The sensei leaves us, but in our spirits he remains. He returns to answer our entreaties; to guide us on our journey; to dissolve our troubles in his wisdom . . ."

One of the lights was wrongly positioned. It was glaring straight into Ono's eyes, almost blinding him. He would remember that. The man responsible would be severely punished.

"The sensei never deserts those who love him. He is ever-present, ever-watchful. *Behold the sensei!*"

The lasers were snapping into position, forming the golden stairway that he would descend over the heads of the crowd. Ono raised his hands high into the air, and the roar of the crowd welled up to meet him. Under the guidance of the disciples in the control box, the mechanism worked smoothly, sliding him down a few feet at a time. He pushed out his knees in an exaggerated walking gesture, moving from step to step of the stairway of laser beams.

A circus trick, perhaps, but the effect was undeniable. The first time had been six years ago, when he had walked across a lake at a dawn celebration of the spring equinox. It had been meant as a metaphor, but afterward he had learned that many of his followers had believed that the illusion was real. He made no comment then or at any time afterward. What was illusory for some could convey a deeper reality for others, and what most people considered real was usually no more than a collection of familiar illusions. Find the reality inside illusions! That was the foundation of his teaching.

He was halfway between the roof and the ground, the invisible wires of the harness holding him stiffly in place. If anyone ever wanted to get rid of him, this would be an ideal opportunity. A flaw in the mechanism, an instant of human error, and he would go plummeting to the ground. He would be killed instantly, and so would two or three of the crowd below. How would his followers respond? They would rip his blood-soaked robe to pieces, perhaps tear his body apart too. Orpheus was ripped apart by the followers of Bacchus, but then his head continued to sing as it floated downstream. He would continue to sing too. His teachings would echo and re-echo throughout the world. They would gain more popularity than ever before.

That was an arresting idea. Perhaps it could be arranged. Perhaps he could convince one of the look-alikes to make the walk down the golden staircase, then arrange a sudden accident. After a while, rumors would be spread that he had miraculously recovered, that he was preparing himself at a secret hideaway. . . . Then he would reappear in public— at the ceremony to commemorate his own death! Imagine the response, the tumult! After that, no one would be able to ignore him again.

These were the thoughts that filled Ono's mind as step by step he drew closer to the ground.

Mitchell was sitting in the research department when the vibrations started. First he felt them in his buttocks, then in his elbows, which were resting on the desk. When the jolt came, he shot to his feet, mouth hanging open. He looked around. No one else was responding, not even the office girl next to him talking on the telephone.

"What's the matter, Mitch?" said Ted Shimano with a grin. "Did the earth move for you again?"

"Yeah," muttered Mitchell, unable to think of a good answer. "These things are getting a bit too frequent for my tastes."

"You're looking pale. Isn't Mitch looking pale, girls?"

Giggles of assent. Mitchell ignored them and sat down heavily in his chair. He was in no mood for joking. Earthquakes affected him physically. They made him break out in a sweat, tensed up his neck muscles. It wasn't just a question of being scared. It was the shock of something fundamental about the world suddenly going wrong. The good old earth on which he had been confidently setting his feet for the past quarter of a century—he could no longer rely on it. The buildings around him, which seemed so strong and stable—they could shake and sway as if they were made of rubber. Solidity and stability were, after all, merely provisional concepts.

Yazawa appeared around five o'clock, when the traders had gone home and most of the salesmen were out drinking green tea at their clients' offices. He strolled into the half-empty dealing room, apparently lost in thought, the jacket of his suit slung over one shoulder. He was wearing a lizard-skin belt with a large silver buckle, and a pair of dark glasses were tucked into the breast pocket of his monogrammed shirt. In most places, Yazawa's dress style would have been unexceptional. In a Japanese securities office, it was well beyond the limit of salaryman chic.

None of the few remaining staff looked up or asked him how his day had gone. Yazawa's unexplained absences from the office had become rather frequent these days. Mitchell stood up and observed him crossing the dealing room to his small office on the other side. When Yazawa reached the door, he suddenly wheeled around, his eyes fixed on Mitchell, almost as if he had sensed that he was being watched. For a strange moment, the two of them stared at each other across thirty yards of office space. Then Yazawa raised a hand and gave an airy wave and disappeared into his room. Mitchell heaved a sigh of relief. That had to be a sign of approval, or at least tolerance.

Mitchell sat down again and tried to concentrate on his spreadsheet. He was just putting his fingers to the keyboard when his phone sounded with the irritating double beep that signified an internal call. Somehow, he knew who was at the other end before picking up the receiver.

"Good afternoon, Mitchell-kun" came Yazawa's unmistakable bark. "Are you feeling in strong spirits today?"

"Excellent, thank you," Mitchell replied cautiously. Yazawa had never inquired after his health before.

"I must have words with you," continued Yazawa. "Something important has come up."

The always slightly metallic tone of his voice was enhanced by the speakerphone he was using. He sounded buoyant, elated even. That, felt Mitchell, was not necessarily a good sign. "I'll come over to your office right away," ventured Mitchell, saving the file on his screen.

"Not my office in this case," boomed Yazawa. "I am in a hurry to do very many things. Come with me to the barber's shop in the basement and let us discuss there in friendly circumstances, man to man."

"But, Yazawa-san, I'm not sure I need a haircut."

Even as Mitchell spoke, he suspected that he was taking a wrong turn. His instinct was confirmed by the immediate response at the other end.

"You refuse this?" Yazawa bawled incredulously, causing the speakerphone to squeak with feedback. "An excellent Japanese haircut supplied by an excellent Japanese barber! Do not refuse! This is certainly necessary for you!"

"No, wait a minute, Yazawa-san. What I mean is—"

What Mitchell meant was that he had just had an excellent Japanese haircut five days before. There was a unisex place in Harajuku that he went to twice a month. He always asked for Mari, a tall girl with braided hair, a lemon-and-honey sort of body scent, and long, strong fingers that kneaded his soapy scalp with a soothing rhythm. She flattered and flirted and knew what he meant when he asked for that Mickey Rourke–style upsweep. Mitchell had an idea that Yazawa's barber would take an entirely different approach.

Another bellow cut him off in mid-sentence. "Very necessary for you, I think! Be in the barber's shop in ten minutes for man-to-man talking and excellent haircut!"

A low-pitched electronic hum signified that the speakerphone had been switched off.

Fifteen minutes later, Mitchell was sitting in the barber's chair in the basement of the building, a sheet covering the upper half of his body, while a silent, gray-haired Japanese man pressed a newly stropped razor against his cheek. In the mirror that covered the facing wall was reflected a face that he scarcely recognized as Yazawa's, since the top third was wrapped in a hot towel and the bottom third was covered with shaving foam. The man looked like a Japanese Santa Claus, leaning back for a nap on his sleigh. But though Yazawa's eyes were closed, he wasn't asleep. He was making light conversation in his own inimitable way.

"You gave this excellent barber many commands," he commented disapprovingly. "There was no need for that. I have already informed him of your special needs."

"You informed him!" said Mitchell, trying hard to fight down his irritation. "And how do you know what kind of styling I want?"

Yazawa opened his eyes suddenly. "Styling? No, you misunderstand the meaning. There is no styling here. Every customer to this shop gets the same haircut. It is the haircut unique to this shop."

"Everyone the same? But I've just given the man detailed instructions. He nodded. He understood me!"

"He is a polite gentleman, Mitchell-kun. He did not want to reply to that insult that you offered him."

Mitchell gazed with alarm into the mirror as the gray-haired barber began to scrape away at the area around his Adam's apple. If it were true that this barber shop produced only one standard haircut, then presumably Yazawa's was a good example of it. Mitchell was not sure he wanted a haircut like Yazawa's—high at the sides, with a severe parting and plenty of oil to keep everything in place. It looked like something out of the silent movies.

Yazawa was smirking slightly, his eyes shut again. An old lady was squatting on a three-legged stool beside him, methodically cracking the joints of his fingers one by one. Mitchell winced at the sound.

"So tell me this, Yazawa-san. If the barbers are such experts here, of what exactly did you have to inform him?"

Yazawa wrinkled his nose. "I mentioned that as a foreigner was coming, maybe they should prepare special instruments—for example, a stronger scissors. You see, foreign hair is much different from Japanese hair."

"It's usually a different color," admitted Mitchell, puzzled.

"Not just a question of color," Yazawa went on without opening his eyes. "The quality is also different. Your hair is coarse, like wild grasses. It grows stubbornly, any way it wants to. Japanese hair is finer and more disciplined than that."

"Really," replied Mitchell flatly. There was absolutely no point in trying to sidetrack Yazawa from a topic that had caught his interest.

"Yes, really. The pubic hair of your women often has the same characteristic. Generally, they have too much pubic hair. In the case of a Spanish lady I met in New York, it ran all the way up to her navel, like a ladder."

Yazawa gave a brief guffaw, spraying a couple of blobs of shaving foam onto the mirror. Mitchell said nothing. He assumed that Yazawa hadn't summoned him here just to discuss pubic hair. The barber began taking the edges off Mitchell's left sideburn. The scraping sound was loud in his ear, which he found even more disconcerting than the crack of Yazawa's knuckles.

"The pubic hair of a Japanese woman is neater, I think," mused Yazawa. "It covers all that should be covered, but no more. It doesn't spread like weeds. Rarely does it cross the perineum. Did you notice that, Mitchell-kun?"

"Notice what?" said Mitchell. His nose was itching badly. He longed to scratch it, but his hands were trapped under the white sheet.

"No hairy ass in Japan," said Yazawa with heavy emphasis on each word.

Mitchell glanced at the two barbers in the mirror. It was impossible to tell whether or not they understood the conversation. They were expressionless, clipping and scraping at the two foam-covered heads as if they were tending bonsai. The elderly lady didn't look up from her careful work. Having successfully cracked every knuckle in Yazawa's right hand, she was now busy with tweezers and scissors. Mitchell leaned back in the creaky leather chair and gazed into space.

"And as for the stock market," said Yazawa, switching the subject with characteristic abruptness, "it will reach a critical point sometime in the cherry blossom season. I have observed the strongest dragon's claw formation on the weekly chart of the Nikkei Index that I have seen for many years. Do you carefully watch for dragon's claw formations, Mitchell-kun?"

"Dragon's claw formations?" said Mitchell dubiously. "I don't know much about chart patterns. Fundamental analysts are supposed to concentrate on profit margins and balance sheets, aren't they?"

"You must study charts more," growled Yazawa. "You must have respect for the actions of the market itself. Only then will you understand the deeper currents."

He put his head to one side, allowing the elderly lady to insert into his ear a steel rod tipped with a ball of cotton wool. Mitchell said nothing. According to Yazawa's predecessor as head of research, the reading of chart patterns was sheer hocus-pocus, on a par with belief in astrology. Once, that had been Mitchell's view too. After all, stacks of academic papers had been written on the subject. The "technical analysts," as the chart-watchers called themselves, had been discredited years ago. The only problem was that Mitchell had been observing Yazawa in action for almost six months now. He didn't understand the techniques that Yazawa favored, or even the language that he used to describe them, but one thing was clear: they worked. On dozens of occasions, Yazawa had called major advances and declines in individual stocks and predicted the week-to-week movements of the Nikkei Index with unerring accuracy. On a regular basis he was doing what the academic papers claimed to be impossible.

"You prefer the truth of numbers to the truth of motion," said Yazawa. "This is typical Western-style thinking, isn't it?"

"It's what investment is all about," replied Mitchell defensively. "The companies produce the numbers. We analyze them and produce our recommendations. Fundamental analysts are the link between the financial market and the real world!"

"The real world? Hah!" Yazawa barked with laughter again, spraying the mirror with shaving foam.

"Don't get me wrong, Yazawa-san," added Mitchell carefully. "I value your stock-picking system highly. The results speak for themselves, no question about it."

The old lady had finished with Yazawa now. She eyed Mitchell expectantly, but he shook his head.

"System?" said Yazawa, wiping the last of the shaving foam from his cheek. "What is your meaning?"

"I'm referring to the system you use for screening out your stock recommendations. You're using nonlinear dynamics there, I suppose."

Mitchell had come across the term in a recent article in *The Economist*. Apparently a couple of rocket scientists in Chicago had developed the ultimate stock-selection system. Based on the principles of artificial intelligence, it incorporated pattern-recognition algorthythms derived from chaos theory. This meant it could model not just changes in profits and the economy, but also the twists and turns of investor psychology itself. The only problem was that the program was too complex for conventional mainframes to handle. You needed what they called "massive parallel processing capability," and that cost an enormous amount of money. Was it possible that Yazawa had somehow come up with a cheaper, simpler version? If so, it could be worth millions.

"Stock recommendations come from the spirit," said Yazawa sharply. "Keep your spirit strong! Watch like a hawk flying above a dark hillside!"

"But no software?"

"All software is in here," said Yazawa, tapping his forehead with a finger.

"So how did you come up with Matsui Paper? I'd be grateful if you could explain the mental processes behind something like that to me."

Mitchell really meant it. Three months ago, Yazawa had insisted that Kent the Mormon write a buy recommendation on a minor paperboard manufacturer that had been in the red for ten years in a row. Kent had duly obeyed, as he always did. Within six weeks, the stock had doubled and people were calling the Mormon a financial genius. There had even been a profile of him in *Institutional Investor*.

Yazawa tugged the cotton sheet from around his neck. "You have heard of the three great warlords from our era of warring states," he said.

"You mean Oda Nobunaga, Hideyoshi, and Ieyasu," said Mitchell. He remembered that much from his history studies in Sheffield.

"Perhaps you also know the legend of their three different ways of dealing with a bird that does not sing. When the bird refuses to sing, Oda would threaten to kill it immediately. That is one way, isn't it?"

Mitchell nodded into the mirror. This bit hadn't been on the course.

"But it is a rash way. The effectiveness is not good. As for Hideyoshi, he would persuade it to sing using many skillful words. That is a better way, I think."

Mitchell admitted that it was.

"As for Ieyasu," concluded Yazawa, "his way is actually the simplest way of all—he waits for the bird to sing. And do you know what happens?"

"What happens?" asked Mitchell, watching uneasily as a great hank of hair fell from the barber's scissors. The man was taking off much more than Mitchell had expected. What kind of hairstyle was he going to be left with?

"The bird sings, of course," said Yazawa joyously. "In the end, the bird always sings. It sings because it is a bird, not a fish or monkey. The bird has no choice in this case. It has to sing! Ieyasu knew that, and so he survived the era of warring states and became the creator of modern Japan. I waited for Matsui Paper like Ieyasu waited for that bird. I waited and waited until the stock had no choice. It had to go up!"

187

Yazawa laughed with triumph. Mitchell watched dumbly as he leaped from his chair and hurled the cotton sheet onto the bench at the side of the room. The stock had no choice but to go up? Sometimes Mitchell wondered quite seriously about the man's sanity.

"Now I must go to some important meetings," he said, standing still while the barber used a small brush to clean his collar. His hair, noticed Mitchell, seemed completely unchanged from when he had sat down in the barber's chair. It was the same length at the sides, with the same glossy swell rising at the same abrupt trajectory.

"I thought you had something to discuss with me," said Mitchell. "Man to man, if I remember correctly."

"We have learned much about each other while talking," said Yazawa solemnly. "For example, I have learned about your appreciation of the hairy ass."

"I have no appreciation of the hairy ass, for God's sake," protested Mitchell. "You're making the whole thing up!"

Yazawa nodded. Mitchell was beginning to understand that when Yazawa nodded, it generally signified not agreement with the other's opinion, but dismissal of it.

"Never mind the hairy ass. I have to know clearly what activities you will be engaged in later this evening. Will you be drinking heavily until you are intensively drunk?"

"I doubt it," said Mitchell.

"Fine," said Yazawa, clapping him on the shoulder again. "Try to keep your head clear, please. There is a chance that there may be an important phone call for you tonight. In such a case, you must give it the best shot."

Mitchell gazed at him in speechless incomprehension. Yazawa took a compact portable phone from his pocket and slipped it into Mitchell's jacket, which was hanging on a wooden stand.

"You must keep this with you at all times tonight," Yazawa continued. "Even if you are being entertained by a lady vigorously at some soapland. You understand that, Mitchell-kun?"

"What kind of phone call?" stammered Mitchell. "Phone call from whom?"

The barber tending Mitchell took a strange-looking electric appliance—something like a flatiron, but twice the size—from a small cupboard under the mirror. He unreeled a length of wire and plugged it into a socket in the floor.

"From investors, of course," said Yazawa sternly. "Many investors everywhere are interested in Otaman these days. The situation surrounding Otaman is getting increasingly bullish on a global scale."

"Otaman! You mean someone is going to call me about Otaman tonight! That's impossible! I haven't finished going through the numbers yet. It's going to take several days before I'm ready to." Mitchell twisted his head around, trying to confront Yazawa directly rather than his reflection. Yazawa was holding out his arms while the old woman helped him on with his jacket.

"Numbers," he snapped dismissively. "These are just broken twigs dancing on the surface of the stream. Remember what I told you, Mitchell-kun. Feel the flow! The flow is what matters!"

The barber placed the rubber-coated face of the strange-looking appliance flat against Mitchell's left shoulder and flicked on the switch. Immediately, his ears were filled with a loud hum and the machine began to vibrate like a washing machine in the last stage of its cycle. Mitchell's shoulders rocked forward as the muscles of his back and neck twitched and quivered in sympathy.

"Hey, what's going on! Stop this blasted thing! Yazawa-san, we need to talk! Yazawa-san . . ."

Mitchell's voice tailed off plaintively. Yazawa's slim figure had disappeared through the swinging door without a backward glance. Meanwhile, the machine was still humming away, the vibrations sending a strange tingling sensation shooting up and down his scalp. He had a violent desire to scratch his head, but still he couldn't move his hands.

"Enough of this!" he shouted, first in English and then in Japanese.

The barber nodded and lifted the machine away from the back of Mitchell's neck. Mitchell heaved a sigh of relief as the tickling sensation faded. "Thank you," he said, struggling to rise from the chair.

The barber smiled politely and pressed the face of the machine down hard on Mitchell's other shoulder. Mitchell's eyes began to water as the vibrations spread through his shoulders, much stronger than before. He could feel his cheeks quivering, and his nose and gums had started to itch violently. With his hands stuck under the white sheet, there was nothing he could do about it.

Trying to distract himself from all the quivering and itching, Mitchell gazed down at the tiled floor, which was dotted with tufts of brown hair. How much had been taken off? It was hard to tell with that towel wrapped around his head, but it looked like a lot. And that large lock of hair between his feet—wasn't it the one on which Mari-san had lavished so much care and attention over the months? Mitchell sank back in his chair, chewing his lower lip in vexation. The massage machine continued shuddering across his shoulders.

Mori spent most of the afternoon going through the documents that Togo had given him. There was only one photo of Ono, but it grabbed Mori's attention instantly. He was standing in the middle of an office, baseball bat held high above his head, while a young salarymen in spectacles cowered below him. In the background was a small crowd of people dressed in the cult's usual robes and several other salarymen, their expressions of fear and panic caught nicely by the camera. Though the cult members were mainly female, there were a number of heavyset shaven-headed men carrying wooden staves. In the newspaper text under the photo, these were described as "soldiers of light," Ono's personal guard.

Mori studied the man's appearance—long glossy hair down on his shoulders, a full beard, and, it was hard to ignore even under the robe, an ample paunch. He had a vague recollection of the incident depicted. It had taken place several years ago, when the scandal magazine *Thursday* had run a sarcastic feature on the "Sisters of Light," pointing out that a couple of them were ex–porno video stars. Ono and a group of his disciples had stormed the head offices of the giant publishing company that produced the magazine, done millions of yen of damage to the furnishings, and put one junior staff member into intensive care with a fractured skull. The prosecutor's attempt to assemble a case against the cult fell apart when the publishing company refused to press charges and its staff members suddenly retracted all their evidence. Ono clearly knew how to apply pressure at the top as well as to the lower ranks.

When he had finished reading through Togo's summary again, Mori stuffed the papers into a manila envelope and found a place for it among the crammed contents of his filing cabinet. He hadn't cleaned out that cabinet in years—not because he liked the dust and the yellowy papers and the smears of cockroach crap, but because there was too much in there that he didn't want to cast his eyes over again. Records of old cases, solved and unsolved; letters from old clients, grateful, angry, sad; newspaper clippings; jotted notes; photos of couples emerging from hotels, mouths wide open in surprise, hands trying in vain to ward off the flash—so much deceit and anger, so much waste. Nothing to be proud of, not for anyone concerned.

At five o'clock, Mori locked up the office and went out to eat roasted eel on rice in a tiny back-street restaurant where every customer was greeted with a shout of "Welcome, company president!" It was a standing joke that usually amused new customers. It also amused Mori, because he really was a company president and had been since the day fifteen years ago when he had set up Mori Economic and Social Research Services Inc. Apart from being president, he was also the company's chief financial officer, marketing director, receptionist, and sole research operative. Over the years, he had tried several secretaries, but it had never worked out. The one girl who had matched that description, and had more charm and intelligence than he had had any right to expect, had quit after one tour of the washroom. Mori had been prepared to buy her the latest model word processor, even to provide her with a secondhand desk and chair, but to rip out the Japanese-style toilet and install a Western-style one—that would have busted his budget for the entire year.

The roasted eel was as good as ever; not too soggy, not too stringy. Mori washed it down with barley tea and a cup of clear soup containing an eel's innards pinioned by a toothpick.

"Many thanks, president! Come again soon."

"I'll be back sometime next week—unless I get ousted from my position, of course. Once you've reached the top, you've got to be on your guard all the time!"

The waiter gave a broad smile as he handed Mori his change. Considering recent events, Mori wondered whether his own joke was really all that amusing. He left the restaurant in a thoughtful frame of mind, digging with a toothpick at a piece of eel liver trapped under one of his back fillings.

Next stop was a large bookstore a couple of blocks away from Shinjuku station. Getting there took Mori twenty minutes on the Honda, easing his way through the early afternoon traffic. He parked in a side street next to a cluster of brand-new mountain bikes, then crossed the road and went inside.

The bookstore, like the nearby jazz coffee bar where he had met Sano, was one of the few places that Mori had remained loyal to ever since he had arrived in Tokyo a quarter of a century before. Although it was one of the biggest bookstores in Tokyo, it was by no means the best organized or most convenient. The small elevator was slow and nearly always full, and the winding staircase between floors was narrow and steep and pervaded with the smell of curry rice. The aisles between the bookshelves were cramped and usually crowded with browsers who wouldn't budge out of the way unless pushed. The books themselves were classified and arranged in a confusing manner that even now Mori wasn't sure he fully understood. Nonetheless, the bookstore's preeminence was unchanged from the late sixties, and probably from many decades before that. In terms of the range of subjects covered and the variety of obscure works nestling in the shelves, there was no competition.

In Mori's student days, the small space in front of the store had been the most popular rendezvous for dating couples in Shinjuku. They were too many to remember, the girls whom he had stood there waiting for, leaning against the wall in his bell-bottom jeans and patched vest. There had been wild intellectual ones; neat, conservatively dressed types, quietly determined to make the most of their three or four years of freedom; semi-professionals who really wanted just to get drunk and have some laughs without any stress; dreamy, mysterious types whom you could never reach, no matter what you did. Mori remembered the faces better than the names. What did these women look like now? What had they become—housewives, mothers, schoolteachers, middle-aged office ladies? They had all slipped through the time tunnel, been sucked away into different worlds. As for Mori, though, he was once again climbing the staircase at the side of the bookstore, breathing in the same old smell of curry rice.

First of all, Mori went to the second floor, where Ono's latest works were piled up in a special display. He picked out two—*Secrets of Enlightenment* and *Secrets of Pure Joy*—and took them to the sales counter. The girl looked at him intently as he handed over his money.

"Are you truly interested in such ideas?" she asked him in a quiet voice.

"That's what I'm going to find out," said Mori. "I never judge a book before I've read it."

"These are wonderful ideas," she said softly as she wrapped the books for him. "If you open your mind to them, you will find true, deep meanings that will change your life."

Mori glanced at her. She was smiling a strange smile, more to herself than to him.

"Thank you for the advice," he said. She carried on smiling, slowly nodding her head up and down like a toy dog.

After that, Mori went up to the fourth floor and spent almost an hour thumbing through books on religion and social anthropology. The jargon was daunting, but he got some idea of how successful cults functioned as "replacement paradigms for the alienated consciousness." Then, following up a reference in one of the sociology texts, he went up to the fifth floor and spent another three quarters of an hour reading an introduction to experimental psychology. He was just skimming through an account of the Gestalt theory of human perception when someone shoved him in the back, pressing him forward against the rack of books. His concentration broken, Mori glanced up from the page he was reading and into a pair of female eyes staring at him coolly over the top of the highest layer of books. Only the top half of the woman's face was visible, but Mori recognized it instantly. It was the woman whom he had seen in the elevator outside Yuriko's apartment. No doubt, she was the same one who had been hanging around outside his office and asking questions in the Chinese restaurant across the street.

"This is quite a coincidence," he remarked dryly.

The eyebrows arched upward in an expression that might have been surprised or mocking or just plain amused, depending on the shape of the invisible mouth. She was almost close enough for him to reach out and grab a glossy lock of hair.

"Perhaps you could recommend a book for me," he went on. "A really good mystery, for example."

For an instant, there was the ghost of a smile in the large oval eyes, then she ducked out of sight. It took Mori several seconds to push his way through the crowd of browsers to the end of the aisle. When he rounded the corner, the place where she had been standing was empty.

He squeezed through to the next aisle and stared up and down it. There was no sign of her there either. Wheeling around, he just caught a glimpse of a tall woman in a red raincoat, long hair flowing onto her shoulders, disappearing past the service counter.

Mori hurried after her, drawing black looks and irritated murmurs from the browsers he shoved out of his way. The woman was fifteen yards in front of him now, walking rapidly toward the elevator. Looking up, Mori noticed that the door of the elevator was open and a small crowd was filing inside.

"Thank you sincerely for patronizing our store," chirruped the elevator girl with a bow. "Now we will descend to the fourth floor, which contains the mathematics, chemistry, physics, law, and management sections."

Mori surged forward, sending a middle-aged salaryman sprawling against a display pile of bestselling paperbacks, which went crashing to the floor.

"What do you think you're doing!" he spluttered at Mori. "Don't you know how to behave like a Japanese!"

"Please prepare for descending," called out the elevator girl. Mori used knees and elbows to propel himself the last few yards. The woman in the red raincoat was at the elevator door now, just about to squeeze herself inside. Mori forced himself between two high school kids standing gazing at the floor guide on the wall and, with a desperate lunge, grabbed her by the shoulder. He was just conscious of the faces in the elevator staring out at him in fascinated anticipation of an "incident."

"Stop! You're hurting me! Let go!"

Mori twisted her around, pushed her against the wall, and then slowly let his hands drop to his sides. The red raincoat was the same type, the height and build were similar, and the hair was roughly the same length, but that was all. The face that was glaring up at him, shocked and indignant, was one that he had never seen before.

"This is a terrible mistake," he muttered sheepishly. "I'm very sorry. I thought you were someone else."

"You behave like an animal," said the woman, slapping the collar of her raincoat back into shape. "You're just the sort of man I can't stand!"

There was something in her eyes that said differently. Somehow, she was enjoying the excitement. Mori looked around. The faces in the elevator were still staring at him expectantly. That must mean the elevator girl was holding the door open. The two high school kids were nudging each other and smirking. Mori shrugged and turned away. From where he was standing, it was clear that the woman he was looking for couldn't have reached the elevator or the staircase next to it. She had to be still on the fifth floor somewhere. He edged his way to the middle of the floor, picked up a computer magazine, then leaned back against a pillar, watching and waiting.

The next time he was sure. It wasn't just the red raincoat and the hair—it was the way she walked as well. He tracked the woman with his eye as she moved toward the far corner of the room, taking a book off a shelf from time to time, then glancing around when she replaced it. Once or twice, he thought she had spotted him, but she kept on going, finally disappearing into the ladies' toilet. Only then did Mori put the magazine back in its rack and make his way deliberately toward the far corner of the room, keeping one steady eye on his destination.

He took up a position to one side of the ladies' toilet and stood there pretending to flick through an encyclopedia of natural history. It was a busy day for the bookstore, and women emerged in a constant stream—middle-aged shoppers clutching carry bags, counter girls in uniform, smartly dressed office ladies, even a nun in full habit. Mori observed them out of the corner of his eye as he bent over the heavy, cumbersome book.

Ten minutes went by, then twenty. Still there was no sign of the red raincoat. It was impossible for him to have missed it. Mori glanced at his watch and compressed his lips. If she thought she could wait him out, she'd better think again. He was prepared to stand there until closing time if necessary. He hefted the encyclopedia back into its place and picked out a slimmer book, an illustrated guide to Japanese wild birds.

An hour and a half later, Mori was still there, considerably better informed about ornithology. No one had entered the toilet in the last five minutes, and no one had come out. His patience finally exhausted, Mori raised a hand to attract the attention of a passing store assistant.

"Excuse me, sister. Can you help me with a small problem?"

"We are always happy to help our honored customers. What is the nature of the problem?" The girl turned a brisk, efficient face toward him and gave him a friendly smile.

"It's my wife. She went into the ladies' toilet quite some time ago and she hasn't come out yet. I'm rather worried because she has a tendency to fainting fits. The doctor has told me to keep a close watch on her."

"Understood! Can I ask you what your wife looks like?"

"She's tall, with long hair straight down her back. She was wearing a red raincoat."

"Understood. I'll go and make sure immediately!"

The store assistant disappeared into the entrance of the toilet, only to emerge again almost in a matter of seconds. The friendly smile had been replaced with a puzzled expression. "Honored customer, she's not there! Are you sure she isn't somewhere else?"

"Impossible!" said Mori tightly. "I saw her go in myself! Maybe my description was not sufficient. Maybe she has taken off her raincoat."

"But there is no one in there at all. I have checked thoroughly."

"There must be another entrance," said Mori, thinking out loud. "What about the window? Was the window open?"

"There is no window in our toilet," said the store assistant, her tone much harder now. "Perhaps you would come with me to the security office. It is necessary to take down full details in this kind of situation."

She was eyeing him with barely concealed suspicion. What was she thinking? That he was a pervert, a shoplifter, a sad fantasist of some sort? Mori glanced for the last time at the entrance of the ladies' toilet. "Must be a mistake," he said quickly. "She's probably downstairs in the fiction department. Sorry to trouble you."

Mori dropped the bird book onto the nearest pile and hurried toward the staircase.

Since coming to Tokyo, Mitchell had, for the first time in his life, begun to drink heavily. It wasn't that he needed to drink to forget or to drown his sorrows or anything banal like that. He had merely developed an enormously strong thirst. And the more he drank, the more powerful it got. In the evenings, especially Friday evenings, it was insatiable. To go home and read a book or watch a video was simply unthinkable. He needed—deserved, demanded—the liberation of alcohol. It was, he told himself, a positive phenomenon, related to the thirsts for sex and work and spending money that had been awakened in him during his time in Japan. Part of a giant thirst for life itself, you could say.

So it was that shortly after eleven Mitchell found himself stumbling alone through the back streets of Roppongi. His companions had gone, and it was too early to go home. Or rather he had drunk enough beer and tequila slammers not to want to go home until he had sated himself on music and images and motion.

It didn't take him long to find the kind of thing he was looking for. At the corner of a narrow street was a sight that immediately grabbed the attention. The last time Mitchell had passed the building, it had been an ordinary concrete box. Now it had been given the facade of a Greek temple, with a large triangular architrave perched on a row of fluted columns. Alcoves in the wall contained plaster statues of gods and goddesses.

More intriguing than the decor were the crowds that were flocking around the entrance—young, female, and dressed in outrageously provocative costumes. Mitchell stood gawking in dumb fascination as the girls lined up to go in: flashing eyes, glossy lipstick, long hair swaying down over tanned shoulders and arms. There were skirts so short that they might have been T-shirts with belts; backless dresses cut low enough to reveal the swell of the buttocks and the first few inches of crevice; strapless halter tops, tight over nipples that stood out like cherry stones. Male customers were present in the crowd too, but they were mostly middle-aged salarymen in rumpled blue suits. They stood clustered together like children on an outing, slapping one another on the shoulders, linking arms, and pretending to be drunker than they really were.

From the dance floor in the basement came the muffled pile-driver thump of the music. Without really knowing what he was doing, Mitchell pushed through the crowd. An escalator clogged with bodies bore him downward. The noise got louder, the pumping beat now overlaid with heavy synthesizer chords. At regular intervals, a woman's orgasmic sigh, stretched out and given a lingering multiple echo, rose and fell like a wave. Looking down, Mitchell saw filtered spotlights—pink, orange, turquoise—sweeping across a mass of shadowy bodies, making weblike patterns on arms, backs, and faces.

The first thing that struck Mitchell about the place was the depth, at least forty feet below ground level. The second was the scale. The dance floor was huge, half the size of a soccer field, and as packed with bodies as Tokyo station at rush hour. He slipped into the jostling throng and began to move with the others, twisting at the hips and raising his hands in the air. There were few other choices of action, since it was almost impossible for anyone to move his feet. The music was gut-quiveringly loud. Mitchell jerked his upper body around to the beat, bumping into a male back that was liquid with sweat, stepping on a toe, taking a sharp elbow in the ribs. He was getting hot, light-headed with the pounding music.

On the other side of the dance floor was a long platform about two yards above it. Mitchell glimpsed tanned limbs flailing about, long hair dashing from side to side. Altogether, there must have been a couple of hundred girls up there, dancing like puppets controlled by a mad puppeteer. Many of them were waving large brightly colored fans, which they opened and closed with a flick of the wrist. Mitchell had never seen anything like that before. He had never felt anything like he did now either. Even from a distance, the sexual energy was hitting him like gamma rays. Impelled to the source, he thrust his way through the wall of salarymen. His whole body felt like a giant erection, steeple-tall and bursting with purpose.

The closer he got, the harder it was to make progress. From the distance of about five yards, all pretense of dancing was given up entirely. The salarymen stood there in rows, gazing upward in a trancelike state, soaking up the barrage of pheromones. Hardly aware of what he was doing, Mitchell bulldozed through, using elbows and knees. He felt giddy. The music had invaded him, the pumping rhythm uniting with his heartbeat, the long soft sigh washing through his mind. One thing he knew—he wasn't just going to stand and stare like all the rest.

Suddenly, a vision appeared in front of his eyes—a tall, heavy-breasted girl with bare feet and long legs. She was wearing a tight minidress that had ridden up her golden thighs almost to the groin. She was rolling her pelvis in slow circular movements, stretching her arms high in the air and rolling her head from side to side, lips spread in a smile of blissful abandon. For an instant, her flying hair spread across her face, covering her eyes and catching in her mouth. Then she flicked it away, and she was gazing right at Mitchell.

Their eyes met, and a bizarre thought flashed into his mind. This woman before him could be a modern incarnation of Amaterasu, the Japanese sun goddess. How did the story go? Hadn't she danced alone in her cave at the dawn of time, keeping the world in darkness? And then what had happened? Someone had coaxed her out again. That would be

Mitchell's role! He would coax the sun goddess out of her cave. He would take her back to his apartment.

The woman was sidestepping away from him now, swaying behind a couple of other dancers. "Don't go," called Mitchell, struggling to the front of the crowd, but his words were lost in the sea of music.

Her skirt had ridden farther up her thighs, revealing a flash of whiteness that was almost blinding. Mitchell caught his breath. It was the woman's G-string, he realized. Evidently it was made of some special luminous material that picked up the glare of the strobe.

"Come back," Mitchell yelled in futile desperation.

She was still gazing at him, smiling euphorically, her brow beaded with perspiration. Her hands stretched out toward him as if she were pulling him in by an invisible rope. Mitchell twisted around. The crowd of salarymen seemed to be frozen into stone, displaying not even an eyelid flicker of movement. The platform was about head-height, supported by a crisscross of steel poles and struts. Mitchell grabbed hold of a strut and began to haul himself upward.

There was pain. Someone had stamped on his hand. He looked up into a female face pinched with anger. That certainly wasn't going to stop him. His vision was dancing just behind, her bare feet sliding from side to side on the plastic surface. Her toenails, he noticed, were painted a glossy red.

Mitchell got his knees up onto the platform, then his elbows and arms. Suddenly, his ear was burning and ringing at the same time. One of the other dancers had smacked him hard across the side of his head with a folded fan. Out of the corner of his eye, he glimpsed the crimson toenails drifting farther away. It was too late to stop. He rolled onto the platform and collected himself into a crouching position just in time to receive another whack of the fan, this time on the cheek. An eight-inch length of wood and paper—it was surprising how much it stung.

There were four girls clustered around him now, their faces masks of rage. When he tried to climb to his feet, they pushed him down by the shoulders. Their squeals rose above the noise of the music. "What are you doing, pervert!"

"Don't you dare touch us!"

The girl who had stamped on his hand pushed off a sling-back shoe and swiped at the side of his head. He ducked, but not quickly enough. The high heel skidded over his scalp. Mitchell gave a little yelp of pain and raised his hand to his head. There was blood, he was sure. He tried to roll free, but it was no good. There were more of them now, and they were closing in, pushing him down with elbows, fists, and knees.

"You won't get away with this!"

"Stop him, quickly!"

A toe jabbed at his groin; a smooth brown knee caught him just under the chin. Mitchell was forced to the edge of the platform, shielding his head as best he could from the swinging shoes and raking nails. The salarymen were staring up at him, amazement on some faces, amusement on others.

The rain of blows paused. The music had stopped at some point that he hadn't noticed, and he could hear the hubbub of the crowd. Mitchell turned from his crouching position to see the crimson toenails just a few inches from his face. His imploring gaze ran up the slender calves, the dimpled knees, the heavy arching thighs. His vision was standing over him, arms akimbo, brow still glistening with sweat. She was staring him straight in the eye, but she was no longer smiling. Mitchell racked his brain for something to say.

"You're a goddess," he mumbled finally. "I think I'm in love with you."

She flicked a wayward strand of hair from in front of her face and turned to the girl with the shoe. "Let's teach this pervert a lesson," she said.

"Push him off," cried the girl with the shoe excitedly. "Quick, everybody—before he stands up!"

"Get ready—push him now!"

Hands were shoving him, knees and elbows jabbing him. Mitchell tried desperately to hold his balance, clutching at a bare ankle attached to a bare foot. For a moment, his grip was tight, but then there was a stabbing pain from wrist to elbow as a high-heel shoe stamped down hard on his lower arm.

"Off the side!"

Mitchell let go. Before his scrambled senses had time to register what was happening, he was reeling backward, clutching at thin air, then sprawling headfirst into the crowd. The previously solid wall of salarymen parted, and he went tumbling to the ground. The impact was jarring. He took it mainly on the right shoulder and hip. For a moment, he lay there looking up dumbly at the faces. It was only when he tried to move that he realized how hopelessly drunk he was.

Someone grabbed him under the arms, somebody else around the waist. He was being abruptly dragged to his feet. Mitchell didn't resist, allowing himself to be backed up against the walkway. He shook his head to clear it and saw a wimpy-looking guy in a Roman toga standing in front of him, forefinger poking at his chest. From the badge on his chest and the walkie-talkie hanging from his belt, Mitchell assumed he was one of the security staff.

"What are you doing!" shouted the wimp in English. "You are the only person to make trouble here. Why do you break our rules!"

He was at least six inches shorter than Mitchell, probably thirty pounds lighter, and had a squeaky schoolboy voice. Mitchell gave a grunt of anger and swatted the finger away with his hand.

"Stop! Listen to what I am saying! I am explaining the rules that you should obey here!"

The stupid uniform, the stupid voice—it was infuriating. And now the wimp was seizing him by the arm, just where it had been bruised by the fall from the walkway. That was too much. Mitchell's self-control suddenly snapped. He swung around and aimed a wild blow in the wimp's general direction. As he did so, he realized, almost as if he were watching the scene from somewhere else, that he was probably making a mistake.

Quite how much of a mistake was soon apparent. The wimp moved like lightning, sliding inside the blow, grabbing Mitchell's elbow and wrist, then twisting and pulling. Mitchell fought to retain his balance, but it was useless. Suddenly, he was rolling over the wimp's jutting hip, his legs bicycling in the empty air. Then the floor came up to meet him with an impact that knocked his breath away. He was vaguely aware of a respectful "Ahh" from the crowd of salarymen, and a scattering of applause.

His cheek flat against the cold concrete, Mitchell glimpsed the girls peering down at him from the walkway. Some were pointing down and giggling, some fanning themselves vigorously, some just chewing gum and looking bored. The woman with the scarlet toenails was nowhere to be seen.

Before he had time to collect his breath, the wimp grabbed him by the collar and dragged him to his feet again. Mitchell tried to break free, but the wimp got behind him, pulled his arm out straight, and suddenly Mitchell was as powerless as a trussed hen. The wimp was using one hand to press down on Mitchell's elbow, the other to twist his little finger upward against the line of his arm. The effect was to turn Mitchell's arm into a lever that forced the top half of his body down to the floor. Mitchell twisted this way and that, but he couldn't break free.

"Make a space," shouted the wimp to the audience of appreciative salarymen. "This customer is being expelled for making a nuisance."

Mitchell stumbled forward, his head forced so low that his knees were butting into his chest. The music had started up again, a bubbling bass track overlaid with a tinkling melody. A corridor opened in the crowd to let them pass. Mitchell scuttled through it, bent double. The strobe was flashing in time with the beat, lighting up a frozen forest of legs to his gaze.

The wimp hauled Mitchell across the dance floor, past the elevator, and through a gray metal door. On the other side was a brightly lit corridor. When the door slammed shut behind them, he let go of Mitchell's arm and let him stand upright. "You don't keep rules," he said and gave Mitchell a shove in the small of his back. Mitchell didn't bother to resist.

Halfway down the corridor was a delivery elevator. The wimp grabbed Mitchell by the elbow and hauled him inside. "Why do you make so much trouble?" he said, shaking his head. "Our disco is number-one disco in Tokyo. Everyone understands that except you!"

He pressed a button on the control panel, then stepped back out into the corridor. The doors clanged shut and the elevator machinery hummed into life. Mitchell felt suddenly exhausted. He slumped into the corner, nursing his injured shoulder, listening to the thump of the music below fading into the distance. When the doors opened, Mitchell found himself in a loading bay filled with black plastic sacks. He glanced around. From the back, the building with the temple facade was just a squat concrete block, with barred windows and a rickety fire escape running up to the roof. The gate to the narrow street behind was locked with a heavy padlock.

Mitchell clambered up it without much difficulty. As he rolled himself over the top of the wire netting, something slid out of the inside pocket of his jacket and clattered down to the pavement. He gazed at in dismay. It was a portable phone. He had completely forgotten about the call that Yazawa had told him to wait for! Hastily, he scrambled down the other side of the fence and scooped it up.

There was a crack down the side of the plastic casing, and the little orange light was dead. He shook it frantically. Something inside rattled. That was a bad sign—the phone must have been damaged in the fracas. Mitchell cursed himself for his folly. He shook it again. To his relief, this time the orange light did flicker weakly.

Mitchell sat down heavily on the tarmac, leaning against the back bumper of a Toyota Deliboy van. He gazed despairingly at the thin oblong of scuffed, cracked plastic. The little orange light was flashing again now, more regularly than before. It took Mitchell a couple of seconds to realize what was happening. Someone was trying to get through to him! The call tone must have been disabled by the battering the phone had taken earlier. Mitchell jabbed at the receive button.

"Who's that?" sounded a vaguely familiar voice. "Are you there, Terry?"

"This is Richard Mitchell, senior analyst at Pearson Darney in Tokyo."

"Rickie baby! This is Dan Rollings here. You're just the man I was looking for."

"Good to hear from you, Dan," replied Mitchell, a sinking sensation in his stomach. Rollings was head of institutional sales at the New York office. A slick, slim jackknife of a man—sharp eyes, sharp nose, sharp teeth—Rollings had risen to his current position a year ago, since then he had been focusing his energies on slapping down, tripping up, and edging out all potential rivals. According to Kent the Mormon, Rollings had the temper of a junkyard dog and an ego the size of a small planet. In short, he was a bad man to have working against you, and an even worse man to have working on the same side.

"You're going to be happy with all the progress over here," continued Rollings. "The trading desk is already committed for a big slice of the action and we have some major players lined up already. Looks like you and Terry have a real winner on your hands."

"Terry?" said Mitchell blankly. He hadn't the faintest idea what Rollings was talking about.

"Terry Yazooer—the head of research, for chrissake! He's been singing your praises, Mitch. He loves the way you developed this idea, single-handed. All the credit goes to Rick Mitchell, he says."

"Idea? What idea?" said Mitchell.

"Hey, come on, don't be modest. I'm talking about the Atomin deal, of course."

"Atomin? You mean Otaman?"

"Otaman, Otaboy—I don't care how you pronounce the goddamn thing! The big funds are raring to go, Rickie. They want to pick up the ball and run with it! But first they need to talk to the analyst directly. That means you."

Mitchell raised a feeble hand in search of his nonexistent forelock, then let it fall to his side again. He was finding it hard to concentrate.

Otaman was now Atomin. Yazawa Terumasa—to give his name in its proper Japanese order—had suddenly become Terry Yazooer. And apparently he had been in close contact with Rollings, singing the praises of the star of the Tokyo operation, the man who deserved all the credit—a brilliant young analyst called Richard Mitchell! None of this made any sense at all.

"You mean they want to talk to me?" repeated Mitchell stupidly.

"They surely do, and you'll never guess who I'm talking about." Even through the stratospheric fuzz, Rollings's voice was pregnant with triumph.

"No, I don't suppose I will," muttered Mitchell, his heart sinking.

"It's Henry Lazarus's people. And Henry himself is going to be there! Well, actually he's in his castle in Mexico, but they're going to key him into the call. How about that!"

Mitchell sat bolt upright. He took the phone away from his ear and stared at it blankly.

Rollings's voice continued to tinkle out of the earpiece. "As you probably read in the *Journal,* Henry's been shifting a lot of money out of Europe recently. The man is hungry for new ideas in Japan. You know his style—when the guy deals, he deals in megasize!"

"Henry Lazarus wants to talk to me!" whispered Mitchell at the shadows. He felt as if someone had kneed him in the stomach, hard.

"Okay—here's the way it looks. They're going to call you on this number at five o'clock Eastern time. What's that going to be with you?"

"That's—uh—five in the morning," he replied, his mind still reeling at the enormity of the concept.

"Well, don't forget to set your alarm clock," said Rollings. "You'll need to be bright-eyed and bushy-tailed for this one. There'll be six of Lazarus's top money managers sitting in their conference room eating up every word you say. In addition to Henry himself, of course. No one has ever pulled the wool over that guy's eyes. Do you hear what I'm saying?"

"Yes," said Mitchell. "I mean no. I mean—"

"Remember, five o'clock Eastern time. Give it everything you've got, good buddy!"

There was a click and the orange light trembled for a few seconds, then went out. Mitchell returned the phone to his inside pocket and pulled himself to his feet. He glanced at his watch. It was already past midnight. Mitchell started walking rapidly, head down as he wove through the crowds. He took a shortcut—around the back of a tiny cemetery, up a flight of stone steps, then out to the big intersection snarling with traffic.

There was a line of around fifty people waiting at the taxi stand. Mitchell took his place at the end and waited. On average, taxis were appearing once every ninety seconds. That meant he wouldn't be home in bed until well after two. Then, less than three hours later, he was expected to wake up and make a telephone pitch about a company he didn't understand to the world's most successful financial speculator. The whole thing was too horrible to contemplate!

Mitchell gazed at the shimmering ziggurats of nightclubs, restaurants, and bars that lined the street. Each neon sign represented a small, self-contained oasis of unreality. Mitchell wished he were safely ensconced in one of those places, being flattered and coddled by the hostesses, with Yazawa, Otaman, and Dan Rollings transformed into fleeting ghosts of his imagination. But they couldn't be dismissed like that. They dominated this strange, dreamlike landscape that he was fated to wander. Somehow his life had turned into a gigantic Nintendo game, with shocks and traps and monsters lying in wait around every corner. Super-Mitchell had to keep going, no matter how many times he was squashed flat by steamrollers or pecked by pterodactyls, no matter that he didn't know where he was going or what he was supposed to be searching for.

At first, Mitchell didn't notice the tiny Suzuki Cappuccino sports car buzzing to a halt on the other side of the road. Nor did he see the driver hop out, slam the door, and walk briskly toward him. When he did look up, he found himself staring into the features of the wimp who had expelled him from the disco.

"You are the troublemaker, aren't you?" he said, nodding his head somberly.

"You know I am," said Mitchell irritably. "What are you planning to do now—throw me out of Roppongi, too?"

"You do not understand the merits of our disco," said the wimp solemnly. "It is the number-one disco in Tokyo. You should visit again, if possible. We do not like to experience a dissatisfied customer, even a troublemaker such as you are."

Mitchell examined the wimps puppylike face for hints of sarcasm. He didn't find any. "You expect me to take you seriously!" he said finally. "After throwing me all over the dance floor in front of those girls!"

The wimp bowed, low enough for Mitchell to see the back of his neck. "I must apologize," he said. "It was a very hateful incident for both of us. I know it is tough to lose face in front of many cute girls, but the number of cute girls in Tokyo is endless. Now you are waiting for a taxi, aren't you?"

"That's right," said Mitchell dryly. "Along with all these other people here."

"Your taxi will not come for a long time," said the wimp, glancing at the line of people. "Let me take you to your house in my car. I have sincere regrets about that hateful incident."

Mitchell glanced across the street to where the Suzuki Cappuccino was parked, engine running. There was a girl in the passenger seat, peering into the mirror as she fiddled around with a contact lens. Even in profile, Mitchell recognized her instantly. It was the sun goddess, now with her hair swept back in a ponytail and a cigarette protruding from her full lips.

"Well, it might be a good idea," he said. "But it doesn't look like there's any room in your car for me."

"We can make room very easily," said the wimp with a dismissive wave of the hand. "This woman has no daytime job, so she can wait here many hours for the taxi if necessary. Her time is not important."

The wimp held out his hand. Mitchell shook it, and they crossed the street together. The wimp rapped on the car door with his knuckle. The sun goddess turned and blew a plume of smoke from her mouth. She was wearing a thigh-length black leather coat with padded shoulders and a gleaming silver buckle. She was younger than Mitchell had first thought, certainly no more than twenty-five, but quite heavily made-up.

"Hey, you," said the wimp in brusque Japanese. "Get out of the car! It's been decided that I will drive this customer home."

The woman glanced at Mitchell, her large eyes signaling no recognition. Close up, she looked amazingly ordinary. "Understood," she said in a bored voice, and unfastened her seatbelt. Mitchell held the door open as she slid her long legs to the ground. The crimson toenails were invisible now, encased in a pair of shiny high-heel shoes. She clip-clopped across the road to join the taxi line. It had grown in length since Mitchell had first arrived, now consisting of sixty or seventy people altogether. When Mitchell lowered himself into the Suzuki's passenger seat, the leather was still pleasantly warm.

The wimp let out the clutch and the tiny car jerked forward, the engine whining like a turbo-charged mosquito. Eyes half-closed, Mitchell atched the fractured neon calligraphy of Roppongi come hurtling toward him.

ELEVEN

Mori read late into the night, scarcely aware of the passage of time. There was something strangely compelling about Ono's vision of the future.

The self-proclaimed "brother of Jesus and Mohammed" was by no means an optimist. The world, he warned, was facing a period of massive turbulence that politicians and the established religions would be completely unable to handle. There would be ten years of economic depression, ethnic conflict, and abnormal weather conditions. America's inner cities were going to erupt into anarchy. Europe would see the rise of another Hitler. For Africa, drought and starvation. For Asia, a host of terrible new diseases that would wipe out millions of "excess humans."

Japan itself was about to experience "The Great Cleansing." According to Ono, within eight years there would be a series of gigantic earth tremors, lasting for months on end. Tokyo would be blitzed with firestorms, underground explosions, and collapsing skyscrapers. The entire coast from Nagoya to Sendai would be buffeted by tidal waves that would sweep away whole towns and villages. Altogether, millions would die, and tens of millions would be left homeless.

That was the bad news. There was good news too, though you had to be a disciple of Ono to appreciate it fully. The Japanese people's faith in empty modern values would be shattered like the concrete buildings that symbolized them. All social institutions—government, schools, companies—would be completely discredited. To satisfy their spiritual disorientation, tens of millions would seek out the True Source of Enlightenment—meaning, of course, Ono and his followers. Its influence would spread over the world, bringing wisdom and contentment to the confused masses of Asia.

Ono's prose wasn't easy to read. There was no logical argument, and each page was stuffed with quotations from Ono's "pre-incarnations," such as Einstein, Lao-tzu, and Nostradamus. Yet the section about the coming earthquakes stuck in the mind. Ono obviously knew the subject well. In a book published in 1991, he had even predicted the time and place of the Kobe quake. That was impressive, Mori had to admit.

So what was the source of Ono's appeal? Why were young people like Yuriko flocking to the chain of mountain hideaways he had set up over the past few years? Somehow he gave them a sense of security, a sense of belonging, and a sense of moral purpose. That was why even graduates of top universities, lawyers and scientists, were willing to turn their backs on the world and join up. It seemed to work with foreigners too. These days there were Peace Technology branches in California, Australia, and the Ukraine. High-profile recruits included an Italian soccer star and a Hollywood heartthrob who was into mysticism and environmental causes.

In a sense, Mori reflected, the world was going Ono's way. It was true that many people had lost confidence in the future. It was true that the old assumptions and values now seemed as reliable as wet cardboard. It was true that the daily news was full of weird and terrible events. People tried to shut their eyes and pretend that everything was still fine, but Yuriko's generation knew differently.

Mori lay back on the sofa, fingers locked under his head as he studied the damp stains on the ceiling. When he had been Yuriko's age, he had believed some pretty bizarre things himself. He had believed that global capitalism could be overthrown by students abandoning classes and trashing the university offices; that Chairman Mao was a political genius who had built the most humane society on earth; that it was reasonable to ambush other students of a different ideological coloring and break their bones with baseball bats. Most remarkable of all, he had believed that the future would always take care of itself; that mistakes had few consequences; that for him personally, everything was bound to turn out well in the end.

What would happen, considered Mori, if he came across his younger self now? Suppose that one night their eyes met in some smoky Shinjuku back alley. The younger Mori wasn't the type to accept any words of advice. He was sensitive to the mildest criticism, quick to anger, always convinced that his own ideas and emotions were of absolute importance. And he certainly wouldn't be prepared to listen to a middle-aged burnout with compromise etched into the lines of his face.

And anyway—what if Younger Mori did listen? Suppose he gave up radical politics, went back to his studies, and graduated, like 95 percent of his fellow students had done, even in those turbulent times. In that case, where would Older Mori be now? Probably working in an insurance company or one of the trading houses. At his age, he would be a section leader, with a team of smiling subordinates, a salary of around ten million yen a year, and a bottle of whiskey waiting for him in dozens of different bars in the Ginza. He would have a company badge, a company loan, and a company apartment, where his company wife would sit patiently waiting for his return from entertaining the company's clients on the company's expense account.

Mori stared at the grubby shapes on the ceiling. The whole idea was bizarre, no more credible than Ono's vision of the future. Perhaps his younger self wasn't such a stubborn fool after all. That kind of life wasn't for Mori, young or old. Never had been, never could be.

Mitchell slept badly, disturbed by a cat yowling somewhere, a couple of helicopters circling overhead, the wind rattling the window screens in their frames. Asleep or awake, his mind was skipping from image to bizarre image, channel surfing through the events of the evening.

There was the sun goddess up on the platform, pelvis jerking, long hair falling over her face. He reached to touch the smooth golden feet, but she slid away from him. Slowly he looked up past the curve of the hips, the heaviness of the breasts, the slender neck—to the face of

Yazawa, covered in shaving cream and glaring down at him with manic glee!

"The name's Terry Yazooer. Happy to meet you, Rickie-kun!"

Long crimson fingernails stretched down toward his face. Meanwhile, somewhere on the other side of the disco a phone was ringing. . . . Meanwhile, somewhere at the other end of the taxi line a phone was ringing. . . .

A phone was ringing! Mitchell leapt out of bed and snatched at the phone on his desk. The voice at the other end was warm and relaxed. It was a voice, thought Mitchell, that was redolent of large sums of money.

"Rick Mitchell? This is Murray Feinman of Midas Investments. You're expecting our call, right?"

"Yes. Yes, I am," said Mitchell, struggling to collect his thoughts. Rick! So now he was Rick!

"Your people in New York have given you quite a buildup. You know, Rick, they say you're the man with the hot hand over there. Actually, we just did a screening of all the recommendations you guys at Pearson's Tokyo have put out over the past six months. The results are phenomenal. At first, I thought there was a glitch in the calculations somewhere." 209

Mitchell took a deep breath. There was no mistake. It was just six months ago that Yasuda had taken over as head of research. Since then, he had been responsible for the timing and selection of every investment idea that the Tokyo office had produced.

"We're very interested in your new ideas, Rick, We've got Henry tuning in from his yacht. Like the rest of us, he's looking forward to hearing what you have to say."

A new voice came in, somewhat fainter and tinnier than Feinman's. "That is certainly correct. By philosophical approach, I consider myself woefully ill-equipped to understand the Japanese markets. The opportunity to listen to an analyst of such distinction is not to be lightly dismissed. Fire away, Mr. Mitchell!"

If Feinman had sounded relaxed, this new voice sounded as if its owner had never acknowledged the existence of time at all. Henry Lazarus's accent was British in the vowel sounds, with a clogging of the consonants that gave away his Central European background. To Mitchell, he sounded like an urbane, Oxford-educated relative of Count Dracula.

Mitchell grabbed the notebook from his bedside table and leafed through it to the notes he had made about Otaman. Balance-sheet ratios, compound growth in earnings, estimates of the breakup value of the company's assets—somehow he knew these things weren't going to be of any use at all. He let the notebook fall to the ground. Feinman's voice was buzzing in his ear. Mitchell made up his mind. He had no choice but to plunge forward.

"Well, gentlemen," he answered. "What I've got for you is a very special concept. The name of the company is Otaman. It's a medium-size trading house—pretty old, pretty dull. Recently, however, there's been a dramatic change in the company's orientation. First let me run you through the historical background, which is very important. It all goes back to a power struggle between two daimyos. . . ."

"You're fading on us a little there, Rick. A struggle between two whats?" That was Feinman again.

"Daimyos," said Mitchell, his eyes squeezed shut in concentration. "They were regional warlords back in the era before the Meiji Restoration."

"You mean the top bananas among the samurai," said Feinman.

"Not exactly," put in Lazarus. "According to my understanding, the daimyo's title was hereditary, whereas the samurai's function was merely professional. Still, that is by the way. Please continue."

"Indeed," said Mitchell nervously. "Now, let me take you back to the early part of the nineteenth century. . . ."

It was basically the story that Yazawa had given to the Scotsman, with a few additional points that Mitchell had gleaned from his visit. He presented no figures, no details of the company's investment plans, no projections of future earnings. He spoke without interruption for about five minutes. When he had finished, there was a brief pause, then came Feinman's smooth drawl.

"Can you put a little more flesh on the bones, there, Rick? What the company was doing way back when is good to know, but we're more interested in how it's going to look in five years' time. After all, we're investors, not antique collectors."

There was a ripple of laughter in the background. Bored and derisive, sensed Mitchell. He winced. Just as he had feared, they were going to pull him to pieces. "It's too early for that," he said, painfully aware of how thin his argument must have sounded. "Future prospects are extremely difficult to quantify at this stage."

"Difficult to quantify! You mean you haven't done any serious analysis of this company at all!"

Here it comes, thought Mitchell, wincing. "I've given you the situation as I see it," he said.

"You have, huh? In that case, I'd say you've been wasting our time in a pretty major way."

You couldn't miss the calculated brutality in Feinman's voice. Mitchell closed his eyes. Dan Rollings would hear about his humiliation tomorrow. Yazawa would cancel his contract. He would be back in his London bed-sit within the month.

"Just hold on there a moment! I don't know about you other fellows, but I found Mr. Mitchell's explanation rather intriguing!"

It was the courtly voice of Henry Lazarus, the East European accent a little stronger now. There was a moment of uncomfortable silence in which Mitchell could hear his own heart beating.

"Sure, it was intriguing," said Feinman eventually. "I'm not saying it wasn't intriguing, Henry!"

"Also potentially valuable," continued Lazarus. "Remember—in all human affairs, past is prologue. That's *The Tempest*, isn't it, Murray?"

"Say what, Henry?" Feinman sounded a lot less relaxed now.

"Shakespeare. You fellows would benefit greatly from a thorough study of Shakespeare. Coriolanus, Henry the Fifth, Lear—these are all prototypes of investment behavior. What about you, Mr. Mitchell? Do you ever find yourself afflicted by uncertainty, like Hamlet?"

"From time to time," answered Mitchell carefully.

"That is the nature of the human condition," said Lazarus. "Nothing in this world is certain. It is not even certain that things are uncertain, if you see what I mean."

"So what are you saying, Henry?" said Feinman. "Should we go with this Otaman thing or not?"

"In view of the extraordinary record of successes achieved by Mr. Mitchell and his colleagues, we should certainly give the idea our most serious consideration, don't you agree? Could you remind me of the size of the bond issue, Mr. Mitchell?"

"One hundred million dollars," said Mitchell quickly.

"That's a nice round number," said Lazarus. "We might be able to take half if the story looked sufficiently attractive. Of course, an investment of such significance would have to be studied rather carefully. That's where you come in, Murray. I want you to work with Mr. Mitchell over the next few days, ironing out the details. We'll reach a decision by the end of the week."

"Just like you say, Henry," said Feinman.

"Excellent! Thank you for taking the time to instruct us, Mr. Mitchell. By the way, are the cherry blossoms out in Tokyo yet?"

"Not yet," said Mitchell, glancing through the gap in the curtains. The sun was already glinting off the tops of the high buildings.

"I've always thought that the cherry blossom season in Japan is over-rated. Rather similar to the stock market, perhaps. Still, that is a matter I am content to leave to an expert such as yourself. Good-bye, Mr. Mitchell."

There was a click, and the phone went dead. Half-stunned by what had just happened, Mitchell sat there staring at it. He had managed to interest a single investor in half the entire Otaman bond issue! And who was the prospective buyer? It was Henry Lazarus himself! Just having the chance to talk to Lazarus was a never-to-be-forgotten event. In Mitchell's mind, the man was a semi-mythical figure, as remote from everyday life as the pope. Here was the man who had left Communist Czechoslovakia with nothing and built up the hottest investment fund in the world; the man who had made two billion dollars in one week of speculation against the European Monetary System; the man whose charitable foundations were channeling hundreds of millions of dollars into environmental research. He was a genius, a philosopher-pirate, the ultimate example of a financial dolphin, sleekly breasting the currents and tides of the world economy. Yet this same Henry Lazarus, speaking directly from his famous ecofriendly estate in Mexico, had expressed clear interest in Mitchell's views! The idea was too immense to absorb all at once.

Euphoria was replaced by depression as Mitchell's thoughts returned to Otaman. So far his inquiries into the Kawasaki project had drawn a blank. He still had no idea what made Yazawa so convinced the stock was a winner. In order to retain his credibility as an analyst, he would need to get to the bottom of all this. And with Henry Lazarus's people breathing down his neck, that would need to be sooner rather than later.

Outside, the city was gradually waking up. Mitchell heard the squeal of a newsboy's bicycle, the rumble of a distant train. He wandered into the kitchen and made himself a cup of coffee, then put on a pair of earphones and lay down on the sofa. Lulled by the sound of waves and rain, he floated—slowly, gently—over the edge of sleep.

———

After getting up at seven, Mori jogged a couple of kilometers to an old shrine set on a hill overlooking the neighborhood. As he did every Saturday morning, hangovers permitting, he sprinted up the fifty-five stone steps and then spent half an hour going through his karate routines under the big red shrine gate. As usual, the place was deserted. There was only a dirty old cat to hear his grunts of effort and observe the stiffness of his joints as he practiced his high kicks.

It took him longer to get his wind back these days. He sat under a stone lamp and rested for ten minutes, browsing through the morning newspaper that he had picked up on the way. When his heartbeat had returned to normal, Mori jogged back down the stone steps, then went to have a "morning set" of boiled egg and toast at a coffee bar. After that, he spent half an hour at a pachinko parlor thinking about nothing except the flow of the silver balls. Mori knew the machines in this parlor pretty well. Once in a while, the owner opened them up and adjusted the pins, but Mori soon got the hang of the new configuration. When he got up from the seat, he had accumulated enough balls to exchange for five packs of Mild Sevens.

213

At eleven o'clock Mori pulled the grimy plastic sheet off the Honda and drove over to Harajuku. There was heavy traffic for a Saturday. As he waited at the traffic lights on Meiji Street, clouds of exhaust fumes swirled around his shoulders like a cape. It looked as if rain was on the way. The sky was completely overcast. The only sign of spring was the warm wind that was gusting through the gaps between the buildings, tugging newspaper scraps from trash bins and sending empty cans bowling along the gutters.

It took Mori over an hour to make the twenty-mile ride. He stashed the motorbike behind a deserted gas station and went looking for Ono's recruiters. From what Togo had told him, he knew that they wouldn't be hard to find.

On weekends the area around Harajuku station is transformed into a teenage aquarium. On display are tame and colorful specimens of most of the species of youth culture that the closing decades of the twentieth century have produced—from rockabilly to Rasta, from cyberpunk to skinhead. The young ones gravitate to the place by instinct. They swim through the boutique-lined back streets, float into fast-food joints, nibble at the wares of the trinket sellers, cluster in schools around street musicians. They blend into the Harajuku scene like parrot fish and tangs blend into coral.

Mori pushed through the crowd, his eyes framing blond wigs, wash-off tattoos, fishnet tights, erect nipples under James Dean T-shirts, young smiles, young eyes, young life. There was no space, no stillness anywhere. The road was jam-packed with cars, the pavement with bodies, the buildings covered with words and images. A truckful of right-wingers was waiting at the crossroads, martial music blaring from loudspeakers at heavy-metal volume. The pigeons on the station roof were screeching like schoolgirls. A couple of TV crews were struggling through the crowd, cameras hoisted on leather-clad shoulders, mike booms lifted high. If Roppongi made Mori feel middle-aged, Harajuku made him feel a hundred years old.

He spotted a group of Ono's disciples at the entrance to Yoyogi Park. It wasn't difficult to recognize them. They were standing in front of a small van covered with posters of Ono and quotations from his works. One of them was carrying a placard emblazoned with the man's bearded features. A tape player had been set on a folding chair. It was playing a catchy popsong about love and happiness and fulfilling your dreams. The singer's bright, rather childish voice was annoyingly familiar. Yumi-chan, guessed Mori. A small crowd had gathered around the van. Mori stood a little way off and watched the performance.

According to what Mori had heard, most of the cults and new religions did their recruiting in pretty sneaky ways, often posing as market researchers or charity workers. Ono's people were different. They proclaimed their allegiance from the start. They didn't look like weirdos, either. There were no twitching eyes, no pockmarked faces. The girls were cute, full of enthusiasm and freshness. They looked you in the eye and smiled. The men bowed politely and talked in measured, reasonable tones. They might have been marketing perfume or sports goods. What impressed Mori most of all was their confidence. They weren't pushy. They seemed to take it for granted that people were interested in what they were saying. That, thought Mori, must be one of the keys to successful marketing—make the customers think that they need you more than you need them. It was a technique that in his own business Mori had never been able to master.

After a few minutes, Mori nudged his way toward the front of the crowd. Most of the listeners were in their twenties or early thirties, like the three disciples of Ono who were making the presentation. One of them, a short girl with bangs that almost covered her eyes, gave him a friendly smile. Clearly, their training had prepared them to deal with people of all sorts, even an ill-shaven middle-aged detective with cynicism written into the grain of his face.

The three disciples in turn fronted the presentation. While one was speaking, the other two would mime and gesticulate in the background, sometimes stepping forward to interject a question. The slick timing suggested many hours of hard practice. The content was nothing new to anyone acquainted with Ono's work. Still, when spoken by an attractive girl in her early twenties, rather than read from a paperback book in a grubby office, Ono's phrases had a mesmeric quality to them. "Cutting out the cancer of despair," "the collapse of corrupted postwar values," "purification by destruction," "spiritual reintegration," "radiating harmony over Asia"—outrageous ideas expressed with pleasant plausibility. Did the audience believe what they were being told? Mori glanced out of the corner of his eye. The people around him were all listening intently. No one was shaking his head or laughing. Ono's cocktail of Buddhism, New Age concepts, and Japanese nationalism seemed to be meeting a satisfactory consumer response.

The presentation lasted about ten minutes. Afterward, Yumi-chan's   215
volume was turned up and the three disciples distributed leaflets and badges to the crowd. Several people asked questions—"Why is Ono sensei so sure of what is going to happen?" "Will the big earthquake affect central Japan too?" "Is enlightenment possible for Americans and Europeans?" The responses were smooth. No doubt they had been given hundreds of times before.

When the girl with the bangs handed Mori a badge, he immediately pinned it to his lapel. "Ono sensei has many great thoughts," he said solemnly. "I will wear his badge with pride."

The girl stopped and smiled at him. Close up, she looked even smaller. The top of her head was hardly higher than his sternum.

"Help me become a member," said Mori urgently.

She looked at Mori so earnestly that he felt sorry for her.

"Will you tell me your name?" she said softly.

"Nakamura," said Mori without a moment's hesitation. He always felt comfortable with that name. There was something straightforward and dependable about it. Nakamura—four simple sounds meaning "middle of the village." In former times, Nakamura would have been a broad-backed peasant, the kind who could shoulder the portable shrine all day long in the village festival. Now, he was an industrial peasant, sweating for little reward in the heartlands of the Japanese economy. Back in his office, Mori had several boxes of Nakamura business cards—Nakamura the cement salesman, Nakamura the construction engineer, Nakamura the warehouse supervisor, and so on.

"You live in Tokyo?"

"Saitama Prefecture! For the last twenty years I have been working—"

"No time for that now, Nakamura-san!" she said, smiling. "Come with me afterwards and you will learn many important things!"

Including what had happened to Yuriko? It was possible. Mori felt more and more certain that the key to her fate lay somewhere within Ono's organization. Beaming with gratitude, he grabbed the girl's hand and squeezed it. "Many thanks, many thanks!"

She went through the crowd, smiling and swapping greetings as she handed out the pamphlets and badges. She looked naturally content, without a problem in the world. Could anything that made people happy be bad? That was a difficult philosophical question. Mori considered it for a moment. What sort of things made him happy? Winning at mahjong or pachinko or at the bicycle track. That cabaret girl from Kyushu with hips like a mongoose and a tongue like a feather. Cracking a difficult case, puzzling out the twists of circumstance and motive. Going out with some good friends, drinking the night away and forgetting about everything. Forgetting—yes, that had to be the key factor. Forgetting made you happy. Without it, the alcoholic drinks business wouldn't exist. And probably neither would Ono's.

"Are you ready now? Come on, let's go." It was the voice of the girl with the bangs, as fresh and enthusiastic as ever. Mori nodded sheepishly. She grabbed him by the sleeve and tugged him toward the van.

He wasn't alone. Half a dozen others from the crowd of listeners were waiting, ready with questions and entreaties. That was impressive. Ono was obviously having no trouble at all in recruiting new disciples.

They all climbed into the van, which nosed out into the gridlocked traffic and jerked and crawled its way to the Tokyo headquarters. Inside the van they were all asked to introduce themselves and explain their personal problems and what they expected to learn from Ono. Five of Mori's fellow recruits were women. Two were students at colleges that Mori had never heard of, two were office girls, and one was a housewife. The sixth, the only other male, was a man in his late twenties who said he was an unemployed taxi driver.

Mori listened carefully as they recounted their woes. In every case but one, the problems they described were vague and abstract—"being unable to talk to people anymore," "feeling lost and exhausted," "isolated and confused." The exception was the housewife. Her complaints were real complaints, uttered with real feeling. She disliked her husband, loathed his parents, distrusted the neighbors, and was having a running feud with the teachers at her son's kindergarten. The girl with the bangs glanced meaningfully at the disciple who was sitting opposite her in the back of the van. They were both smiling their usual euphoric smiles, but Mori could sense that they didn't approve. In Mori's opinion, the housewife would soon find that the invisible gate was mysteriously barred.

"How about you, Nakamura-san? Now it's your turn to share your problems."

The girl with the bangs was looking him straight in the eye, an encouraging smile on her face.

"Share my problems . . . But it's so difficult . . . I don't know . . ." Mori mumbled, staring at the floor of the van. He sucked air through his teeth, shook his head, and lapsed into sullen silence.

"Come on," said the girl gently. "This is a new beginning for you. Relax and speak your troubles, then your mind will become like clear water."

"But I'm not even sure what the matter is. I have these feelings . . . confusion, heaviness . . ." Mori spoke in a dull, hesitant voice, his eyes trained on the girl's feet. "So much is happening in the world, so many things I don't understand. It's like being in a foreign country, where you don't speak the language, don't have any friends, don't know where to go or what to do."

"A foreign country," said the girl approvingly. "You're right. These days, Japan is a foreign country, even for the Japanese."

Mori nodded somberly. "Sometimes I wake up in the morning and I don't remember anything anymore. I've forgotten my own address, my age, my job, where I was born, everything."

"You forget these things because they are not important. The only thing that matters is developing your inner light so that it will shine like a beacon and give encouragement to others."

"Together, a hundred million beacons will shine like a mighty sun!"

"You remember well!" said the girl delightedly. "Those are the exact words of the sensei. Now please tell us more about yourself, Nakamura-san. If we know about your background, we will know something about the source of your confusion."

"Yes, of course," sighed Mori. "Though it is embarrassing for me to say these thing—"

"Don't worry. Drain away the muddy water, and what remains will be clear."

Mori turned his eyes to the floor again and embarked on a long, stumbling self-description. The Nakamura that he sketched was a sad case indeed. The small machinery company that he had been working for since high school had made him redundant last year. It had been a shattering experience. For several weeks afterward, he put on his suit every morning and left home at seven-thirty, pretending to everyone, including himself, that nothing had happened. He would sit for hours on park benches or in coffee bars, spend sunny afternoons wandering around department stores. Then Nakamura's wife called his office one day and found out the truth. The next week, she moved back to her parents' place, full of angry complaints. Meanwhile, his eldest son had dropped out of high school to join a motorbike gang, and his sixteen-year-old daughter had been picked up by the police for sniffing glue. On top of everything else, there was a stress fracture in his back, which made it hard for him to sleep without tranquilizers. The neighbors thought he was going crazy. His children despised him. He couldn't help it, but recently he had started looking forward to dying. . . .

All this Mori recounted in a mumbling monotone. He had prepared the story in advance, but as detail mounted on depressing detail, he found it satisfyingly convincing. He was even moved himself. Nakamura had relied on fate to see him through, and fate had betrayed him. He was so passive, so uncomprehending. There was no hope for the guy, none whatsoever.

When he had finished, the girl with the bangs gazed at him, her eyes shining. "That was very good," she said, radiating the pleasure a teacher shows to a favorite pupil. "You should have no trouble with the tests, I think."

"Thank you for your help," said Mori, ducking his head in a gesture of modest gratitude. The eyes of the other six potential cult members were boring into him. Mori looked away, smug in the knowledge that his performance had totally eclipsed them.

It wasn't long before they arrived at the complex of squat concrete buildings that housed the cult's Tokyo headquarters. There were half a dozen similar vans parked in the center of the courtyard, the vacuous cheeriness of one of Yumi-chan's pop songs spilling from one of the loudspeakers. In the flat gray desert of the courtyard, where nothing moved except for the security cameras, the music had a disembodied, slightly sinister tone.

The three disciples ushered them out of the van and into a smaller courtyard, also gray and empty. They marched in silence toward the entrance of a large building at the back of the complex, the girl with the bangs leading the way. There was an arch in the low wall on the far side of the courtyard. Turning and bending slightly, Mori peered through it. On the other side was some sort of parking area. He was just able to make out several radiator grilles, all the same tall dignified shape, familiar from movies rather than the streets of Tokyo. Rolls-Royces—at least three of them nestling in the shadows.

One of the male disciples noticed Mori peering through the archway. The smile faded from his face like the image from a switched-off TV screen. "That is a private area," he said. "Do not look there. You must keep looking straight in front."

So here they were, valuable potential recruits visiting the Tokyo headquarters for the first time, and they were being ordered not to turn their heads. So how would the full members be treated in those secret "training sessions"? Mori recalled a section from Ono's book about "enlightenment through obedience" and "making incorrect thoughts dissolve like ice in hot tea." He sensed that beneath all the smiles and the pop songs, there was a disciplinary regime that would make the average karate practice look like a picnic under the cherry blossoms.

At the entrance to the building, the girl with the bangs used the remote-control device to open the outer door. They stepped into a small anteroom with another security camera a few feet above a small control panel set in the wall. The lens rotated toward them like the barrel of a gun. The girl raised a hand to wave at it. With her cute smile and one hundred and fifty centimeters of height, she might have been waving to her teddy bear.

"Requesting permission to enter," she said into the microphone grille in the center of the control panel.

"Please input your identification number," came the polite, elder-sister voice of the central security system. Mori watched as the girl's fingers pushed a series of buttons on the control panel. Four digits, with a slight pause after the first two. People usually didn't have much originality when it came to thinking up these secret numbers. Mori was willing to bet that she was born on the fifth of February, or possibly the second of May, in 1973. You could never be quite sure of the order of month and day.

"Input completed," she said cheerfully.

"Permission to enter approved," replied the smooth synthetic voice. The inner door slid open and they passed through to the large hall inside.

The first thing that Mori noticed was Ono standing in the middle of the hall wearing a long white robe and raising his hand above his head in a gesture of welcome. Even from thirty meters away, Mori could see that the man's complexion was a strange purple-pink, the same color he had once seen on the face of a construction ministry official dangling from a light fixture in an Osaka love hotel. Almost in slow motion, Ono's hand dropped to his side. His mouth dropped open, revealing shimmering white teeth, and his lips spread into a huge parody of a smile. The girl with the bangs signaled for them all to stop, and the three disciples made deep bows in the sensei's direction, their foreheads almost parallel with the floor. Ono nodded stiffly and his head inclined in a small bow of acknowledgment. Then he raised his hand above his head again, took a step backward, turned sideways, and disappeared. The three disciples lifted their heads and motioned their seven guests toward the elevator as if

nothing had happened. But the recruits stood rooted to the spot, openmouthed with amazement.

"Ono sensei," breathed the taxi driver. "He must be the possessor of superhuman abilities."

"The sensei is a miracle-maker," said one of the students. "A true brother of Buddha and Jesus."

Mori gazed at the spot where Ono had been standing. He could just make out the faint glint of glass. "Excellent technology," he muttered respectfully to the girl with the bangs. "That is the most realistic holograph I have seen in my life. The designer must be a man of high skills."

The girl looked at him keenly. "You are right," she said. "It is a work of genius. The designer was Ono sensei himself."

"Really! The sensei is a man of many talents."

"That goes without saying," cut in the disciple who had reprimanded Mori for looking at the Rolls-Royces. "But you sound quite knowledgeable about such complicated technologies, Nakamura-san. Please tell us—where did you obtain this information?"

He was staring Mori straight in the eye, his arms crossed in front of his chest. It was a powerful stare, hard to look into, hard to look away from. Mori felt like a schoolboy being quizzed about cheating on a test.

"Well . . . at my company . . ." he muttered. "That is, the company I used to work for—we used to supply equipment to one of the big electronic makers. I visited their research center several times in those days—"

"So what products were you selling?" asked the disciple, his stare not wavering from Mori's face.

"We were only a small company," said Mori apologetically. "We didn't have so many products . . . just some simple ones for specialist usage in laboratories and so on."

"What kind of products?" snapped the disciple.

"Mostly engineering plastics," said Mori. "Supertensile laminates; pressure-resistant, shape-retentive moldings; reinforced styrene monomer substrates—that sort of thing."

The disciple gazed at him blankly.

"Our products may not have had a large market scale," said Mori. "But their reputation for reliability is very high. If the sensei ever requires any supertensile laminates or reinforced styrene substrates, I still have my contacts at the company. I can still do my best—"

"Not necessary," cut in the disciple. "The sensei is a religious leader, not a laboratory technician! Please speak of him with more respect. Now stop chattering, all of you. We must hurry."

"Understood!" came the collective answer. The girl with the bangs led the way into the elevator, and the doors closed behind them.

There were certain people in this world, thought Mori, whom you only had to address in a certain tone of voice and they would obey without question. They had a deep desire to be told what to do. He seemed to be with half a dozen examples of this type right now. Then there were others who had a deep desire to do the telling. Put the two types together and what did you have? You had a religious cult that was spreading like a new virus. Come to think of it, you also had schoolyard bullying, politics, big business, bureaucracy, the Gendai Giants, and everything else.

They got out on the third floor and were led into a large hall. The lights clicked on automatically as they stepped inside, illuminating several rows of white stone benches, an array of wooden masks on the wall, and, at the other end of the room, a thick-trunked mandarin-orange tree with clusters of mandarins hanging from its leafy branches.

"The sensei's skills are amazing," said the taxi driver, pointing at the tree. "That looks almost real."

"It does, doesn't it?" said one of the students. "Those oranges look so delicious."

"They are delicious," said the girl with the bangs with a smile. She walked over to the tree, reached up into one of the branches, and plucked out an orange. She peeled it as she walked back, handing a slice to each one of the visitors. The housewife stared at the segment of orange lying flat on her palm as if she expected it to disappear at any moment. Finally she lifted it to her mouth and took a tentative bite.

"Hydroponic cultivation," said the disciple who had questioned Mori before. "Do you have any idea how that is done, Nakamura-san?"

"None at all," answered Mori truthfully.

"So you don't know everything after all! Well, it's done by a regulated flow of nutrients that are fed directly into the roots of the tree. You can't see anything, of course. There's a special chamber sunk into the floor."

"Amazing," said Mori, shaking his head with admiration. "Did the sensei develop this technology himself too?"

"Yes, he did. Not on his own, of course. There are several research groups working under him. Each has a different subject assigned to it."

"You people are really advanced, aren't you? It's very impressive."

"It is necessary for us to understand many scientific fields," said the girl brightly. "Everything has to be ready in time, you see."

"Does it?" said Mori without thinking. "Ready in time for what?"

"For the great purification, of course," said the girl. "It should happen within the next seven years, you know. We must be fully prepared to seize the opportunity that fate will deliver to us."

She spoke in a calm, matter-of-fact voice, as if she were describing what she was planning to have for dinner. Mori tugged the lobe of his ear. She was looking at him, expecting a response, and none came to mind.

"You're right," he said finally. "Good preparation is vital in all types of business. Good preparation gets you nine-tenths of the way to success. That's what the president of our company always used to say, and he was a very smart man."

The male disciple frowned. "What your president said is irrelevant!" he exclaimed with obvious distaste. "The sensei is steadfastly planning for the major turning point in the development of human consciousness! Please do not mention him in the same breath as the owner of some back-street sweatshop! Understood?"

"Understood," muttered Mori sheepishly.

The disciple gave a grunt of approval, then left the room through the door they had come in by. Mori caught the girl looking at him. He gave the quiver of a smile. She wrinkled her nose in an expression between amusement and annoyance that he found unexpectedly alluring. She was, if he was right about her birthday, just at the age when she should be finishing up at college. What could have happened to turn her into an unquestioning follower of the sensei? Mori followed her with his eyes as she walked toward a door at the far end of the room. The slender legs, the tanned arms, the roll of her buttocks as she walked—from the back, she looked like the kind of girl you see window-shopping in Shibuya, a smooth-cheeked, floppy-haired young boyfriend hanging onto her shoulder.

The remaining male disciple instructed them to wait silently until their names were called, then took up a soldierly stance half a dozen yards in front of the bench. Hands clasped behind his back, without a quiver of the facial muscles, he was scrutinizing them all closely in turn.

The first to be called was the housewife who had eaten the mandarin orange. The others watched expectantly as she followed the girl with the bangs to the door at the end of the room. She reappeared ten minutes later, looking slightly flushed. She smiled brightly at no one in particular, bowed at the male disciple, who reacted not at all, and left the hall without saying a word. Mori had a strong suspicion that she wouldn't be coming back.

One by one, the others followed. The expressions on their faces when they emerged gave Mori a good idea of how they had fared. The taxi driver looked confused. The two office girls both looked lost in thought. They had all passed, guessed Mori. They were already thinking ahead to the next stage. One of the students came out looking calm and serious; the other walked quickly, with a fixed smile and her eyes on the ground. The principle there was quite simple. The one with bad news was disguising it because she was ashamed. The one with good news was disguising it not to excite jealousy.

Finally, it was Mori's turn. He crossed the hall into a small room equipped like an office, with desks, filing cabinets, and a personal computer. Again, Mori was struck by how quiet the place was. There seemed to be no one else around. The girl was sitting at a desk waiting for him. She seemed to have guessed what he was thinking.

"Not many people are here today," she said. "Everyone is cleaning up after the annual festival in the Nippon Dome."

The Nippon Dome was the home of the Gendai Giants baseball team. Mori had never been there in his life. "Annual festival? What happens there?"

"It is the celebration of our togetherness with the sensei. We conduct such a ceremony every year, just before cherry-blossom time. There were many songs and dances, many weddings too. Thanks to the sensei, much happiness was created."

"If I had been there, maybe I would have been able to get married, too," said Mori wistfully.

"You might," said the girl with a laugh. "That would have depended on whether you were chosen or not."

"Chosen by whom? Some kind lady like you?"

"Chosen by the sensei, of course. It is the sensei who leads us all to our happiness. Everything else is human selfishness, isn't it?"

"I suppose so," said Mori, meeting her simple, steady gaze. "All the same, I would not be disappointed if the sensei provided someone like you."

She looked at him and wrinkled her nose again in that cute way. "I don't think we're the same type," she said archly.

"We should be," said Mori. "After all, we're both Aquarians!"

It was a gamble, but he felt pretty confident in the outcome. She had to be either Aquarius or Taurus.

"You're an Aquarian, too? That's a big coincidence, isn't it? But, wait a moment—how did you know?"

"I could sense it when we first met," said Mori, pressing home his advantage. "There is some strange connection between us; don't you feel it?"

"Well, I don't know," she said, faltering. "It's possible—I feel something, I think."

"Yes, it's certain," said Mori, holding out his hands in front of his chest. "I can feel it. The waves of your *ki* force have almost the same frequency as mine. There is no difference at all!"

"You have the power to feel these things?"

"Don't say anything more! Stay absolutely still!" Mori got up from his chair and placed the palm of his hand on top of her head, then breathed deeply in and out a couple of times. "No question about it," he said finally. "The frequency is absolutely the same. That means that we must have been born on exactly the same day."

"The same day? That would be amazing!" Her eyes were glowing with interest. "But can we be sure? You must tell me—when is your birthday, exactly?"

"The fifth of February," said Mori without a second's hesitation.

The girl sat up straight in her chair, her eyes wide. "You were right!"

she said. "Our *ki* forces are matched like brother and sister. I thought I could feel something unusual when we first met back in Harajuku. There was something different about you from all the others who come to listen to us."

"I suppose you have had the honor of meeting the sensei many times face to face," probed Mori.

"Not many times. Just three, actually. The most recent time was last week, when he visited our office here." She was smiling a radiant smile. The memory was obviously still fresh in her mind.

"Did you have the chance to have some conversation with him?"

"Conversation?" The girl looked shocked. "The sensei does not have conversations with people—certainly not with a low-level instructor like me. But he did notice me, I am sure of that."

"How do you know?" asked Mori.

The girl gave a little frown of determination. "That's a secret. I'm not supposed to tell anyone!"

But what's the point of having a secret if no one knows about it? She was bursting to tell someone, that was obvious.

"Any secrets relating to the sensei must be guarded closely," said Mori. "You should keep them locked up in your heart. But remember—we have exactly the same frequency of *ki* force. That means we are closer than brother and sister. You can tell me anything and I swear that no one else will ever know."

"Do you promise me?"

"Of course! I promise on my life."

Her eyes were shining like rock pools in the sunshine. She was so naive, so easy to deceive. Something must have gone wrong with her education, reflected Mori. She hadn't learned that the world is full of deceivers and cheats. Such as Ono and his type. Such as Mori himself. This time, though, Mori wasn't actually lying. He had no intention of passing her secret on to anybody.

"All right, then, I'll tell you." She leaned forward across the desk, her voice dropping to an excited whisper. "The news I received last week is the best news of my life. The sensei has chosen me to become one of the Sisters of Light. That means I will have the honor of devoting my life to his comfort."

"Really," breathed Mori. "That really is great news. When do you start?"

"Special training starts this weekend in our headquarters. I must go there secretly, without telling anyone. Not my parents, not my friends, not even my colleagues here in this branch office."

"Don't worry," whispered Mori back across the table. "This information is safe with me. By the way, how many other girls have become Sisters of Light?"

"I don't know. Not many, I think. It is a great honor to serve the sensei directly. Only the most loyal and sincere girls are chosen."

Meaning only the most compliant and credulous girls. Did that include Yuriko? It was at least possible. "What about from members recruited from this branch? Are you the only one to be chosen, or were there any others this year?"

The girl's face clouded over. "These things are secret. We are told in private by the senior disciples. No one else should know what is happening."

"But there must be rumors. Girls who suddenly disappear from their normal positions—what do people say about them?"

"Yes, there are rumors," said the girl, her brow furrowing at the thought. "Some girls are jealous, you see. They cannot bear the thought of others having the honor of serving the sensei. I hate such talk. I never listen to any rumors, whatever they may be saying."

"Did you hear any rumors earlier this year?"

"Maybe there were rumors," she said abstractedly. "One girl who was recruited last year. She was already a junior instructor."

"And she became a Sister of Light?"

"She left us suddenly, without saying a word. That was unusual. So some of the other girls started talking. They were jealous of her good fortune, I think."

"Were you a friend of Yuriko's?"

Mori had to try, but as the words left his mouth he knew he was going too far. Suddenly, she was staring at him with a confused expression on her face.

"How did you know her name? Are you related to this girl in some way?"

Mori beat a hasty retreat. "Related to her? Of course not! The only Sister of Light I know is you!"

"Hush! Do not say such things! Nothing is decided yet. There is special training, and then an interview by the sensei himself! Only if everything goes perfectly will I qualify."

Mori gazed at her flushed face. "You'll qualify," he said gently. "I can sense it for sure."

That was the truth. The legs, the breasts, the fresh smile, the eager eyes, the simplicity, the intense urge to believe—Mori reckoned she had everything that Ono would be looking for.

"Now let us finish this talk," he went on. "As we agreed, we will never mention the subject again. It will be a secret just between you and me. So do your best, and be careful."

"Careful?" She looked puzzled. "Careful about what?"

Mori stared at her in silent exasperation. Be careful of the dangerous lunatic that you call sensei; be careful that you don't end up with your lungs full of the greasy water of Tokyo Bay; be careful not to believe all the lies and nonsense that people foist on you—that's what Mori wanted to say. If he had, it might have made him feel better, but it wouldn't have had any effect. That was obvious. So he changed the subject instead.

"By the way, you haven't told me your name yet," he said.

"My name?" said the girl, frowning slightly. "We don't usually give our names to nonmembers. The sensei instructs us that unnecessary personal entanglements always start from trivial exchanges."

True enough, thought Mori. At least, that had been the entire basis of the approach to women that he had developed in his university years. The idea was that perseverance was always rewarded. If your hit ratio was one in thirty, then you had to be prepared to make thirty pickup attempts. If it was only one in sixty, you could get the same result, but twice the effort would be required. It was always arithmetically possible to be successful. The problem Mori had these days was that his hit ratio had fallen so drastically that in order to be sure of success he would have had to spend all his time doing nothing else.

"Unnecessary personal entanglements," repeated Mori thoughtfully. "Yes, I can understand that. Still, it's strange, isn't it? I mean, we share the same *ki* force, but I don't even know what to call you!"

She looked him straight in the eye, then nodded. "My name is Miki," she said in a quiet voice. "It's written with the characters for 'beautiful' and 'tree.' "

Mori was ready for that one. "Another amazing coincidence," he said. "My own given name is Yoshio, and it is written with that same character for 'beauty.' "

"Really!" she said, startled again. "We seem to have a lot in common, don't we!"

"Probably more than we'll ever know," said Mori.

They stared at each other in silence for half a minute. "Well, then," she said finally, glancing at the clock on the wall. "Let's get back to the reason that you are here. You are supposed to take the test to see if you are properly attuned to the sensei's thinking."

"Ah, the test!"

"It shouldn't be difficult. Not for someone with a strong *ki* force like you!"

"I will try my best," said Mori, making a modest little bow.

Miki tapped a few commands into the laptop computer, then registered his name and age. As she had said, the questions that she read off the screen weren't exactly difficult. There were a dozen of them—all highly abstract, all relating to the subject's attitude toward life, happiness, and the sensei. Mori carefully molded his answers to suggest the maximum self-pity, feebleness of spirit, and confusion. After every answer, the girl gave a little grunt that might have been of either approval or disappointment and tapped away at the keyboard. What sort of comments was she inputing? Unfortunately, the screen was tilted in such a way that he couldn't see.

"How do you expect the sensei to help you?" was the final question. Mori didn't hesitate.

"I have no expectations, just hopes," he muttered. "I want the sensei to carry on his plans for Japan and Asia. Just to be alive at the same time as the sensei is a big enough reward."

He watched her response. Was that overdoing the self-abasement? No, evidently not. Miki nodded to herself and gave another little grunt.

"Are you ready for the results?" she said, finally raising her eyes from the small liquid-crystal screen. "The computer has already calculated the score."

"So quickly?" Mori was starting to feel edgy. He had an instinctive dislike of exams that went back to his junior high school days.

"It's instantaneous. Our information technology research group created the program specially. Of course, a little bit depends on what categories the instructor sorts the responses into."

She gave Mori a reassuring smile. She knows I'm going to pass, he realized in a flash. She probably graded my answers in a way that makes it impossible to fail.

The laptop gave a long, drawn-out beep. "Congratulations," said Miki warmly. "You've passed with excellent marks—one full standard deviation above the average!"

Despite himself, Mori couldn't help feeling rather proud. "Does that mean I'm now an official member, just like all the others?"

"Yes, it does. I'll make out a membership card for you right away. From now on, you are eligible to participate in all our activities, including the special training sessions run by the sensei himself."

Mori pricked up his ears. There would be no better way than the special training course to view Ono from close range, perhaps to talk to some of the higher-ranking disciples. "Ah—that would be a big benefit to me, I think. When and where is the next one of these special training courses?"

Miki laughed, her nose wrinkling in an expression that made her look like a fifteen-year-old. "You are keen, aren't you!" she said, switching off the laptop. "As a matter of fact, the next one begins on Tuesday. It's only a short, two-day session, but it would be very unusual for someone who has just joined us to attend."

"Really," said Mori, disappointed. "Why is that?"

"Special training is very intensive, you see. Most people have several weeks of study and preparation here at the Tokyo headquarters before going."

Mori pushed out his lower lip. "This is a great shame," he said, casting his eyes down to the table. "Seeing the sensei face to face, listening to his teachings—that would make such a big difference to my life. I'm sure that all my confusions would disappear like—like an ice cube in a cup of hot tea."

Miki nodded gravely. "The sensei has that effect on many people," she said. "You will have another chance—probably in the early autumn."

"The autumn is so far away," said Mori plaintively. "I am not young anymore, you know. My health is not what it used to be."

She looked at him in silence for a moment, then gave a sigh of defeat. "All right," she said. "I'll put your name into the list of applicants. But turn up as early as you can. There may not be room for everyone." She switched the laptop computer on again and tapped in more commands.

"And where is the special training session going to take place?" pressed Mori. "Will it take many hours to get there?"

Miki shook her head. "Unnecessary questions," she said. "Do not discuss such matters with anyone, either before or afterwards. Leave everything to the wisdom of the sensei."

"Understood! I'm just excited to have passed the test. This is one of the best days of my life."

That brought the smile back to her face. "As soon as I saw you, I knew you were going to pass," she said, her fingers tapping at the little keyboard. "My *ki* force could sense it immediately."

Which controls which—does the *ki* force control the person, or does the person control the *ki* force? That was a question that Mori was still pondering five minutes later when Miki led him across the courtyard, down a narrow passageway, and out onto a bustling Ochanomizu side street.

After she had used her security card to open the gate, Mori turned and faced her. For a moment, the two of them stared at each other. After the silence inside the complex, the sounds of everyday life on the street outside—the motorbikes, the chiming traffic lights, the animated voices of the passers-by—seemed unnaturally loud, like a movie soundtrack in a cheap cinema.

"Take care of yourself," said Mori suddenly. "Bad things can happen, you know."

"Bad things?" said Miki, frowning. "How can that be? From now on, I am under the direct care of the sensei!"

"That's exactly why you've got to be on your guard."

"What do you mean by that?" She looked angry. Mori knew he should walk out of the open gate and disappear into the crowd, but for some reason he just stood there gazing at her. How could someone be so nice and so dumb at the same time?

"What do you mean?" she repeated, hands on hips. "These words of yours need explanation, I think!"

"Listen to me," he said, grabbing her by the wrist. "The best thing for you is to forget all this. Forget the sensei. Forget the Sisters of Light. There are bad things going on. They'll deceive you. They might even hurt you."

"Hurt me!" She looked stunned by the idea, then outraged. Mori plunged on regardless, speaking in a low rapid voice.

"Don't go to the headquarters. Go home to your parents. This is good advice I'm giving you."

"My parents!" she squealed angrily, pulling away from him. "Are you joking! I haven't seen my parents for years. They understand nothing! Why are you saying such stupid things!"

It was hopeless. He shouldn't have said anything in the first place. He let go of her wrist and stood back, hands on his hips. "All right," he said. "You know best. Forget everything I said. But just take care of yourself, do you understand? Don't believe everyone is as nice and kind as you are, because they're not."

Miki looked at him, bemused. "Saying such bad things about us— you're not the right kind of person at all! I should go back at once and change your test result to 'failure.' "

"But you won't, will you?"

"No, I won't, because I believe that you're a kind man. That's what I thought when I spoke to you for the first time in the park. You are a kind man, aren't you?"

Mori reflected on that one for a moment. "I suppose so," he said finally. "Compared to the average, anyway."

"In that case, you'd better take care of yourself, And no more bad words! Just this once I'll pretend I heard nothing."

She slammed the gate shut and ran back up the passageway. Mori sighed a sigh for both of them as he stepped out onto the pavement. Miki wouldn't change. He wouldn't change either. You couldn't force people from what they were to what you wanted them to be—not your friends, not your women, not yourself. He had seen enough to know that, so why did he always find it so hard to accept? Cursing his own stubbornness, Mori slipped into the stream of Saturday afternoon shoppers.

TWELVE

Shortly after dawn one Sunday morning in late March, a white Mercedes with darkened windows eased out of a hotel parking lot in central Tokyo, negotiated the tangle of overpasses and tunnels at the city's core, then sped along the northbound expressway.

The sun was slanting through layers of orange cloud strung across the eastern sky. The roads were almost empty; just a few long-distance trucks that had been thundering through the night and some taxis on the way home. Silent in the back seat of the Mercedes sat a man wearing a white silk shirt open at the neck, white slacks and loafers, and a pair of sunglasses so dark that they seemed to swallow the light of the new day. On his knees rested a notebook computer with the liquid-crystal screen raised ready for operation. The screen, however, was blank except for the blinking of the cursor. Behind the black lenses of the sunglasses, the man's pink and lashless eyes were focused on the cityscape scrolling past the car window.

Snowbird couldn't help but feel frustrated. Here was a superb dawn, just a few days before the cherry blossoms were due to appear, with the outline of Mount Fuji clear and huge even from a distance of three hundred miles—it was a scene that should have inspired him to add several more haiku to the long sequence that he had been working on for over a year. But nothing came—his creative urge was completely blocked. In fact, for the past couple of months he had been finding it more and more difficult to write, which was a strange and unsettling experience for a poet once criticized for facile and shallow over-prolificness. That was a fault that Snowbird had long recognized in himself, and sought to remedy by limiting his creative efforts to moments when the conditions were absolutely right. Now was such a moment, but all that came to mind was trite and clumsy, the sort of stuff that Snowbird himself would have dismissed with a sneer if he came across it in some local newspaper. Once again, the magic syllables—the ones that immediately looked and sounded and felt absolutely right—refused to form in his head.

The cause of the problem was obvious—the persistent nervous tension that felt like a huge knot tightening in the depths of his chest. To capture in words the beautiful uniqueness of the moment, it was essential to be perfectly relaxed, at peace with yourself and with the universe. Snowbird did not follow a strict Zen approach to haiku writing, but he had always been able to prepare his spirit for the moment of creation, regardless of the circumstances. One of his best efforts, a sequence of four linked haiku that had been widely praised in a top-grade literary magazine, had been composed lying prone on a rooftop squinting down the sights of a rifle. The young Snowbird had lain there in the dark for three hours, waiting for the right man to appear at the right window. The autumn moon big in the sky, the warm wind stroking the hairs on the back of his hand, the chirrup of the insects in the trees—it was all still fresh in his mind.

Snowbird switched off the little computer and flipped down the lid. The farther north the Mercedes traveled, the tighter grew the knot in his chest. It would be futile to resist, now that they were drawing ever closer to the source of Snowbird's nervous tension.

What was it about Ono that disturbed him so much? The man was half-mad, probably more than half, but that wasn't it. Snowbird had worked with crazy people before. It hadn't bothered him. In fact, for many of the jobs he had organized, normality would have been a disqualification. And Ono was harmless enough on the surface. He wasn't given to violent tantrums. He didn't try to lie and cheat his way out of obligations. He didn't treat Snowbird's professional reputation as some sort of personal challenge. No question about it, he was an intelligent, highly educated man. On a good day, it was possible to have a conversation with him about screen paintings of the Kamakura period, or Schopenhauer. But those good days were few and far between. Most of the time Snowbird had to endure disjointed harangues about the twenty-first century or watch bizarre fits of "mind opening," when Ono would writhe about on the floor, his head bouncing from side to side, his tongue lolling from his mouth. One such fit had occurred in the middle of an important business meeting to which Snowbird had brought some high-level contacts from west Japan. Kansai yakuza tended to be of a conservative disposition. The three senior officers of the Yoshimoto Alliance reacted with astonishment when Ono suddenly called for a special rug to be brought into the meeting room and then spent ten minutes floundering about on it like a dying carp. The deal that Snowbird had been planning made no further progress.

The problem was that Ono couldn't be controlled. How could you frighten a man who genuinely believed that he was a god? That was something for which Snowbird hadn't been prepared. It had come as quite a shock. When he had first heard about Ono, he had assumed that the man was a sharp operator, the kind who might have been a successful real estate developer or show business tycoon. Other new-religion people whom Snowbird had done business with had fallen into that category. Snowbird hadn't liked or trusted any of them, but he had respected their special acumen, their unfailing instinct for human weakness. And in every case he had been totally confident of his ability to impose his will on them. As soon as he met Ono, Snowbird knew that he was moving into different territory. He clearly remembered the first words that Ono spoke to him.

"For a man so familiar with death, you are strangely afraid of dying. Why is this?"

Not "I look forward to cooperating with you," or "Sincere gratitude for your presence today." Instead, words of death, spoken with utter tranquility while those unblinking eyes—the wide pupils like mineshafts to the center of the earth—held him tight in their gaze.

"I'm no different from anyone else, sensei. Isn't it said that the deepest desire of all creatures is to persist in their own being?"

"Aristotle made some such comment, but as you know there are many serious flaws in his thinking."

"The idea makes sense to me. It is a question of instinct, not bravery—the same for human beings as for animals or insects. Aren't you also afraid of dying, sensei?"

Ono gazed at him in silence for a moment, those large eyes empty of emotion. When he spoke, it was in a murmur so soft that it seemed to be massaging the words. "I was once, a very long time ago. It was the first time."

"The first time?"

"The first time to die. It was a murder carried out by a professional, someone much like you. He was a soldier in the personal guard of my brother, the pharoah. Until then, I had thought he was my friend."

The pharoah? Snowbird opened his mouth to speak, but no words came to mind, so he closed it again.

"He cut my throat while I was bathing," Ono went on dreamily. "Then he pushed me down under the water, and I watched the blood swirling away from me like a scarf in the wind. Can you imagine the terror as I realized what was happening?"

235

Snowbird nodded dumbly. The image was so vivid, he could imagine the whole scene. Ono's speech entranced him, took him further into the story.

"I put my hand to my throat, but the blood was unstoppable. His arms were so strong, squeezing and pulling me down . . . It was then that I knew that I was going to die and I was scared. I kicked and twisted and cursed both my brother and the man who was holding me. But it was no good. My mouth just filled with hot water and blood. That salt taste is unforgettable, no matter how many centuries pass. Think of it—the taste of your own blood as you struggle for life!"

Snowbird swallowed dryly. There was a tang of salt in his own mouth. Ono closed his eyes and took a deep breath. After a pause, he resumed his story.

"I carried on struggling until all the water in the bath was red. Then my strength left me and there was a rushing sound in my ears. I knew there was no point in being scared anymore, and I relaxed every muscle in my body."

Normally, Snowbird would have laughed at a story of that kind, but there was something about the way that Ono spoke that sent a shiver down his spine. "It sounds like an unpleasant way to die," he commented.

"Yes, it was. And I sense that it could have been you who was the murderer. After all, you are a man who has cut throats many times."

Snowbird didn't like that.

"That's rather unlikely, isn't it? I mean, it would be a strange coincidence for the same two people to come across each other in different lives, wouldn't it?"

Ono smiled serenely, his eyes still closed. "Not at all," he said. "There are strong connections between people that can stretch through the eons. Patterns can repeat themselves over and over again, until they are finally resolved. In your case, you have certainly committed many murders, and always for reward. Never through jealousy or anger. This karma is so powerful that it will not change in lives to come."

"Lives to come? You believe that you know my future lives too?" This time he couldn't keep the incredulity out of his voice.

"I do not know exactly, of course," replied Ono. "That would be impossible. But I sense a pattern powerful enough to bring us together again and again—in past, present, and future. Many times you are filled with the desire to murder me. Once or twice you even succeed, but many times you fail."

Snowbird smiled his flapping wound of a smile. "Fail? That would be most unusual, sensei. I am a very careful planner."

"You fail because you are frightened. Over the eons, you kill many times, but many times you are killed. Yes, in every life so far, you have died with screams on your lips."

Ono suddenly opened his eyes and gave a little gurgle of laughter. It was all nonsense, of course, no more than the sort of skillfully concocted rubbish peddled by street-corner fortune-tellers. Nonetheless, Ono's words echoed in Snowbird's mind for weeks afterward. He couldn't get rid of them. Snowbird had never been a superstitious man, but he had never dismissed those things either. Anyone who thought of himself as a true poet had to be aware of deeper realities beyond the banal mechanics of everyday life.

From the start, the relationship between the two men was supposed to be one of equals. That was what Ono had demanded, and Snowbird had readily agreed, assuming that it was just a form of words, a sop to the pride of the egomaniac who was used to being treated like a shogun. After all, Snowbird was the professional. It was no exaggeration to say that it was thanks to Snowbird that Ono had achieved what he had. If it hadn't been for his influence, the Peace Technologists would have remained a small-scale outfit trapped in a fantasy world, with no access to finance, no protection, and no means of ever converting their wild ideas into detailed plans of action.

So what had happened to that relationship of equals? As time had passed, Ono's behavior had grown more bizarre and more arrogant. He had taken to ringing Snowbird up in the middle of the night about trivial security questions that should have been the province of his own people. His rambling speeches were growing longer and even less coherent. He delayed the schedule and made senseless changes without telling anyone. In short, Ono's behavior was of a sort that Snowbird would never have tolerated from a fellow professional of no matter what rank. The man was unreliable, and in Snowbird's world that was one of the most serious offense of all. Still, for the time being Ono was essential to the success of the project. That was recognized by all concerned. There would come a time—Snowbird didn't know when, exactly—when the situation would be different. The whole structure of the project would need to be changed, to be put firmly in the hands of professionals. At that point, Ono's role would be over. Snowbird knew exactly what his instructions would be then. He couldn't say that the prospect displeased him.

The Mercedes sped through the northern suburbs of the giant city. There was more traffic now: a couple of empty buses, some delivery trucks making an early start. The sun had risen well above the horizon, and the orange underglow of the clouds was starting to fade and shrink. Far to the west stood the bulk of Mount Fuji, a huge broken-topped molar scraping against the heavens. Snowbird didn't give it another glance. His mind was already at his destination, and the knot in his stomach was tightening.

Ono woke with the dawn as he did every day, no matter where or for how long he had been sleeping. For a few minutes, he lay motionless on the cushions, gazing at the shapes and figures on the ceiling—a lotus blossom crowned with flames, a dancer with a diamond set in her forehead, a white bird with the head of a dog. They were part of a panorama painted by one of his favorite disciples, a girl called Kazue. She wasn't with him now. She wasn't yet of high enough grade to enter the Inner Chamber of Earthly Delight. If she passed through the next stage of her progress—and Ono would make sure that she soon did—she would enter the elite group of Sisters of Light who were allowed admittance to all the chambers in all the different temples.

Ono rolled over on the soft, delicately perfumed cushions and picked up his robe. The two girls who had accompanied him in his meditations last night were still asleep, exhausted by their physical and mental exertions. That was normal, since it had been the first experience of this chamber for both of them. They would probably sleep right through the day. When he stood up, one of them rolled over onto her back, a hand sliding down to cover her groin. Her eyes stayed firmly shut. Modest, even in sleep—but not so modest when the inner doors of her mind were pried open last night. The other was lying facedown, a few beads of sweat standing out on her smooth back. She was breathing heavily, which caused Ono a flash of worry. There had been accidents before with first-timers. He put his foot against her buttocks and gave a sharp prod. The girl gave an incomprehensible mumble of protest and wriggled away from the invasive toe. That was all right, then. She would be completely back to normal in a couple of days. Ono left them there and stumbled groggily down the low corridor that led to the Temple of Inner Refreshment.

Half an hour that seemed like eternity. Gamelan music like crystal raindrops passing through his latticed flesh . . . A rainbow of scintillating perfumes, each one never experienced before . . . A wave that swept through his mind, carrying away all impurity and weariness . . .

When Ono emerged into the small garden on the other side of the pleasure complex, his senses were as sharp as a razor. Walking barefoot across the lawn, he felt every single dew-laden blade of grass. He heard every single bird, every single insect, and understood the terrible urgency of their noise. He knew that if he wanted to he could remember every single thing that had happened to him over the past week with total accuracy. Each scene could be recalled as vividly as if it were appearing on a screen in front of his face.

But there was no point in calling to mind past trivialities when there was an endless succession of new trivialities that had to be faced. Today was a day that Ono would have liked to spend meditating, sitting alone on the tiny island in the middle of the lake, his spirit soaring as high as an eagle above the dull world of events and plans. Unfortunately, it wasn't to be. There was an unpleasantness that had to be confronted. The colorless man was coming to see him. He would be arriving soon, full of suspicious questions and tedious demands. It was important to satisfy him, if only for the reason that dissatisfaction would certainly lead to more frequent visits, more prying, and more suspicion. Ono didn't want that. For the time being, he was willing to make use of the colorless man, who was undoubtedly a valuable instrument to have at one's disposal. But there would come a point in the not too distant future—Ono couldn't be sure of the exact timing—when he would have to break his connections with such people once and for all. They had taken his ideas, his science, and were using them for purposes of their own too banal even to bear thinking about. He didn't complain because he had received much help in return, albeit of a very basic sort—logistical, financial, and so on. The problem was that the colorless man and his friends were starting to forget the simple point that they could have done nothing without him—that he was the originator, the developer, the inspiration of the whole project. Without him, they could assemble all the capital, all the distribution capability, all the security they wanted and it would do them no good at all. There would be nothing to finance, distribute, or protect.

The colorless man was accustomed to being feared. To Ono, he was no more than a cruel child wreaking his vengeance on a nest of insects after a scolding by his parents. He was half-amusing, half-sad; not frightening, and certainly not complex enough to be interesting. He was of course capable of killing Ono—indeed, Ono sensed that he had thought about it many times—but that was not frightening either. The colorless man's karma was to be a killer. He made no attempt to break free of it. That he should think about killing those who stood in his way was natural and inevitable, just as a scorpion would always think about stinging its enemies. Ono would have to watch him closely to make sure that his tedious demands were met. And in the end, when the time came to take what had been created out of the hands of the criminals and their contacts—at that point something suitable would have to be prepared for this empty parody of a human being.

When the white Mercedes swished through the security gates and drew up outside the main hall of the temple on the hill, Ono was waiting on the forecourt, dressed in a billowing white robe with a purple sash and flanked by half a dozen of the Sisters of Light. Snowbird didn't wait for his chauffeur to come around and open the door, but bounded out of the car. The Sisters announced his appearance by banging on the tambourines and little drums that they held, and shouting out greetings in shrill voices.

"Sensei," called out Snowbird as he mounted the few steps to where

239

Ono was standing. "It is a great pleasure to have the chance of meeting you on such an excellent spring morning."

"The pleasure and honor are all mine." Ono beamed. "You must be tired after a long journey at such an early hour. We are sincerely grateful for your presence."

Snowbird made a formal bow, returned by Ono at exactly the same gradient. The two men went inside, laughing and joking, but not wasting time. They knew that there was much to discuss.

Mori went to the bicycle track with Ida, a cop whom he had been swapping information with for the past twenty years. Ida was a solid, good-humored guy, but these days there was more and more disappointment creased into his face. At his age, he should have made inspector level a long time ago. All you had to do was keep your mouth shut and smile at your superiors and turn up for work at the right time every morning and it should happen automatically. For Ida, it had never happened. In what should have been the prime of his professional career, he had been shunted from one administrative job to another, ending up in a traffic-and-crowd-control position at the police station next to the Nippon Dome. Mori concluded that Ida must have said or done the wrong thing somewhere along the line. What that thing was, Mori had never asked and never would and he knew that Ida would never tell him. After all, what was the point?

Mori wasn't such a keen bicycle-race fan as Ida. He assumed that most of the races were fixed. If they weren't, it meant that the yakuza weren't doing their job properly, and Mori had more respect for them than that. Ida didn't care. He analyzed the form of the riders in different conditions and over different distances, and studied the way they limbered up. Then he bet cautiously, only on the races where he felt confident and only after he had worked out the probabilities on his pocket calculator.

It wasn't a good day for Mori. As usual, he bet on all twelve races, using a two-rider quinella each time. Mori's system was to find two reasonable outsiders with individual odds of around twenty to one. These weren't the rank outsiders—Mori was too old to believe that rank outsiders stood a chance of anything in life—but somewhere in the bottom quarter of the list of odds. The advantage of this approach was that if both riders managed to place, Mori stood to turn his two-thousand-yen stake into two hundred thousand—enough to buy an air-conditioner for the office, get a new turntable for his stereo, and replace all his scratched and worn-out LPs. The disadvantage was that it seemed to work only once every couple of years, and today wasn't one of the lucky days. Mori didn't manage a single success, dropping twenty-five thousand yen altogether. That, he tried not to register, was equivalent to two weeks' rent on his office.

Coincidentally, twenty-five thousand was also the amount that Ida won. He bet on only eight races, and he won six times, using a combination of bracket quinellas and single-shot plays. Most times, Ida included the favorite in his system, and most times the favorite romped home in one of the first three places. Mori didn't understand how Ida could do that. The odds he was getting were so boring—just four or five to one on his quinellas. So he was turning two thousand yen into eight or ten. What could you do with that? It wouldn't even buy you an hour in a low-grade pink salon.

The last race ended with the favorite zooming home half a wheel ahead of the second favorite. Thousands of losing tickets were ripped up and hurled in the air and fluttered down on the heads of the crowd like cherry blossoms. For the twelfth time of the day, Mori's was among them. Ida grinned as he guzzled his way through a stick of octopus dumplings.

"You're a good citizen, Mori-san," he said indistinctly. "Your contribution should be highly esteemed."

"How do you mean?" said Mori, gazing disconsolately at the results board. He had been called many things in his time, but good citizen was not usually among them.

"Look at this stadium—it used to be so shabby until it was rebuilt. Now they have the finest facilities for the riders, comfortable seats in the stands, these video screens everywhere. That's all thanks to people like you, Mori-san." Ida licked a few drops of soy sauce from his big, pawlike hand and grinned.

"What you say is true," grunted Mori. "Without people like me, none of this could have happened. And people like you would get even worse odds on the favorites than you get already."

"That's understood, but the odds on the outsiders would get more attractive. I might even bet something on one or two of them myself. You see, the problem right now is that a lot of people bet like you, Mori-san. That means the odds on the outsiders are usually too short compared to their real chances. On the other hand, the odds on the favorites may look boring, but quite often you find they're too long if you work out the probabilities."

Ida tapped his pocket calculator with a stubby finger. Mori shook his head and smiled at that one. He could never bet on a favorite, no matter what the calculator said.

"Anyway, your contribution deserves some reward," Ida went on. "There's a yakitori place not far from here where they have excellent gizzard and liver."

"Sounds good," said Mori. "Let's give it a try."

So for the sixth time in a row, the evening would be on Ida. Mori didn't want it to happen that way, but as long as he kept losing he had no choice. To refuse would be to imperil a long and valuable friendship. Mori resolved that the next time he won, they would celebrate not with yakitori but with the finest sushi, followed by scotch whiskey in a smart Roppongi bar.

They stayed in the yakitori place for a couple of hours, draining half a dozen sake flasks and sampling pretty well everything on the menu.

Mori steered the conversation toward Peace Technology and the big meeting at the Nippon Dome.

"It's a crazy business—all those girls getting married to people they've never met. You wouldn't want your daughter to get involved with something like that, would you!"

"Of course not—though from a certain point of view, it solves a lot of problems. No more worrying about finding arranged-marriage partners, no need to employ guys like you to investigate family backgrounds!"

"That's true. But this whole event must have been a huge headache for you guys. Forty thousand young people meeting in the dome. I'll bet there were quite a few incidents with parents trying to grab away their kids and that sort of thing. And Ono has his own security staff, doesn't he? Somebody in the police department must have had the job of keeping them in line, making sure that they didn't harass people unduly and so on."

Ida shook his head. "It wasn't like that," he said. "Actually, we took a much lower profile than we do at the regular Giants games. Ono's security people handled everything themselves."

Mori blinked at Ida in surprise. "You let them do that? There was a huge crowd in a state of excitement, a cult leader idolized by his followers and hated by many others. What if there was a riot? What if someone tried to shoot him? Everyone would want to know what the police were doing!"

"That can't be helped," said Ida, gnawing on a ball of ground chicken meat. "It wasn't a public event, where everybody can buy a ticket and go in. Ono's people hired out the dome for the evening. They could do what they wanted in there, as long as they didn't cause any offense to anyone else. That's what we were told, anyway. The instructions that came down from above were to keep the police presence to a minimum and stay outside at all times."

"That's a little strange, isn't it?"

Ida's face was flushed with sake. "Plenty of strange things go on in the police service, Mori-san. It's just like any other bureaucracy—it's got its own special priorities. There are certain powerful politicians who can be very helpful on budget and personnel matters. Also every year a dozen of our top people descend from heaven into lucrative low-stress jobs in the private sector. Someone has to recommend them for those jobs."

Mori looked at his friend thoughtfully. There was anger in Ida's voice. Mori had never heard him talk like this before. "So, what are you saying? That the decision to go soft on Ono was the result of political pressure?"

"I didn't say that. All I know is what I've told you. You're the detective—you draw your own conclusions."

Ida drained his sake cup with a loud smack of the lips. That was his way of signaling that the subject was now closed.

243

In Tamura's eyes, weekends had become as precious as gold. The daily routine at the office was a torment spent racking his brains for a way out of his dilemma, cringing every time the phone rang. He couldn't concentrate on anything. It was no use trying to hide what he felt—he wasn't that sort of man. His juniors knew something was wrong. He could see it in their faces, and that made him feel worse. They probably assumed it was some family trouble or a health problem. They had no idea that it was something that, if ever revealed in public, would bring unbearable disgrace not just to him but to the branch as well and all his colleagues, indeed to the whole of CBJ.

He had gone farther than he had ever imagined possible. First, he had gotten involved in the death of a young woman, becoming the prime suspect in a murder that had yet to be discovered. Next, he had turned into an accomplice of the yakuza, planning a massive fraud on the bank that had recruited him from college, trained him, and promoted him to the rank of deputy branch manager. Until the nightmare had started, Tamura hadn't realized quite how much his life was built around the Commercial Bank of Japan. For the past quarter of a century, he had been drinking in the evenings with CBJ colleagues, playing golf with them on weekends, attending their weddings, sometimes as the official go-between. Until his own marriage, he had lived in the CBJ dormitory, then afterward for ten years in the bank's married quarters. The house that he had lived in these past ten years had been bought with a special low-interest loan that CBJ had provided. Without CBJ, Tamura barely existed.

When the weekend came, Tamura felt safe, remote from the humiliation and misery that dogged his every minute at the office. Everything at home seemed so ordinary, so reassuringly unchanged. His wife cooked the same sort of meal that she had cooked every weekend for the past twenty years. His daughter, Mika, practiced the Mozart piece on the electronic keyboard he had bought for her fifteenth birthday. At ten o'clock on Saturday morning, he heard the tape-recorded cry of the seller of bamboo washing poles and the whine of his tiny van negotiating the narrow lanes outside. At eleven o'clock, it was the scrap-paper collector, singing out his readiness to exchange old newspapers and magazines for rolls of toilet paper. These simple routine events now seemed charged with a special meaning that they had never had before. Suppose he were arrested for murder, fraud, concealing a dead body, and all the other crimes they would think up. The washing-pole seller and the scrap-paper collector would still steer their vans past the house at the same time every Saturday morning. Mika would still do her piano practice. The only difference would be that Tamura himself would be somewhere else—being interrogated in a police station or alone in a prison cell.

It was possible, of course, that nobody would find out about the fraud for a long time, several years, even. There was even a chance that he might be able to cover it up entirely. Recently, the bank had been occupied with writing off huge amounts of bad loans. The head office might not inquire too closely if he spread the damage around in a plausible way. If he could only stay in his current job for another four or five years, there might be some hope. But what a five years that would be! Better to assume that all would be revealed at some point, that he would go down in disgrace and disaster. And what then? What would he do? The answer came to him not as a dawning realization, but as something that should have been obvious from the start. There was only one way out! It would be easy, painless—a relief for everyone. He would leave a letter for Mika explaining what had happened to him—how he had been ensnared in a trap from which it was impossible to break free. She would understand. Not immediately, perhaps, but when she was older and had seen how the world worked.

So there was neither any use in worrying nor any use in hoping. All he could do was enjoy each weekend as if it were the last of its kind.

They noticed the difference, too, Mika and Etsuko. He saw it in their eyes. It was unusual for him to get up so early on weekends; to sit there in silence listening to Mika trilling through the sonata in C major; to offer to drive his wife to the Daiei supermarket and then wander around in her wake, staring at the brightly packaged items as if they were sculptures.

Had he been a good husband and a good father? Probably not. For one thing, he had been working too hard. He had spent too many evenings drinking with clients, too many weekends away golfing. There had been whole months at a stretch when he had seen Mika only for a few hours on Sunday evenings. They hadn't had a family holiday for so long. It was at least five years since they made the trip to Guam. Nowadays, he simply couldn't afford to take the time off. The Shinjuku branch of CBJ was too busy, too important to the success of the bank as a whole. It was not surprising that Mika seemed to have grown up so fast.

Then there were the women—the hostesses, the "companions," all the other girls from the "water-trade." There had been many of them over the years. At first, he had tried to hide it from Etsuko, taking care to wash away the perfume before going home, emptying his pockets of the business cards and matchbooks that he had collected in the Ginza and Akasaka. Soon he had given up the effort. Etsuko had worked at CBJ herself for four years after leaving college. She knew what went on in a major bank. She knew that it was all part of the job. He didn't spend time with those women because he wanted to, but because he had to. If he had been a teetotal puritan who went home every evening at eight o'clock, he would never have risen to the position of deputy branch manager and CBJ would have lost important clients. It was all for the benefit of CBJ. Etsuko tolerated the situation, but of course that didn't mean she liked it. Tamura understood that—no woman would.

"Let's go out this evening," he said when they got home from the supermarket. "All three of us. We can go to the movies, have a meal in a restaurant—whatever you like."

They looked at him as if he had said something totally absurd. "The movies?" said his wife disbelievingly. "These modern films—I don't know if they're really suitable for families. . . ."

"Don't be so conservative. There's no reason for us to be left behind by all the new trends. We have modern minds, don't we?"

"Modern minds!" said Etsuko with heavy irony. "You certainly haven't got one. As for me, well—to tell the truth, I'm quite comfortable being left behind!"

That was typical of Etsuko. Tamura did his best. He came up with a suggestion that would be fun for all of them, and she knocked it down immediately. It had almost become a reflex action. Still, he refused to be discouraged. It was just her way of showing that she wasn't to be taken lightly.

"All right, it was just an idea," said Tamura with a shrug. "Tell me what you'd like to do. Let it be your choice today."

"Let it be Mika's choice," said Etsuko. "Make it a birthday treat for her!"

That one stung. He had been on a business trip on the weekend of his daughter's eighteenth birthday two months ago. It had been absolutely unavoidable, relating to the financing of a huge new resort development in Hokkaido.

"How about going to a soccer game?" said Mika. "All my friends have been going to J-league matches this year. The Yokohama Marinos have this cute guy who scores all their goals. He studied soccer in Brazil and he has long hair down to his shoulders and he's in commercials for body lotion, you know the one where he comes out of the shower with his chest all wet and shiny and says—"

"Good idea," said Tamura, glancing at his wife. "We've never been to see a soccer game, ever. I've often wondered what makes them so popular."

"You mean it," said Mika excitedly. "We're really going to see Kinoshita-kun!"

"Kinoshita-kun?"

"He's the star striker of the Marinos, you know the one who comes running out of the shower with his skin all glistening and shouts out—"

"It's decided," said Tamura, holding up his hand. "We're going to see Kinoshita-kun and his teammates."

"It'll be difficult to get tickets, Papa. They've been sold out since before the beginning of the season."

"No problem," said Tamura with full paternal authority. "Leave everything to me."

Indeed it wasn't a problem—as long as you were prepared to pay. They got to the grounds fifteen minutes before the kickoff. Tamura left Mika and Etsuko at the entrance to the main stands and went off to bargain with the scalpers, who were dotted at strategic points around the venue. What they told him came as quite a shock. The best seats had a face value of eight thousand yen, which was expensive enough to start with; the scalpers were demanding thirty thousand for each. Altogether, he had to peel over one hundred thousand yen of banknotes, almost as much as he would have paid for a few hours at a top-class Ginza club.

"How come this match is so popular?" he asked the scalper, a man with nicotine on his fingers, sake on his breath, and cigarette burns on his polyester trousers.

"It's the Kinoshita effect," grunted the scalper, folding Tamura's banknotes into a fat little wad. "Everybody wants to see this Kinoshita play. That's why our prices are thirty percent higher than last year."

"So what happens if he gets transferred to another club?"

The scalper lifted his polyester shirt to reveal a grubby fanny pack cradling a bloated paunch. He carefully inserted the wad of banknotes between it and the wall of gray flesh. Tamura glimpsed many similar wads, maybe twenty or thirty in all. No wonder the man's paunch looked on the point of bursting out of the fanny pack.

"That's not going to happen," he said flatly. "You can be sure of that."

The game was quick and confusing; the crowd, mostly young and female, wildly enthusiastic. Mika got to her feet and joined in the screams of excitement whenever Kinoshita-kun ran with the ball, his long hair streaming out behind him. Etsuko cheered as well, shouting out the names of the players through a plastic funnel she had bought. Tamura wanted to cheer, but he wasn't sure when the moment was right. The ball being booted high into the stands; a tackle that sent an opponent spinning to the ground; the goalkeeper hurling the ball downfield with all his might—these seemed like good moments to cheer, but no one else did. Then there were perfectly good goals disallowed because of something called an offside trap, which, the way Etsuko explained it, was just ignoble, underhanded trickery, not at all worthy of a manly sport.

So that was soccer. Certainly lacking in the subtler fascinations of sumo or baseball, but still good fun to watch in the festive atmosphere of the stadium, accompanied by the steady banging of the big *taiko* drums and the chanting of the fans and the wave shapes made by the crowd. It put Tamura in a cheerful mood that lasted for hours afterward.

When the match was over, they went to a Brazilian restaurant that Mika had read about. Tamura and his wife were the oldest people in the place by a good fifteen years, but that didn't matter. The noise of the voices and the flavor of the meat and the clean taste of the beer banished all thoughts of age and position. Suddenly, he was laughing a lot without really knowing why. Mika was laughing a lot too, and even Etsuko was smiling and making jokes. When a group of Brazilian musicians appeared on the tiny stage next to the kitchen and started up the hypnotic samba beat, he knew exactly what he wanted to do.

"Come on," he called to Mika. "This is your chance. I'll teach you what real dancing is!"

"Not here, Papa," she protested coyly. "This is a restaurant, not a disco."

"Don't be so boring!" he said, grabbing her by the arm. "This music was made for dancing!"

"No, Papa, don't!" she squealed in embarrassment. "Everybody is looking at us! Please let go!"

"If you won't dance with me, then I'll dance alone. I don't care whether people are looking or not. This is carnival time—time to relax, time to enjoy!" He got to his feet and pushed his chair back into place. Mika hid her face behind her hands.

"Well, if your daughter won't dance with you, perhaps your wife can act as a substitute."

Etsuko was looking up at him, a humorous smile on her face. He hadn't seen her smile like that for years. "Come on, then," he said, and helped her to her feet. "Let's pretend we're in Rio."

The eyes of the restaurant were on them—a middle-aged couple cavorting in front of four grinning Brazilian musicians while their daughter pretended she had nothing to do with them and the waiters dodged past, plates of sizzling meat held high above their heads. Etsuko was smiling at Tamura the whole time, telling him things with her eyes that she never had and never could tell him in words. When the music finished, there was a round of applause from the customers and the musicians. Tamura turned and bowed.

"*Gracias, señores,*" he said and led Etsuko back to the table. Mika was sitting there with her chin cupped in both hands. She was looking at him quizzically.

"Papa, are you feeling all right?"

"I'm feeling fine," he answered truthfully. "Actually, I've never felt better."

"You missed your chance," said Etsuko, with a shake of the head. "Your father only does this sort of thing once every ten years."

"So next time I'll be twenty-eight," said Mika brightly. "That's pretty old, isn't it! Will you dance with me on my twenty-eighth birthday, Papa?"

For a moment, Tamura stared at her blankly. When Mika got to the age of twenty-eight, the world would be a different place. She would think of her father in an entirely different way. There would be no bossa nova, no soccer, no smiles.

"What's the matter, Papa? What are you thinking about?"

Tamura fixed his gaze on his daughter's puzzled face. "I was just wondering about something," he said slowly. "Has anyone ever showed you how to sing karaoke properly? I mean, with real professional technique."

"Karaoke?" said Mika and Etsuko in unison.

"Come on," said Tamura, getting to his feet again. "I know a place with over two thousand songs available. Let's go and sing until our voices disappear!"

The two women looked at each other and shrugged.

They stayed in the karaoke bar for three hours, singing the songs that had been around in the years before Mika was born. That style of pop ballad, with the quiet backing and the serious lyrics—at the time it had been known as "new music." Well, it certainly wasn't new anymore, but the songs still sounded fresh to Tamura. His own favorite singer-song-writer was a man who had produced a long string of moving ballads while working in the international section of Maruichi Bank. His first successful album had earned him enough money to quit his job, but he chose to stay on instead. That impressed Tamura immensely. Here was a man who thought and felt like a poet, but had the courage and en-durance of a loyal salaryman. He was everything that Tamura would have liked to have been.

It was ten o'clock in the evening when the three of them got out of the taxi at the corner of the street where they lived. Tamura hadn't drunk much—just a few beers to soothe his throat—but he was feeling light-headed. Etsuko had always had a weak head for alcohol. Just half a glass of wine had been enough to turn her face as red as a paper lantern. The calmest of the three of them was Mika, whose tolerance for alcohol was already closer to her father's than her mother's. She was talking about how much she enjoyed studying English, how determined she was to get into Tamura's old university. Tamura had had his doubts whether she was going to make it but now he was starting to revise his opinion. Perhaps his daughter was going to turn into one of those sophisticated, interna-tional types, like the newscasters on TV. Perhaps she really was a lot smarter than her father and mother. He sincerely hoped so.

At the gate of their tiny house, Tamura stopped and took a deep breath of cool night air. The fat yellow moon was impaled on the TV aerial of the apartment block opposite. The street was deserted except for a couple of schoolboys on the way home from weekend school and a man walking a small dog that was yapping continuously. He had it on a short lead, but it kept trying to pull away from him.

"Those little ones have bad tempers, don't they?" muttered Etsuko, taking the house key from her bag.

"You can say the same thing for human beings too," said Tamura with a laugh.

The man put down the bulky shopping bag that he was carrying and patted the dog on the back, but still it wouldn't stop yapping and pulling on the lead. Tamura found the sight strangely fascinating. The dog and the man hadn't gotten used to each other. For the moment, it seemed, it was the dog that was the master.

"Are you coming inside or not?" called Etsuko as she opened the door.

"I'll be there right away," said Tamura.

As soon as the words left his mouth, the man shot a glance in his di-rection. Instantly, fascination was replaced with cold dread. The man smiled and raised his hand. "Good evening," he said.

"Come on," shouted Etsuko from inside the porch. "What are you doing out there?"

"Go and run the bath," Tamura shouted back hoarsely. "I'm just talk-ing to someone!"

The man reached into the shopping bag, took out a dog biscuit, and dropped it onto the pavement. "Good weather today, wasn't it!" he said, staring down at the dog. "I hope you enjoyed the soccer match!"

There was no mistake. It was the same voice that Tamura had heard before, on the train and in Shinjuku park. The young man had altered his appearance slightly—he had much shorter hair now and was wearing a pair of steel-rimmed glasses—but he was still instantly recognizable. Tamura strode across the street.

"What are you doing?" he hissed. "This is my home!"

The dog crunched into the biscuit, not even looking up.

"I know that," said the young man softly. "I've come to give you a message. If you want Mika-chan to carry on studying in a good frame of mind, if you want her to enjoy university life and meet some nice boys, if you want everything to carry on as smoothly as before—then you have to do exactly what we say. Do you understand this?"

"I understand," said Tamura, suddenly sweaty despite the cool breeze.

"The first loan must be made available in two weeks' time. Don't even think about telling your colleagues or your wife or going to the police. We always follow through on our pledges. You know that, don't you!"

Tamura nodded. The young man smiled. "It's good that you see the situation so clearly," he said. "Anyway, I may pass by from time to time, just to be sure that there are no problems."

With that, he reached down, grabbed the little terrier by the scruff of the neck, and dropped it into his shopping bag. The dog immediately started yapping again. "Shut up, Taro," said the young man. "People are trying to sleep around here!"

Tamura watched him swagger down the street, swinging the bag from side to side. Only when he had rounded the corner to the main road did Tamura go in through the gate of his house.

"What happened?" called Etsuko from upstairs. "You've been such a long time out there!"

"There was someone wanting directions," responded Tamura, locking the front door behind him.

"And it took you so long to explain?"

Tamura didn't answer. So he wasn't safe even here! He had forgotten that yakuza weren't like salarymen. They didn't take weekends off and they didn't make any distinction between home and office. They would never give up, never leave him alone.

He pulled off his shoes and sat down on the step of the porch, staring dully at the wall. He had been dreaming a brief and pleasant dream, but now he had woken up again to the nightmare that his life had become. Try as he might, the nightmare would never be shaken off, and the fleeting dream would never be recaptured.

After saying good-bye to Ida, Mori took the train home. If any one of his quinellas had worked, he would have taken a taxi. As it was, he didn't arrive in the suburb of Chiba, where he had been living for the past two years, until ten o'clock.

Mori had always wanted to own his own place. Unfortunately, his timing had been disastrous, right at the peak of the real estate bubble. His choice of location had been far from ideal too, but it was all he could afford. The real estate broker had assured him that the area was up-and-coming, that the number of new projects being started would keep resale values soaring for years to come. Well, within a year that guy had gone bust, several big developments had been scrapped, and resale values were in free-fall. As a result, the district had never quite made the full transition to residential status. There were brand-new apartment blocks standing next to paddy fields; brightly lit convenience stores standing next to junkyards piled with smashed-up car bodies. The whole area looked unfinished, and as if it never would be finished.

There was a fifteen-minute walk from the station to the small apartment block where Mori lived. At this time, the streets were more or less deserted. In the waiting area in front of the station, there were just a couple of salarymen sitting on a bench drinking beer from cans and a taxi driver dozing with his stockinged feet sticking out of the passenger window. Mori took the usual shortcut—through the bicycle park at the side of the station, and then down the path next to the stonemason's yard. He walked quickly, pondering what Ida had told him about the Peace Technology congress. It was strange that someone like Ono could have that kind of influence.

Mori had almost reached the end of the path when a figure moved to block his way. Even at the distance of twenty yards, Mori could see that it was one of the salarymen who had been sitting in front of the station. Where was his friend? Mori had a feeling that he knew the answer even before he turned around. Yes, there he was, standing at the other end of the path, hands on his hips. Altogether, it was an unusual pattern of behavior for two men having a last drink together on Sunday night.

Both men started walking toward him. The silly smiles had gone, and there was something about their slow, purposeful gaits that didn't match their blue suits and flapping raincoats at all. Mori examined the possibilities. The path itself was no more than a couple of yards wide, its surface hardened mud. Probably the best plan would be to take one of them on, disable him, then make a dash for it. The only trouble was that Mori didn't fancy his chances. The sake was fuzzing his reactions, and he had a feeling that they weren't the kind of men who could just be shoved out of the way.

Mori glanced behind him again. The salaryman was no more than ten yards away, not hurrying at all. He was holding something in his hand, a steel pipe with one end covered in taping. That was to stop his hand from slipping if it got sweaty. The other guy was pulling a chain out of his pocket, wrapping it around his right hand. He walked slowly too, the end of the chain scraping along the ground.

It didn't look promising. Mori took a deep breath, grabbed the fence, and swung an ankle over the top of it. The wooden slats gave a creak of protest. There was a grunt of surprise from one of the salarymen, and the sound of feet jogging toward him.

Mori levered himself upward, using knees then elbows to scrabble astride the fence. He was on the point of sliding down into the stonemason's yard when there was a fizzing sound next to his ear and a jolting impact across his back. The pain was like an electric charge. Out of the corner of his eye, Mori saw the salaryman flicking back the chain in readiness for another swing. The other one was cocking the steel pipe, aiming carefully at Mori's stretched forearm. Mori pushed away from the fence just in time and dropped to the ground. The pipe smashed into the top of the slats, breaking up the half-rotten wood.

"Come on, let's get him. There's nowhere to run to in there!"

Mori rolled over on the hard ground, sprang to his feet, and looked around. The stonemason's yard was fairly large, about the size of two tennis courts. It contained urns, statues, and reliquary objects of all shapes and sizes. Mori wove his way between them, hoping to reach the fence on the other side undetected. Beyond that lay a major road, well lit, with plenty of cars passing. If he could only get to it, he would be safe.

The two yakuza dropped over the fence, and Mori slipped behind a multihanded statue of the goddess of mercy. There were no voices, no footsteps as they edged through the shadows of the larger statues. One of them was working his way through to the fence, the other edging down the row of stone objects, checking each one in turn.

Mori picked up a handful of gravel and tossed it toward the fence, then ducked behind an incense burner shaped like a blooming lotus. He heard one of the salarymen turn sharply a couple of yards away, the sole of his shoe scraping on the ground. Mori slipped back into the shadows, moved soundlessly around the incense burner, and emerged behind the man's back. Standing completely still, staring in the direction that Mori had tossed the gravel, he was just a couple of paces away. Mori glided forward like a ghost, hands stretching out to grab and choke.

The salaryman must have heard something. He suddenly wheeled around, the steel pipe ready in his hand. Mori ducked and the pipe went swinging into the incense burner, smashing the lotus bloom to fragments. Momentarily, the impact knocked the salaryman off balance. Mori moved fast. His first blow was a good one, his knuckles driving into the neck area just below the ear. The salaryman reeled back against the incense burner. Mori feinted another swing with his right hand, then charged in close for a knee jab to the groin. The steel pipe clattered to the ground, and the man doubled up against the incense burner. Mori heard the sound of running feet behind him. He reached down, picked up the steel pipe, and swung it with some precision against the inner side of the kneecap. The salaryman gave a yelp of shock and collapsed to the ground. Mori dodged back into the shadows behind the incense burner.

The footsteps stopped. The man with the chain was on his own now. Would he give up and go home? Somehow Mori doubted it. He slipped into the shadows behind a walking Buddha and waited. Five minutes passed, then ten minutes. Mori kept scanning the yard. All was quiet, the stone faces pale in the moonlight, the chiseled fingers motionless. Finally, he moved away from his vantage point and padded toward the pathside fence. The salaryman whom he had left on the ground in front of the broken incense burner was no longer there. Mori cursed himself for not hitting the guy hard enough.

He stopped in front of the goddess of mercy statue and turned back toward the mason's shop. For a moment he thought he saw a movement somewhere in the blackness of the window, between the silhouetted reflections of the Buddhas. No, that would be impossible. Neither of the salarymen could have gotten to the shop before he did. He edged away, until out of the corner of his eye he saw another small movement in the blackness. He paused to scrutinize the window again, then suddenly wheeled around and dove to the ground.

It was almost too late. The movement was not in the window at all. It was the statue that was moving, toppling off its plinth and crashing down toward him. There was a heavy thud as it fell to the ground, both arms snapping off and the torso shattering into a thousand fragments. Hollow plaster, thought Mori as he rolled sideways and jumped to his feet.

The salaryman with the chain scythed the air a few times, forcing Mori backward against a life-sized Buddha. The first full-blooded swing came at head height, too fast to see in the murky light. Mori dropped to his knees, judging the timing from the movement of the man's wrist. The chain thwacked against the Buddha behind him, knocking the head clean off the shoulders and sending it flying toward the mason's shop. The next swing was too low to be ducked. Mori caught it with the steel pipe, but the end of the chain lashed around it and cracked him on the arm just above the elbow. He sprang sideways, the whole of his right arm numb with the impact.

The salaryman moved forward with the lightness of a dancer, swiftly feeding the chain from left hand to right and back to left again. The next swing could come from either side, high or low. Mori edged backward, eyes fixed on the chain. He had to time his rush, to make sure with the first blow of the pipe.

He heard the sound behind him an instant too late, twisting around to catch the blow from the spade full on the chest. The force sent him reeling against a block of polished marble. Mori glimpsed the other salaryman, face still smeared with blood, limping forward, shovel in hand. The chain! Where was the man with the chain?

The man with the shovel swung again. Mori deflected the blow with the steel pipe. Sparks flew from the shovel's metal head, and it went clanging against the marble block. Mori grabbed the handle and pulled, priming himself for a full swing. This time he was going to make sure.

Strangely, he missed his target completely, the pipe sailing through the empty air. Why was that? Why had he lost his balance, and why was he falling? Just before his head thumped to the ground, Mori glimpsed the chain wrapped tightly around his ankles. That was a skilled move. This guy had definitely been doing his homework.

Mori tried to keep from rolling sideways, but he was being dragged backward by the ankle. He flipped over onto his knees and tried to grab the chain with his hand. A thumping blow in the small of the back knocked him flat on his face again. Just as he was levering himself up a second time, a boot caught him full in the belly, and all the breath left his body.

Mori lay flat on the ground, gasping for air. The man with the shovel was standing a couple of feet away, readying himself to smash the blade down on Mori's head. The other one had removed the chain from Mori's ankle with a couple of dextrous flicks of the wrist. "This is your chance," he said to the man with the shovel. "Make sure he never gets up again!"

The man with the shovel nodded. "This is a dead man," he said, and raised the shovel high above his head.

Painfully, Mori twisted himself around in a crescent shape. The steel pipe had fallen to the ground a couple of yards from where he was lying. If only he could have one last chance to use it! But the man with the chain was watching him like a hawk. Any sudden move and that chain would come slashing down on him again.

There was a muffled thump from the far corner of the yard. The man with the chain held up his hand. "Wait! What's that noise!" They stood listening in silence, but there was nothing more.

"I'll go and check. Make sure this one doesn't move a muscle."

He made a couple of turns around his wrist with the chain, then padded into the shadows behind the marble block. The man with the shovel brought it down to chest level and took a half-step nearer Mori. If he could just be distracted for a second, Mori might be able to make a lunge for the pipe.

The salaryman seemed to read Mori's thoughts. He glanced at Mori, then in the direction of the pipe. Without taking his eyes off Mori, he bent down and scooped it up. "Thanks for bringing it along," he said. "I thought it was lost somewhere."

Mori said nothing. Things were looking bad. If there was only some way he could grab the shovel, twist it away from the man . . .

From over on the other side of the mason's yard, there was a crashing sound, as if another statue had fallen over. The salaryman backed away from Mori and peered into the gloom.

"Sounds as if there's a problem," said Mori softly. "It's not too late to get away, you know."

"It's certainly too late for you," the salaryman sneered. He took a step forward and swung the edge of the shovel into Mori's face.

Mori saw it coming and rolled sideways. The salaryman dropped the shovel and came charging forward. Mori launched himself headfirst at the man's midriff. He was fast enough to avoid the first swish of the steel pipe, and managed to plant a fist in the side of the belly. The momentum sent them both staggering back against the statue of the goddess of mercy, rocking it on its plinth. Then there was a jarring blow to Mori's ribs as the steel pipe crunched home.

Mori lay there, stunned by the pain. He blinked, bracing himself for a second blow that never came. Finally, he scrambled and twisted to face the salaryman. He was leaning against the goddess, the steel pipe dangling at his side. For a moment, he regarded Mori thoughtfully. Then without a word he crumpled to the ground, a single trickle of blood running down his brow. Mori maneuvered himself into a squatting position and peered into the shadows behind the statue.

"You can come out now," he called. "This one won't be getting up for a while."

Several seconds passed, then a slim figure moved out of the shadows. Black training shoes, black jeans, black baseball cap on back to front. And when it was lifted off the head, plenty of long black hair falling to the shoulders. Mori shook his head to clear it. No, there was no confusion. She was still there, and she was human. Behind her the goddess was still standing on the stone plinth, staring gravely into nothingness.

"What happened to the other guy?" he said finally, hauling himself to his feet.

"Over there in the corner. He won't be troubling anyone for a bit either."

She was young, Mori realized, no more than twenty-four or twenty-five. Even in the dim light, he could see that she was exceptionally attractive—tall, with large eyes and a high forehead. It was hard to be sure, but he thought he might have seen her somewhere before.

"It's a pity about the statues," she said.

"Don't feel guilty," he said, glancing at the headless Buddha behind her. "Keeping me alive is a good enough cause."

"What about those two men? Won't the police make them pay?"

Mori smiled at that one. "The police? They'll never find out what happened here tonight. They'll probably file it as random vandalism by a motorbike gang."

"I doubt that," she said, shaking her head. "You see, I called them ten minutes ago and explained what was happening."

"You did what!"

There was indeed a siren wailing somewhere in the distance. The girl pulled a portable phone out of her jacket pocket. "I called them on this," she said. "Just before I came over the fence. They said they would send someone right away."

The siren was much louder now. Mori could hear the engine of the patrol car as it roared up the main road from the station. He stepped forward and grabbed her by the wrist. "Come on," he said. "Let's get out of here immediately."

"I can't leave now," she said, pulling away from him. "We are instructed to offer the police maximum cooperation."

Mori stared at her in disbelief. The headlights of the patrol car were raking through the slats of the wooden fence. If the police got hold of her, the whole incident, Mori's part in it included, would end up splashed all over the newspapers.

"What are you saying!" he hissed frantically. "There's no time to lose!"

The car door slammed shut, and there was a clatter of footsteps on the pavement. The girl took a step forward, then stopped and shook her head.

"But rules are rules! This is in our manual of correct procedures!"

"But it's not in mine!" growled Mori, snatching her wrist again and giving it a jerk that almost pulled her off her feet. "Now let's move!"

Tugging her after him, Mori raced for the fence. There was a hammering on the door of the mason's shop, then the crunch of boots as a couple of cops ran into the yard. Mori helped the girl over the fence and onto the path, then scrabbled up himself, the pain in his shoulder temporarily forgotten.

"I see one of them!"

"There—lying on the ground."

The cops spread out, their flashlight beams playing over the stone faces of the statues. Mori and the woman crept along the path, heads down, as quiet as a pair of cats.

Ten minutes later, they were safely inside Mori's apartment. He cleared a place on the floor for a couple of cushions and got out a bottle of Suntory Royal and a couple of chipped glasses and some snacks. They squatted in silence for a few moments, savoring the rough taste of the whiskey. The woman glanced around her new surroundings with an air of surprise that was by no means approving. That irritated Mori. By the standards of some other private detectives he knew, what she was inspecting with such condescension was close to luxury—one hundred square yards of floor space altogether, with a bath, central heating, and a tiny balcony on which he kept his cactuses.

As for the decor and furnishings, Mori's attitude had always been the less the better. There was a battered old cabinet containing several hundred LPs; on top of it the silver karate cup he had won at college and a stack of Russian novels. There wasn't much else—no chairs, no tables, no sofa. Just peeling paint and sun-faded tatami mats, a few piles of bucks on the floor, album covers, newspapers, coffee cups. Looking through her eyes, Mori understood that it wasn't exactly what she was used to. Indeed, in some respects, it could be described as a mess. But, on the other hand, it was what he was used to. It was Mori's mess, and he liked it that way.

"Not quite what you expected when you started following me around?" he ventured.

"Following you?" she said without looking at him. "What do you mean by that?"

"Don't play games," said Mori coldly. "Who are you working with? The Kawashita syndicate? That hitman on the motorbike?"

"You think I'm working with yakuza? What a crazy idea. If that were true, why would I just save you from being beaten up?"

"Maybe because you don't want me to be beaten up. Maybe you've got a contract to kill me."

"Right," she said, taking another sip of Suntory. "And now I've got an excellent opportunity. Here in your own apartment, with no witnesses."

Mori watched apprehensively as she unzipped her thin leather jacket and slipped a hand inside. The cushion she was kneeling on was four or five feet away—just about in range for a swipe with the whiskey bottle. But she was fast, as she had shown in the mason's yard.

"Here, let me introduce myself properly."

It wasn't a gun. It was a wallet of red plastic, emblazoned with a cartoon Snoopy, from which she took a business card.

"My name is Sachiko Kuwata. I'd like to request your cooperation and guidance. I am just a beginner in this business."

She bowed low, thick tresses of hair flopping onto the tatami mat in front of her. Mori inspected the business card. It described her as "Trainee Investigator" at the Shinjuku office of New Japan Research Bureau. Mori recalled the pestering phone calls, the insolent threats. So she was working for an organization that was trying to put him out of business. He took out his scuffed leather wallet and tossed one of his own business cards onto her lap.

"This is a big honor for me," she said, sliding it into her wallet. "You are a famous man at our company, Mori-san. You are known as the most experienced and successful freelance investigator in Shinjuku."

Successful! Mori had never been called that before. Still, when you thought about the others, it wasn't so much of a compliment. Small-time extortionists, fantasists, punch-drunk ex-boxers—compared with the average, Mori was a genius.

"In that case, why are your people trying to put me out of business?"

Sachiko looked surprised. "That is a misunderstanding," she said, tucking away the plastic wallet. "The policy of New Japan is to create cooperative relationships in all the areas that we enter. Our business philosophy is simple—in the future, investigative services will just be one part of an integrated security industry. Data protection, crisis management, industrial espionage—we want to cover all these aspects of our customers' needs."

"Industrial espionage?" said Mori, raising an eyebrow.

"That means prevention of industrial espionage," she answered solemnly. "For example, we recently identified a high-level employee of Mitsutomo Heavy Industries who had been infiltrated into the Sumikawa Electronics R&D center as a receptionist."

"Amazing," said Mori, genuinely impressed. "How did you manage that?"

"We found a small inconsistency in her educational history, so we got her health insurance records, credit card purchases, and so on and ran a cross-check on our mainframe. There was a close correlation with the profile of a Mitsutomo employee who was supposed to be on a two-year research course in America. It turned out she hadn't attended a single class. Our researcher checked it all out on the Internet."

"The Interwhat?" said Mori, unable to hide his bemusement.

"The whole inquiry only took a couple of hours," Sachiko continued airily. "And our researcher didn't even need to get up from his desk."

All done from his desk! It was hardly fair to call a guy like that an investigator. He was just another kind of salaryman.

"This is no longer the era of the freelance investigator," she continued, sensing his shock. "We're using the best software, the most sophisticated statistical techniques. No freelancers can compete with this kind of work, not even you."

"You may be right," said Mori, pouring them both a refill. "But that doesn't seem like a good reason for following me around."

"At the moment, our company is very strong in information management, but we lack expertise in field work. That is where your methods are very interesting, Mori-san. Our branch manager believes they are worth close study."

"Your branch manager?" said Mori, dropping an ice cube into each glass with a plop. "Would that be a guy called Kadota, by any chance?"

"That's right. Do you know him?"

"We've spoken," said Mori laconically. "Anyway, is it correct to assume that Kadota-san ordered you to follow me around?"

"He told me to observe you and study your working methods as closely as possible."

"And what reason did he give for all this?"

"He is very interested in your capabilities, Mori-san. He said that he wants to make an agreement of cooperation with you. We would supply you with our information systems and a steady flow of new business."

"I see; and what would you people get out of the deal?"

"Well, we'd get your experience in field work and your contacts and reputation in the area. Our branch manager respects you greatly, you know."

Kadota obviously had a strange way of showing his respect. Still, Mori shouldn't complain too much. If Kadota hadn't set Sachiko on his trail, those two yakuza would probably have left him for dead in the stonemason's yard.

"Your interest is much appreciated," he said. "But what your boss calls cooperation, I call subcontracting. I've got no desire to get absorbed in the New Japan *keiretsu,* no matter how many computers you've got at your disposal."

"I thought that would be your first response," she said, nibbling at a chunk of squid.

"It's also my second response, my third. I take the cases I want to take, and I handle them my own way—without any help or interference from anyone. That's the way I've always worked, and I'm not planning to change."

Mori cracked an ice cube between his teeth. They were both silent for a few moments. "Are you interested in jazz?" he said finally.

"Jazz?" She tilted her head reflectively. "Well, I like acid jazz."

"You like what?"

"Acid jazz—it comes from London originally. It's very big in the clubs these days."

Mori glanced at the wedge of dog-eared album covers in the cabinet.

How many were there—three hundred, four hundred? All meaningless to someone of Sachiko's generation. It was stupid to ask, really.

"So what made a girl like you get involved with this kind of business?" he said, changing the subject.

"It's simple," said Sachiko, brushing a stray strand of hair out of her eyes. "When I left college two years ago, many big companies suddenly stopped recruiting female graduates. They still accept high school graduates because they think they can get nine or ten years of work out of them before they get married. And they accept men, of course. That's not fair, is it!"

Fair—that was a word that Mori hadn't used for a couple of decades. He tried the unfamiliar shape of it on his lips. "So is New Japan what you call fair?"

"More or less. Men still behave like men, and they expect me to behave like a woman. But they gave me good training."

"Well, from what I saw in the mason's yard, you must have been a good student."

She smiled modestly.

"I shouldn't say this myself, but I had the highest marks on the training course. There were twenty-five others, and all of them were men."

"Congratulations," said Mori, raising his glass. "By the way, there was one other thing that has been puzzling me. You got away from me in the bookshop last week. Was that some technique they taught you on this training course?"

"Yes, it was," she said, flushing slightly. "We practiced it many times."

"How does it work?" said Mori, genuinely curious. "I was ninety percent certain that I saw you going into the ladies' room."

"You were right. I did go into the ladies' room."

Mori hadn't been expecting that answer. He had assumed that she must have ducked away somehow when he was rushing through the crowd. "But there are no windows, no other doors. It's impossible to get out!"

"I got out the exact same way I went in," said Sachiko proudly. "In full view of everyone. Actually, you looked me straight in the eye. For a moment, I thought you'd recognized me."

Mori stared at her in disbelief. He tried to recall the scene in the bookshop, the suspicious shop assistant, the stream of women emerging from the ladies' room. It was no good. He had no idea.

"Give up," he said with a shake of the head. "You'll have to tell me how you did it."

"The nun!" said Sachiko, with more than a hint of smugness in her voice. "I was the nun! Don't you remember?"

Mori did remember the nun—a middle-aged woman with thick spectacles and a stooping walk. So, the nun had been Sachiko! No question—it was a brilliant disguise. Still, he should have been more careful. He should have checked her shoes, her hands, the other obvious points.

"Nobody looks twice at nuns," Sachiko went on, pleased at his obvious discomfiture. "People respect them so much."

"Not me," growled Mori. "Not from now on, anyway. I'm going to watch them like a hawk. I'm going to sniff them for perfume, I'm going to get down on my hands and knees and look up their habits to see if their legs are shaved!"

"Poor nuns!" she said with a laugh. She drained her glass, stood up, and twisted her hair into a kind of bun, which she covered with the baseball cap. Mori made just one half-hearted effort to persuade her to stay.

"Are you sure you're all right? These people are dangerous, you know!"

"Don't worry—it's you they're looking for, not me. You must be careful, Mori-san."

A smile and a wave of the hand and she was gone, the best-looking detective that Mori had ever seen in his life. Acid jazz, the Internet—she had opened a door into a world that Mori knew little about and usually cared less. For the first time, he was beginning to think that it might be worth stepping inside.

THIRTEEN

The whole research department was in the big meeting room. In the center of the circle of chairs was Yazawa, pacing to and fro as he expounded his market strategy for the coming week.

"The pebble floats while the dead leaf sinks," he mused, apparently to himself. "Is such a thing possible? Yes, yes, yes—it is certainly possible! These days, such things are happening in the market with rapid frequency. So what must we do, Mitchell-kun? What is the right strategy to master this problem?"

"Uh—I'm sorry, Yazawa-san. I don't quite get that—"

"Wake up, Mitchell-kun! You are dreaming, I think. In your mind, you are feasting on the special ladies' sushi which you enjoy so much!"

"No, actually not—I mean—I was just—"

"Silence! Concentrate your mind on the market! Give it all the love and respect you give to your favorite ladies' sushi! Respect the market a little more and you may understand it a little more! Do you see my meaning?"

Actually, Mitchell hadn't been reflecting on either women or the stock market. His mind had been entirely focused on Terumasa Yazawa. "Yes, I think so," he said. There was no point in provoking the man this early on a Monday morning.

"Good! Now let us search for those floating pebbles. Kent-san, please tell me what is your idea for this one?"

The Monday strategy meeting was a weekly ritual. Today, Yazawa was putting on the standard performance, featuring bizarre metaphors, brutal interrogations of unsuspecting analysts, and sudden leaps of logic. Mitchell watched with more than usual fascination as poor polite Kent the Mormon was tweaked and teased. What sort of man had Yazawa been in the early 1980s? What twist in his character had made him throw away a fast-track career with one of Japan's major city banks, something that most salarymen would have considered a prize above all others?

"Check the daily stochastics," he was now snapping at the mortified Kent. "Check the oscillator. Look at the reversal on the weekly point-and-figure chart. Do these basic things before making such a suggestion again!"

"Okay, I understand," said Kent, coloring a deep crimson. "I guess I was just kind of thinking that machinery stocks look—"

"Please do not kind of think," roared Yazawa with gleeful savagery. "Give up kind of thinking at once! Everything that you think, everything that you dream, everything that you have the power even to imagine—*has already been totally discounted in the market!*"

"Yessir!" Kent winced.

Mitchell recalled the details recorded in the press. Swimming pool parties in rented villas; weekend trips to the Caribbean; shopping sprees in Paris—it was hard to reconcile all that with the intense, coiled spring of a man who was standing in front of him now. Yazawa had never struck Mitchell as an extravagant type. He certainly had unconventional tastes—in food and women, for example—but they were not expensive. His favorite barber charged only one thousand five hundred yen, less than the price of the special shampoo that Mitchell used. The Ray-Bans, the snakeskin belt, the Isuzu Mu—again these were distinctive, but far from luxury items.

Yazawa was staring at the ceiling now. "There are four different approaches to investment, Kent-san. Do you know these four approaches?"

"Uh—no—maybe no . . ." said the Mormon sheepishly.

"Then let me explain. There is the approach of water, which proceeds to its goal slowly and predictably. That is a good way for a methodical person like you, isn't it! Choose the way of water, Kent-san!"

"Uh—yuh—sure. The way of water it is."

So what was it all about? What was it that made the man tick? The theory that Mitchell came up with was hardly reassuring. If Yazawa hadn't committed the fraud for the money itself, then he must have done it for the sheer hell of it, for the joy of knowing he had everyone fooled!

There was a sound like a rifle shot as Yazawa cracked a knuckle. "Then there is the way of the mountain. Nothing can move the mountain. It stands still in its place and endures all weather. This is a good way for a long-term investor, such as a pension fund."

One thing was clear about this man, reflected Mitchell—he loved playing games. That was an aspect of his character that hadn't changed at all since the early eighties.

"Another approach is the way of the wind. It comes silently and disappears without a trace. This is the way of an excellent stock-picker, I think."

And of course Yazawa was a born gambler too. When he was in Los Angeles, he gambled with commodities and options and he gambled with his career. What was he gambling with now? That was a question that Mitchell would have dearly loved to answer.

Yazawa was standing still now, hands on hips. "And the last way is my own way. Do you know that way, Kent-san?"

"Uh—no, I guess not."

"It is the most dangerous way—the way of fire. When your spirit is on fire, you can burn through every obstruction. Nothing can halt your progress. Do you understand this?"

Kent nodded vigorously.

"But there is a big problem with this one. If you burn too strongly, then everything you touch will be consumed also, and finally you will be consumed yourself. That is why the way of fire is a dangerous way. Nothing and nobody can control it. That is exactly the problem of my own investment style, I think!"

You could be right, thought Mitchell. But what happens to the people who happen to be standing too close?

"Now back to Mitchell-kun," said Yazawa, spinning around as if he had read Mitchell's thoughts. "I have a big question for you too. What can you report on my number-one recommendation for this month and all subsequent months?"

"You mean Otaman?" said Mitchell, suddenly forced to log out of his ruminations. "Well, um, there's good news, actually. Over the weekend I managed to speak to one of the biggest investment funds in the United States."

"Really!" said Yazawa, dropping his voice to a melodramatic whisper. "This is promising, I think!"

"I think so," said Mitchell smugly. "The response was very positive. They're considering a major commitment, maybe as much as half of the entire issue!"

"One half!" hissed Yazawa. "Did you say one-half?"

He approached Mitchell's chair and fell to his knees on the carpet. Kent and the other analysts observed in silent anticipation. This wasn't their problem any longer. Now it was Mitchell's turn.

Mitchell looked down into Yazawa's eyes, which were at stomach height, about four feet away. He had never viewed Yazawa from this angle before. It was a curiously unsettling experience. The man's head, he noticed again, was almost perfectly round.

"Mitchell-kun," breathed Yazawa. "There is no longer any doubt about this. You are an excellent person, a true James Bond of the Great British Empire!"

Mitchell was sitting in a revolving office chair. He tried to push it backward, but it was already flat against the wall. The other analysts were gazing at him, trying their best to conceal their smiles. Surely, Yazawa would get up now and carry on the meeting. Surely, his little joke was over. But no—Yazawa waddled forward on his knees until his face was no more than a couple of feet from Mitchell's navel. He stared up at Mitchell like a mad doctor at an unsuspecting patient.

"One half of the whole issue!" he said, shaking his head in wonder. "You deserve much for your fine efforts!"

"Thank you," said Mitchell nervously.

Yazawa rested a hand on each of the chair's arms and eased himself forward. Mitchell squirmed backward, but there was no escape. Yazawa's chin was hovering just a few inches above Mitchell's lap, his unblinking eyes gazing into Mitchell's. "I want to show respect for your work," he said. "If I were a woman, do you know how I would show my respect for you now?"

"No!" croaked Mitchell, his spine rigid against the back of the chair. This was beyond a joke now. The man was out of control.

"You don't know? I am surprised. You should have had this experience many times in Japan, and also in your home country."

"I mean yes! Yes, I do know!"

Yazawa looked around at the stupefied faces of the other analysts. Mitchell's thighs tingled with the man's presence. It wasn't a pleasant sensation.

"In such a case, Japanese ladies pay respect more sincerely than Western ladies. I know this from personal experiences in more than fifty different countries. Compared to foreigners, Japanese ladies are always one hundred percent diligent and sincere. Do you not agree, Kent-san?"

"Hum—yuh—you could say so, I guess . . ." said Kent, his face even redder than before.

"Mitchell-kun deserves some special reward for his efforts," said Yazawa, his voice dropping to a purr. "If I were a lady, I would give him his special reward with all the gentleness and diligence in my capacity. I would be one hundred percent sincere."

There was a moment of heavy silence. Mitchell felt as if his legs and torso had been rubbed with itching powder. He tried to look away, but there was no avoiding the glaring eyes, the shiny cheeks, that disturbingly round head. Suddenly, without a hint of warning, Yazawa sprang to his feet, pushing away violently from the arms of the chair. The chair's wheels went shrieking sideways across the wooden floor. Mitchell jerked forward, barely stopping himself from falling to the ground. Yazawa skipped back to the center of the room.

"But I am not a woman!" he bellowed, pounding his fist into his hand. "I have other ways to show my respect! Many other ways!"

Kent the Mormon was sitting there, his mouth hanging open. Ted Shimano was busy trying to keep a straight face.

"Mitchell-kun will have a substantial bonus this summer," shouted Yazawa, fixing his glare on each of them in turn. "It will enable him to enjoy to his heart's desire. Follow Mitchell-kun! Do like Mitchell-kun and there will be many rewards! Is that understood?"

"Understood!" roared the analysts in unison. Mitchell said nothing. He was overcome with a sense of relief that lasted for the remainder of the meeting.

Getting back to his desk in the research department, Mitchell called up a twenty-year chart of the Otaman stock price on his computer screen and sat gazing at it for several minutes. What did it mean? If you believed someone like Yazawa—as opposed to the trained economist who had preceded him—there was a way of looking at this long squiggle that would tell you what was going to happen in the future. The idea was that there were certain patterns that repeated themselves because they were manifestations of the unchanging rhythms of crowd psychology. All you had to do was identify them and then you could predict how stock prices would behave. The introduction to charting that Mitchell had studied was full of references to "pennant formations," "double bottoms," and "golden crosses." These patterns were easy to spot, though it seemed that in practice they gave many false signals. But nowhere had Mitchell found any explanation of "the headless warrior" or "thunderclouds over the mountain," or any other of Yazawa's favorite patterns.

Mitchell stared long and hard at the pictorial history of the Otaman stock price. What did it resemble? A strip of jagged coastline? A dying man's cardiograph? The scrawl made by someone trying to get a pen to work? It looked so random, so unformed. He pushed his chair back and glared at the chart from a distance of six feet, then put his head on the desk and squinted at it sideways. It was no good. The chart refused to surrender any meaning. He cleared it from the screen, shaking his head in frustration.

269

"Are you thinking sufficiently with your reptile mind?" said the familiar voice just behind his shoulder. "Do not use your monkey mind! Use your reptile mind instead!"

Mitchell swiveled around on his chair to confront Yazawa's grinning face. Would the man never leave him alone?

Yazawa took a silver cigarette case out of his pocket and thrust it in Mitchell's direction. Mitchell shook his head. "The monkey mind is good for using tools," continued Yazawa reflectively. "It is also good at manipulating information and such tasks. We need the monkey mind, which gives us many excellent things, such as technology and economics and laws."

"And the reptile mind?" said Mitchell dryly. "What does that give us?"

Yazawa paused to inhale deeply. Mitchell had never seen him smoking before. He wielded the cigarette like a weapon. "The reptile mind is the old brain, which contains such things as fear and lust and greed. This is what gives us our choice of ladies and our choice of leaders and also our choice of stocks. Love, war, speculations—all these things are controlled by the reptile mind. This is called by scientists the limbic brain. Do you know the limbic brain?"

"The limbic brain?" said Mitchell. "No, I don't believe so."

Yazawa blew a plume of pungent smoke into his face. "Good investors must pay attention to the activities of the reptile brain," he said sternly. "By the way, I hope I didn't surprise you in the strategy meeting. I wanted to praise you and I wanted to encourage other analysts to make good efforts on a similar level. The meaning of what I did was that they should not easily forget."

Easily forget? No one present was likely to forget Yazawa's performance for a long time to come. It would be engraved in their memories, as it was engraved in Mitchell's.

"I see," said Mitchell. "Well, that's okay—though you had me rather worried at one point."

"This is excellent advice for you, Mitchell-kun! Silence your monkey mind, and listen to the cry of the reptile deep within you. At that stage, the movement of the market becomes not so difficult, I think."

At that, he flicked some ash into Mitchell's trash can and marched off into the dealing room.

Mitchell mulled over their brief conversation. Yazawa was making a big effort to keep him happy. But why? Mitchell would have liked to think that it was out of respect for his potential as an analyst, but he knew that the real answer was simpler and less flattering. It was because of Otaman. For Yazawa, Otaman was not just another recommendation, like Matsui Cement or Sanwa Electric. It was much bigger than that.

Mitchell shifted his gaze back to his computer screen, where the message icon was flashing. His electronic mailbox contained a detailed request from Murray Feinman for additional information about Otaman. Midas were still serious about Otaman, he said, but they needed more detail. They needed to know why the balance sheet had started expanding so rapidly and why investments in securities were being carried at acquisition cost instead of market value. Also, why had the method of calculating depreciation been suddenly changed, and how come so few affiliated companies were included in the consolidated accounts?

Mitchell spent the next hour answering Feinman's queries as best he could, then turned his attention to the stock exchange documents in his in tray. According to Ted Shimano, these should be a good starting point for tracing out the patterns of financial power behind the Otaman stock price. For any company, the thirty largest stockholders were listed every six months. So the half a dozen faxed pages that he now held in his hand should give him a reasonable picture of who had been buying the Otaman stock and who had been selling. With a bit of luck, that would give him a better idea of what to expect next than the uneventful sideways wriggle that the twenty-year chart had depicted.

The faxed pages were hard to read. Mitchell pored over them for twenty minutes, scribbling the main points into his notebook. When he had finished, he stared in surprise at what his little notebook was telling him. Ted Shimano had been right. There was a subtle pattern developing that he would never have gleaned from any other source.

Over the past ten years, the big Japanese institutions had been steadily reducing their holdings of Otaman shares by an almost identical amount each year. As a result, the proportion of the company's shares held by the ten largest investors had fallen from 50 percent to less than 20. Finding what had happened to those holdings was more difficult. From what Mitchell could tell, they had been absorbed, not by one or two other large institutions, but by a number of small investors, each of which held less than 1 percent of the total. So over the past decade, Otaman had changed from a company controlled by the usual group of establishment institutions to one with a much wider spread of shareholders, probably small companies and individual investors. He stuffed the papers into a file, then locked them up in the bottom drawer of his desk. The last thing he wanted was for Yazawa to observe this unorthodox bit of research that he had been doing.

One of the research assistants was sitting on the far side of the research department making some clippings from the Nissho newspaper. He walked over to her desk. "Thanks for arranging this stuff to be sent through," he said with a pleasant smile. "It's been a big help, really."

The girl smiled back. She had one tooth that was completely crooked; an imperfection to the Western eye, but a powerful "charm point" for most Japanese men. Just out of a two-year women's college, with a tiny nose and mouth and the pale complexion that was said to be worth seven types of beauty, no doubt she would soon be in strong demand.

"It was no trouble," she said. "I'm happy to help you, Mitchell-san."

"I'd be grateful if you didn't mention it to anyone yet. It's all part of a new method of analysis I'm developing. I want to keep it secret until the flaws have been ironed out."

Was he being foolish, trying to cover everything up like this? Perhaps he was creating more suspicion than he was removing.

"Understood! By the way, Mitchell-san, I think I saw one more sheet come in this morning. Would you like me to check?"

Could he really be bothered to look through another sheet of blurred Japanese script? He decided that he could. He didn't have anything better to do. "Uh—yes, you might as well," said Mitchell, going back to his desk.

The girl trotted over to the fax machine and leafed through the incoming documents, finally turning up another sheet of filings. She dropped it on Mitchell's desk as she passed on one of her frequent visits to the ladies' room. Mitchell glanced at it without paying much attention at first. It was, if anything, even harder to read than what he had received already, and the format was different. Squinting at the blurred and smudged characters, he gradually pieced together what it said. Here was at least part of the answer to the mystery of what had happened to the Otaman stock dumped by the big institutions. According to the filing, a company called Heisei Lease had declared a 5 percent holding in Otaman just two months before. That made the company one of the top ten holders of Otaman stock, its purchases having happened too recently for it to be included in the biannual list of the thirty biggest holders. Without the filings, Mitchell would never have known that Otaman suddenly had a substantial new shareholder.

So what kind of outfit was Heisei Lease? Why had it decided to take a stake in Otaman? Checking through his company handbook, Mitchell confirmed that it wasn't listed on any of the official stock exchanges, nor was it included in the ranks of major unlisted companies. He walked over to the tiny library section in the corner of the research department and picked out the most recent directory of the Japanese leasing industry. Surprisingly, there was no mention of Heisei Lease here either. So it wasn't one of the top five hundred leasing companies, even though it had the financial resources to buy a good chunk of Otaman shares. That was odd, to say the least.

Mitchell returned to his desk and rang up directory inquiries. There was only one number given for Heisei Lease, and the address was somewhere in Nippori. At first, Mitchell was doubtful whether he had the right company. He had been expecting an address in Otemachi, Akasaka, or one of the other central business districts, not in a down-at-the-heels entertainment area. He decided to make absolutely sure. Mitchell dialed the number. There was no reply for over a dozen rings. They must be busy over there, thought Mitchell, drumming his fingers on the desktop. He wondered how many staff the company had, what kind of products it specialized in leasing.

"Yes?" a gruff voice answered eventually.

"I'm looking for Heisei Lease," said Mitchell, taking maximum care with his Japanese. "Is this the right number?"

The response was a suspicious growl. "What do you want? Who are you, anyway?"

"The name is Kitano, chief of the personnel department at Otaman." Was Mitchell's Japanese really good enough to get away with that? With some careful pronunciation and the help of the background noise, he hoped that it was.

"Otaman? Yes, of course! Are you having any problems over there?" The man's tone had changed totally. The suspicion had disappeared, replaced by an urgent concern.

"Yes, a few small problems," said Mitchell, moving the receiver farther from his mouth. "Nothing too serious, I think."

"Security again, is it?"

"That's right. Some small security problems."

The voice at the other end sounded agitated. "Look, I've told your people before not to come here with that sort of thing! Talk directly to the men we have sent you. They are specialists! Do you understand?"

"Yes," said Mitchell. "I'm sorry for bothering you."

"What did you say your name was again?"

"Kitano of the personnel department."

The man clicked his teeth in vexation. "Look, I don't think we've ever met, Kitano-san, but you should understand that contacting us here goes totally against the procedures we established."

"Understood!" Mitchell hastily put the phone down and gave a sigh of relief. His ploy had succeeded, but what exactly had he learned?

Heisei Lease was clearly no ordinary leasing company. Apart from owning a chunk of Otaman's equity, it also appeared to be supplying some kind of security service. Mitchell recalled the tough-looking men in uniform he had encountered during his visit to the Otaman research center. Were they employees of Heisei Lease? It was certainly possible. In that case, what kind of company was it? Who owned Heisei Lease? That was going to be much more difficult to find out.

Mitchell refused to let himself be discouraged. In the last few minutes, he had learned enough to convince him that the trail had to be followed farther.

Mori's meeting with the dragon lady wasn't going well. The two of them sat in the coffee shop of the Isetan department store, a pseudo-European emporium of luxury brands that always made Mori feel edgy. The women were so perfectly dressed, coiffed, and perfumed—how could you even think of touching them? And the men were as smooth as fish, the type of guys who rubbed creams and oils into their faces and had their arms and legs electronically depilated. Mori had nicked himself shaving in a couple of places, and the Korean pickles and *shochu* rice-spirit that he had consumed the night before were still hot on his breath. He sat slumped in the corner of the coffee shop, defiling the place by his presence.

The dragon lady was eating a cake and smoking at the same time. The cigarette was a long thin one, some foreign brand that he had never seen before. She listened in a bored manner to his explanations of the difficulties of the case.

"You are telling me the truth, aren't you?" she said suddenly.

"What do you mean?" said Mori, taken aback by the ferocity of her gaze. He found her eyes disconcerting enough at the best of times. The wrinkled skin around them was crusted with a patina of violet and silver makeup. The eyelashes were false, the eyebrows had been shifted upward, and Western-style folds had been fitted into the lids by cosmetic surgery.

"He hasn't got to you too, has he?"

"Got to me?"

"You know what I mean." She blew out a stream of tobacco smoke and used her fork to spear a piece of the strawberry gâteau. Mori gaped at her, astonished by the implication of what he had just heard.

"You're suggesting that your husband has influenced me in the conduct of this case? Is that what you're saying?"

"You work it out. You're the detective, aren't you?" Irritably, she stubbed the cigarette into an ashtray. It was only half-smoked, with a ring of lipstick discoloring the filter.

Mori was too amazed to be angry. Over the course of the years, he had been accused of many things, sometimes fairly, sometimes unfairly. This, however, was the first time that anyone had accused him of working against the interests of a client.

"If that's what you think, we might as well stop right now." He pushed back his chair and got up to leave. As he had hoped, the woman put out her hand and grabbed him by the jacket.

"Wait a minute," she said. "That was a stupid comment I made. I apologize for it."

"Let me tell you something," growled Mori, standing by the side of the table. "We're not a bunch of conmen or thugs. There are business ethics in this world, and we understand them just as well as doctors or lawyers—or architects, for that matter!"

She ran her hand down the inside of his thigh and patted his knee. "Sit down, Mori-san," she cooed. "I know that you're doing your best. It's just that you don't seem to be concentrating as much as you were at the beginning."

Mori was glad to sit down, though he didn't show it. He could ill afford to walk out on this case before presenting the final report. It was the most lucrative job that he was working on these days, and there was little else on the horizon. Having professional pride was all very well, but without fees there would be no profession to have any pride in.

275

Back in his office, Mori reflected on the conversation as he swilled coffee out of his aluminum mug. In a sense the dragon lady had been right. He hadn't been concentrating on her problems, and with good reason. There were more important things going on. For the second time in a month, he had just managed to escape an attempt on his life. But what had he done to merit that kind of attention? It had to be related to the Yuriko case. Somebody somewhere was prepared to devote thought and money to halting his inquiries for good.

The death of Sano's daughter had taken Mori into something much bigger and more complex than he had imagined possible. He couldn't see the pattern yet, but he could feel its existence. And before too long the outlines ought to become a little clearer. Tomorrow a certain sad case called Nakamura was due to join the Peace Technology's training camp at an undisclosed location. The whole Yuriko case was finally coming to a head.

When Mitchell left the office at six o'clock, Yazawa was sitting in the middle of the dealing room staring at the ceiling while his favorite female graduate stood behind his chair massaging his neck. That was the third time since lunch that she had been summoned. Over the past few

months, Mitchell had come to believe that there was a reasonable correlation between the state of Yazawa's neck muscles and the state of his
mind. It looked as if in both areas the tension was rising to abnormally
high levels.

Mitchell went home and changed into jeans and a T-shirt, then took
the Yamanote loop line to Nippori. As usual, the train was jam-packed.
After almost two years in Tokyo, Mitchell still hadn't got used to the
pressure of other people's bodies against his. It put him on edge, made
him sweat. In the London Underground, he was used to occupying a
certain space—it only had to extend a few inches on all sides—that he
could claim as his own. In Japanese trains, no such personal space existed.
All space was available for use, even that between your legs or next to
your ear. People registered no response when others trod on their toes,
poked their buttocks with umbrellas, or fell asleep on their shoulders.
When squeezed together face to face, they would shut their eyes rather
than stare at each other. Nobody ever reacted, nobody ever said anything.

As the train approached Nippori, the crowd thinned out a little. Some
people even took out newspapers and started reading them, an impossi-
bility in the full crush of the rush hour. Mitchell turned his gaze to an
advertisement for anti-stress medicine made from ancient Chinese herbs:
"The salaryman's friend." He could do with a spoonful of that stuff right
now. Sometimes he felt that he was getting out of his depth these days.
Or rather, that he no longer knew where his depth was. It might be a
couple of inches below his toes or it might be a couple of hundred feet.
If he didn't keep moving with the current, if he stopped to consider
what he was doing, Tokyo might just drown him.

He got out of the train at Nippori, trying to look as inconspicuous
as possible. But how could he look inconspicuous? He was a head taller
than everyone else, had different color hair and different color eyes.
Everyone was watching him; he felt sure of it. On the train, people had
been peering at him over the tops of the books and magazines they were
reading. The ticket collector stared at him, stared at the ticket he was
proffering, then stared at him again, eyes narrowed, as if there were a
possibility of a forgery. When Mitchell walked through the station, he
was followed by the gleaming eyes of a tramp sitting slumped against a
wall. On the platform, schoolgirls shot glances at him and whispered to
their friends. He might as well have been carrying a sign that read, "Here
I am, a strange foreigner called Richard Mitchell engaging in suspicious
activities."

Or he might have been imagining it all. Maybe the ticket collector stared at everyone like that. Maybe the schoolgirls were exchanging stories about their boyfriends. Maybe the tramp was gazing at some delirium-induced hallucination. Maybe the people on the train were just concentrating on the top line of the page they were reading. It was impossible to be sure.

Using a map to guide him, Mitchell made his way around the back of the station into a low-grade entertainment district. Well-muscled men in undershirts squatted on their haunches, slurping noodles from paper cups. Women dressed in chiffon negligées and school uniforms stood in the hallways of pink salons and cabarets, smoking cigarettes and calling out to male passersby in throaty voices. A few of them were desperate enough to include Mitchell in their invitations.

"Hey, handsome boy—just two thousand yen for thirty minutes' service time! Welcome inside, you!"

It was not the kind of district in which Mitchell would have expected to find the headquarters of a major leasing company. Still, where Otaman was concerned, he was immune to surprises by now. He turned left into a side street lined by noodle restaurants and dingy love hotels, checked his map in the light of a flashing purple sign, then emerged into a small square containing a tall windowless structure that he recognized as a vertical parking garage. Next to it was a squat concrete box of six storys that, according to the map, housed the headquarters of Heisei Lease. It also housed a porno video shop in the basement, a money-lending shop on the ground floor, a mah-jong club, and a number of small businesses of uncertain category. Mitchell looked around. The square was empty, lit only by the flickering brightness of the video place.

Mitchell stood in the shadows for ten minutes, then stepped out into the square and approached the front of the building. He tried to walk confidently, as if he were there on a perfectly normal errand—though he had no idea what he would say if he were challenged. Immediately inside the building was a cramped lobby area, with the entrance of the money-lending shop on the left and the scratched and peeling doors of an elevator in the middle. Next to that was a metal door with "Emergency Exit" painted on it in red characters. After assuring himself that there was nobody visible in the money lender's shop, Mitchell strolled into the lobby, pausing in front of the board on the wall that listed the building's tenants. Heisei Lease—there it was, on the sixth floor. Mitchell thought about using the elevator, then decided against it. Instead, he pushed open the creaking metal door on his right and stepped onto the unlit staircase on the other side.

After the door had swung shut behind him, Mitchell stopped to let his eyes get used to the darkness. There was a rustling sound a couple of yards ahead of him, and he held his breath. There was no recurrence. It was a rat, he decided, probably gnawing its way through a discarded trash bag. He squeezed his eyes shut for a moment, then opened them again. He could see a little better now, at least enough to make out the shape of the steps ahead. The rat made another rustling sound. Mitchell ignored it. He had seen rats before, long gray ones scuttling up the alleys of inner London. They were unpleasant little things, but if you didn't bother them, they wouldn't bother you.

One hand feeling for the wall, Mitchell slowly mounted the concrete staircase, crunching through old cigarette packs, balls of newspaper, plastic cups. The rat seemed to be getting more active. In fact, there seemed to be two or three of them scrabbling around the heap of old cardboard that he could dimly make out on the first-floor landing. Mitchell deliberately trod louder, hoping to scare them off. Harmless they might be, but he had no desire to have one come running up his trouser leg.

Strangely enough, his approach had the opposite effect to what he had expected. The rustling and scrabbling grew louder. Mitchell stepped gingerly onto the little landing. There was a fetid smell in the air that he found quite nauseating. How big were these Japanese rats anyway? Could they have mutated somehow, grown fat and fierce on a diet of toxic waste? He still couldn't see anything. They seemed to be under the cardboard somewhere, making more noise than ever, actually trying to thrust their way upward through the many layers.

Mitchell tiptoed over the mound of rotting cardboard. Was living in Tokyo driving him slightly crazy? Maybe his suspicions about Otaman and Yazawa were no more real than the giant rats lying in wait for him under the cardboard. Certainly he was coming up with the weirdest ideas these days, getting increasingly paranoid. For example, that scrap of paper poking out between the sheets of cardboard looked exactly like a human hand. There was the shape of a wrist, even the line of a curled finger. It was strange how your eyes played tricks when your nerves were keyed up. Jaw clenched, Mitchell put his foot down hard on a particularly lumpy section of cardboard. No squealing rats emerged. He gave a sigh of relief and stepped onto the next flight of stairs.

Except that he couldn't put his foot down. Something was preventing him from moving forward! He glanced down, then instantly froze to the spot, his heart leaping in his chest. There was a hand! It was grabbing onto his trouser leg, pulling him back onto the landing. And the hand was connected to an arm, and the arm to the body of a man who was slowly dragging himself out from under a sheet of cardboard! A second ago, Mitchell had actually been walking on top of him!

Convulsed with panic, Mitchell kicked, twisted, hopped, tried to pull himself away from the man's grip. It didn't work. Instead, he lost his footing on the slippery surface of the cardboard and fell to the ground. The man changed his grip from Mitchell's trousers to his arm, hauling himself up close. Mitchell squirmed away through the cardboard, but the man was too strong. There was no shaking him off.

"I've been waiting for you!" he croaked, pushing his face into Mitchell's. "You brought me a present, didn't you? You must have brought something!"

Mitchell was trapped, his back flat against the wall. He gazed at the bloodshot eyes, the straggly beard, the sunken cheeks. "What do you mean?" he muttered faintly.

"I need a new toothbrush. Look—this one is no good now!"

The tramp pulled a pink toothbrush out of his ragged coat and waved it in Mitchell's face. Mitchell tried to edge away, but the man's grip on his wrist was like a steel band.

"Let go of me," Mitchell said desperately. "I'm a foreigner! I haven't got a toothbrush!"

"So where is it?" came the fierce whisper. "In your own country?"

"That's right. I left it back in England." He had stopped struggling. It was important not to make any more noise. Someone there on the first floor might hear them and open the door to find what was going on. The police might be called. Mitchell might end up being arrested for vagrancy! The vagrant financial analyst—he wouldn't last long at Pearson's if that story got out.

"England, you say." The tramp brought a rheumy eye much closer. "Manchester and Liverpool! I like the Beatles very much. I remember when they came to Japan. Do you remember that?"

The tramp was squeezing his wrist tighter now. This was a strong man, maybe an athlete of some sort in better days. Mitchell thought fast. The only sure way to shake the man off would be a full-frontal attack with fists, elbows, and knees. No doubt he would try to cling on, probably giving Mitchell a good raking with those talonlike fingernails. In the

279

end, Mitchell would have to shove him down the stairs, and that would make a big disturbance. Someone would come and grab them both, Mitchell would spend the night in a cell, cooped up with junior yakuza and glue-sniffing bikers, and then in the morning he would be taken to Narita airport and deported. And all because he had chosen the staircase over the elevator!

"Wait! I'll have a look."

Mitchell dug into his pocket. What did he have there? Just his wallet, containing twenty thousand yen, a credit card, his fitness club membership card, and a condom. He wasn't going to hand over any money, and somehow he didn't think the tramp would find much use for either of the other items. What else? Suddenly, he remembered something. There was a comb in his pocket, a long curvy one he used for slicking down his forelock. Thanks to Yazawa's barber, he wasn't going to be needing it again.

"How about this?" he said, taking it from his pocket. "It's a comb, a very good one, actually. I bought it in a famous English department store. Look, there's some writing in English."

There was indeed—"Quality Hair Products" in wavy gold script. It was a decent enough comb, made of toughened plastic that made a euphonious sound when you ran your thumbnail over the teeth. Mitchell did that now and was gratified by the tramp's reaction. He let go of Mitchell's arm, took the comb, and studied it closely for a few moments. Then he dragged it through his long straggly hair. It was just about strong enough for the job.

"Next time, I'll bring a toothbrush," said Mitchell, slowly rising to his feet.

The tramp continued combing his hair, slowly and carefully, as if he were afraid of breaking his new possession. Mitchell left him there and made his way up the next section of staircase.

Nerves still jangling, he gradually felt his way, stumbling and tripping several times, up to the sixth floor. Once there, he paused for several minutes, ear to the metal door, but there was nothing to be heard. Finally, he turned the door handle a little at a time, trying to minimize the squeak it made, then pushed the door a fraction of an inch open. What he saw through the gap was an empty hallway lit by a flickering neon light, an elevator, and on the other side a glass door engraved with the name "Heisei Lease." The door was, he noted, a few inches open. From inside he could hear the murmur of voices, too low for him to understand what was being said.

Mitchell waited for another few minutes, then stepped out into the hallway, gently closing the metal door behind him. He tiptoed across to the glass door. There was an empty reception desk on the other side of it, behind that a couple of tables, some filing cabinets, and a stack of beer crates. The voices seemed to be coming from the far end of the office, next to the window. There were two of them, one of which Mitchell recognized from the phone call in the morning. He flattened himself against the wall next to the door and listened.

"Remember this," said the first voice. "We must preserve security at all times. Every detail of this operation must be exactly right."

"Understood. That reminds me—actually, a strange thing happened here today."

That was the man who had been so domineering on the phone. He now sounded utterly deferential. Mitchell edged closer to the door. He had a strong premonition of what the man was going to say.

"A strange thing? What do you mean?"

"There was a phone call from someone who said he was a section chief in the Otaman personnel department. I checked with one of our people over there, and there were no records of him at all."

"No records! What kind of questions did he ask?"

"He didn't ask any questions at all. That was strange. Also, he spoke strange Japanese. He sounded like a foreigner, in fact."

"There are no foreigners working for Otaman."

"That's what I thought. Already I have informed higher-up people and inquiries are being made."

"Good. Now I must go. All praise to the sensei."

"Praise to the sensei!"

There was the sound of a chair leg squeaking on the floor, and suddenly the senior man was stalking toward the entrance. Mitchell leapt across the hallway on tiptoes and into the emergency exit, swinging the metal door shut behind him. It made a dull thump.

"What was that?"

"What?"

The two men were out in the hallway now. Mitchell could hear the senior one's voice no more than two yards from where he was standing in the dark.

"There was a noise. It sounded as if it came from the emergency exit over there."

"Really? It must be that tramp again. I've had him thrown out a dozen times, but he keeps coming back."

"Can't you do anything about it?"

Mitchell held his breath. If they opened the door and came after him, he would have to run for it. Rushing down the staircase in the dark would be pretty dangerous. One false step, and he would end up in a crumpled heap on the next landing. And then they would grab him. . . .

"I should give him a good beating—he deserves it. But there's a problem."

"What's that?"

"He's so dirty. Nobody wants to get close."

The senior man laughed, and then there was a hum as the elevator arrived. Mitchell closed his eyes in relief. The two men said their farewells and the elevator door banged shut. Mitchell waited for five minutes, slumped against the wall, then edged his way carefully down the staircase. This time the tramp was nowhere in sight. Finally, Mitchell emerged into the empty square and dashed down the narrow lane toward Nippori station.

So anxious was he to put distance between himself and the Heisei Lease office that he didn't pay any attention to the headlights that had turned into the lane until they were a dozen yards away. He stepped into a doorway to let the car pass, and then suddenly ducked down behind a trash can, heart banging like a drum. The car was a black Isuzu Mu, and the driver's features were horribly familiar.

Had Yazawa seen him? He showed no sign of it. His eyes were fixed to the front as the car glided toward the Heisei Lease office.

FOURTEEN

When Mori arrived at the Peace Technology branch in Ochanomizu, the main gates were already open. A long line of people was edging inside, along a pathway marked out by chains hanging between metal posts. Several disciples strode up and down the line, bellowing instructions through megaphones.

"Stay in single file."

"Have your membership certificates ready."

"Everybody will have their chance soon enough, so don't jostle the people in front."

Mori took his place in the line and shuffled forward. Peering ahead, he could see several disciples sitting at a long table, questioning each of the new recruits in turn and tapping information into laptop computers. Behind them, there were half a dozen buses in the courtyard, the long, capacious type that companies used for transporting their workers. They were surrounded by a milling crowd of several hundred people. Mori was relieved to see that he wasn't by any means the oldest recruit present. Although the average age was in the twenties, he could make out a number of middle-aged men in the crowd, most of them gazing around and looking lost.

Approaching the long table, Mori recognized the disciple standing closest to him. It was the man who had driven the little group of potential recruits from Harajuku. When he saw Mori, he frowned.

"You! What are you doing here?"

"I have come to learn more about the sensei's teachings," said Mori. "It is my hope to renew myself and work for the enlightenment of Japan."

"Work for enlightenment? How are you intending to do that?"

"By throwing away the shell of my wasted life," said Mori, handing over his membership card. "By washing off the dirt of useless experience. By digging deep into the mine of the spirit."

"Good, Nakamura, good. Perhaps I was wrong about you before."

Mori gave a grateful smile and little bow. The disciple entered his details into the laptop, then printed out a ticket and handed it to him.

"That's your number for the training session. Don't lose it, whatever you do."

Mori took out his wallet, carefully put the ticket inside, then went to join the crowd in the courtyard. There were eight coaches, each with a capacity of forty or fifty. Looking around, Mori estimated that over three hundred people were waiting. One of Yumi-chan's recent hit songs was blaring from a loudspeaker. A dozen disciples strode through the crowd, checking tickets and shouting instructions through megaphones.

"Be sure that you board the bus that corresponds with the number on your ticket."

"Do not push, do not cause confusion. Wait until the order is given."

Among the crowd there was an atmosphere of subdued excitement. Few of the recruits seemed to know one another, so there was little talking among them. At least three quarters of them were women, mostly in their early twenties, shy looking, but otherwise totally normal. The men were the same—no different from the students and office workers to be seen flooding through the streets of Shibuya every weekend.

The disciples were closing the front gate now, turning away fifty or sixty people who were still waiting in line. From what Miki had told him, they would have to wait for the next training session in three months' time. And where was Miki today? Mori scanned the crowd but couldn't see her. That was strange. The three other disciples whom he had met on Saturday were present, striding through the crowd and yelling instructions. Was it possible that what he had tried to tell her had actually had some effect, that she had decided to break her links with Ono's people? If true, that would be a ray of sunshine. It would mean that he had accomplished something, even if the Yuriko investigation made no further progress.

Mori waited until the disciple who had checked his papers at the gate was walking past, then stepped out of the line and tapped him on the shoulders. "Excuse me," he said timidly. "It's about the young lady who gave me the entry test on Saturday. I don't see her anywhere. I was wondering if something might have happened to her."

"Happened? What do you mean?"

"Well, I was wondering whether she might be sick or have left or something. . . ."

Mori was hoping against hope. The disciple stared at him incredulously. "You mean turn her back on the sensei's teachings? Impossible! She will never leave us!"

"That's good news," said Mori dully. "You see, I feel some personal obligation to her as the person who led me into this new life."

"That's old thinking, Nakamura," snapped the disciple. "You must learn to clear it out of your brain. Obligation, duty, gratitude—these arise from personal interactions that are merely random, like the Brownian motion of gases. The only constant forces are growth and decay. This is the basis of all the sensei's thinking."

"I understand that," said Mori, lowering his gaze. "Personal matters which look as big as mountains are just grains of dust in the eye. Still, it just seemed surprising that she is not here. "It's not important, I know . . ."

"The reason she's not here is simple," said the disciple. "She received special instruction to go alone to the training center yesterday afternoon."

"A special instruction? What does that mean?"

"What does it mean?" echoed the disciple, with an enigmatic smile. "It means that it was the sensei's will that she should be there yesterday night. Don't ask too many questions, Nakamura. Before asking a question, always ask yourself why it is important to know the answer."

"The questions of fools and the answers of experts—together they make a dialogue of croaking frogs."

The disciple patted him on the shoulder and moved off toward the next coach. Mori stepped back into the line, which was finally edging forward. So Miki had been summoned to the training center a day early. The special instruction must have come suddenly—she had given no hint when speaking to Mori on Saturday. What inferences could be drawn from that? There was only one that Mori could be sure about—that she had taken absolutely no notice of his words of advice. Understandable, of course. Had he really expected her to listen to the warnings of someone like Nakamura, a man so defeated by life that he was applying to join a religious cult at the age of forty-five?

Mori took his seat in the bus next to a young man wearing a single gold earring and a dreamy expression. Mori caught his eye and smiled. "This is truly an exciting experience," he said. "I feel privileged this opportunity has come to me so soon."

The young man nodded. "Six months ago my eyes were opened by the sensei's teachings and already I have been given the privilege of special training three times."

Mori noticed that the young man never really closed his mouth. His lips and teeth were always half an inch open, which gave him an air of perpetual surprise. Surprised by being alive, thought Mori. It wasn't hard to imagine what he must have looked like when he was three or four years old.

"So you probably know where we're going?" murmured Mori.

The man frowned and shook his head. "I was told not to discuss that subject with anyone."

Mori felt like grabbing him by the lapels and roaring, "Can't you think for yourself for once, instead of doing whatever you're told?" But there would have been no point—the answer was obvious. "Can't you at least say how long we'll be in this bus?"

"It doesn't matter," said the man with the earring. "All time spent with the sensei is precious. Time without him is dead time."

"But we aren't spending time with him now, are we?" said Mori.

"We can if we wish." The young man opened his shoulder bag and took out a cloth headpiece interwoven with wire cord, which he wrapped carefully around his head.

"What are you doing?" said Mori.

"Haven't you seen one of these before? This machine was developed by our medical electronics unit. It enables me to receive the sensei's *ki* waves at any time, just by pressing a button."

He took a battery pack out of his bag, connected it to one of the wires, and switched it on. The headpiece gave off a quavering hum, like a faulty refrigerator. The young man laid his head back against the seat and stared into space. His mouth was still that half-inch open.

Mori's bus was the last to leave. He glanced out the window as it pulled out of the gateway into the streets of Ochanomizu, so full of ordinary busy people going about their ordinary business. Inside, the bus was a different world—of quiet men and women staring down at Ono's words on their laps or receiving his *ki* waves through headpieces or listening to Yumi-chan singing her eerily saccharine songs. The video screens at the front of the coach were showing fast-changing images of amoeba replicating, H-bombs exploding, giant lotus blooms opening up, huge waves rolling across a bay. Nobody else was looking out of the window. The coach eased into the line of traffic. Mori pulled one of Ono's books from his bag and stared blankly at the page.

What kind of place would Ono have chosen for his training center? Would they take the expressway that pointed north through the Kanto Plain to the Japan Alps, or the highway that would swing northeast along the coastline, or perhaps the permanently clogged artery that went west through Yokohama to the Izu Peninsula? The coach rumbled through the heavy traffic, down taxi-lined shopping streets, past giant department stores and office blocks. Surprisingly it showed no sign of making for any of the major routes at all. Instead, it headed due south through the heart of the city, the Ginza, the financial district, and finally into the warehouse area of the waterfront.

Mitchell spent the morning in the office, answering more queries from Feinman and staring at the numbers blinking on the giant board on the wall. Advancing prices were marked in red, declines in green. Today everything was green, just as Yazawa had forecast in the strategy meeting. The market was collapsing. There was no particular reason. Intelligent people had been buying those same stocks all last week. Now, suddenly, nobody wanted them. That was an eerie phenomenon, thought Mitchell. Was his own world about to collapse just as the Nikkei Index had suddenly done a few years ago? Was his own stock about to enter a dizzy downspiral? It was possible. After that moment outside the Heisei Lease office last night, all the assumptions on which he had been acting had started to look rather frail.

Had Yazawa seen him lurking in that doorway? So far there was no way of telling, since Yazawa had yet to put in an appearance in the office. According to the girl who doubled as his masseuse, he had departed on a sudden business trip. Mitchell didn't know whether to be glad or fearful. He wasn't looking forward to their first meeting, but neither did he relish several days of uncertainty.

"Is something the matter, Mitchell-san? Would you like a cup of coffee?"

It was the girl who had brought him the stock exchange fax about Heisei Lease. She was called Keiko, Mitchell recalled. She had joined the company just one month before on the personal recommendation of Yazawa. So what was the relationship between them? Could Yazawa have put her there to keep a watch on him?

Mitchell resisted the impulse to snap a refusal. "Certainly," he answered with a rather forced smile. "That's very kind of you."

There was a notebook lying open on his desk in which Mitchell had listed a number of doubts and worries about Otaman. Keiko was glancing at it as she put the coffee cup down on his desk. Or was she? Mitchell watched her out of the corner of his eye. With her long, fluttering eyelashes and perpetual half-smile, it was hard to know what she was looking at.

"You seem tired, Mitchell-san. Is there anything else I can do for you? Would you like me to massage your neck?"

And meanwhile look over my shoulder and read all the documents on the desk? Absolutely not! The best thing you can do for me is get out of my sight as soon as possible! So thought Mitchell. What he said was rather more tactful.

"No thank you, Keiko-san, but it's nice of you to offer. A woman like you will make an excellent wife one day."

She giggled dutifully and walked back to her seat with little tripping steps. Mitchell took a gulp of coffee and swilled it around his mouth. He could imagine Keiko twenty years older, bringing a cup of coffee to her elderly husband with that same half-smile on her face. There would be just enough cyanide in it to do the trick. Immediately after the funeral, she would fill out the claim on the life insurance policy. Then, still dressed in black, she would call her young lover on the phone. Incidents of that sort really happened. They were reported in the papers almost every week.

He ate lunch on his own in a small curry-rice restaurant in the basement of the building. It wasn't Mitchell's favorite place by any means, but it was fast and filling. You bought a meal ticket from a machine at the door, waited for a space to open up at the eating counter, then straddled a stool and tossed your ticket onto the greasy Formica. In a matter of seconds, a plate would be slapped down in front of you, together with a glass of water and a hand towel.

Mitchell ordered a medium-hot beef curry, which he proceeded to spoon into his mouth with the relentless determination that the etiquette of the place demanded. Around him, nobody was saying anything. The only sounds were the scraping of spoons on bowls and the noises of sauce being slurped. The customers were all male. Some of them were skimming through weekly magazines laid flat on the counter, others staring at the small TV set perched on a shelf. The program was a preview of the baseball season. Mitchell watched it in a desultory fashion. Anything would do to take his mind off Yazawa and Otaman.

"So how do you evaluate the Giants this year?" the interviewer asked the retired catcher with the permanently bewildered expression. "They managed to win at the Kawasaki stadium last night, but are they really playing well enough to win the upcoming series against the Porpoises?"

"There is still room to strengthen their spirit as a team," said the catcher cautiously. "They are relying too much on individual performances. Without those two home runs from Kawasaki, the position would have been very doubtful."

"Kawasaki-san usually achieves fine performances at the Kawasaki stadium," said the announcer. "He certainly kept up that record last night, didn't he!"

"That's right," said the catcher with a clumsy grin. "Maybe if there had been a baseball field bearing my name, my home-run hitting would have been a little better."

Mitchell chewed more slowly, toying with a gristly lump of beef between tongue and teeth. Finally, he stopped chewing altogether and sat staring at the TV screen. What had they said that he found disturbing? It was the mention of Kawasaki, symbol of his general frustration with Otaman. He was no nearer finding the truth about the Kawasaki project now than he had been when he first heard about it kneeling on the floor of the Otaman toilet. But wait a moment! The TV people had been talking about some baseball player called Kawasaki, who always did well at the Kawasaki stadium. Kawasaki was not just a place name. Like most Japanese place names, it was a surname too. So when he had heard those two Otaman employees talking about the Kawasaki project, why had he

289

assumed that they meant a project based in Kawasaki? They might have been referring to a project led by a man called Kawasaki! It was equally likely, in fact.

Mitchell dropped his spoon into the half-full bowl, splattering curry sauce on his tie. Suddenly, he didn't feel hungry.

"Have you finished already?"

Don't just sit there staring into space—not in the hour between twelve o'clock and one when we do 90 percent of our business! Either pick up that spoon and continue shoveling curry rice into your face, or get up and go! All this and more was communicated by the cook's beady glare. Mitchell took the hint. He emptied his glass of chlorinated water, wiped his mouth with the hand towel, and left.

Back in the office, the research department was deserted—no analysts, no research assistants. Ted Shimano was probably strolling through the boutiques of Ginza, Kent the Mormon standing in Hibiya Park trying to interest some middle-aged housewife in the teachings of the Latter-Day Saints. And Keiko? Perhaps gone for an assignation with Yazawa in some nearby love hotel. Mitchell sat down at his desk. The task ahead of him was quite simple. He had to find out whether Otaman had a senior employee—a man powerful enough to head a project bearing his name—called Kawasaki. He tried not to let his hopes rise too high. So far there had been too many disappointments. He felt as if he had been wandering around a darkened room, banging his shins on the furniture from time to time but failing to find the door. In the end, he had started to doubt whether there was a door at all.

He unlocked his desk drawer and pulled out all the information he had collected about Otaman—annual reports, product brochures, financial statements in both English and Japanese. For the next twenty minutes, he scanned every page for the names of employees. He found a Kawamoto who was head of the textiles division, and a Yamazaki in the import division, but no Kawasaki. Perhaps he was wrong again, he thought gloomily. Perhaps he had simply misunderstood what was being said. Then he remembered the allergic reaction the mention of the Kawasaki project had provoked in Wada, the stressed-out finance director. No, the Kawasaki project certainly existed. Mitchell was convinced that it was the key to Yazawa's bullishness on the stock.

He dumped all the documents back into his desk drawer, then went over to the filing cabinet and pulled out the company file that Pearson's maintained on every listed company. He had already taken out most of the material, so all that was left were a few publicity pamphlets from the mid-eighties. "Otaman announces promising diversification into soybean milk products!" "Otaman sets up helicopter transportation subsidiary!" Mitchell took them over to his desk and leafed through them. As far as he knew, almost all these ventures had ended in failure. Golf course development, for example—Otaman had begun that in 1988, just in time to catch the peak of the bubble economy two years later. Mitchell glanced at the photos of smiling middle-aged men in tartan trousers practicing their golf swings. "Otaman's strong tradition of golf," ran the caption. "Our company's executives at the recent company golf tournament."

Mitchell gave a sigh. How could he recommend a company like this to someone like Lazarus? Otaman had the kind of management who would diversify into golf course development for no better reason than they enjoyed playing the game themselves. Under the caption were a few paragraphs explaining the company's deep attachment to the game of golf, which apparently stretched back to the prewar era of old Manjiro Ota. "In today's Otaman, the traditional love of golf is as strong as ever," the article fluffed on. "Many senior executives are keen golfers, including West Japan Sales Director Keizo Eda and last year's tournament winner, Strategic Planning Department Deputy Leader Yoshio Kawasaki (extreme left of photo)."

Mitchell jerked to attention. He closed his eyes and opened them again. No, he wasn't imagining it. The name was still written there on the page—two Chinese characters that spelled not Kawamoto or Yamazaki this time, but Kawasaki. Unmistakably, incontrovertibly Kawasaki. Otaman did indeed have a senior employee called Kawasaki. Mitchell now knew that for sure. He also knew the man's title and even what he looked like. Of course, this was all historical information. By now, Kawasaki's hairline would have receded farther, and there would be a few more wrinkles in those plump features.

Mitchell slid the pamphlets back into the file and returned it to the cabinet. It was a quarter to one. In ten minutes or so, the analysts and research assistants would be returning from restaurants, boutiques, hotels, or wherever else they had been spending their lunch breaks. There was just enough time for him to confirm his thoughts.

He called the operator at the Otaman head office. "Please give me

Kawasaki-san of the Strategic Planning Department," he said curtly. This time he wasn't going to allow them enough time to identify him as a foreigner.

"Do you mean Director Kawasaki?"

Not a mere department chief, but a director. Kawasaki had obviously done well over the past few years. "Yes," said Mitchell.

"Excuse me, but who shall I say is calling?"

Mitchell hadn't been prepared for that question. He hesitated for an instant, then an idea sprang to mind. He wasn't sure whether it was a good idea or a bad one, but it was the only one available. "Yazawa of Pearson Securities," he replied casually.

"Understood," sang out the operator. "Please wait for a moment while I put you through."

She sounded quite accustomed to the name, thought Mitchell. The phone was ringing—once, twice, three times. Then a man's voice came on the line, cautiously respectful.

"Yazawa-san? Didn't Kawasaki tell you? He's gone on a business trip to the Oshima facility."

Mitchell put the receiver back into place without saying anything. Finally, he was making progress. Otaman did indeed have a senior executive called Kawasaki, whose staff appeared well acquainted with Yazawa.

There was a noise behind Mitchell's back and he swiveled around, half-expecting to see Keiko. Instead Kent the Mormon was standing in the middle of the room staring open-mouthed at the giant stock-price board. More or less all the prices were green now, including the machinery stocks about which he had been so optimistic the day before.

"This is terrible," he moaned. "What's going on?"

"Isn't it obvious, Kent?" said Mitchell, getting to his feet. "All the dry leaves are sinking!"

"But why!" said Kent indignantly. "I mean, these are good stocks!"

He really did believe that, thought Mitchell. That was the difference between Kent and the rest of them. Kent believed wholeheartedly in the virtue of his machinery stocks, just as he believed wholeheartedly in Joseph Smith and his golden tablets. Nothing could shake his faith, not even the fact that the stocks had been in a downtrend for nearly two years now. Whatever happened, Kent would continue to follow the way of water.

Mitchell went over to the bookcase next to Keiko's desk and pulled out an illustrated guide to Japan. There was Oshima on the map—the largest of a string of little islands that looked as if they had been excreted from the aperture of Tokyo Bay. He turned to the summary page of facts and figures at the back of the book. Oshima, he read, is the largest of the seven Izu Islands, a volcanic chain stretching three hundred miles into the Pacific Ocean. Administratively part of the Tokyo metropolitan area, it has a population of thirty-five thousand and an area of fifty square miles. The women of the island, called *anko,* wear dark cotton kimonos with white splashes and carry their burdens on their heads. The island is dominated by Mount Mihara, an active volcano whose last eruption in 1985 caused the entire island to be evacuated. The main industries are the production of camelia oil and milk.

So Greater Tokyo spread three hundred miles into the Pacific Ocean and included a lava-spouting volcano. So there were Japanese women who carried bundles on their heads. The information was certainly interesting, but it didn't give him much help. And it was unlikely that the Kawasaki project had much to do with camelia oil or dairy products. Mitchell turned back to the map and stared at it.

"What are you up to, Mitch? Are you planning to take a vacation in Oshima or something?"

Mitchell looked up into Ted Shimano's smiling face. For a moment, he was lost for words. No credible explanation came to mind.

"What about these *anko* girls?" said Mitchell lamely. "The book says they're the most conservative girls in Japan. I'd like to see that for myself."

He wished fervently that Ted would go off and dewax his ears or clip the hairs out of his nose or whatever it was that he was planning to do. But for some reason Ted was finding the subject too amusing to leave alone.

"Can you beat that!" said Ted, turning around to appeal to Kent the Mormon. "Mitch is planning to go to Oshima and try his luck with the *anko!*"

It was then that Mitchell noticed Keiko standing in the doorway, listening to the conversation with evident attention. Her cheeks, he thought, were looking rather flushed. She walked across to her desk, glancing at the map that Mitchell was holding as she passed.

"Feel free to ask me about Oshima," she said. "I have many relatives living on Oshima, you see."

Mitchell found himself struggling for words again, trying to think of some way of changing the subject. Ted shook his head in amused disbelief and left the room. Keiko stood there watching him, that same little half-smile on her face.

The phone on the desk in front of him rang, and he stared at it for a moment.

"Do you want me to get that for you, Mitchell-san?"

Mitchell snatched at the receiver. The last thing he wanted was Keiko intercepting his calls.

"Hello, Mr. Mitchell. How are you today?"

At first, he didn't recognize the female voice on the other end of the phone. The accent was so much more British than his own. Was it someone from the embassy, or a journalist from the BBC?

"Uh—fine," he replied, still not catching it. "And how are you?"

"In excellent form, actually. Remember, I said I'd call. Well, here I am—calling."

The sly giggle gave it away. "Eiko!" he said, suddenly elated. "It's great to hear from you. I've been thinking about you all the time."

A lie, of course, but one in a good cause. In fact, Mitchell had more or less forgotten about Eiko, such had been his troubles with Yazawa, Otaman, and the rest. Now, the memory of her pushed everything else aside—the flashing eyes, the perfect mouth, the mischievous, mocking Eiko-ness that was in her every gesture.

"You're a good talker, Richard Mitchell."

"Not just a talker! Next time we meet, you can judge for yourself!"

Her laugh was like a sparkling wave in a sunny bay. "That's why I'm ringing, actually," she said. "I'd rather like to see you as soon as possible."

Eiko wanted to see him as soon as possible! Mitchell was going up in his own estimation all the time. He turned around to check whether Keiko had been monitoring the conversation. She hadn't. In fact, she wasn't even sitting at her desk anymore.

"There's no point in waiting," said Eiko briskly. "What about tonight?"

"Tonight!" She was desperate for him! It was the only possible explanation.

"Yes, it's my night off, you see. I thought it would be nice if you could come around eight o'clock. I'll prepare my pièce de résistance for you—jolly old mixed grill and mashed potatoes!"

Jolly old mixed grill and mashed potatoes! Mitchell wouldn't have cared if she'd said fish paste sandwiches. One of the most beautiful women Mitchell had met in his life, an elegant creature who worked in a top-class Ginza hostess club and spoke superb, educated English, was inviting him home for a meal that she would prepare with her own hands! This was the kind of thing that could only happen in Tokyo. Never in Hackney, never in a thousand years!

"I'll see you tonight, then," said Mitchell after scribbling down the directions to her apartment.

"Cheerio, Richard. Don't be late, now. I'll be creaming the potatoes specially for you!"

Mitchell put the phone down, amazed by himself yet again.

Mori sat on his assigned bench at the back of the lower deck and gazed out of the grimy porthole beside him. Craning his head, he could see the ship's wake, a gray froth spreading out on the filmy waters of the bay. A strange thing about Tokyo, Mori reflected; the farther away, the better it looked. From this distance, separated from the eye by five miles of water, with the citadels of concrete and glass lit up cleanly in the spring sunshine, the place looked manageable, almost placid. You couldn't hear the roar of the streets, nor get jostled by the crowds, nor sense the city's disordered metabolism.

It took almost two hours for the ship to grind its way past Yokohama, along the Miura Peninsula, then into the heavier swells of the open sea. Although there was little wind, the water was rough enough for the ship to develop a pronounced pitch and roll. Tokyo soon became a distant blur glimpsed through the spray-lashed porthole. Mori was wondering whether the ship would bear east around Noto, then follow the coast north or cut across toward the Izu Peninsula. Again, though, there was no deviation from the route due south. This time Mori knew what it meant. They had to be heading for one of the Izu Islands.

On the bench next to Mori sat the man with the earring. He had finished with the headpiece and was now absorbed in Ono's latest book, underlining important sentences with a yellow marker. In Mori's experience that was a sure sign of mediocrity. It was a way of pretending to yourself that you had absorbed things that you hadn't.

"Looks like we're heading for Oshima or one of the other islands," said Mori.

"The place is not important," said the man with the earring, glancing up briefly. "The sensei has chosen this place for reasons that must be good."

No doubt about that, thought Mori. Only a couple of hours from central Tokyo, yet remote from the attentions of the authorities and inaccessible to snoops and troublemakers. And, of course, a place that was hard to get to would be equally hard to get away from.

The other recruits were almost as quiet as the man with the earring. They hadn't been told that it was forbidden to get up and wander around the boat, but nobody did. Instead, most of them had their eyes fixed on a large screen that had been set up at the prow end of the ship. So far it had shown a number of short clips about Ono, his teachings and prophecies. In one, he used sophisticated computer graphics to demonstrate the series of giant earthquakes that he was predicting before the end of the century. Mori watched in uncomfortable fascination as the ground under central Tokyo liquefied, toppling skyscrapers, flattening bridges, and releasing curtains of fire. The detail was close enough for him to make out Shinjuku, where the eighty-eight storys of the city hall had crashed to the ground and the Kabuki-cho entertainment district was being quickly reduced to cinders. His own office was only a few miles from there. The building was several decades old, with foundations so weak that the whole structure rattled and swayed in high winds. In the event of an earthquake on the scale Ono was predicting, it would probably be the first building in all of Tokyo to collapse.

In another clip, Ono was being interviewed by a pretty young woman who Mori remembered seeing on TV news programs several years ago. From the way she asked the questions, it sounded as if she were a fully paid-up member of Peace Technology.

"Your disciples have called you a great scientist and philosopher, spiritual leader and also a living god. What does it mean to be called a living god?"

Behind his bushy beard, Ono smiled genially. "It is not difficult to be a living god, actually. All human beings have this capacity, if only they were aware of it."

The woman's eyes went big with exaggerated surprise. "You mean everyone can be a living god? Including me?"

"Yes, you too, Kyoko-chan! You have that capacity just the same as everyone else. Unfortunately, most people are unable to kill the human being in themselves and bring the god to life."

"Kill the human being? What does that mean, exactly?"

"It's a rather difficult expression, I know. What it means is that you have to reject all the false information that has been imprinted on you by the circumstances that you were born into. Jobs, family, friends, housing loans, worries about education and marriage—these are all part of the human being that you have accidentally become."

"But these things are important, aren't they?"

Ono threw back his head and laughed, revealing an impressively regular set of teeth. "Yes, of course. They are important in your daily life as a human being. But that is all. They are what limit you as a human being and prevent the release of the life force that lies deep within you. This is why most people are unable to bring the god within them to life."

"So what must I do to become a living god?"

Ono nodded, suddenly serious. "It needs much training, much spiritual exercising. It is not enough to forget the human being; you must actively kill it. It is the role of our organization to enable this to happen on a national scale. As a result of our efforts, the god force will grow stronger and stronger in Japan."

"Thank you very much, sensei."

After that, the screen flickered blankly for a few seconds, then went back to the first clip that had been shown, a collection of the highlights of Yumi-chan's recent concert tour. Most of the recruits continued watching, even though they had seen the whole thing just an hour before. Mori glanced out of the window. He couldn't make out the mainland any longer, just the sky and the wheeling gulls and the gray churning sea.

It took almost three hours to get to Oshima. The ship pulled into the harbor, and the disciples directed the disembarkation of the recruits as efficiently as they had directed the embarkation on the Tokyo waterfront. A carpet of rush matting had been laid along the side of the quay, and the recruits were instructed to sit down cross-legged on it and wait for further instructions. Again, Mori found himself next to the man with the earring, who was still absorbed in the teachings of Ono.

"What is happening now?" Mori muttered.

"We are waiting," said the man with the earring. As on the coach and on the boat, he was sitting with his earring side to Mori. After his statement of the obvious, Mori felt a strong temptation to seize the thin gold loop between finger and thumb and give it a hard downward jerk.

"Yes, but why wait here on the quay?"

"Why not? The sensei's people know what they are doing, I think."

Such trust. This was the sort of man who was born to be deceived—by women, door-to-door salesmen, politicians, religious leaders, anyone.

He had probably believed in monsters and water goblins well into junior high school. Mori tried to control his contempt. After all, everyone had a little of the same impulse. Everyone wants to believe in something outside their own experience. Women read romantic comic books about true love, even though every hour they spend with a man is a living contradiction. Men watch movies about heroic samurai, heroic cops, even heroic yakuza, even though they've never met anyone like that and never will. Reality is weak compared with the urge to believe.

The older generation of politicians and businessmen—all of them had once believed things that sounded ridiculous in retrospect: that "one hundred million spirits acting as one" could defeat the material strength of the Western nations, even when there were no more warships or fuel; that the eight corners of the world could be united under Japanese rule; that the imperial family was descended directly from the gods. Now these men were controlling huge organizations, making hundreds of complex decisions every year. You could believe stupid things and not be at all stupid yourself. It just depended on the environment.

"Did you study hard during the voyage, Nakamura?"

Mori looked up to see the disciple standing in front of him on the rush mat. "I did my best," he answered. "I read the sensei's words on the great purification and meditated on them."

"Good," said the disciple, turning away. "That is one of the key parts of the sensei's teaching. Tomorrow you will be guided through some meditation exercises that you will never forget for the rest of your life."

The big ferry ship that had brought them here was nosing out of the harbor, ready to make the journey back to Tokyo. Mori stared across the quay at the little port town. The last time he had been on Oshima was twenty-five years previously. He remembered the scene well—the hammering heat of August, the trees and bushes fizzing with cicadas, the smell of baked clams. A first-year student called Kazuo Mori had come for three days fishing with a couple of friends from the university karate club. In this same little town, they had met a group of high school girls on their annual class trip. Mori had the task of approaching the best-looking girls he could find. There was something in the air that midsummer's day, something that made it natural and innocent to laugh and share secrets with three seventeen-year-old girls; to become close friends in just a couple of hours. Later in the evening—the six of them diving naked off the rowing boat, pale bodies ghosting through the clear water, then settling down snug on the gritty sand, listening to the crash of the waves and the buzz of the insects and the little noises made by the others, gazing up into a sky splattered with more stars than Mori had seen before or since. Next day—smiles and waves and an exchange of phone numbers that everyone knew would never be dialed.

Everything new and easy for the young, all experience waiting to be picked like a ripe persimmon. Mori wouldn't want to see the women now. He wouldn't want to see the three of them stepping out of that little souvenir store on the corner, with bulging handbags and too much makeup and loud voices shrieking out jokes. And he wouldn't want them to see him either. As for the little town itself, though—nothing much seemed to have changed. The fishing boats in the harbor were newer; there were some satellite dishes peering skyward like giant sunflowers; one or two more advertising signs. That was all. The streets were as empty and dusty as he remembered them; the old women peering out of the doorways crinkle-eyed and dark-skinned; the cluster of wooden houses as small under the looming bulk of the volcano.

After another ten minutes there was a whine in the distance, then the sleek forms of three hydrofoils appeared around the headland, skimming across the bay with a gentle bucking motion that disguised their speed. The ferry seemed to be standing still in the water as they raced around it and entered the harbor. The disciples raised their megaphones, and all the recruits were instructed to prepare for boarding. As usual, not a word was said about where they were going or how long it would take.

There were a couple of men making some repairs to one of the fishing boats in the harbor. Mori watched their reaction as the hydrofoils pulled up at the quay. They glanced over a few times, as the boat they were working on bobbed about in the wash, but that was all. Obviously, they had seen it happen many times before.

Three hydrofoils, each with a capacity of thirty or forty—it was going to take at least two trips to transport everyone. That suggested that their destination couldn't be all that far away. Most likely, they were bound for a smaller island, one that didn't have a good enough harbor to allow the big ferryboat to moor.

The disciples checked that everyone was present, then issued the instructions for boarding. Mori was gratified to learn that this time his group was due to be among the first to embark.

Once inside, they were told to fasten their safety harnesses and stow their bags safely under their benches. The hydrofoil started gently, gliding out of the bay and only picking up speed when they were beyond the headland. Then they were hurtling across the open sea, the direction obscured by the lashing of spray on the window. A few times they hit larger waves, and there was a booming sound as the entire craft lifted out of the water.

After ten minutes of this, the girl sitting beside Mori took off her *ki-wave* receiver and raised a hand. The disciple leaning against the wall didn't notice or pretended not to notice, so finally she called out.

"Excuse me—I have a request. Please listen to my request!"

"What is it?" snapped the disciple.

"My stomach is in a bad condition. I would like to request permission to use the toilet facilities, please?"

The disciple approached her seat, using the handrail to stop himself from stumbling. The woman looked up at him appealingly. "First, try meditation," said the disciple sternly. "With correct meditation, it is possible to overcome the rebellion of the body."

The woman nodded. She was breathing heavily now, beads of sweat standing out on her forehead. Her eyelids were fluttering shut.

"Forget your stomach," said the disciple in a low monotone. "Forget your body and forget your mind. Renew yourself in the cleansing fire, stare unblinking into the great golden eye . . ."

"The great golden eye," murmured the woman, her own eyes fluttering shut.

"The great golden eye that never closes," droned the disciple, pressing the palm of his hand onto her forehead. "You cannot look into the golden eye with your two naked eyes. You must open your hidden eye, the third eye that is now stirring to the warmth of my hand, opening like a lotus bud . . ."

The woman was making little gulping noises. Her face had lost all color. Mori leaned back in his seat and opened his book. It was obvious what was going to happen next.

"Bathe yourself in the flood that washes away all that is old and useless . . ."

"The flood that washes away . . ."

It didn't take long. She took a deep breath, then suddenly stood up, shoulders heaving. Possibly because she had been repressing the impulse for several minutes, the first heave of her stomach was a powerful one, sending a jet of puke streaming over the well-polished boards of the deck.

"What are you doing?" yelled the disciple, hurriedly taking a step backward.

That was a mistake, because she turned toward him, looked up, and tried to say something. Instead of words came the second heave of her stomach, not as powerful as the first and less liquid in content. This time the disciple was badly positioned, and the puke rained down on his lower legs. Coffee, noted Mori, and sweet corn and lumps of bread and white meat—Kentucky Fried Chicken, perhaps. The disciple was wearing trousers with cuffs, down into which the larger gobs of puke were slowly sliding.

He grabbed the woman by the upper arm, this time taking care to stay behind the line of fire. "Go to the toilet at once," he said tightly. "Get cleaned up!"

The woman put a handkerchief to her mouth and scuttled off obediently to the toilet. The disciple stared around at the other recruits, then disappeared through the door that led to the upper deck.

After another twenty minutes, the hum of the motor dropped to a lower pitch and the hydrofoil began to slow. The spray lashed the window less frequently, and Mori was able to make out the outlines of their destination—a small, heavily forested island that rose steeply from a rocky shoreline to a single peak. As they drew closer, more detail became apparent—the high cliffs on the west side, the clump of flat concrete buildings on the near shore, some sort of communication tower peeking through the trees. Closer still, Mori could see the artificial harbor and the boats within it—two more jetfoils and a number of smaller craft. There were no fishing boats, no cars in the quayside area, no billboards on the roofs of the concrete buildings. Mori guessed that it wasn't going to be a good place to buy souvenirs.

The hydrofoil glided into the harbor and the recruits disembarked according to the disciples' instructions. The girl who had been sick was given a cloth and bucket and told to go back inside and clean up the mess on the floor. She looked a lot better after throwing up, but she was crimson with embarrassment. Pity she didn't aim a little higher, thought Mori. A stream of hot puke down the inside of his shirt might have made him shut up about the great golden eye for a long time to come.

FIFTEEN

If Eiko's instructions hadn't been so precise, Mitchell would never have been able to find her apartment. Only a few hundred yards from the main road, it was set in an exclusive residential district of narrow winding lanes and high walls. Glancing into the parking areas of luxury apartment blocks, Mitchell saw Porsches, Rolls-Royces, a Morgan, an old gas-guzzling Chevrolet with giant fins.

Each car would have cost its owner double the price overseas, and all for the sake of grinding forward from one jammed junction to the next. In Mitchell's view, keeping a high-performance sports car in such conditions was almost an act of cruelty, like keeping a hunting dog in a skyscraper block. One day he intended to own a Morgan himself. One day he would be the kind of person who should own a Morgan—fiendishly successful but carefree—and he would drive it where it should be driven. He would squeal around the winding roads

of the Scottish Highlands or thunder through the Loire Valley, resplen-
dent in goggles and long scarf flying in the wind. There would be a
woman in the seat beside him, of course—a mysterious, sophisticated
type who looked like Nastassia Kinski or Isabelle Adjani. Come to think
of it, she might look like Eiko. Yes, Eiko would certainly do.

There were trees everywhere—an even surer status symbol than the
cars. Not just a few obligatory cherries, but leafy evergreens running all
the way up to the brow of the hill, where the silhouette of a shrine gate
stood in the moonlight. The streets were quiet—no blaring loudspeakers,
no subway trains shaking the ground beneath your feet, no karaoke
booming away in back rooms. An expensively dressed woman was kneeling down scooping up the mess made by her poodle. A young man in a
tuxedo got out of a taxi and pressed the buzzer on a door in a high stone
wall. There was no name on the door, no sign on the wall to indicate what
lay behind. That, thought Mitchell, was a better indication of the prestige
of the area than the trees or the cars. Here you could buy privacy.

Eiko's apartment block was set some thirty yards back from the road.
Mitchell crunched his way across the gravel, passing a giant lichen-en-
crusted stone lantern with a Ferrari nestling in its shadows. The main
door hummed open on his approach, giving entry to a lobby of gleaming black marble, silent and empty. Mitchell keyed Eiko's apartment
number into the entry phone and glanced at the mailboxes. Only half of
them had names, of which three belonged to foreigners. Eiko, he noted,
was among the residents who preferred anonymity.

"Richard! Don't be such a nosy parker!"

Mitchell gave a little jump at the sound of Eiko's voice, immediately
provoking a snort of laughter from the metal grille above the entry
phone. He couldn't see the security camera, but it was obviously there
somewhere. It was lucky that he hadn't been picking his nose or adjusting the hang of his boxer shorts.

The heavy security door gave a whirring sound. Mitchell went
through it and into the plush, leather-lined elevator.

He glanced in the mirror. What he saw met with his approval. He was
freshly shaven, hair slicked back to disguise the damage done by Yazawa's
barber. His slacks, pastel green with a baggy seat and pegged ankles, had
been bought at a boutique in Harajuku a couple of weeks ago. Mitchell
was especially proud of his shirt, a billowy number featuring an eye-bend-
ing wave pattern in bright yellow superimposed with European newspaper headlines. "BASTA!" it said on his collar, "BRONCA!" on his left cuff.

When had Mitchell started dressing like this? Back in London, he had been happy with Marks and Spencer's underwear, C&A jeans, a leather jacket bought in a street market. Clothes were just something you picked up in the morning from a heap on the sofa and got into without thinking about. A shirt was a shirt. Any one was as good as another, until it became too grubby to wear any longer and got flung into the laundry bag or sometimes back into the closet. He bought an item of clothing only as a replacement for another item that had worn out or gotten lost. Now he spent Sundays browsing through the boutiques of Harajuku, his credit card primed for action. He had spent more on his boxer shorts than he would have previously spent on an entire outfit. It was all part of the new Mitchell, an individual who refused to accept the lukewarm mediocrity of existence. He was ready to challenge whatever the world had to offer.

What the world had to offer him tonight was Eiko. She was waiting to greet him at the elevator door; barefooted, dressed in a long T-shirt and cutoff jeans. He moved forward to give her a peck on the cheek, but she saw it coming and skipped backward.

"Great perfume," said Mitchell, refusing to be put off his stride.

"Chanel Number Nineteen, limited edition. It's one of my favorites."

"Now it's one of mine too." Mitchell would never be able to pick it out again. Nonetheless, he recognized that there was something special about Eiko's perfume. Its lingering redolence attested to serious expenditure.

"What an amazing shirt!" she said with a giggle as he eased off his shoes.

"I'm glad you like it," said Mitchell.

"I didn't say I liked it, did I!"

It was a huge apartment. The living room alone was more than twice the size of his own place, and one entire wall was a picture window with a spectacular view of Tokyo Tower. Gleaming bare boards, batik screens, soft light from angled lamps—it was quite unlike the cramped, gadget-packed clutter of the usual Japanese home. Mitchell felt as if he had walked into an advertisement in a design magazine. Several pictures hung on the walls, the sort of abstract slashes and smudges that he detested. Nonetheless, they gave off the indefinable aura of having cost large sums of money. The same could be said for the large Chinese vase near the door, the Persian rug, and the walnut dining suite.

The leather couch gave a satisfied hiss as it received his weight. "Quite a place," murmured Mitchell. "I didn't realize you were such a wealthy young lady."

"I'm just a poor working girl," she said, with a laugh. "I'm borrowing this apartment from a friend of mine, actually."

This friend was unlikely to be a woman, thought Mitchell. A place like this would cost several million pounds. Still, from the expression on Eiko's face, she wasn't going to tell him any more, and he wasn't going to ask. At the far end of the room, next to the dining area, was a piano—not an electronic keyboard, but a baby grand with the lid up. Mitchell glanced at it. There was a sheet of music ready in the stand. He could just make out the title, Erik Satie's third étude.

"Do you play a lot?" he ventured.

"Not as much as I should," said Eiko. "I simply don't have enough time to practice."

They lapsed back into silence. She must be interested, Mitchell reassured himself. After all, she had rung him up and invited him to her apartment. She wouldn't have done that unless she had already made up her mind. They were going to make love tonight. It was more or less ordained. They both knew it and that was why they were both feeling a little tense.

"So what would you like to drink?" said Eiko suddenly. "G and T, or a glass of champagne, or possibly a beer?"

Mitchell would have dearly loved to gulp down a preliminary gin and tonic, just to calm his nerves, but he intended to be careful with alcohol tonight. He wanted to be in peak condition. It was going to be memorable for both of them. A woman like Eiko deserved no less. "Champagne would be great, thanks."

Eiko disappeared into the kitchen and emerged holding a bottle of Dom Pérignon. "Voilà," she said. She peeled the foil off the top and sat down on a chair, the bottle squeezed between her legs.

"Here, let me help you with that," said Mitchell, getting to his feet.

"No, I can manage myself, thank you," said Eiko, hunching over as she slowly eased out the cork. She gave a little grunt and the cork emerged with a *pop,* sending a short-lived column of froth cascading onto her jeans. "Damn and blast," she said matter-of-factly, and began pouring the champagne into the tall crystal glasses on the table.

Mitchell watched in silence. A dark patch was spreading along the inner thigh of her left leg where the champagne was soaking into the bleached denim. She caught his gaze and giggled.

"What are you staring at, Richard?" she said. "Does it look as if I've peed in my pants?"

Mitchell felt himself flush. What was going on here? Why was he feeling so ill at ease? After all, it wasn't he who had just spilled champagne on his trousers! He got up to accept the glass that she handed him, and they clinked a *"Kampai."* He drank fully, his mouth and throat luxuriating in the tiny explosions.

"Thirsty, aren't you?" she said, and he realized that his glass was almost empty. She pointed the bottle at him, and he held his glass out for a refill.

Eiko sat down on the sofa, legs curled up underneath her. She had excellent feet, Mitchell noted. Most women took inordinate trouble over their legs—waxing and tanning and muscle-toning—but treated their feet like slaves, distorting the natural shape and letting bunions and calluses develop. Eiko's feet were like pieces of sculpture: long narrow heels, delicately curving arches, creamy skin that revealed the blue map of the veins. There was only one thing that was wrong. On each foot, four of the toes were long and straight, but the fifth was squashed and bent. There was no nail either. For some reasons, the image of those neglected, brutalized little toes stayed in Mitchell's mind through the meal that followed. It was an imperfection at the remotest part of her body, the only imperfection that he had been able to identify.

The next couple of hours were difficult. After the champagne, there was a bottle of Beaujolais. Mitchell drank most of it to help ease the tension. The mixed grill was not bad, neither was the sponge cake that followed. Mitchell tried to steer the conversation onto Eiko's background and interests and ambitions, but he was repeatedly nudged back to his own experiences. Once again, just as at the Ginza club, Mitchell found himself doing most of the talking, and mostly about himself. Eiko smiled and filled his glass and made wry little comments, but gave away nothing. It had been Mitchell's intention to hint that Eiko was wasting herself as a hostess, that she should find a job that would make better use of her talents. Now he wasn't so sure. Eiko was as much of a nightclub hostess in cutoff jeans as she had been in a strapless cocktail dress.

Did he like her? Not as much as he had expected. A lot of what she said was dull or obvious. The conversation was often heavy going, the gap between their personalities and interests too wide to bridge. Did he desire her? Absolutely—indeed, the less he liked her as a person, the more he desired her as a woman. She was so controlled, so unreachable. He was determined to make her lose that control, to wake up the neighbors in this silent, super-discreet neighborhood. But would he have the chance? Perhaps she had just invited him round for dinner and conversation. No, that was impossible. This was a woman who had decided to make her living in the "water trade." Furthermore, she had been educated in a private girls' school in England. She knew what the score was.

Mitchell was not disappointed. After the meal, they moved to the sofa. Eiko brought him an Irish coffee and sat perched at one end watching him drink it, like a cat observing a goldfish. She used a remote-control device to turn down the lights and activate the compact disc player.

"Do you like Chopin?" she murmured, patting his knee with her hand.

"Of course." What other answer was there? Was there anyone who would say that they didn't like Chopin in these circumstances—with the meal finished and the lights low and a beautiful woman edging down the sofa toward you? Still, there was something unnatural about the atmosphere. Mitchell should have been the protagonist in this scene. Instead, Eiko was taking the lead, treating him like a rich middle-aged businessman whom she was rewarding for spending lots of money at the club. Mitchell felt even less at ease than before. He gazed into the whirl of cream rotating in his coffee cup. For the moment the new Mitchell, the confident, ever-positive challenger of new experiences, had disappeared.

She reached out and brushed his cheek with her hand. "You've got a nice profile, Richard," she said. "It reminds me of that movie actor. You know, what's his name . . ."

"Mickey Rourke?"

"That's the chap. He's got a naughty mouth, just like you."

She was sitting next to him now, her forefinger running along his lower lip. She was expecting him to nibble it, so he did. Is this what it feels like to be a woman? thought Mitchell. Is this what it feels like to be seduced? His physical responses were just as vigorous as he had hoped, but mentally he was totally disengaged. It was as if he were standing in front of the sofa looking down and giving himself instructions—that's right, nibble a little more—now right hand moving up slowly to cup the breast, brushing the nipple upward—turn and kiss on the half-open mouth, pushing her backward . . .

"Like your ears too," she whispered. Her breath tickled as she took his earlobe between her teeth.

The stream of instructions continued. Good—now under the T-shirt, caress the flat of the stomach, the jut of the rib cage—weigh the breast in your hand, jiggle it slightly—there, fork the nipple softly between your fingers—okay, keep moving—don't bore her, remember . . .

Did Eiko have a similar invisible coach standing in front of her giving a similar commentary? She certainly had the kind of expertise that only came from considerable practice. Take the way she was treating his ear. She didn't chew it like a piece of bacon, or sponge around inside like a doctor, but tickled and teased, making hot shapes with her lips and uttering little purring sounds that sounded almost natural.

The invisible coach was now telling Mitchell to roll Eiko backward on the sofa, to slide his hand over the place where the champagne stain had flowed, to kiss her again, slowly and rhythmically.

"Naughty mouth," she said, biting his lower lip hard enough to hurt. "Just as I thought."

"You've no idea just how naughty," said Mitchell.

"You don't know how naughty I am, either," she said, fingers digging into his buttocks.

But he was dying to find out. The coach's commands were coming thick and fast now. All right—keep the variety going—slide down and kiss her throat, not hard enough to leave any marks—remember, she works for a living—good, now stroke her cheek with your left hand—she wants to put your fingers in her mouth, don't ask why, she just does—let her chew on them for a while, but you're going to need them soon—okay, this is a difficult bit—with your right hand undo the top button of her jeans—ease it, don't twist it—now undo the zipper, slowly, like unwrapping a parcel—these jeans are tight, but don't worry, she's going to help you, she's going to raise her hips off the sofa—that's it, toss them on the floor—silk panties, it feels like, with see-through panels at the side—warm, isn't she, but leave that for the moment—now she wants to undo the buttons of your shirt, so turn sideways—let her get on top . . .

Mitchell lay there, listening to the instructions in his head. Chopin was tinkling. The champagne was coursing through his bloodstream. Eiko was sitting astride him, hair falling across her face, bare thighs pinning him to the sofa. Her warmth was flat against his.

Still while she bites your nipples—right, now she's undoing your belt—trace her backbone with your finger, there, right down through the cleft of her buttocks—a little tickle, nothing more, not at this stage, you don't want to distract her when she's trying to pull your trousers off—good, she's lying on top of you—bite her shoulder, bite like you mean it—but no marks, remember—next the T-shirt, slip off the T-shirt—now flatten her breasts against your chest, separate her legs with your knee—slide upward, just a little pressure so she knows what to expect—good, now look into her eyes and kiss her again—harder this time, plenty of tongue . . .

The coach's voice was slipping farther and farther into the distance. Mitchell was breathing hard, his pulse throbbing through all the obvious places. Eiko raised herself above him, hair brushing over his eyes, breasts swinging lightly across his face. Then suddenly, without any warning at all, she stood up, leaving him lying flat on the sofa.

"Come on," she said. "It's time to take a shower."

Mitchell looked up, startled. The coach had disappeared completely. "But I had one before coming out tonight."

"That doesn't matter," said Eiko severely. "Honestly, you Englishmen are so primitive!"

The bathroom was brightly lit. For some reason, Mitchell felt embarrassed to strip off his boxer shorts under Eiko's supervisory gaze. He turned his back, which made her giggle. When he turned around again, she was naked herself, standing with her hands on her hips. Mitchell managed to keep his eyes on her face, though they were being dragged downward with intense gravitational force. She led him by the hand into the shower, as if they were brother and sister.

Mitchell had never been washed as thoroughly as Eiko washed him— at least, not since he was an infant. He stood motionless under the shower, barely able to see through the streams of water pouring down his face. Eiko sat beside him on a little plastic stool, a soapy cloth in her hand, meticulously sudsing and squeezing and probing areas that had never been probed before. Gradually, a heavy numbness spread through the entire area of his groin and thighs.

"What a healthy young man you are," she said, giving him a playful tweak.

Blinking down through the gushing water, Mitchell was astonished. He had never been this healthy before. It both looked and felt as if he had been injected with quick-setting cement.

"All right, now it's my turn," he said, reaching for a sliver of soap.

"I'll do it myself, thanks," said Eiko, rising from the stool. "You go and wait in the bedroom."

Mitchell wrapped himself in a bathrobe and went into the bedroom. There was a large round bed in the middle, the black silk sheets folded down invitingly. He picked up a remote-controller from the bedside table and experimented with the brightness of the concealed lighting. Was Eiko the kind of girl whose passions would be stimulated by a near-daylight glare that left nothing to the imagination? Or would she revel in the fumbling mystery of total darkness? It was a difficult choice. In the end, Mitchell opted for a compromise, a level of dimness that revealed the outlines of everything but the detail of nothing. He then lay down on the bed and waited. This was a strange experience, he reflected as he gazed at the ceiling. With Japanese women, he was used to feeling in control. You couldn't help it, really. No matter how meek and mild a man might be, they had a way of making him feel like a cudgel-wielding caveman. But with Eiko he didn't feel dominant at all. He felt as if he were playing chess with a much better player.

It was at least ten minutes before Eiko appeared in the door, also clad in a white bathrobe. She adjusted the light down further, then approached the bed, hands behind her back. Mitchell reached out a hand to grab the belt of her robe, but she skipped away from him.

"Do you like games, Richard?" she said, looking him straight in the eye.

"What kind of games?" said Mitchell, sitting up on the edge of the bed.

"Exciting games. The kind to play in a bedroom."

Under the circumstances, that was like asking if he liked Chopin. "I like most kinds of games."

"You Englishmen are such good sports, aren't you! All right, first of all, just close your eyes for a moment. I've got something for you here."

Mitchell closed his eyes and felt an eye mask being slipped over his head. It was quite tight, pressing against his lids. When he opened his eyes again, he couldn't see anything. Eiko stroked his cheek with her fingernails.

"That suits you nicely," she said. "Now put your hands behind your back. Don't be frightened, Richard. It's only a bit of fun."

"Hey, who says I'm frightened?" said Mitchell, smiling in the direction of Eiko's voice. He didn't sound convincing, even to himself. He put his hands behind his back and felt them being bound at the wrist. She did it quickly, tightening the knot with a jerk.

"And now for the ankles," she said, sounding like a school monitor talking to a student. "Kneel down on the bed and put your legs out straight behind you."

He obeyed without saying anything this time. What was she using to tie him? It wasn't cloth. It was hard and thin, like some kind of thong. And it hurt. Mitchell had no idea what to expect. He had never done anything like this before. He recalled certain pictures he had seen in the low-grade magazines that salarymen sometimes read on the train. Women trussed up like hams, candles dripping hot wax onto bare flesh, whips, savage-looking metal clips. Pain! Mitchell didn't like the idea of pain at all. Whoever thought there was something erotic about pain must be crazy. Was going to the dentist erotic! Was burning your hand on the stove erotic! Now she was running a cord between his ankles and wrists, forcing his whole torso to bend like a bow. The best thing, he decided, was to play along with her wishes, however bizarre they might seem. As long as there were no hot candles.

Eiko gave him a push between the shoulders, and he fell flat on his face. She laughed. "You look so funny, Richard," came her voice from somewhere above him. "Now stay still while I put this gag in place."

"Gag! For God's sake, Eiko . . ."

Her fingers closed around his nostrils. He opened his mouth to protest, only for it to be crammed with what felt like a giant ball of putty. He tried to spit it out, but there was a strap that was being closed around the back of his head. He couldn't move his tongue. He couldn't do anything but grunt.

This was going too far. He was plunging into the world of the low-grade weekly magazines, but with one important difference: in the magazines, it was always the women who were bound and gagged and had hot candle wax dripped on them. The idea was that, despite all the moaning and twisting about, they were secretly enjoying it. So far, Mitchell was not enjoying this experience at all. The ardor that had manifested itself on the sofa, then developed in the shower to awe-inspiring proportions, had now vanished entirely. The quick-setting cement had been replaced by icy water.

Mitchell rubbed his face against the bed, trying to slide the mask upward, but it was no good. The fit was too tight.

"Don't be a silly boy, Richard," cooed Eiko. "There's no point trying to pull it off. All these things have been designed so they can't be shifted."

Mitchell made a gurgle of protest. Eiko laughed again. "Do shut up, Richard," she said. "I've got no idea what you're saying. Now I'm going to slip out for a little while. Be a good boy when I'm gone, won't you?"

Her footsteps moved away, then the bedroom door opened and

closed. He was alone, thousands of miles away from his bed-sit in Hackney, trussed up on a bed in an apartment owned by an unknown millionaire. His fate was in the hands of a woman who was quite unlike any other Japanese woman he had ever met; unlike any woman of any nationality, actually. Surely, this kind of thing wasn't standard practice in the Ginza. All those rich Japanese businessmen whom he had seen sipping whiskey—they weren't paying huge sums of money for this, were they?

Eiko was playing with him, he could see that now. She had invited him here, seduced him, then rendered him helpless. But why? The possibilities were shudder-inducing. Hadn't there been a movie about a Japanese woman who had hacked off her lover's genitals, then carried them around with her for days? Apparently, the Japanese considered her some kind of national heroine. Could Eiko be a fan of hers? Or what about organ theft? His liver and kidneys might be extracted, then sold on the black market. . . . These were all crazy ideas, of course, the sort of things that common sense told you could never happen. But the situation that he was in now was also one that common sense told you could never happen. Since Mitchell had been living in Japan, common sense hadn't been much help at all.

He wriggled to the edge of the bed and dropped onto the floor. That wasn't such a good idea, it turned out. With his hands and legs tied, he couldn't break his fall, and the side of his head banged hard against the ground. He lay there for several minutes, half-stunned. Eiko had been right. The mask and gag and thongs were immovable.

Finally, he heard the bedroom door click open, and footsteps padding toward him. He raised his face in the direction of the door and made some gurgling sounds that conveyed, he hoped, impatience and irritation. For several moments nothing happened, so Mitchell levered himself up into a kneeling position, back resting against the bed, and made some more gurgling sounds, this time more imploring. That was when he smelled the smell, and his heart began to beat much faster. It was a hospital smell, the kind you associated with operating rooms and rubber gloves.

Suddenly Mitchell was grabbed by the back of the head, and there was a cloth over his face, cold and wet. The fumes that he was breathing were strong, scouring his nasal passages as they rushed upward, bringing tears to his unseeing eyes. He didn't want to breathe them in again, but he was sliding sideways and his stomach was nauseous and he didn't have the strength to hold his breath any longer. It felt as if a black cloak were slowly descending over his head. He shook his head to clear it, but the slow descent of the cloak couldn't be stopped. He slumped to the floor, this time hardly feeling the impact. His face was numb, his heart a slow drumbeat in his ears. The black cloak was covering his entire body now, wrapping him in its folds.

Mitchell's breathing became steady and slow. The wet cloth moved away from his face, and fingers fiddled with the mask. Deep in the coils of the black cloak, Mitchell rolled over onto his back. He registered a shaft of bright light forcing its way into his brain, the gag being pulled from his mouth.

"Eiko," he mumbled through huge, heavy lips. "What—whuh—wheh?"

The wet cloth was put back under his nose. A face was hovering above him, just out of focus. It wasn't Eiko, he realized dimly—there was not enough hair. In fact, it wasn't a woman's face at all. It was someone Mitchell recognized from the shape of the head, which was perfectly round, like a football. . . .

The heavy black cloak was descending again now, wrapping him more securely than before. Through a small, shrinking aperture, Mitchell saw the man's face looming closer. "Guh!" he grunted weakly. "Why are you here . . ."

Yazawa gave a harsh laugh. "That is the question I should ask you," he said. "After all, I live in this apartment."

"Yuh-pah-mah-tuh. But—"

Mitchell was vaguely aware that the words were sticking to his rubbery lips and tongue. He squinted up through the fast-closing aperture.

"Sleep well, Mitchell-kun. When you awake, we have very many things to discuss."

Mitchell tried to move his mouth, but it was impossible. The black cloak was everywhere, closing all the gaps, invading all his senses. Mitchell embraced the black cloak and let it gently bear him away.

313

The Peace Technologists were not great believers in luxury accommodation. Mori found that out when he was led to the building that was to serve as the trainees' living quarters. The sleeping facilities consisted of a large room with a tiled floor on which all of them, men and women, were to sleep. The walls were stacked with futons that gave off a damp, musty smell, suggesting that they hadn't been washed for quite a while.

The only decor was supplied by the many posters of Ono—on a mountaintop at dawn, standing in the middle of a lake, levitating several inches above his purple meditational cushion. Loudspeakers in the ceiling boomed down a program of Yumi-chan's songs interspersed with readings of Ono's prophecies. Adjoining the sleeping quarters was a locker room in which the clothes that the recruits had come in were exchanged for thin kimonos. Next to that were a large washroom and a row of six doorless toilet cubicles. In its appearance and smell, the whole place reminded Mori of his high school days.

Disciples walked among the trainees, ordering them to be silent and concentrate on the sensei's image and words. Mori went over to the window and surveyed the scenery. The building they were in was on the eastern side of the mountain, about halfway between sea level and the peak. To get there had taken almost an hour of slogging up a steep, mud-ridged path that curled through the trees. Mori judged that the complex of buildings that he had seen from the hydrofoil was somewhere to their west, a few hundred yards lower. There was no sign of it from the window, which looked out on an asphalt-covered square backed by dense forest dropping away to the flatness of the sea. There must be another way down, thought Mori. The equipment and materials needed to build a place like this couldn't have come up the narrow path from the harbor. And yet the building was encircled by a thick screen of trees. Staring through the fading light, Mori made out a narrow patch of the forest that looked different from the rest—paler and somehow unaffected by the strong sea breeze. He remembered the hologram of Ono in the Ochanomizu branch office. The Peace Technologists were masters of dissimulation.

"Enjoying the view, Nakamura?" It was the disciple who had befriended him earlier in the day.

"Yes," said Mori solemnly. "The sight of the sunset and the peaceful forest has calmed my spirit and helped me to reflect on many things."

"That is good," said the disciple. "But do not concentrate too much on what is outside. After all, the forest and the sea and even the sun have no reality to those who understand the sensei's teachings. Instead, you must concentrate on the world inside you, purifying and cleansing it."

"Understood!" said Mori, moving away from the window.

"Tonight you will begin to purify and cleanse your thought in the Chamber of Prophecy. That is the place where you will learn of the beauty and terror of the sensei's visions. But first it is time to eat and drink. Everyone is weary after the long journey."

Mori nodded. No refreshments had been provided since he had arrived at the Ochanomizu branch at ten in the morning. He was extremely hungry and thirsty, and so, he guessed, was everyone else.

The trainees were told to form lines ordered according to the numbers they had been given and sit cross-legged on the floor. Five disciples whom Mori hadn't seen before—heavyset young men with shaven heads—entered the room. One was carrying a tray heaped with plastic cups and plates, the others aluminum barrels and cardboard boxes. They set down their burdens at the end of the room and refreshments were prepared and handed back down the lines. Sitting near the back of his line, Mori was one of the first to receive his plate and cup. Hot green tea and a few cubes of bean jelly—it wasn't exactly a feast, but after nine hours without food Mori was grateful for anything. The bean jelly was much too sweet for him, so he slipped half into a pocket and washed down the rest with several gulps of tea. The tea wasn't good either: it had a strange metallic aftertaste.

Mori was one of the few trainees who didn't put up a hand when the disciples asked if anyone wanted more. Of course, they were mostly in their twenties and early thirties—a generation that had been brought up with peanut butter and doughnuts and milkshakes. Mori had no sweet tooth. He detested sweet sake and rum and cola, and the only time he had ever tasted a piña colada he had immediately spat it out over a nearby rubber plant.

After they had finished, the cups and plates were cleared away by the men with the shaved heads and then the trainees were divided up into the usual groups again. They waited in silence, contemplating the sensei's image and listening to the prophecies booming from the loudspeakers. Mori watched as the first group, made up of twelve young women and four men, filed out of the room, a disciple leading the way and another bringing up the rear.

In about half an hour's time they were back. It was a shocking sight. Several, men and women, were weeping uncontrollably, and the rest were in such a state of glassy-eyed shock that they could hardly walk. The disciples ordered them to pull some futons off the pile. As soon as they returned to their places, they slumped to the ground, falling asleep immediately or staring blankly at the ceiling. The prohibition against discussing their experiences was entirely unnecessary. They were incapable of it.

"Don't worry," said the disciple who was directing Mori's group. "You will get used to it soon enough. The session later tonight will be less of a shock, and the one tomorrow morning even less. By the end of the three days, you will enjoy your entry into the world of the sensei's thought."

That sounded reasonable, thought Mori. After all, it was unrealistic to expect to understand the sensei's teachings fully without a certain amount of struggle and suffering. The sensei was directing the trainees to reject their useless previous lives in favor of something purer and more valuable. That was no simple thing to do. It meant tearing away prejudice and random emotions like branches from a dead tree. Some emotional distress was only to be expected.

"Get ready, Nakamura. It's time for your group now."

The disciple was standing in front of him, looking down. Mori stared back, then leapt to his feet. For a moment, he had forgotten that he was supposed to be Nakamura, the burned-out middle-aged salaryman. The weight of his own life as Mori, the burned-out middle-aged detective, had been pressing down too heavily on his shoulders.

They were led out of the large room, down the steps at the main door, then along the side of the asphalt square to a windowless hut that was attached to the main body of the building. In front of Mori was the young man with the earring; in front of him the woman who had puked her breakfast onto the disciple's trousers. The dusk had faded into night by now. The moonlight illuminated the concrete of the building, but all around the forest was dark. Gazing at the rustling trees, Mori was overcome by a childish fear. It was the right sort of setting for a horrible fairy tale. What kind of creatures might live inside? And once you entered, would it be possible to find a way out again? Or would the trees and creepers somehow block your way, condemning you to stay with them for the rest of your life? Much better, surely, to stay away from the forest; much better to stick to the paths and open spaces. As they were guided in through the low door in the hut, Mori noted that his heart was beating quite fast and, despite the cool wind, he was sweating profusely.

On the other side of the door was a small, dimly lit room. The recruits squatted down on the floor, so close together that Mori felt knees and elbows prodding him. But he didn't mind. The opportunity of experiencing the sensei's visions directly was enough to drive away all sense of bodily discomfort. He clutched his hands together in his lap and sat in eager anticipation.

There was soft music—the simple but beautiful melody of a children's song repeated over and over on a Japanese flute. Gradually an organ welled up in the background and the tempo began to accelerate, rising faster and faster until the melody drowned in a thundering crescendo of cymbals and tympani. At that point the wall that Mori was facing slid away to reveal the crowded streets of Shinjuku. They must be on the roof of a building, thought Mori. Not a very tall one, since the skyscrapers towered far above their heads and the faces of the people on the street were visible.

Little by little, the music was rising in intensity. He felt a threatening undertone there somewhere in the shifting organ chords and the quavering bass notes of the Japanese flute. Something terrible but inevitable was going to happen. Mori didn't want to know what it was, but he couldn't shut his eyes. The fascination was too strong.

There was a sudden jolt that sent Mori sprawling, followed by a shuddering vibration which ran through his body like an electric shock. When he looked up, the whole world seemed to be shaking itself apart. Tall buildings were swaying, solid concrete fissuring and crumbling, cars slewing across into crowds of pedestrians. He could hear screams of panic, not just from the people on the street, but from the recruits around him. In fact, he was screaming too, rolling over and over in fear and confusion. The darkened room was filled with moans of desperation as the recruits writhed and thrashed their limbs. A small voice in the depths of Mori's brain was saying "computer graphics," "high-definition video." Other, louder voices were saying "Throw the others out of the way," "Hide yourself in the ground."

Then came another jolt, stronger than the first, and the ground rose to hit Mori a stunning blow on the forehead. Dazed, he looked up to see a giant crack opening up in the road below, and cars and buses toppling inside. The air was full of noise: the wailing of sirens, screams, crashes, the thump of distant explosions. A train slipped off a railway bridge and hung in midair like a wounded snake. There was a roar close by as one corner of a department store building slumped to the ground, throwing up a huge cloud of dust. In a mirrored skyscraper, the windows suddenly shattered, raining shards of glass on the street below, spilling bodies from the gaping holes. Black smoke was billowing through the narrow streets; orange flames flickering from burned-out taxis.

And still the vibrations did not stop. Mori tried to get to his feet, but it was like walking on jelly. Instead, he lay curled up into a ball, covering his head with his hands as huge chunks of masonry smashed to the ground. Many of the other recruits were huddling together, their screams of shock having turned to groans and whimpers as the vibrations continued, shaking them to their bones and teeth. A new smell wafted to Mori's nostrils—the sharp smell of urine.

There were emergency drills you were supposed to follow, places of refuge you were supposed to find. But it was no good. Buildings were crumbling, roads splitting, overpasses collapsing, fireballs and smoke clouds spreading everywhere. And still the vibrations got stronger.

Nothing could save them now. Slumped among the moaning, twisting bodies of the recruits, Mori wept bitter tears. Everything he had known was gone, smashed and burned beyond all hope of repair. In a few minutes, so much had gone to waste, all the efforts and hopes of so many human beings. There was no point in running for shelter. There was no point in struggling to survive, because a world in which this could happen was a meaningless place. Gripped by despair and grief, the most intense he had ever felt, Mori sat there in a stupor, waiting for the flames or the gas or the falling concrete blocks to end his misery.

A disciple's voice rang out, stern and strong. "Be silent, be still! Hear the words of the sensei!"

A golden staircase had formed in the sky above the city. A white-robed figure was slowly descending, his arms stretched out in front of him. Around Mori, the moaning and thrashing of limbs stopped. Just the presence of the sensei was calming and comforting. The sensei's face was visible now. It radiated gentle strength and concern for the suffering below. He turned in a circle, moving his hands slowly up and down. Listening to the music of the sensei's voice, Mori let his muscles go limp, and a feeling of great warmth and tenderness spread through his body. What the sensei said was true! What the sensei said answered all his doubts and fears!

But what did the sensei actually say? Afterward, Mori found it difficult to remember. After he had waved good-bye to the recruits and ascended the golden staircase, the walls of the room misted over again, the music surged, and then they were confronted by a kaleidoscope of colorful shapes that danced and pulsed in hypnotic patterns. Meshed lines formed into a whirling vortex that dragged you in. Slowly rotating spirals flashed mauve and orange. Amoebae of light twisted and merged and turned themselves inside out.

Mori's head was aching, and his mouth felt unusually dry. The air was bad inside the room. He longed to be outside in the cool of the evening, far from the dizzying kaleidoscopic motion and the loud music, which was starting to be irritating. Looking around, he could see that most of the other recruits were staring at the shapes on the wall with total concentration. All were sitting still, and some were breathing deeply through open mouths. It was as if they were asleep with their eyes open.

Eventually, the shapes faded away and the lights were switched on. Some of the recruits had to be helped to their feet; others were sobbing, biting their lips, wiping away tears with shaky hands. No one said anything as they stepped outside onto the asphalt. How long had they been in there? Just thirty or forty minutes, if the first group was any guide, but it seemed like hours.

Mori sucked in the good air of the forest night. Little by little, the strength was returning to his body and the aching in his temples was easing. He glanced at the waving branches of the trees. On the way to the Chamber of Prophecy, they had somehow reawakened long-forgotten childhood nightmares. That was strange. They didn't scare him now.

The disciple led the recruits back to the entrance of the building and into the large room where the others were waiting. They took their bedrolls off the stacks lining the wall, laid them on the concrete floor, and flopped down.

"How do you feel, Nakamura?" asked the disciple who had accompanied them. "Have you managed to understand more of the sensei's prophecies?"

"I have understood this," said Mori, without pausing to think. "Without the sensei's teachings, there is no purpose to human life. It is not worth living."

The disciple nodded sympathetically.

"That is what many people say after their first session. Now contemplate on what you have seen and make use of it."

Mori lay flat on the futon, a dull tiredness creeping over his body. He closed his eyes and teased at the questions that were bothering him. Many things were strange. The Chamber of Prophecy, for example. How had those effects been created? Everything had been so realistic—not just the images and the sound, but the physical sensations as well. The sensei was strange too. His words had impressed Mori greatly, but now he couldn't remember them. And, not least, Mori himself was strange—thinking strangely, acting strangely. The sight of a bunch of trees waving in the wind had given him goosebumps. He had wept and screamed in the Chamber of Prophecy. When the disciple had asked him how he felt, he had answered, without a moment's hesitation, in the guise of Nakamura.

Pretending to behave like Nakamura all day was beginning to make him think like Nakamura. Now, that really was scary! Nakamura meant no harm to anyone. He was much sadder than he deserved. And where else but from Ono were the likes of Nakamura ever going to find any comfort?

These were the tangled thoughts of a tired brain. It wasn't late, but Mori felt sleepy. He heard the next group filing out of the room on their way to the Chamber of Prophecy, but he didn't open his eyes. Instead, he let Ono, Nakamura, and everything else dissolve in the spreading darkness of the forest night.

Mori wasn't asleep long because when he awoke, the last group was coming back from the chamber. The recruits took the last of the futons from the stack and lay down in the same exhausted state as the others. The disciples dimmed the lights, walked up and down the lines of sleeping bodies, then all but one left the room. The remaining disciple squatted down at the far end, back against the wall, and stared into space. After a while, he took a book from his pocket and began to read it by the light of a small flashlight.

Mori checked his watch. It was only ten o'clock, yet most of the recruits were sprawling on their futons, deeply asleep. Glancing behind, Mori noticed the young man with the earring lying flat out on his futon, arms flung out on each side. His permanently open mouth was now gaping to maximum aperture, and a series of long rasping snores was emerging. Beside him, the woman who had thrown up in the hydrofoil was sitting up on her futon, looking about her with a puzzled expression on her face. When she saw Mori staring at her, she smiled, pointed at the snorer, and wrinkled her nose. Mori glanced at the disciple at the other end of the room. He was buried in his comic book, apparently oblivious to everything around him. The snores suddenly broke into a series of grunts and wheezes, and the guy with the earring shifted onto his side. The girl behind him giggled. Mori leaned over toward her.

"This man makes much noise," he whispered. "It must be hard for you to sleep."

"I don't mind," she said. "But why has everyone got so tired suddenly? It's much too early to go to sleep." She appeared to have made a good recovery from her seasickness. There was a bright smile on her face, and she was looking around with obvious curiosity.

"We've all had a grueling experience," he said. "Participating in the prophecies of the sensei must have drained away our energy."

"It didn't drain my energy. It was just like watching a cartoon on TV, that's all. No reason to scream and roll around on the floor, I'd say!"

Mori gazed at her in silence. She wasn't pretending. It was clear that she hadn't been disturbed by the experience at all.

"Anyway," she whispered, "I don't want to go to sleep yet. I can never go to sleep on an empty stomach. You see—" She stopped and bit her lip, aware that she had said something that she shouldn't have.

"Empty stomach?" pressed Mori, his mind starting to work a little faster. "You mean, you didn't eat the bean jelly?"

The woman gave a guilty nod. Even in the dim light, Mori could see that she was blushing. "That's right. I was still feeling nauseous, you see."

"What about the tea? Did you drink that?"

She shook her head. "It would have upset my stomach too, so I poured it into a crack in the floorboards. It was a bad thing to do, I know, but I didn't want to be sick again. You see, I felt so ashamed in the hydrofoil. . . ."

The bean jelly, the tea! It was so obvious. Mori could have kicked himself for not thinking of it before. He lay back on his futon, hardly aware of the cadenza of snores from behind.

Shortly after eleven, the disciple at the other end of the room stood up and walked over to the doorway, where he stood muttering into a walkie-talkie. After that, he turned to the control panel in the wall and switched the room lighting from dim to maximum brightness. In the same instant, Yumi-chan's voice began to blare from the speakers in the ceiling—loud enough, Mori reckoned, to be heard halfway to Tokyo Bay.

Several of the recruits sat up on their futons, yawning and staring around blankly. More than half, however, remained flat on their backs— motionless or with just a hand or foot stirring. In a matter of minutes, the five shaven-headed disciples had reappeared, again carrying the cups and boxes and barrels. One of them was also carrying several bamboo staves under his arm. While three disciples busied themselves with preparing the bean jelly and tea, the others walked between the lines of futons, thwacking the sleepers on the legs with the staves.

"Yow," yelped one girl, who had received a stinging blow on the back.

The disciple who had delivered the blow stopped in his tracks and wheeled around. He was a heavily muscled man with a broken front tooth. "Learn to forget the illusion of pain," he roared. "Learn to accept the reality of the stick which rouses the spirit from your dull body!"

"Understood!"

"Now get up! Close your eyes and stand on one leg. Whatever happens, do not fall!"

He hit her again, a cutting blow on the buttocks with a full swing of the wrist behind it. She didn't make a sound this time, but the force of the blow sent her sprawling forward onto the tiles.

"Hopeless," said the disciple, shaking his head with grim satisfaction. "Before this course is complete, you will learn to stand still."

When the tea and bean jelly arrived, Mori followed the example of the woman next to him. Making sure that none of the disciples was watching, he poured the tea into a crack between the floorboards. The bean jelly he flattened out and slipped into a pocket. All the other recruits, including the woman who had been sick, were busily eating and drinking, no doubt realizing that this would be their last refreshment until morning. Many of them put up their hands when the disciples offered second helpings.

Eventually everything was cleared away. The disciple who had struck the woman with the stick stood in the center of the room. He turned slowly, gazing watchfully in each direction in turn. "You have eaten enough and slept enough," he said. "Now it is time for tonight's final session, in the Chamber of Light. All that you have experienced so far will be consolidated and strengthened. After this, you will be filled with the deepest joy and gratitude."

This time, the recruits were divided into two large groups. Mori's was the first to file out of the dormitory and down the steps. They were led along the side of the asphalt square, past the Chamber of Prophecy to a block that jutted out from the back of the building. The room inside was twice the size of its neighbor, and the floor and lower part of the walls were covered with padded mats. The disciple who had been reading the comic book stood in the center of the room and demonstrated a series of gestures and motions that the recruits were supposed to imitate.

"Your spirits have become too familiar with your bodies," he explained. "Now you must learn the way to make them strangers again. Train your body to do what is unfamiliar."

He began with breathing "from the stomach"—long shuddering breaths that would overoxygenate the brain. Next he proceeded to "make strangers of the eyes," rotating them clockwise, then counterclockwise at increasing speed. That was just a preparation for the difficult bit—rotating the head in one direction while rotating the eyes in the other.

"Hommm!" he boomed as his head swung around like a piece of broken machinery. "Hommm! Hommm! HOMMMM!"

There were also things to do with the arms and fingers, twisting them together and pulling in a way that set muscle against muscle. The recruits tentatively copied the routine. "HOMMMM!" boomed fifty voices, Mori's included. Soon several of the recruits were experiencing minor convulsions, their hips and knees jerking about uncontrollably.

After a while, the disciple paused. "Good progress!" he said. "Now we can begin in earnest. Be ready for your spirit to struggle with your body! Open your mind to the new impulses that will soon arrive!"

Loud drum music started up. The overhead lighting was switched off, replaced by a number of narrow bright beams that raked around the room like searchlights. The recruits continued with the routine. The five disciples walked up and down the room, occasionally thwacking a recruit on the shoulders, pulling a head around faster, roaring "HOMMMM" into an ear from point-blank range.

Mori didn't want to be the last to start twitching. Copying the woman in front of him, he flailed his arms from side to side and screwed up his face into a grimace. The bull-necked disciple approached and inspected them both for several minutes. His verdict on their progress was a lash across the buttocks for the woman and for Mori a pair of lips pressed against his ear followed by a deafening roar of "HOMMMM!" As the disciple was walking away, the woman suddenly threw herself to the ground and started beating her head against the padded matting. She glared up wildly at Mori, a hunk of foam rubber protruding from her mouth. Concerned that she might sink her teeth into his ankle, Mori skipped a yard backward. She rose to her feet, then hurled herself to the ground again, rolling over and over until she hit the wall.

She was only the first. The drumming picked up speed and the lights began to flash in accompaniment. Mori glimpsed many more of the recruits thrashing about on the floor, beating their heads against the padded walls. The disciples supplemented their sticks with elbow jabs to the pit of the stomach and kicks to the back of the knee. Fewer of the recruits were standing now. As the music and flashing lights were rising to a climax, Mori felt a shuddering movement underfoot. Amazed, he glanced down. Nothing could be seen in the whirling, flashing light, but there was no mistake—the floor was vibrating.

The vibrations quickly gathered in intensity, then suddenly there was a sharp bucking sensation. Mori estimated that the whole floor must be jerking several inches up and down. Even above the roar of the drums, he could hear the screams of the women around him. The ones who had been standing pitched forward onto their faces. Those who had been flailing and jerking on the floor flailed and jerked with even greater intensity. As the vibrations subsided, Mori found that he was the only recruit left standing. Instantly, he plummeted to the ground and began to pound the matting with his arms and legs.

The session continued for what seemed like an eternity. The drumming thundered in his ears. The flashing lights seared his brain even when his eyes were shut. Finally, one of the disciples stood in the center of the room, manipulated a metal object the size of a cigarette, and everything stopped. Mori glanced around furtively. It looked as if he were in a war zone. Bodies were lying around, limbs sticking out in unnatural positions. The air was full of moans and sobs, and a couple of people were making weird jabbering sounds, as if they were trying to imitate a foreign language. Gradually, with the help of numerous prods and swipes from the bamboo staves, most of the recruits managed to pull themselves to their feet. Faces were pale and sweaty; mouths twisted into strange, lopsided shapes.

There was one figure that didn't move. It was the girl who had been scolded back in the dormitory. She lay there, her face locked in an expression of goggle-eyed panic. Blood was trickling from her open mouth, and there was a large bloodstain on the matting next to her head. The bull-necked disciple approached her from the other side and poked her in the small of the back with his stave. She responded with a gurgle that seemed to come from deep within her chest. The disciple lifted the stave to elbow height and cracked her hard on the buttocks. She gave a longer gurgle, and a stream of frothy blood spilled over her lower lip.

"Stop!" called out Mori. "This woman is in bad condition."

The disciple's gaze ranged across the group of recruits standing before him, finally coming to rest on Mori's face. "Did I hear something?" he said softly.

"The woman," muttered Mori. "Her condition is bad."

"Her spirit is bad," said the disciple, prodding her in the back with his stave. "Some special hard training is necessary in her case."

"Look at her face," said Mori. "There is blood running from her mouth."

The disciple stepped over the prone body, glanced down, then stared at Mori again, a mirthless smile on his lips. "You notice such a thing very well, I think. Come here!"

Mori stumbled forward, his head lolling slightly from side to side. For good measure, he gave a couple of twitches with eye and mouth, and made a noisy gulping sound like a man about to be sick. It was obvious what was going to happen next.

The disciple raised the stave, this time gripping it with both hands like a baseball bat. "I will rouse your spirit to deeper reality," he said through clenched teeth. "I will make it rebel against the dullness of your body!"

The stave swished through the air in a vicious blow aimed at Mori's groin. Mori turned away at the last moment and let the stave catch him on the fleshy back of the thigh. The disciple grunted as the stave hit home. Mori gave a little yelp and collapsed to the ground, twitching as if he had just been electrocuted.

"Excellent, Nakamura," shouted the disciple gleefully. "At last it seems your spirit has been truly roused!"

For several seconds, Mori thrashed around facedown on the floor, jabbering nonsense syllables at the top of his voice. Then he twisted over on his back; glassy-eyed, drooling an accumulation of saliva from the corner of his mouth.

"Learn from Nakamura," said one of the other disciples. "The key to superior awareness is the sudden release of the wakened spirit."

When they were led out of the chamber, Mori gave a last glance at the padded floor. It was several feet higher than the ground level outside. Enough space, he guessed, for a second floor underneath and a mechanism to create that bucking motion. And no doubt the Chamber of Prophecy would have been designed in exactly the same way—hence the terrifying sensations of the earthquake. Ono had taken a lot of trouble to plan the effects that he wanted.

SIXTEEN

For several hours, Mitchell drifted in and out of consciousness, or dreamed that he did. The aperture in the black cloak would open a few inches and he would watch things being done to him, or dream that he was watching things being done to him. Then it would close again and he would return to his dreams, or dream that he was returning to his dreams.

He was being lifted up, carried to a car. The air was cool on his cheek. A door slammed right next to his ear. Now Eiko was sitting beside him, her expensive perfume filling his nostrils.

"Wha's happening?" he mumbled.

"Richard! You sound so funny! I can hardly understand a word you're saying!"

He shook his head sorrowfully. *"We were making love. Why did you do this to me?"*

"Don't be ridiculous, Richard. I could never make love to a man who has such bad taste in underpants."

"Eiko, you don't understand! I forgive you for working as a hostess. I forgive you

for screwing all those businessmen who treated you like an object. I won't treat you like an object. I'll take you driving through France in my Morgan, your hair flying in the wind . . ."

"You haven't got a Morgan, Richard. You haven't got anything. You're on the verge of being sent back to London, to live on supermarket beer and takeout kabobs."

"I'm not going anywhere."

"You're certainly right about that. You've been such a nuisance, going round poking your nose into things that don't concern you at all. Now we're going to have to kill you!"

"Kill me? Why? I haven't done anything."

"The human sacrifice will take place at dawn, on the dot. Afterward, your kidneys and corneas will be removed and sent to Brazil. At last, you'll be some use to someone, you useless thing."

Mitchell moaned in terror and his eyes fluttered open, or was it shut? Anyway, they were fluttering. The car was moving fast. He fell forward, and his brow hit something hard. Then the aperture in the black cloak was closing, or he dreamed that it was closing. . . .

The car stopped with a jolt. Mitchell was lifted out, into an elevator, into a brightly lit corridor. His bare feet trailed on the carpet. Now he was slumped in a chair, legs splayed out in front of him. There was the sound of blinds rattling down just behind his head. Somebody was talking to him, tapping on his cheek. His hands hurt because his wrists had been tied together too tightly. His head hurt because there was a chemical smell rising into his skull and it was tearing at the black cloak, pulling it away layer by layer . . . Bright light, bright pain, the tapping on his cheek stronger and stronger. Now the black cloak was fading to gray . . .

Mitchell opened his eyes. Yazawa was standing in front of him, hands on hips. Another man was holding a wet cloth under his nose and slapping him alternately on the left and right cheek.

"Wake up, Mitchell-kun," said Yazawa. "We've got urgent business to discuss."

The man holding the cloth stepped back. He was an ugly-looking character with a frizzy "punch perm" hairstyle. Mitchell thought that the face looked vaguely familiar. He took a deep breath and shook his head to clear away the last misty tatters of the cloak.

"This is completely illegal," he muttered thickly. "You're holding me against my will."

"I'm afraid there's no other way," said Yazawa, shaking his head sadly.

"You completely betrayed my trust. Now it's time for you to face the consequences."

That made Mitchell almost as angry as he was scared. What an outrageous statement! Yazawa had kidnapped him from a woman's bedroom, drugged him when he was defenseless. Clearly, Yazawa was crazed by jealousy. That was the only logical conclusion. "How was I supposed to know about you and Eiko?" he protested. "You should have told me about your relationship, then I wouldn't have gone near her!"

"Our relationship?"

What was the problem here? Mitchell didn't seem able to get through. Had Yazawa's male pride been bruised so badly that he wouldn't admit anything? "Yes, your relationship!" said Mitchell with sarcastic emphasis. "I assume you and Eiko are having some kind of relationship, aren't you?"

Yazawa laughed the harsh laugh that Mitchell had heard so often in the Pearson office. "In a way, I suppose. After all, she is my sister!"

"Your sister," muttered Mitchell in astonishment. "Eiko is your sister! That doesn't make sense!"

Could Yazawa really be the type to commit a criminal act in order to defend his sister's honor? If so, what century was the man living in?

"Why not!" said Yazawa crossly. "It makes plenty of sense to me!"

"So what was Eiko doing in England? And why is she prostituting herself in a Ginza nightclub?"

Yazawa stepped forward and cuffed him hard on the side of the face. Even in its numbed state, Mitchell's cheek stung with the impact. "You talk like that, you know nothing about this country. You know nothing about anything!"

Yazawa's voice sounded different. Why was that? No, it wasn't his voice, exactly. It was his intonation, which was smooth and relaxed. With a shock, Mitchell realized that his boss was suddenly speaking perfect English!

"Wait—I didn't mean any disrespect. It's just a little strange to think of your sister working as a hostess, that's all."

"What's strange?" snapped Yazawa. "It's a prestigious occupation. Her mother's been working in the Ginza for more than thirty years."

Not "our mother" but "her mother." This was too confusing for Mitchell to handle. He was still dreaming. That was the only possible explanation. Maybe if he blinked and shook his head, he would wake up. Mitchell blinked and shook his head vigorously. He didn't wake up. All that happened was that the ache in his temples got worse. Yazawa leaned down until their eyes were at the same height.

"Listen—I'd like to give you my family history, but this really isn't the time and place. You're the one who needs to do the explaining, not me!"

"What do you want me to explain?" wailed Mitchell, stretching forward in the chair. "Why have you brought me here? I don't understand."

Yazawa turned and made a sign with his hand and the man with the punch perm left the room. It was only when his back was turned, revealing his warty neck, that Mitchell recognized him as one of the security guards at the Otaman head office. So all this had to do with Otaman! It was nothing to do with jealousy about Eiko or samurai revenge or any of that nonsense. Suddenly Mitchell felt as if he were sinking into a bottomless ocean.

"You're going to tell me everything," said Yazawa slowly. "Who you're working for, how much you've told them. I want to know the exact details."

Mitchell swallowed dryly. "I'm not working for anybody."

"Don't stonewall, Mitchell. You've been snooping around, making phone calls, doing all kinds of shit. Tell me everything, and I'll see what I can do. You may get out of this in one piece yet. Do you understand what I'm saying?"

Yazawa was speaking in a rapid, excited voice. Mitchell looked up at him curiously. Two related ideas struck him at the same time. First, that Yazawa was lying, and not expertly either. Second, that he was nervous. Mitchell had never seen Yazawa so agitated before.

He kicked his lower lip and nodded. He understood the meaning of the words clearly enough. He also understood that the whole Otaman business was bigger, more complicated, and more dangerous than he had ever thought possible. He was trapped in a game whose rules had never been explained to him. All the time, he had been trying to play Snakes and Ladders on a Go board.

"Okay, I'll tell you what I know. But first of all, untie my hands. I can't think straight like this."

He pulled at his hands, hard enough to rock the chair onto its back legs. Yazawa turned to the door and flicked his fingers loudly. The Otaman staffer with the punch perm came back in.

"Untie him," Yazawa snapped in Japanese.

"But there are instructions."

"Do it. He is my responsibility."

Hands free at last, Mitchell rubbed his wrists, then started to describe his unofficial investigations into Otaman. Yazawa paced up and down in front of him, pausing occasionally to shoot out a question. It took less than ten minutes. When Mitchell had finished, Yazawa stood staring at the ground, frowning and shaking his head.

"Why did you disobey my instructions?" He sighed. "Everything would have turned out fine for you."

"You mean it won't turn out fine now?"

"I'm afraid not. But this is all out of my hands now. I'm going to have to ask for further instructions."

Ask whom? What kind of instructions? All sorts of questions were on Mitchell's lips, but he wasn't given the chance to voice them. Yazawa made a sign with his hand, and the Otaman staffer moved forward and grabbed Mitchell by the arm. Mitchell tried to push him away, but only succeeded in toppling the chair over and banging his own head against the floor. The man sat astride his chest and took out a cloth from a plastic bag. Mitchell thrashed his arms against the floor, but it was no good. He couldn't move.

The cloth covered Mitchell's mouth and nose, filling his nostrils with the pungent chemical odor. Before his brain had registered what was happening, the black cloak was forming in the air above him, then dropping down to bury him in its folds. Suddenly he felt as if the hands beating against the floor on either side of him belonged to someone else. The heaving chest with the heavy weight on it belonged to someone else. And all the dangerous confusion belonged to someone else too.

Outside the cloak everything was complicated and frightening. Inside, everything was soothing and simple. Mitchell was glad to drown in the simplicity of the black cloak. And as he slowly drowned, rolling over and over in its dark folds, he dreamed.

He dreamed that he was dragged down a corridor, thrown into the back of a car. He dreamed that the car drove fast, and his head banged against the door. He dreamed of the splash of water, spray hitting his cheeks, the wind tearing at his hair as he raced through the night at breakneck speed.

Then he opened his eyes, and the dream faded into nothingness. He was sitting at the wheel of his bottle-green Morgan, charging down the open road with a lovely woman by his side. Who was she? It didn't matter. The sky was blue, the sun warm on his brow, and a warm welcome was waiting in the chateau on the hill.

Snowbird stood in the lounge of his hotel suite, shirtsleeves rolled up to the elbows, his hands moving smoothly as he talked. From behind the barrier of his black sunglasses, his eyes roamed around the room, occasionally glancing out of the big picture window. The scene that met his gaze was an inspiring one—the shimmering circuitry of nighttime Akasaka. Yet tonight he was not in a mood to enjoy it. Business, after all, was business.

He turned away from the window, took a sip from his glass of milk, then resumed his presentation. The three Chinese men were sitting in armchairs, their eyes fixed on him. Snowbird held a pointer in his right hand, with which he occasionally rapped the video monitor on the table beside him.

"The reason I have invited you here today," he said, dropping his voice for dramatic effect, "is to discuss a proposal that could change the shape of your business out of all recognition."

He paused and glanced at each of the three in turn. The expressions on their faces were impossible to read. "Go on," said the eldest of them. "We're listening."

"Let me be frank. At the moment, you've carved out a niche for yourselves as middle-ranking regional players. That's a fine enough position for the time being, but it won't last forever. The competition is getting hotter all the time. In order to stay ahead of the game, you need a real comparative advantage. That's exactly what we have to offer."

"It's a surprise that you are so concerned with our problems."

The eldest man was a plump Taiwanese with a soft, round face like a Chinese steamed bun. In his youth he had been known as the Tiger of Taipei and was renowned as a martial arts expert. Snowbird had heard that he had once killed an ox with a single blow on the skull. Now he was as fat as a sleepy old ox himself. It wouldn't be long before a younger Tiger appeared from somewhere and hit him so hard that he didn't get up again.

"I examined your competitive position because I recognized the compatibility of your interests with ours. We also are not big players. Like you, we need alliances, partners, good long-term relationships. When it makes sense to do a deal, we seek out the most suitable partner and we do it."

"And you think it makes sense now?"

The speaker was a slender young man from Hong Kong who was wearing a chunky gold signet ring, a gold bracelet on his right hand, and a Rolex on his left. He also had matching gold cuff links and collar studs, gold-rimmed spectacles, and a couple of gold teeth glinting in the side of his mouth.

"Absolutely," said Snowbird, thwacking the pointer into the palm of his hand for emphasis.

"Meaning for you or for us?"

"For both. Look—what we are dealing with here is a product with exceptional potential. There will be sky-high margins, secured by an un-challengeable, monopoly position. I'm not exaggerating, gentlemen—this is a twenty-first-century market opportunity ready to be exploited by those with twenty-first-century vision and acumen."

Snowbird launched into the main body of his presentation. This was the third time he had been through it, and each time he found his own arguments more convincing. How could anyone have any doubts? The merits of the case were self-evident. Even the Americans, with their no-torious short-term perspective, had been able to appreciate the opportu-nity, and the deal had been clinched without difficulties. In terms of scale . . . America was of course the most important market, followed by Europe, but in terms of future potential the Asian market was the most promising. That was why Snowbird had gone to such lengths over this presentation. Nobody was going to accuse him of neglecting the Asians.

"Pretty bullish, aren't you?" said the man from Hong Kong, leaning back in his armchair. "But what you're suggesting is a leap into the un-known. This is a product that would run directly across our other inter-ests. We're going to need some pretty strong arguments before we sign off on something like this."

"You shall have them," said Snowbird. "Whether you accept their va-lidity is a matter for your judgment. But let me make myself clear—the product will reach the market with your help or not. We will need a fi-nal decision in a matter of weeks."

He spoke in English, articulating each word with careful emphasis. None of the other men present was a native speaker of English, but all the same he paid attention to his grammar and sentence structure. Snow-bird prided himself on his command of English, even though there were others in his business—men who had spent half their careers in Hawaii or California—with greater fluency. They had absorbed it from necessity and used it functionally, gracelessly. Snowbird was different. He had learned English out of intellectual curiosity, in order to be able to read the poets whom he admired in the original. Snowbird had been a middle school student when he had first come across the works of Eliot, Frost, Auden, and the rest. Immediately, a new world had opened up, but the translated versions, he had sensed, were only capable of giving him a fraction of what was really there. After long years of study those early instincts had been confirmed. Nowadays he read voraciously—not just poetry, but also novels and biographies of great literary figures. Set against that, the ability to negotiate directly with representatives of foreign crime syndicates was a minor accomplishment.

"A matter of weeks? That's crazy. We haven't even seen the product. We have no idea of its capabilities. How can we make a decision like that in a couple of weeks!"

"I understand your concerns, Ambrose-san," said Snowbird, forcing himself to smile politely. "First of all, though, let me express my total confidence in the performance of the product. Don't just take my word for it. The folders on the desk in front of you contain summaries of experimental data collected in top-class laboratory conditions."

The three listeners picked up the folders and shuffled through the papers inside.

"Now, who put this stuff together?" said the man from Hong Kong, his stubby forefinger tapping on a sheet of pie charts and graphs. He spoke in the sort of sloppy West Coast drawl that always grated on Snowbird's sensibilities. The sort of man, thought Snowbird, who thought Auden was a brand of European luxury car.

"Our R&D people, of course. Every important aspect of the product was examined and refined during the development phase. That is the Japanese approach, gentlemen. The idea was to create the optimum product, one with a unique package of features that will guarantee market dominance."

"All chemical compounds can be reproduced," said the Hong Kong man flatly. "There's no patent protection in our business, you know."

He turned to the other two for approval. The Tiger of Taipei gave a perfunctory chuckle. The man from Shanghai, who had flown in earlier that day, looked up from the data sheet he was reading and gave a twitch of a smile. Snowbird guessed that he understood only half of what was being said.

Snowbird's eyes narrowed behind his dark glasses. Mentally he counted to ten before replying. "If you study the documents a little more closely, you will understand what I mean by uniqueness. We are not dealing with an ordinary chemical compound of the sort that could be cooked up in some back-alley factory in Kowloon. This is a bioengineered product, created by recombinant DNA technology after years and years of basic research."

"And what does that mean exactly?" The humor had gone out of the Hong Kong man's voice. Clearly he was anxious not to lose face in front of the two older men. Snowbird softened his tone again. You had to be accommodating to important customers, no matter what obnoxious little creeps they might happen to be.

"It means that this is not a synthetic product which can be broken down and reverse-engineered in the usual way. It would have to be grown."

"Grown?" The Tiger of Taipei looked puzzled. "What, you mean it's alive?"

"In a manner of speaking, yes. It's an organically derived material which our people have created from scratch and then succeeded in culturing on a mass scale. Believe me, there are few organizations outside the pharmaceuticals giants with the ability to come close to our achievements. Gene-splicing is not like stitching together fake Louis Vuitton handbags, you know. It requires huge capital investment—high-purity clean rooms, process-control apparatus of incredible sensitivity. For this we had to go to special sources in the United States and Russia."

"And you think you can hold a monopoly position in the face of all the competition?"

"I'm absolutely certain we can. In the modern world, monopolies are created by the overwhelming deployment of technological resources. Believe me—no one will be able to produce anything similar for decades. The partners that we select will enjoy a significant and long-lasting advantage over their competitors."

He didn't overstress that "we select," but he wanted to let them know that there were other options. There were the Thais and the Vietnamese, for example. Also, the Russians were handling the European market. It would be quite possible for them to take East Asia as well. Snowbird was in two minds about the Russians. They were, after all, the people who had produced Pushkin, Pasternak, Mayakovski. But would they be able to handle the complex logistics that were required? Snowbird would certainly prefer the Chinese to take the East Asian market. Ambrose was certainly objectionable, but once the decision had been taken his people could be relied on to do a good job. Snowbird had worked with them on several occasions before, and he had not had any complaints.

"Okay," said the Hong Kong man, tossing the folder back on the table. "I'll have our people check this stuff out. Now, what about the product samples? When will we be able to inspect the real thing?"

"All in good time," said Snowbird, aware that he was sounding irritable again. "There's no point in making samples available until there is a clear in-principle agreement in place, and we're not at that stage yet. What we are trying to do today is to help you understand the true potential of Buddha Kiss."

"Buddha what?" frowned the Hong Kong man.

"Kiss," said Snowbird, pursing his misshapen lips in a gesture of illustration. "There is another name too, of course—a scientific name that describes the molecular structure of the material. This is what you might call our pet name. It was bestowed on the product by its inventor. He claims that its effect on the psyche is akin to a kiss bestowed by the Buddha."

"Is that right?" The Tiger of Taipei looked lost for something to say.   335

"A screwy kind of guy, sounds like," commented the Hong Kong man, determinedly unimpressed.

If only he knew how screwy, thought Snowbird, smiling thinly to himself. "A certain measure of eccentricity usually accompanies high scientific achievement. Historically speaking, breakthrough products have rarely been created by people of standard bourgeois mentality."

"So what effects is this nutty professor of yours referring to?"

"I cannot speak from experience," said Snowbird, picking up a remote control. "Not having either used the product myself nor been kissed by the Buddha. Nonetheless, Ambrose-san, after watching this video I have prepared, you should have some idea."

One click of the remote control dimmed the lights, another set the video rolling. Snowbird sat still, his chin resting on his hands. He had always considered himself a long-term strategic thinker, not a deal-maker. In his current position, though, he was having to take direct responsibility for all the key aspects of the project, including marketing. There was simply no one else with the right kind of experience. Really, what he was doing now—second-phase contacts with overseas distribution channels—should have been handled by someone of lower rank. The three Chinese were medium-ranking representatives of their organization, certainly lacking the authority to make any binding commitments themselves. It wasn't really appropriate for Snowbird to deal with them directly, even less to engage in demeaning debate with the man from Hong Kong. Snowbird glanced at him disapprovingly, leaning back in his armchair, one foot casually hooked over a knee. Loud designer tie, ugly watch, too much aftershave—the man's taste was on a level with his grammar. Furthermore, he had no respect. Snowbird was offering him something that his own people couldn't create in a hundred years, and still he was acting like a bored teenager. Some said that the Chinese were overtaking the Japanese as the dominant force in Asia. They had the numbers—no question about that—but did they have the necessary dedication, the thirst for achievement, the humility? Looking at Ambrose Ho, Snowbird had his doubts.

The video presentation that Snowbird had put together was simple, but effective. The opening clip showed a man of Middle Eastern appearance smiling broadly, then breaking into a fit of giggles that gathered in intensity until he was rocking to and fro in his chair, gales of laughter issuing from his mouth. The camera tracked back to a full-body shot. It revealed that the man was sitting in front of a wooden table, staring at something in front of him on the table as he laughed. Only when the camera came in again could you be certain that it was indeed what it looked like—a finger.

A figure whose face was out of the shot appeared behind the seated man, grabbed his left hand, and slammed it down on the table, palm open. The little finger of the hand was missing, and the stump was spurting blood across the tabletop. The man stopped laughing and looked almost comically surprised. The faceless figure stepped back out of the picture. A heavy sushi knife appeared, was waved back and forth theatrically, then came slicing down on the seated man's thumb. His hand shot back to his side, leaving the severed thumb on the table. His eyes widened as he registered what had happened. He looked down at the stump, looked at the finger, then his lips broadened into a smile of euphoric glee. He threw back his head and gave out a long, shoulder-shaking gurgle of laughter. The exercise was repeated twice more, and each time the seated man found the experience of having a finger chopped off more hysterically funny than the time before. At the end of the clip, he was shaking his head helplessly, tears streaming down his cheeks as he guffawed with unstoppable amusement.

The man was an Iranian. He belonged to a gang that had double-crossed some low-level yakuza in a deal relating to forged telephone cards. His Iranian colleagues got scared and grabbed him one night and handed him over, hoping to avert any larger conflict. An old friend had happened to mention the subject to Snowbird, who had immediately had the bright idea of making use of the punishment session. The old friend had been only too happy to oblige, as Snowbird's old friends invariably were.

In Snowbird's view, the secret of good marketing was to leave the customer with an unforgettable image in his mind. This was particularly necessary with the Chinese, who were unlikely to respond well just to charts and statistics. He had been looking for an unforgettable image, and quite by chance he had found one. As a result, there was now a six-fingered Iranian walking the back streets of Osaka who had unknowingly starred in the world's first commercial of its kind.

The introductory clip ended, and the video moved on to an explanation by a masked laboratory worker of the biological principles on which the product worked. The laboratory worker described how various chemicals acted on the pleasure centers, as revealed by isotopic scanning. Next, there was a comparison of the properties of selected psychotropic agents and stimulants. According to the voiceover, the Buddha Kiss development team had begun by studying the whole range of mood-altering drugs, synthetic and natural, from alcohol to morphine, from peyote to crack. Each had been marked for plus and minus factors—euphoric intensity, ease of use, damage to the central nervous system, etc. The target was to engineer a new product that would maximize the ratio of pluses to minuses. The result was Buddha Kiss, which combined low toxicity with intense and immediate effects on the brain's pleasure centers. Low doses induced powerful feelings of contentment and confidence without affecting motor functions. Rats given small doses were twice as sexually active as the control group for as long as the experiment continued. Monkeys became extremely docile and were more easily trained to perform simple tasks. Larger doses had stronger psychotropic effects, in which bursts of high activity alternated with long, trancelike states in which the animals refused all food and drink.

The next shot was of Snowbird himself, standing in the middle of the laboratory, talking straight to the camera. Buddha Kiss, he asserted, was unlike every existing drug on the market. It would be acceptable to a wide range of social classes and age groups, from autoworkers to architects, from secretaries to the "silver market" of married retirees. It could be sniffed, smoked, injected, dissolved in a drink, or chewed in a gum. Side-effects were negligible, high levels of repeat use as good as guaranteed. Without a doubt, he concluded, Buddha Kiss was superbly suited to the demands of the times. It had the potential to outmode the current generation of recreational drugs as thoroughly as video had outmoded silver-halide photography. Their future was as low-margin, second-choice products. The future of Buddha Kiss and its derivatives, on the other hand, was as the single-malt scotch of the twenty-first century.

An exaggeration, of course, but one that should grab the attention of the Chinese. Snowbird's purpose was to reinforce the message that Buddha Kiss represented a different generation of product, one that had been developed according to the principles of functionality and customer acceptability. This wasn't some kind of medical spinoff, originally developed to tranquilize sheep or stabilize psychotics. It was engineered specifically to satisfy a defined set of consumer needs. Were the Chinese farsighted enough to understand what that meant? Snowbird hoped so, but from the expression on Ambrose Ho's face, the outlook was not encouraging. As the lights went up, he still had that little smirk on his chubby face.

"Sounds like a science fiction to me," he said, glancing at the Taiwanese. "You really expect us to believe this stuff is going to take off just like that?"

Snowbird got up from his chair and looked down on them, arms folded in front of his chest. "Your response is natural," he said. "Throughout history, major innovations have been greeted with scepticism. That's the way it should be. The new has to work hard to displace the old. In the end, though, the consumer will be the judge, and I've got no doubt that the verdict will be highly favorable—and highly profitable for those involved."

"But why is it so special?" said Ambrose Ho, scratching the side of his shiny little nose. "I still don't get it. I got to tell you straight-up here—I just don't see what all the big fuss is about."

Snowbird walked over to the window, the pointer still in his hand. He stared out onto the lights of Akasaka, trying to calm his rising vexation. Had Ambrose Ho actually absorbed anything or had he just been sitting there dozing? No doubt, the man had never been confronted with this kind of responsibility, but instead of acting with due humility he seemed to lack any sense of his own shortcomings. Of course, he owed everything to his father, who was a big man in the organization. Without family help, he would never have risen above the level of the manager of a "wet fish" bordello in Wanchai. The same could be said about the silent man from Shanghai, whose father was a high-ranking general in the Red Army. Nepotism, thought Snowbird, was the great weakness of Chinese society. In contrast, Japan was meritocratic. He himself owed nothing at all to his family's influence. Everything he had achieved, he had achieved by his own efforts.

"Seems to me like there's plenty of gaps in this story," went on Ambrose Ho. "I mean, what's supposed to be happening here in Japan, for example?"

"I'm not sure I follow you," said Snowbird, turning from the window.

"Your domestic market's pretty huge, isn't it? When's the thing going to be launched here? Who's handling the marketing? What about the pricing? All this could be valuable information for us, you know."

"Wait a minute," said Snowbird, holding up a hand in front of his chest. "We supply the product. You conduct the marketing in the specified markets whatever way suits you best. That's your business, and what we do in Japan is our business."

"Sounds to me like you're looking for a fall guy," said Ambrose, a sarcastic edge to his voice.

"A fall guy," said Snowbird, waggling the pointer impatiently. "What is that supposed to mean?"

"It means you want the profits, but you want someone else to take all the risk for you. The way you've got it figured, no one's even going to know this stuff comes from Japan, right? All the world's going to see is the other end of the deal. It'll be those goddamn Chinese who take all the heat!"

"This is business," said Snowbird angrily. "You can be sure that the financial terms will be structured to reflect your contribution."

"And to reflect our risk," said Ambrose. "Which is going to be a whole lot bigger than yours, I'd say!" He was stabbing his finger in Snowbird's direction, his face puffy with arrogance.

"You're being totally unrealistic," snapped Snowbird. "We took a huge risk in developing the product in the first place. Now we're taking the whole risk of going to mass manufacture and global distribution. The risk in marketing is on an entirely different scale!"

For a moment, the two men glared at each other in silence. Snowbird stood with his arms folded, the pointer sticking up from his shoulder like an antenna. Ambrose sat in his armchair, brow furrowed in an unpleasant scowl. The Tiger of Taipei looked on in some consternation. He had been around long enough to know that the silence of a man like Snowbird was a bad sign. Ambrose's grandfather had come from the same village in Hainan as his own grandfather. It was his responsibility to see that the headstrong young man kept out of trouble.

"Let's try to avoid misunderstandings here," he said, a pacific smile on his pudgy face. "We have the basis of an interesting relationship, I think. There are just a few details needing to be cleared up. After all, we're sure to be asked a mountain of difficult questions by our own people."

Snowbird made a slight bow. The older man was doing his best to defuse the tension.

"For example, can you give us some idea when commercial-scale shipments will be ready?"

"Our target is early next year," said Snowbird. "To be frank with you, there are some uncertainties, but that is our current schedule."

"Uncertainties?" queried Ambrose Ho with a curl of the lip.

"Yes, uncertainties. The scale of the financing required to establish mass-manufacturing facilities and global distribution channels is probably well beyond your comprehension."

Ambrose Ho sat up straight in his chair, his brow like thunder. He was just about to deliver his reply when there was a knock on the door.

"What is it?" called out Snowbird, switching to gruff Japanese.

"Sato here. Something urgent has come up."

"I thought I told you to make sure I wasn't disturbed."

"But it's the sensei."

"Especially by the sensei. I haven't got time to waste on his crazy whims."

"He says it's serious. A security breakdown that requires immediate attention."

Snowbird glanced at the Tiger of Taipei, who was still smiling his conciliatory smile. He was old enough to have been educated under the Japanese occupation. That meant he had probably got the gist of what was being said.

"All right," said Snowbird, switching off the video monitor. "Wait outside for me."

He made a brief apology to his three guests, then slipped out the door. Sato was standing in the corridor, a look of trepidation on his face. After a few minutes of hushed conversation, Snowbird returned to the room.

"I hope you will accept my sincere apologies," he said smoothly. "There is a little problem that requires my immediate attention. I'm afraid I must ask for this meeting to be adjourned."

"What, you mean right now?"

Snowbird nodded. Ambrose gave a meaningful glance to the man from Shanghai, who was looking more confused than ever.

"We can resume discussions tomorrow or the day after, at any time convenient to you."

"These things happen," said the Tiger of Taipei, nodding sagely. "And always at inconvenient times." He hauled himself to his feet, revealing a paunch like a sack of rice.

"You're right there," said Snowbird grimly. "They shouldn't, but they do." Without looking, he knew that the sarcastic smirk had returned to Ambrose Ho's face.

Mitchell squinted through flickering eyelids. It was a strange kind of chateau, he thought. You got there by elevator, then you were driven through the grounds in a golf cart. The staff were mainly men with shaven heads, and their idea of hospitality was pretty rough and ready. Two of them carried Mitchell by his shoulders and feet, swinging him about as if he were a stuffed doll.

He glimpsed Yazawa talking to one of the staff who had a back like an oak door. What was going on? Yazawa seemed agitated. The big servant was shaking his head. Mitchell wanted to call out and tell them to get his bed ready quickly, but his mouth wouldn't work. In fact his eyes wouldn't work either. He was falling asleep again, dreaming the same kind of strange dreams.

That he was lying down in a brightly lit room, with a crowd of people around his bed.

That someone picked up a syringe and slid the needle into his arm, just above the elbow on the inside.

That Yazawa bent down and kissed him lightly on the cheek.

That someone told him an extraordinary joke, the best joke he had ever heard in his life.

The exhausted recruits were led back to the dormitory, where the second group were preparing for their session. Mori copied the others, walking with head bowed, muttering gibberish under his breath. The recruits slumped down on their bedrolls and lay motionless, some instantly asleep despite the noise, others staring at the ceiling, their lips moving silently to the chants blaring from the overhead speakers. One bedroll was unoccupied. The woman who coughed blood had not returned from the session.

Half an hour later, the second group came back in the same state as the first. After they had slumped onto their bedrolls, the lights were dimmed and the loudspeaker finally went silent. The lone disciple squatted at the far end of the room, reading his book. It wasn't long before the man with the earring resumed snoring. He was lying spread-eagled, one arm thrown over his face. The woman behind him was curled up on her side, mumbling quietly in her sleep. Just half an hour after the second group had returned, there were only two people awake in the entire dormitory—Mori and the disciple. An hour later there was only one. The disciple had stuffed the book into his pocket, taken down a bedroll, and switched the lights off completely.

The only light was the faint glimmer of the moon through the window. He gazed at the outlines of the unconscious bodies stretched out on all sides of him. It looked as if he were in a morgue. If he wanted to find out more about Ono's operation lower down the mountain, there was unlikely to be a better time to make a move.

Mori rose to his feet. Half-crouching, he padded down the gap between the bedrolls. Once or twice, as he was stepping over a sleeping body, there was a cough or the stirring of a limb, which caused him to freeze on the spot, but most of the recruits were deep in slumber. The lone disciple at the far end of the room was as silent and still as the others, no doubt lost in dreams of the sensei and his prophecies. Mori slipped through the doorway. Having checked that no one was lurking in the washroom, he took a pair of sandals from the rack in the hallway and crept out into the night.

There was a gentle breeze brushing through the trees, and the air was cool and refreshing. Mori's feet crunched the asphalt as he made for the patch of forest that he had identified earlier. As he got closer, the shimmering of the hologram became more apparent. Mori stepped through it to the track on the other side, which made a winding descent of the mountain.

Once the training center was out of sight, Mori stopped and listened. An owl hooted. A small creature of some sort—lizard, weasel, squirrel?—

went scooting across his path. The wind hummed, and there was a deeper hum beneath it—the hum of electricity. Mori moved forward carefully, since the downward gradient was steepening and even in the clearer areas there was plenty of undergrowth. The dark cotton kimono he was wearing offered little protection against the nettles and thorn-bushes that he occasionally brushed against, but at least it made for excellent camouflage in the shadows of the forest.

Mori walked for twenty minutes, following the path as it curled down the mountain. The electrical hum got louder and louder. Finally he glimpsed bright light through the trees, then the outline of a flat concrete roof. It was the complex of buildings that he had glimpsed from the sea. He was now approaching it from the back.

No "Keep Out" signs were visible, but there was a fence—twelve feet of tight steel netting topped with hoops of barbed wire. It had been put up several years ago, Mori guessed, since the vegetation of the forest had already encroached on some parts, spearing it with branches of bamboo and looping it with strands of creeper.

Mori crept to within a yard of the fence and observed the complex of buildings from behind the trunk of a camphor tree. It was a much bigger, more elaborate setup than he had been expecting. In the center was a six-story building that looked as if it had been transported intact from the Otemachi business district. The lights were shining on almost every floor. Immediately behind was a long flat building with blinds covering the windows. At the very back were two smaller blocks with TV aerials and clotheslines on the roof. Those, Mori assumed, were the living quarters. If so, then there had to be at least fifty people based here. What were they doing? What could justify an operation of this sophistication? Using tree trunks as cover, Mori moved down the length of the fence. He soon found the electric generator responsible for the loud hum. It was located near the front of the main building, housed in a kind of roofed cage that would protect it from the elements. Mori didn't know much about generating capacity, but the thing was on a different scale from the compact machines that he had seen at camping grounds. It looked large enough to supply the needs of a whole village.

The main building looked out onto a concrete area about the size of a baseball diamond. It was lit with the bright overhead lights that Mori had glimpsed through the forest. The building itself, he could see now, was divided into two sections. The section facing his side of the fence was structured like an ordinary office building, with windows on every floor. The other side didn't have any windows on the first, second, and third floors. Instead there was a large sliding door, such as might be found at a truck depot. In front of the door and leading away across the concrete square were two thin strips of metal that Mori would have been unable to make out if they hadn't gleamed dully in the overhead lights. They were rails.

Suddenly, there were voices at the front door. Mori ducked behind a clump of bamboo as a disciple emerged, turned, and gave a deep bow. Mori recognized him instantly. It was the broken-toothed one who had beaten him to the ground "to rouse his spirit." The disciple walked across the square and disappeared into a shed on the other side. When he emerged a few seconds later, he was sitting in a golf cart, which gave off a high-pitched whine as he steered it over the concrete.

Mori watched the cart cruise up the slope toward the sleeping quarters, then edged away from the bamboo. Moving like a wraith, he carried on his exploration, following the rails down toward the sea. It looked as if Ono had designed some kind of vehicle to connect the main building with the lower part of the complex. What could be the point of that? Presumably not to accommodate the needs of sightseers. It had to be there for transportation purposes. But to transport what and where? The more Mori discovered about Ono's operation on the island, the more unanswerable questions were occurring to him.

The grounds of the complex got narrower as the incline got steeper. There was no lighting, but Mori could make out the rails from the raised concrete bedding in which they had been set. At this level, the forest was thinning out into a scrubbier terrain, in which a few trees were interspersed with bushes and clumps of couch grass. Lower still, Mori glimpsed the silhouette of another building, this time completely dark. He hurried toward it, scrabbling over bushes and loose earth.

The sight that confronted him there was a spectacular one. He was standing on the edge of a sheer precipice, the sea thundering against the rocks hundreds of feet below. The building was actually a concrete block that had been set on a narrow outcrop of cliff. On three sides there was nothing but air. Looking more closely, Mori noted the big pulley on the roof and the single strand of heavy cable taut against the sky, and he understood what the designer had had in mind. The block was there to house some kind of winch mechanism, linking the complex with the shore below.

The block's windows were just spaces between the concrete slabs. A good design for withstanding typhoons, thought Mori. He gripped the steel netting of the fence with his hands, dug his toes into the stony earth, and tried to work himself right up to the wall. Once or twice his feet missed their place and a shower of stones went ricocheting down the face of the cliff. It was a long way down, all right. He tried not to think about it.

Finally, he reached the point where the fence ended and the concrete wall began. There was a tricky three yards to the nearest window in which Mori had no handhold and just a six-inch ridge for his feet. He took a deep breath and slowly edged along it, cheek and palms flat against the concrete wall. The wind tugged at his kimono. Far below, the waves crunched against the rocks.

He didn't let out his breath until his elbows were resting firmly on the window ledge. Then he wriggled inside, dropping shoulder first onto the damp floor. He rolled over and sat on his haunches while his eyes got used to the murky light. The room in which he found himself was filled with machinery, wiring, the smell of oil. On the opposite wall was a control box with a single red light glowing dully. Looking up, he could make out the shape of a giant winch set on a stand. It was from this that the heavy cable ran, winding through a system of wheels and then out through a slotlike opening in the high ceiling.

Breathing more easily, he moved through the doorway into the large room on the other side. The visibility was much better here, thanks to the moonlight flooding in through a space in the front wall large enough to drive a truck through. There was no guardrail or ledge, just a sheer drop to the sea below. Mori approached it and peered out. The heavy cable was hanging in the air, just a couple of yards from his face. Mori followed it down several hundred feet with his eyes, right down to the shore. Immediately below the tower was a small bay protected from the open sea by a curling promontory covered with trees. It was an ideal natural harbor, and that was how it was being used. Mori counted a dozen boats of various shapes and sizes drawn up alongside a quayside. Thanks to the promontory, it would all be invisible from the open sea.

Looking into the limpid black water was making him feel giddy. Mori took half a pace backward. Suddenly, there was a loud clang from the next room, followed by a gathering rumble and then the squeak of the pulley wheel above his head. The elevator was in operation! He peered over the edge again. Yes, the small white rectangle on the quayside was gradually getting bigger.

Mori thought about hiding in the room with the winching machinery, but if anyone entered and turned on the light he would be trapped. And as for the room he was in—it was empty of furnishings, except for a ladder lying on its side. It had to be there for a reason. Mori glanced upward. Just as he had thought—one of the panels in the ceiling had been taken out. Moving quickly and surely, Mori leaned the ladder against the wall, climbed up to the gap in the ceiling, and swung himself through it.

The space on the other side was only just tall enough to stand up in. There were no windows, but the weak light from the far end made it possible for Mori to keep his footing on the wooden beams. He moved uncertainly toward the source of the light, which turned out to be a half-open sliding panel in the ceiling. Mori slid it completely open and stuck his head out. This ceiling was actually the roof of the block, and he was within spitting distance of the squeaking pulley wheel. He ducked back again and returned to where he had left the ladder. Should he pull it up out of sight? Probably, but it was too late now. The elevator was humming toward him. He could even hear the sound of voices inside.

The rumbling and squeaking stopped, and the elevator engaged with the metal bracket. Peering through the gap in the ceiling, Mori saw two men hop out onto the concrete floor. One was a tall disciple in a brown robe. The other was a middle-aged man in white overalls, a white peaked cap, and steel-rimmed spectacles. He was being treated with a deference that Mori had never observed in any of the disciples before.

"Fujita-kun should have been here to meet us," said the disciple, gazing around the elevator room. "Please wait a few minutes until he arrives."

"I have no intention of waiting for this Fujita-kun!" said the man in the white coat angrily. "Open the door and let me out at once!"

"But there are security procedures that must be followed. Temporary residents such as yourself must be accompanied at all times."

"Forget the security procedures! Were you not told not to bother me with trivialities? I am afraid that you have no understanding of the mind of a scientist!"

Evidently cowed, the disciple took a bunch of keys from his belt. The two men passed directly under the missing panel in the ceiling and disappeared from Mori's sight. There was the sound of a heavy door being swung open. When the disciple came back into view, he was alone. Mori heard him cluck his tongue in exasperation as he walked slowly toward the elevator. He turned, and then for the first time his gaze fell on the ladder. His brow wrinkled and he stopped dead, his eyes traveling up the rungs to the ceiling and the open panel.

The man was certainly no quick thinker. There was plenty of time for Mori to duck out of the way, but as he did so his foot slipped off the rafter and he came down with all his weight on a panel of the ceiling.

Mori froze and listened. There was no sound. Then he noticed the top of the ladder vibrating slightly. The disciple was coming up. The damage had been done, but all the same Mori took care with his footing as he edged down the length of the rafter to the sliding panel in the roof. Was the disciple slow-witted enough to put that sudden noise down to the wind or some other natural cause? Mori doubted it. The man would follow his security procedures, making sure that all parts of the building were thoroughly checked. And that was bad news for Mori.

As quietly as possible, he lifted himself out onto the roof, taking care to ease the panel shut behind him. He hunkered down beside the pulley mechanism. It didn't give much cover, exposing his body from the shoulders up. If the disciple came onto the roof, he would be spotted easily. It didn't make Mori feel any better to know that two yards behind his back was a straight drop of several hundred feet.

The disciple had been well trained. Mori heard a creak from the rafter below, then a few seconds later a faint tinkle from the bunch of keys as he slid open the panel. Mori hunched down, hoping that his silhouette would blend with the shape of the machinery. It didn't.

"You there!" hissed the disciple. "What do you think you're doing?"

"This mechanism," Mori muttered indistinctly. "I thought it needed some attention."

The situation was unpromising. Mori rose slowly to his feet and gave a little bow. The disciple hauled himself up onto the roof and approached him. Their eyes met.

"I don't think I've seen you before," said the disciple. "What part of the operation are you working in?"

"Repairs and maintenance," said Mori.

"And you always do this work after dark?"

"Not always, but it can be convenient to do routine checks when the equipment is not being used. It is my personal responsibility to ensure that everything is in perfect working order."

The disciple was silent for a moment. "I see," he nodded finally. "Anyway, your behavior is contrary to several security regulations. You must come down immediately."

Mori bowed again. His hopes were rising. The man was obviously the kind to believe anything he was told. After all, that was why he had joined Ono's organization in the first place. He moved away from the pulley toward the panel in the roof. The disciple was standing next to it, arms crossed in front of his chest.

"You go first," he said, a little too quickly for Mori's liking. There was a slight quaver of suppressed tension in his voice. Mori bent down toward the panel, his nerves suddenly on edge.

Without looking up, he saw the feet adjusting to a different stance, heard the sharp intake of breath as the blow was delivered. He leaned away just in time, and the fist that was intended to crunch into his jaw thumped harmlessly against his chest instead.

"You thought you could fool me!" snarled the disciple, following up with a savage kick to the stomach that Mori managed to half-parry. "But I am not fooled. You are an outsider, a spy. It is obvious from your words!"

"You're making a mistake," gasped Mori, rolling away just in time from a stomp to the groin.

"No mistake. No one here would talk of personal responsibility. There is only the will of the sensei!"

He stomped again, this time catching Mori on the side of the knee. Mori fell forward, grabbing the other man's foot with both hands and twisting. The disciple collapsed to the ground, the other foot scything at Mori's face. Mori jerked out of the way and dived onto the man's back, hands scrabbling for his neck.

That turned out to be a miscalculation. Before he knew what was happening, the disciple had grabbed Mori's fingers and was sinking his teeth into the flesh of his hand. Mori snatched the hand away, sliding sideways. The disciple twisted free, and an elbow jab caught Mori full in the stomach. He rolled back, fending off the disciple's lungeing fists and feet.

Mori used the pulley to haul himself to his feet, but he wasn't quite fast enough. The disciple charged, his forehead thumping into Mori's chest, a flying fist catching him on the point of the chin. Mori reeled backward, half-stunned, just managing to break his fall with his shoulder. He was trapped in the corner of the roof, much too close to the edge.

Another couple of yards, and there would have been nothing to break his fall but the rocks far below.

Mori struggled to his knees. The disciple sidled forward on the balls of his feet. He was fit and strong, but totally predictable. In this position, he wouldn't come forward unless he was sure. He would just feint and block and use his feet to force Mori to the edge. Then a well-aimed reverse kick would send Mori spinning into space. Mori needed him to charge. He needed to get close.

"You said I didn't pay enough respect to the sensei," said Mori rising awkwardly to his feet. "You were certainly right there."

"Too late for apologies," grunted the disciple. He kept moving, weaving from side to side, ready to block any thrust for safety that Mori might make. Instead, Mori took a step back. He was no more than a yard from the roof's edge. The gusting wind was whipping the kimono hem around his knees.

"This sensei is nothing but a cheap charlatan."

The disciple stood bolt upright, his nostrils flaring as he sucked in air. He had stopped moving from side to side. "Liar," he snarled. "The sensei is the greatest genius under heaven. Admit that before you die!"

"A great genius at swindling people's money," smirked Mori. "He talks of ascetic disciplines, but look at that big fat belly! It must be stuffed with beer and pizza!"

The disciple gave a roar of anger and then charged forward, hands scrabbling for a chokehold. That was just what Mori had been hoping for. As his high school judo teacher would have pointed out, the disciple's posture was all wrong—the center of gravity way too high, the legs too far behind. Mori caught a flailing hand and swiveled his hips in a single fluid movement. Not much strength was needed, just steadiness in the legs and a good, smooth follow-through as he guided the wrist downward.

Almost in slow motion, the disciple's feet left the ground and he tumbled over Mori's knee in a perfect arc. He hit the ground shoulder first, and the momentum carried him right to the edge of the roof. Keeping his eyes fixed on Mori, he stretched an arm behind him to steady himself, but there was nothing there. The momentum was rocking him backward and his hand was clutching thin air and his eyes were registering shock, panic. And then, like a magician's rabbit, he had disappeared from sight.

Mori peered down. He thought he saw something dark bouncing off the cliff, then a splash far below that might have been a wave breaking against a rock. He heaved a sigh of relief and checked the knee that the disciple had stomped on. It was bruised, but he could bend his legs without too much pain. He quickly made his way along the creaking rafter and clattered down the ladder to the elevator room. He took the ladder down and leaned it against the wall in the position in which he had found it. What about the elevator? It would probably be a good idea to send it back down to sea level.

Mori was just about to step inside and press the start button when he heard the main door squeak. He wheeled around, to be confronted by the man in the white cap, who was standing in the doorway staring at him.

"What are you doing here?" he snapped.

Here we go again, thought Mori. "I'm from repairs and maintenance. It's more convenient for everyone if machinery is checked when it's not being used."

"That's a point, I suppose. Anyway, what happened to the other guy? He's still holding my security pass."

Mori moved toward the door. "Oh, him—yes, I think he's down below somewhere."

"Down below!" said the man, glaring at Mori accusingly. "That's impossible. The elevator is still here."

"Perhaps he didn't use the elevator," said Mori. "Perhaps he found a shortcut to the bottom."

The man in the white cap looked puzzled, then the light of realization dawned in his eyes and he glanced behind him. Suddenly, he looked scared. Mori raised a finger and shook his head. "Careful," he said. "Or you'll be using the shortcut too."

The man made a rush for the door. Mori caught him halfway, turned him around, and hit him once, hard, in the pit of the stomach. He gave a grunt of shock and collapsed to his knees. Mori picked him up by the armpits, flattened him against the wall, then delivered a carefully aimed uppercut to the side of the jaw. The white cap flew off his head, and he slumped sideways to the ground. Mori prodded him with a foot, but there was no response.

Mori went through to the winch room and searched around on the floor. When he had found the materials that he needed, he returned to the elevator room and hauled the unconscious man up the ladder to the next floor. After binding him hand and foot with wire cord, he tied him to a beam and gagged him with pieces of old newspaper. The Mori who descended the ladder was dressed in white overalls and had a pair of steel-rimmed glasses in his upper pocket. All he needed now was the white cap. He picked it up and planted it on his head, pulling the peak down over his eyes. The overalls were a little too short and the cap was a little too big, but otherwise the fit wasn't bad. Mori smacked the dust off his trouser legs. Did he really look like a scientist? He put on the spectacles and squinted aggressively through them. He only hoped that he wouldn't need to think like one as well.

Mori stepped outside and closed the big door behind him, clicking the padlock that the disciple had left hanging on the hasp. After checking that no one else was around, he started up the slope toward the distant cluster of buildings.

About a hundred yards from the sea, the area enclosed by the fence widened in a V shape. Most of it was overgrown with wild grass and thornbushes, but in the middle was a channel, quite a bit wider than a Shinjuku back street, that had been sanded over. Bisecting the sanded ground was the raised concrete bed. Mori scuffed through the sand and gazed at the rails. They were a couple of inches wide and about five feet apart. That suggested a fairly heavy vehicle. Why would a religious leader need heavy industrial equipment? For that matter, why would a short-tempered scientist be brought here by boat in the middle of the night? Mori was as perplexed as ever.

SEVENTEEN

Mori was already halfway to the main building when he glimpsed movement in the brightly lit square. One of the golf carts had emerged from the hed at the side. There was a disciple sitting in the driver's seat, his shaved head as pale as a melon under the lights. The cart wheeled around in an arc and began to follow the rails down toward the cliff. Mori glanced around. In his white overalls there was little chance of concealment. It was too late anyway. The disciple in the golf cart had spotted him and was waving a hand in the air and shouting something. It didn't sound threatening. Mori stood up, put on the spectacles again, and pulled the peak of the cap down over his forehead. It was time to look scientific.

The little cart was only a couple of hundred yards away now, trundling down the slope at a speed that caused it to buck and bobble on the stony ground. "Please wait there," the driver was shouting. "Do not tire yourself by walking farther!"

Mori crossed his arms in front of his chest and waited. The cart finally rattled to a halt in front of him, and the disciple skipped out and made a low bow. "Forgive me for keeping you waiting for so long," he said. "Let me take you to your quarters at once."

Mori gave a grunt of displeasure and climbed into the back of the golf cart.

"Our scientific personnel must be treated as the treasure of the organization. Those are the sensei's own words."

"Wise words," said Mori, giving a sigh of irritation that indicated the conversation was at an end.

The disciple got back into the driving seat and turned the cart toward the bright lights of the square. There was silence between them. Mori became uncomfortably aware that he was being scrutinized from the side.

"Is something the matter?" he growled as they approached the main building.

"Of course not," stammered the disciple, looking hastily to the front. "It's just that your face is unfamiliar. We are trained to recognize all the scientists at a glance."

"Then your training needs some improvement," said Mori. "You should know me. After all, I know you well enough."

"You do?"

"Yes. Isn't your name Fujiya, or something like that?"

"Fujita. How did you know?"

"You've earned yourself a good reputation here, Fujita-kun. Now you must make efforts to keep it up!"

"Thank you," said the disciple. "Look, I must apologize again for keeping you waiting. It was an inexcusable mistake."

"No more foolish words," said Mori. "Stop chattering and drive!"

They skirted the square in silence, then followed the white line that led to the two buildings at the back of the complex. The disciple brought the cart to a halt at the door of the larger one, stepped out, and bowed low enough for Mori to count the folds of flesh on the back of his neck. Mori gave a grunt of dismissal, stepped into the building, and closed the door behind him.

And stopped dead, his nose pressing against a thick glass panel. He pushed, but it didn't move; fumbled for a door handle, but there wasn't one. Looking around, he saw that there was some sort of security lock set into the wall. Unless that were activated correctly, there was no way in, and activating it incorrectly could be a bad mistake. He waited for the whine of the golf cart to fade into the distance, then slipped outside again and edged around the corner of the building.

At the back, there were only a few feet of space between the wall and the fence. Mori eased himself into the gap, taking special care with his footing. The ground was sticky, thanks to a steady drip of water from an overflow pipe, and there were a couple of empty beer cans visible in the dim light. There was a row of windows on the ground floor, several of which were half-open. The one in the middle had a light glimmering from between the curtains. Ducking under the darkened windows, Mori edged toward it.

There was just enough of a crack between the sides of the curtains for him to peek inside safely. What he saw was the upper bodies of two men dressed in the same white overalls as Mori. They were looking down, apparently immersed in thought. Rising onto his tiptoes, Mori observed that they were sitting on a tatami floor, with a shogi board and two beer cans between them. Saxophone music was coming from a portable CD player near the window. Mori recognized the number—Coltrane's "My Favorite Things," the majestic version recorded live at Newport in 1962. It was one of his personal favorites.

After a few seconds of silence, one of the men stood up and said something. The other pointed at the window, causing Mori to duck beneath the level of the ledge. The window squeaked open, the curtains yanked apart, and Coltrane was suddenly louder. Mori squeezed against the wall, trying to make himself as small as possible. For a few seconds, there was no movement. The man was just staring into the forest, apparently waiting for something to happen. Then something did happen. A thin stream of liquid looped high over Mori's shoulder and splashed to the ground on the other side of the fence. The man was too absorbed in his shogi game to make it to a toilet! Mori silently cursed all scientists and turned his face to the wall, ignoring the stray drops pattering down on his back.

Eventually the window slammed shut, and Coltrane went quiet. Mori peered through the slit in the curtains and confirmed that the two men were gazing at the shogi board once more. The lights were off in the next room, and the window was half-open. Putting his face to the gap in the curtains, Mori saw the shape of a man's body curled up on a bedroll in the middle of the floor. From the sound of his breathing, he was deeply asleep. Just under the windowsill was a small table on which Mori could make out a wallet. He snaked his arm between the curtains and stretched out his hand. The wallet was just out of reach. He stood on tiptoe and made a little jumping motion, but his scrabbling fingers succeeded only in pushing the wallet farther down the table. There was no other solution. If he wanted to examine what was on the desk, he was going to have to get much closer.

Stealthily, using his elbows and knees, Mori eased himself up onto the window ledge, then pushed his upper body through the gap in the curtains. The man's sleeping face was just a few feet from the window. Mori moved slowly, like a cat stalking a bird. Finally, when his whole upper body was craning into the room, he bent down and gingerly lifted the wallet between finger and thumb. Also on the table were some small polyethylene bags containing a white powdery material. Mori clamped the wallet between his teeth, stretched his arm out again, and just managed to get his fingertips to one of the bags. Holding his breath, he wriggled his body forward another inch. That proved to be a mistake, as a plastic card slid from the wallet and clattered onto the table. The man rolled onto his back, muttered something unintelligible, and lifted a hand to his face. Mori froze, pulse thumping. The hand rubbed an eyelid, which twitched and flickered but, to Mori's intense relief, did not open. He hung there, just a couple of feet from the man's face, until the hand returned to the sleeper's side and the deep, regular breathing began again. Then he reached down to pick up the polyethylene bag and eased his way back through the window.

Mori used the light from the shogi players' window to examine what he had found. The contents of the wallet were unsurprising, but nonetheless revealing—a small amount of money, a couple of business cards, and a security card with an IC chip built in. Mori slipped the security card into the pocket and glanced at the business cards. The first belonged to Professor Kimura, director of the Japan Neurobiology Center; the second to Kenji Ito, research chief of Sumikawa Pharmaceuticals. Ono's people appeared to have some highly prestigious contacts. He opened the polyethylene bag, dipped a finger into the white powder, and put a few grains to his tongue. The effect was like electricity. He gathered the saliva in his mouth and spat. Even such a tiny amount left a strong aftertaste, bitter and slightly metallic. Where had he tasted something similar to that? He tried to remember. Of course—it was the tea! The stuff that had turned the trainees into a collection of nervous wrecks.

Levering himself up into the darkened window again, Mori put the wallet and the bag back on the table. Then he crept along the alley to the other side of the building. All was still, except for the breeze ruffling the trees and the clouds drifting across the moon. Mori heard the distant buzz of the generator, the hooting of an owl deep in the forest. He decided to check the neighboring building as well. It was some thirty yards away, across a patch of rough ground. Mori moved quickly, stumbling a few times on knots of undergrowth.

This building had the same proportions as the one that housed the scientists. Mori edged into the space between the outer wall and the fence. Again, there was a row of half a dozen windows, several of which were open. There was just one light at the window farthest along. Noiselessly, Mori made his way toward it.

What he observed was another four-and-a-half tatami mat room, with the same bare furnishings as he had seen in the first building. Stretched out on the floor was a bedroll containing a sleeping figure huddled under the sheet, with thick strands of hair falling across the pillow. The occupant of the room was a woman, a young and attractive one, if the curve of the neck was any guide. Mori crept along to the next window. A similar sight greeted him there, and at the next one too. He had found the Sisters of Light. He was finally closing in on Yuriko's trail.

The window in the last, lit room was a few inches open. Mori stopped and pressed himself against the wall. There had been a sudden noise in the room, something between a hiccup and a moan. He strained his ears. Yes, there it was again, slightly louder this time. He recognized it as the sound of a human being in misery.

Mori edged closer to the window, moving his eyes to the narrow gap between the curtains. There was no bedroll in this room, just a woman curled up in the fetal position on the bare mat. Her hands were covering her face, and her whole body was jerking as she sobbed, as if the physical effort was using up her last reserves of energy. Something about that jerking motion told Mori that she had been sobbing for a long time already.

He watched for several minutes, unsure what to do. The convulsions came in waves, a powerful one breaking up into small shudders that continued while she built up strength for the next effort. Mori was on the point of moving away, when a particularly strong one shifted her body around, enabling him to glimpse her face.

The shock was jarring, and not just because he knew her. The woman Mori was staring at was Miki, and at the same time not Miki. She had Miki's face, but the expression it carried was completely alien to that of the young woman whom Mori had met just a few days before. She hadn't been capable of the depth of anguish conveyed by that grimacing face and that terrible sound.

It was a pitiful sight. It was also an opportunity. Mori's mind worked quickly. If he confronted her, would she raise the alarm? Doubtful. After all, she hadn't wiped out his membership that time, even though there had been ample reason. But would she be any use in this semi-hysterical condition? Hard to say, but nothing would be lost by finding out.

Mori emerged from the alley and padded around to the front of the building. With the clouds covering the moon, visibility was poor, but there was no sign of movement anywhere. He opened the outer door and slipped inside. The security lock was the same as the one in the other building. Mori took the security card from his back pocket and inserted it in the slot. A red light winked for several seconds while the machine read the chip. Mori eyed it warily. Finally, there was a click, and the lock in the glass door disengaged. Mori pushed it open and made straight for the farthest room on the left.

He didn't bother to knock, kicking his shoes off and sitting beside Miki before she even realized he was there. She turned to look up at him, the shock of recognition making her temporarily forget her grief.

"Why?" she said in a small voice that disappeared into a gulp.

Her eyes were bloodshot, the pupils dilated. Mori smiled, shook his head, and raised a finger to his lips.

The sobs came again and she hunched up with her face pressed against his knee. Mori didn't say anything but just sat there stroking her hair. They stayed in that position for over a quarter of an hour, Mori sitting still, Miki not lifting her face to the light. Finally the sobs started to die away and her breathing became a little more regular.

"What are you doing here, Nakamura-san?" she said finally, dabbing at her swollen eyes with a tissue.

"The sensei has asked me to help with some work. I have some technical knowledge—in laminated plastics, remember."

"You are helping the sensei?" she said, shrinking away from him. "You're one of them, aren't you? You're pretending to be my friend, but you're on their side really!"

She gave a wrenching sob and collapsed onto the tatami. Mori picked her up and clapped his hands in front of her face. She looked dazed, her eyeballs rolling sideways to the floor. Mori clapped again, more loudly. "I'm not with them," he hissed in her ear. "I'm with you. Don't you remember? Our *ki* forces are exactly aligned! That's why we've come together again like this."

"Are you a good man?" she said, brow furrowed. "You said you were a good man!"

"I said relatively speaking," said Mori. "Meaning compared with the average."

"The average is bad, very bad. That's what I think now."

She swallowed a sob and took a deep breath. Mori waited for the right moment. "Come on," he said gently. "You can tell me what's wrong. We're like brother and sister, right?"

Mori held out his hand and Miki pulled herself up into a sitting position. He remembered how small she was, a head below him even when they were both squatting on their haunches. She had dark rings under her eyes that had not been there three days before, and she was paler and thinner in the face.

"Everything is hopeless," she said suddenly. "My whole life is a stupid mistake."

"That's an exaggeration, isn't it?"

"No, it isn't. I want to die. I don't care if they kill me like they killed that other girl. It doesn't matter one bit."

She jutted out her lip and shook her head vigorously. Mori got up, closed the window, and clicked the hasp on the door. "Go on," he said, sitting down on the tatami again. "Explain to me exactly what you mean."

The story that Miki told was a simple one. She had arrived on the island on Sunday, together with ten other girls who had been chosen from branches all over the country. On the first night, they were taken to a room in the main building and instructed in special techniques of meditation. That was when Miki's troubles started. While the others were achieving blissful experiences, she suffered a series of terrifying hallucinations. In the dim light, the prone bodies of the girls turned to corpses, the disciples to scavenging animals tearing at their limbs. Miki ran for the door and screamed but one of the disciples beat her to the ground. At some point she must have lost consciousness, but the hallucinations grew in intensity. The details were so vivid: sounds, smells, physical pain, fear so strong that it was suffocating.

She had no memory of being taken out of the room, but the next day she woke in a large room with three other girls sleeping on futons. They were older Sisters of Light who had been sent to guard her. It was what they told her that had scared her the most. There had been other girls who had reacted badly to the meditational exercises. They were given several chances, but in the end if they failed to make progress they were punished severely. Instead of being allowed to serve the sensei directly, they were given to the senior disciples, who could do what they wished with them. These girls were considered so unreliable that they were never allowed to leave the island. Some weeks ago one girl had indeed tried to escape. She had been captured soon enough, and that was the last that anyone had heard of her.

Miki had understood the warning. She had to work hard at her spiritual exercises, otherwise she would suffer the same fate. Unfortunately, in the next training session the hallucinations were even more terrifying, and she lost consciousness almost right away. Again, she woke up in the room with the three Sisters of Light. The sensei, they told her, didn't tolerate spiritual weakness. When the Great Purification took place and Japan became the beacon of light to Asia, the unworthy would be cast aside. Polluting elements would be washed away, and the world made new and fresh.

The same thing had happened again today. Afterward, they told her that she was not worthy to enter the era of enlightenment. She would be cast aside in the Great Purification, an idea that terrified her more than being sent to serve the disciples.

"The sensei is a great genius," she said, still sobbing weakly. "But he has no interest in what is good and bad, only in his own power. I have come to think that he is a destroyer, not a savior."

She stopped and gazed anxiously at Mori, trying to read his reaction.

"I understand," he said sympathetically. "But for your own safety you must hide these thoughts. Try to pretend that you're responding to the meditation just like the others."

"But how can I do that?" said Miki, dismayed. "The visions are unbearable. You don't know what they're like."

"Do exactly what I say and you won't get any more of these visions. Don't drink the tea they give you. Pretend to drink it, but get rid of it when no one is looking. And stay away from that bean jelly too."

"The tea and the bean jelly? Why? What do you mean?"

"No more questions," said Mori, rising to his feet. "Just follow that advice and you'll be all right. Then you must imitate what the others are doing. Pretend you're a movie actress playing a part. Do you understand me?"

Miki nodded obediently. She still looked confused, but some of the old brightness was back in her face. Mori shuffled on his shoes and pushed the door a couple of inches open. There was no sign of activity. He turned, gave a wave, and stepped out of the room. What he needed to do now was to get off the island immediately. It wouldn't be long before the missing disciple and the scientist were discovered.

The moon was shuttered behind the clouds, making it difficult to see more than a few yards ahead. He made his way across the open ground, intending to work his way back down toward the tower. He was halfway between the two buildings when he heard a trilling whistle several yards behind, the sort of sound that a songbird might make as a preliminary clearing of the throat. The only problem with that explanation was that soon afterward another whistle sounded somewhere off to his right, followed by one a few yards in front. Mori didn't know much about the bird life of the region, but he doubted that three insomniacs of the same species would be found quite so close together.

He paused and squinted through the gloom in the direction of the last whistle. There was something there, all right—something dark and a whole lot larger than any bird that Mori had ever seen. Then there was a rustle in the undergrowth behind him. He wheeled around to face it, but too late. A ferocious blow caught him just above the waist, knocking him sideways. Something was swooshing toward his left ear, and he threw up an arm to protect his head. The stave smashed against his elbow, numbing the arm from the fingers to the shoulder.

"What's going on?" he called out through gritted teeth. "There must be a mistake!"

"No mistake this time, spy," hissed a familiar voice. It was the young disciple who had driven him to the building in the golf cart.

"Hoi—Fujita-kun!" said Mori desperately. "It's me—don't you remember!"

The butt of a stave jabbed hard into the small of his back. Mori grunted with the impact, stumbling forward. Another blow came lashing in against the back of his knees, sending him sprawling to the ground.

"Fujita lacks experience," said a deeper voice, with a jeering tone. "He has only been here five days. Hardly long enough for any scientist to remember his name!"

Mori rolled onto his side and looked up. There were four shadowy figures standing above him, all big guys with staves held ready. He thought the closest was Fujita. One of the others grabbed Mori by the elbow and wrist, another got a forearm around his neck. Mori didn't resist as they pulled him to his feet.

"Wait a moment," said a disciple who had not yet spoken. "Let me have a better look at him!"

That was another familiar voice. The disciple whose arm was squeezing his neck relaxed a little. The one who had just spoken loomed closer, revealing a shaved head, heavy shoulders, and ugly little eyes.

"Well, what a surprise," the disciple said gleefully. "Welcome, Nakamura-san! I hope your stay with us has many benefits for your spiritual progress."

He grinned, and the broken front tooth was visible even in the murky light. Then suddenly he shifted his stance and thrust the stave at Mori's groin. Mori read it from the angle of his shoulders. He pulled to the left, driving his elbow into the stomach of the man behind. The stave thumped harmlessly against his hip, and the armlock on his neck loosened. Mori threw himself at the disciple with the broken tooth, connecting with a knuckle jab to the Adam's apple, then pulling him into a head butt.

361

The timing was better than the aim. Mori felt the man's broken tooth tearing across the skin of his forehead. Then another stave lashed against the back of Mori's calves, and he went down. He tried to keep rolling, but a foot thumped into his chest, knocking him back. Suddenly, staves were pounding into his back and shoulders. One cracked against the side of his head, then another, and lights were dancing in front of his eyes.

"Beat the spy!" Fujita was shouting. "Beat him like a dog!"

Mori found himself lying facedown in the grass, the blows raining down from staves and feet. He covered his head with his hands. The disciples were grunting with the effort. Mori's mouth filled with bile and blood, and then he heard and felt no more.

Ono stood stroking his beard as he gazed at the prone body lying on the concrete floor.

"And what have you discovered about him so far?" he said to the two disciples who had dumped the body in front of him ten minutes before.

"Not much, sensei," said the senior one. "He entered the training program under the name of Nakamura and managed to slip away when the others were asleep."

"Slip away? Wasn't anybody watching over them?"

The disciple bowed his head sheepishly. "The discipline was unforgivably lax, sensei. Those responsible will be punished severely."

"See to that personally! And find out everything you can about this man! Follow every step that he made. All the facts must be gathered as soon as possible."

The other disciple stepped forward and bowed. He was a heavyset man with small, piggy eyes and a split lip that looked like a piece of raw liver. "May I make a humble suggestion, sensei?" he said thickly. "When he wakes, I will dig the information out of him personally. I would consider it a unique privilege to be given that responsibility."

Ono held up a hand in front of his chest. "Your diligence is commendable. Indeed, if all were as diligent as you, this regrettable incident would never have happened in the first place. Unfortunately, however, it has happened. Our friends in Tokyo must be informed. This is another matter for them."

"But, sensei, this is an internal problem," protested the disciple with the bloodied lip. "Surely we can deal with it ourselves!"

Ono shook his head. "Perhaps we could, but it would not be sensible. This is more than a simple breach of security. Enemies are circling around us, plotting to destroy our plans. We must be extremely cautious in our responses."

"Understood!"

Ono stalked out of the room, down the corridor, and into the small elevator that led up to his private quarters. Until recently, he had been spending the nights in the Chamber of Delight on the top floor. It had exactly the same specifications as the Chambers of Delight in all his other residences—the same perfume in the sprinklers, the same crystal music murmuring through the hidden loudspeakers, even the same pattern on the cushions. For the past few nights, though, he had chosen to sleep alone in his private study. It was part of a conscious effort to win back control. The experiences of the chamber had become too powerful, too draining of his mental energy. And the flashbacks had been becoming more and more intense.

Just yesterday, he had been sitting in the meeting room listening to Kawasaki bumbling on about the distribution system. Kawasaki's words were dull, and Ono's mind had been wandering over distant vistas of time and space when suddenly he started to experience shooting pains in his toes. They developed into a burning sensation that spread through his feet to his ankles, and his nostrils filled with the smell of burning flesh. He stared at the others, who were still calmly listening to Kawasaki. Weren't they aware of that smell? Didn't they realize that Ono's feet were on fire? In the end, he had been forced to rush out of the room and dose himself with tranquilizers.

Ono opened the door of his study, glanced at the psychedelic mandala pattern on the wall, then immediately looked away. The pattern was a vortex of streaming colors made up of tiny dots. If you gazed at it long enough without blinking, it would rotate, gently at first, but then at increasing speed until the watcher felt himself being sucked inside. Originally, it had been developed by the cognitive psychology research group as a prototype for some more advanced work in ambient video. Ono had taken a liking to it and ordered copies to be put up in meeting rooms in all the branches. For the past few days, though, he had been hesitant even to look at it. He didn't want to be sucked into that vortex, where anything might be lying in wait.

He locked the door, lay down on his sofa, and closed his eyes without turning off the light.

Eight floors below, the two disciples hauled Mori into a storeroom and threw him onto a damp futon. The disciple with the split lip pulled up a wooden box and sat down on it, resting his chin on his hand. The senior disciple walked out of the building, entered the shed where the carts were kept, and chose one. Seconds later, he was sitting behind the steering wheel, humming down the bumpy track toward the elevator tower. In obedience to the sensei's orders, he had to retrace the path the intruder had taken so that a full report could be made to the man the sensei called the "specialist." The disciple had seen this specialist several times before and had heard something of his reputation. But that didn't mean that he respected him. The man was ugly and unhealthy. He was making use of the sensei, pretending to understand the range and depth of his thought. The disciple believed that if it ever came to a straight fight between the specialist and himself, man against man, then the specialist's reputation would prove to be of no account at all.

When the disciple was within five hundred yards of the tower, he stopped the cart and got out. This was where Fujita-kun had told him that he had found the man in the scientist's uniform. He would now trace the intruder's path, step by step, just as the sensei had ordered.

As he walked away from the cart, there was a crackle from the walkie-talkie fastened to his belt. He unclipped it and raised it to his mouth. "Yes, what is the matter?"

"A message has just come in from one of our friends. It sounds like something we should deal with at the most senior level."

"That's impossible. I am engaged on a high-priority security investigation on the direct orders of the sensei! Everything must be completed by the early morning."

"This also concerns a security matter. The friend will be arriving here in the morning. He says he will need to speak to the sensei and Kawasaki-san. Someone should tell them immediately."

"The sensei must not be disturbed again tonight. That is essential. As for Kawasaki-san, I will decide whether it is worth waking him after all the details have been made clear."

"Understood!"

The disciple shook his head in vexation. After everything had been running so smoothly for so long, two security problems cropping up in the same night! It defied belief. Or rather, as the sensei had said, it indicated that enemies were circling around, preparing to destroy everything that had been created. That could be why the sensei seemed so exhausted these days, so absentminded and withdrawn—it was the spiritual effort of preparing for these cowardly assaults. The disciple seethed with silent rage. He would not let the sensei take the strain alone. He would beat down these cowardly schemers until they cried out for mercy!

Yoshio Kawasaki woke at six-thirty, as he had every morning for the past thirty years. It didn't matter where he was—in Otaman's living quarters for married men, in a cheap business hotel in Nagoya, in the apartment of some Ginza hostess—he didn't need an alarm clock. Still, it was strange to wake up on the island, so far from the familiar noise of cars and trains. This was his twelfth visit in the past year, but he hadn't gotten used to it yet.

He hadn't gotten used to dealing with Ono either. Without question, the man had a brilliant mind. The research personnel whom Kawasaki had sent to the Peace Technology laboratories all had high regard for his creativity and scientific knowledge, which spanned an unusual number of diverse fields. At the same time he was a businessman's nightmare, forever changing his mind, as full of whims and exaggerated suspicions as a spoiled child. And he had definitely changed for the worse since

Kawasaki had first met him. Physically, he was at least ten pounds heavier, and he often gave off a strange smell. The rumor was that he wouldn't bathe for days after the sex sessions that he conducted with his female followers.

Mentally, the changes were just as striking—the sudden shifts in mood, the pauses in midsentence, the replies to questions that had not been asked. The cause could have been easily inferred without listening to the gossip of the scientific personnel. Ono was overindulging in the products of his own research. For the private use of his inner circle of senior disciples, he was cultivating versions that had been rejected because of the unpredictability of the side effects. Of course, Ono had never accepted that there were any significant side effects, no matter what the dosage. Research that showed otherwise had been destroyed and the scientists responsible dismissed. Kawasaki had met some of those men. He had heard firsthand about sudden shifts in the brain's biochemical balance, which could lock hallucinations into the user's consciousness for months, perhaps years, afterward. He had heard about the monkeys who had starved to death even though fresh bowls of food were set before them every day.

Ono, Yazawa, the albino yakuza—in all his long years of corporate service, Kawasaki had hardly known that such people existed. Now, in a manner of speaking, they were his colleagues. It was a curious thought. For almost thirty years, Kawasaki had been a normal salaryman, with hopes and fears that didn't extend beyond the environment of the company. Within the heart of the normal salaryman there was supposed to be the readiness to do anything—absolutely anything—for the benefit of the corporate entity to which he was committed for life. The members of the Otaman board had tested this loyalty, and it had not been found wanting. When they explained to Kawasaki that the company's financial plight necessitated his undertaking an unconventional and dangerous new project, he hadn't hesitated for an instant.

At seven o'clock, one of the disciples brought in a tray containing a bowl of rice, two sardines, and a raw egg. As always, he asked Kawasaki whether he wanted to join the early morning meditation session, and as always Kawasaki refused. Instead, he did thirty push-ups and spent fifteen minutes on controlled breathing exercises. The sea view was beautiful, but lonely for a man used to the bustle of the city. Kawasaki preferred the chiming of the level-crossing gate near the Otaman living quarters to the screech of the seagulls.

As soon as he had finished the exercises, another disciple appeared at the door and he was taken downstairs to the big meeting room. The others had yet to arrive so, after arranging his papers, he went down to the lobby and waited there. The door to one of the smaller meeting rooms was half-open, and someone was pacing up and down inside, metal-tipped heels clicking against the tiled floor. He peered in through the door, and found Yazawa standing at the window. There was briefly an expression on his face that Kawasaki had never seen before. It was the expression of a man in an agony of indecision.

"Ah, Kawasaki-san," he said. "It's good to see you here. The early mornings are splendid at this time of year, are they not?"

"Indeed they are," said Kawasaki, unable to hide his surprise. "But I wasn't expecting to see you here. When did you arrive?"

"Late last night," said Yazawa. "A problem came up that needed to be discussed immediately."

Kawasaki said nothing. He had grown close to Yazawa over the months they had been working together. The furious energy with which the man worked, drank, sang, and enjoyed women was deeply impressive. Once, after a secret conference in a Peace Technology temple in the Japan Alps, Kawasaki had watched him ski down a mountainside studded with rocks and tree stumps. He skied like a demon, roaring with laughter as he sailed into the air. Yet now something was obviously wrong. Normally, Yazawa would have no business here on the island. Raising capital was his responsibility, not manufacturing or distribution. A problem that required immediate discussion at this level would have to be a serious one. Kawasaki hoped that his new friend hadn't made some sort of mistake. Among the other members of the project team were people who didn't look on mistakes with indulgence.

"In a matter of days the cherry blossoms will arrive," said Yazawa. "Do you still enjoy the cherry blossoms?"

"Enjoy?" said Kawasaki, nonplussed by the question. "Well, the members of my department usually have a blossom-viewing party somewhere. We drink lots of beer and sing karaoke. At my age it's more a question of duty than enjoyment."

Yazawa shook his head vigorously. "Age, age! You're always talking about your age, Kawasaki-san. Look—I want to invite you to a special cherry-blossom party next week. My kind of party. It will make you forget about age completely."

"What kind of party is that?"

"Have you ever embraced a woman after watching her dance naked in a storm of falling cherry petals?"

Kawasaki gazed at Yazawa. As was often the case, it was hard to know whether he was serious. "No, I've never had the chance," he said cautiously.

"Then next week will be your first experience of real blossom viewing! There will be two girls for you, two of the most elegant hostesses in all Ginza. You will drink the finest sake from cubes of scented pinewood. Then you will embrace them on a carpet of cherry blossoms, with cherry blossoms falling all around you!"

"Two girls just for me?" said Kawasaki, smiling. "What about you?"

Yazawa shook his head. "This year I will be unable to attend, I think. You must hold the party in my place. Look—I will write a number down for you. Call when you get back and tell the mama-san that Yazawa has sent you for a cherry festival. Everything will be prepared."

He took a business card from his pocket and scribbled down a Tokyo phone number. Kawasaki took it and slipped it into his wallet. "Thank you," he said quietly.

"Remember—when these girls hear that you've been sent by me, they will expect much. You must put your whole being into embracing them. Do it like a mad animal! Do it as if you are in your last moment on this earth."

Yazawa laughed uproariously, walked up to him, and suddenly did something unusual. He stuck out his hand, like a foreigner would do. When Kawasaki tentatively put out his hand too, Yazawa grabbed it and pumped it up and down.

"Do it like a mad animal," he repeated, a strange agitation in his eyes, then suddenly turned and walked over to the window.

Kawasaki left him there. His friend's mood swings were always hard to read, but Kawasaki could guess what lay behind this one. As he walked toward the large meeting room, which was now open, his heart was heavy.

Shortly after nine, Snowbird's limousine slid out of the hotel's underground parking lot and edged into the crawling, fuming traffic. At night, Akasaka looked like a piece of abstract art—an installation the size of a small city. But in the morning rush hour every shred of beauty was stripped away. Everywhere was noise and disorder and brutally ugly angles and surfaces. Great gouts of humanity were being disgorged from the subway exits, then surging over the maze of pedestrian crossings. It was a depressing sight at the best of times. And today the smog-ridden air did not even permit a compensatory glimpse of Mount Fuji.

Dismissing the chaos around him, Snowbird pointed his remote controller at the disc player, lay back, and closed his eyes. The music that welled from the speakers was one of his favorite pieces, Glenn Gould playing the "Goldberg Variations." Snowbird waited until the end of the tenth variation, the fughetta, before turning the volume down and regretfully picking up the phone. It took six rings to get through.

"Are you on your own?"

Snowbird glanced at the back of Sato's crew-cut head. A good man, Sato. He was afraid of nothing in this world. Except, of course, for Snowbird himself. "One of my men is driving the car," he said.

"No one should hear what is to be said."

Snowbird leaned forward and pressed a button in the back of the driver's seat. There was a hum as the glass screen rose. "Sorry about this," he called out just before it closed. Sato nodded an acknowledgment. Snowbird didn't like to keep too many secrets from his best men, but in this case he had no alternative. He put the phone to his mouth again.

"All right, I'm ready now," he said. "It's just you and me."

They spoke for almost twenty minutes, time enough for the limousine to pass through the Ginza and over the first set of bridges to the waterfront. When Snowbird put the phone down again, he was so preoccupied by what he had heard that it was several minutes before he remembered the glass screen. Even then, it was only after he noticed Sato's quizzical eyes in the rearview mirror.

"Is everything proceeding in a satisfactory manner?" murmured Sato when the glass screen had hummed back into its place.

"Satisfactory? Hmmm—we shall see," said Snowbird pensively. He stared out the window at a dingy warehouse bordered by the oily black waters of a canal. It was ugliness exemplified, but he didn't look away. He didn't even see it.

Sato concentrated on the road ahead. He knew his boss well enough to realize that events were likely to turn extremely unsatisfactory for someone before too long. Snowbird stared out the window, lost in Glenn Gould's world of musical geometry.

EIGHTEEN

Mori was woken by the pain. He wanted to stay unconscious, but the pain wouldn't let him. Pain shooting through his arms, shoulders, and neck. Pain like a cord tightening around his skull. His eyes flickered open, and the bright sunlight shining in his face made his head throb with additional pain.

He was lying on a grubby futon. His hands were tied behind his back, but apart from that he was free to move. He pushed himself up onto his knees and tried to piece together what had happened.

The rumble of the elevator machinery—the two scientists playing shogi—Coltrane soaring like an eagle—then the disciples' faces glaring down at him through the darkness—the grunts of effort as their staves thumped into his body—rolling over in the undergrowth, trying to get away from the pounding of the staves.

The images came flooding back. Well, they had him, all right. It had been one of the most comprehensive beatings he had ever endured. He sucked in a deep breath and gingerly tried out his joints, starting by wiggling each finger in turn. Fortunately, no bones seemed to be broken, though it felt as if a rib might have been cracked and it was hard to find any part of his body that wasn't covered in bruises and welts.

And where had they taken him? It seemed that he was in some kind of storeroom that also served as a convenient holding place for people. Apart from a few stacks of cardboard boxes, the only pieces of furniture were the moldy futon on which he was lying and a couple of wooden chairs. The ceiling was high. On the outside wall was a narrow window, not large enough even for a child to get through. Sunshine was pouring through it onto the futon. His watch had been taken, but he could tell from the angle of the sun that it was already about ten in the morning.

He pulled himself to his feet and tried out his ankles and knees. Walking was painful but not impossible. What he needed was three or four days of rest and recuperation, gradually toning up the bruised muscles, learning to live with the pain. That's what his massage sensei always said when the pressure of his peglike fingers drew a wince of protest from Mori: "Don't fight the pain, learn to live with it." If Mori ever managed to get back to Shinjuku in one piece, there would be a couple of months of extra business for that massage sensei.

But how was he going to do it? He was on a tiny island fifty miles south of Tokyo Bay populated by a cult that was quite prepared to eliminate its own members, let alone an intruder like Mori. The disciples had captured him in the act of spying. There were no police, not even ordinary citizens who might notice his plight. He was completely isolated. Mori lay down again on the futon and waited. They would come soon. He would have to have something pretty good to tell them.

What actually happened was not what he was expecting at all. A face appeared behind the smoky glass panel in the door, and he heard the key turn in the lock. The door swung open, and two disciples appeared in the door. One of them he recognized at once. It was the heavyset man with the small eyes and the broken tooth. Except that he didn't have the broken tooth anymore. His lips were bloodied and swollen, and when he opened them to snarl out a comment, Mori noticed that both the tooth and its neighbor had disappeared completely, leaving a gap half an inch wide. The stinging sensation in his own forehead told him there was a gash there a couple of inches wide.

"Get up, spy! We have important news for you!"

The other disciple, an older man, held him back with a hand and pointed at Mori with his stave. "You wouldn't like to tell us your real name, would you, Nakamura?"

"Real name?" said Mori groggily.

"It doesn't matter. If you want to be called Nakamura, that's fine with us. Coffee and toast will be brought in a minute. Will you want milk in your coffee?"

"No milk," said Mori, retching slightly as he remembered the vial of cloudy liquid that Togo had shown him.

"You must be wondering about this hospitality," said the senior disciple. "The reason is that a man is coming from Tokyo to see you. He has requested that you should be in good condition."

"That was thoughtful," said Mori dryly.

"Let me tell you about this man, Nakamura," said the senior disciple. "He is a specialist at getting information out of people. We are not specialists. We will leave everything to him."

"Unfortunately we must," grinned the gap-toothed disciple. "But we will study his actions closely. Maybe he will permit us to practice when he has finished."

The two of them shut the door and locked it. Some ten minutes later, the senior disciple swung the door open and the gap-toothed disciple walked inside. He was carrying a tray containing a cup of coffee, a slab of toast dripping with butter, and a hard-boiled egg.

"This is for you," he said, dropping the tray with a clatter onto a heap of cardboard boxes. Coffee slopped onto the toast, and the egg rolled from one end of the tray to the other.

"That's impressive," said Mori, sitting on the floor with his back to the wall. "There may be hope for you yet. When this operation finally falls apart, there should be a job for you in a coffee bar somewhere."

"You talk like a child!" snarled the disciple. "The sensei's plans are meeting with greater and greater triumph."

"I wouldn't be so confident of that. Anyway, let me give you some advice. When you take the customer's order, always ask him how many minutes he wants his egg done. That's the mark of a true professional!"

"You will regret those words!" The disciple took the stave from his belt and swung at Mori. He fell sideways onto the futon, and the stave swished over his head and cracked against the wall.

"Stop this at once!" The senior disciple stepped forward and grabbed the gap-toothed disciple by the shoulder.

"This man has disrespected the sensei. His insolence merits serious punishment!"

"Silence! The sensei himself has ordered us to leave him for the specialist."

The gap-toothed disciple wagged the end of his stave in Mori's face. His nostrils were wide, his face flushed with anger. "Tonight I will ask for a favor," he hissed. "I will beg to be allowed to assist in this work."

Mori wriggled into a squatting position. "I apologize for causing trouble," he said mildly. "But have you got some salt? I really can't eat a boiled egg without salt!"

The gap-toothed disciple made a sudden lunge forward, but the other man held him tightly by the sleeve. "Go and get the salt," he said. "This is a valuable lesson for you, a man who has so much to learn. You must learn how to kill your hate, or one day it may kill you. Remember the philosophy in which you have been trained."

"Understood!" muttered the younger disciple, his eyes still flashing with anger.

"Does the mongoose hate the snake whose throat it rips? Does the owl hate the mouse when it swoops down silently from the tree? Feel oneness with your enemy as you swoop down on him! Those are the words of the sensei!"

"Understood! I will bring the salt immediately!"

"And some pepper too," called out Mori as the gap-toothed disciple disappeared through the door.

The senior disciple looked down at Mori and smiled. "I also like to have salt and pepper with a boiled egg," he said.

Mori nodded and said nothing. This, he thought, is a very dangerous man. A few minutes later, the gap-toothed disciple returned with the salt and pepper. The senior disciple instructed him to untie Mori's hands, and they watched in silence as he ate and drank.

"I suggest you get some rest now," said the senior disciple solicitously when Mori had finished. "It's important for you to recover your energy fully."

Important for whom? thought Mori as he dabbed the crumbs of his plate with a finger. The gap-toothed disciple stepped forward holding the cord that had been used to bind Mori's wrists. As he bent down, for a moment Mori had the wild idea of making a grab for the man's groin, pulling and twisting him to the floor. A knee across the throat, an elbow smash to that ugly mouth—it would be over in a couple of seconds. But then there was the senior disciple standing at the door with his stave poised. He would have been a formidable barrier to Mori in prime condition. With a swollen knee, one eye half-closed, and every joint in his body aching, Mori didn't feel hopeful about his chances at all. And even if by some miracle he did manage to get past the man—what then? There were probably dozens of other disciples patrolling the grounds. No, there was no point. It would be more sensible to take the senior disciple's advice and build up his energy, watch and wait.

Mori let the gap-toothed disciple retie the cord, flexing and twisting his wrists slightly to give himself some extra room. The disciple was so intent on pulling the cord as tight as possible that he hadn't noticed that Mori's wrists weren't straight.

"Try to relax," said the senior disciple as he closed the door. "Remember, the way to enlightenment is like smashing the mirror in front of your face."

"Or like diving off the Kegon Falls into the raging torrent below," said Mori.

"You know the sensei's words well," said the disciple approvingly. The door shut and the key turned in the lock. Mori lay down on the bedroll and stared at the ceiling, wondering how he was going to make that spectacular plunge.

Time passed. From the movement of the sun across the floor, Mori guessed that it was nearly midday when the key clicked in the lock and the door was pushed open. This time there were four disciples—the two who had brought the coffee, Fujita-kun, and one other. They were pushing a gurney on which lay the prone figure of a man. Ignoring Mori entirely, Fujita-kun threw a futon down on the other side of the room. They lifted the figure off the gurney and dropped him like a sack of potatoes.

"Here's some company for you, Nakamura," said the gap-toothed disciple. "I hope he doesn't disturb your sleep."

Mori waited until they had closed the door before walking over to the other side of the room and giving the newcomer a closer inspection. The man was lying on his back, eyes closed, hands at his sides. There were two features of his appearance that were immediately notable. First, he was a foreigner—tall, with dark brown hair. Second, although his eyes were closed, his mouth was not. It was stretched so wide that his whole face was creased with the effort, and from it emanated a sporadic gurgling sound. Mori stared down at him in amazement. The foreigner didn't budge an inch. He just lay there, chest quivering, his face contorted with bursts of helpless laughter.

Snowbird's boat pulled up at the quayside in the early afternoon. As usual, he had insisted on steering it himself. Sato was an accomplished pilot—in fact, he had once been an enthusiastic powerboat racer—but Snowbird enjoyed the sensation of thundering across the sea too much to turn the wheel over to anyone else. Driving on land was an activity in which he took no pleasure whatsoever. Especially in Tokyo, there were always too many cars, too many traffic lights, too many blocked junctions. Today, for example, it had taken over an hour to get from the hotel to the anonymous-looking warehouse among the wharfs and storage tanks where the boat was kept. Snowbird loved that boat. He loved the way the sleek fiberglass prow cut through the wavetops. Out on the ocean, you could steer where you wanted. There were no signals that had to be observed, no other travelers to get in your way.

Sato sat strapped into the backseat, his occasional words of advice lost in the roar of the engine. Snowbird sat at the controls, spray thwacking against a plastic windshield inches from his face. Of course, it was hardly the ideal kind of boat for the open sea. In a heavy swell, there would be trouble. But Snowbird was not the kind of man to spend his life avoiding risks. The boat was fast, and the ride was exhilarating. And with nerves tingling in the whipping wind and eyes focused on the shifting wave pattern in front, he was fully distracted from the business ahead.

There was a group of four disciples waiting to greet him at the quayside. They bowed low and made polite inquiries about his journey. Snowbird let Sato answer. He was in no mood to talk, and anyway, he didn't trust these disciples. Among them was a tall man, one who walked softly like a big cat and who frequently looked at him out of the corner of an eye, gazing up and down in a way that Snowbird recognized. In that gaze was resentment, fear, the will to prove himself. The disciple stood behind Snowbird in the elevator, which was a clear breach of etiquette, but Snowbird let it pass. After all, Sato was watching carefully the whole time.

A cart was waiting for him outside the elevator tower. Snowbird climbed in, and one of the younger disciples drove him up to the main building. Over the past few years, Ono had summoned Snowbird for urgent meetings in several different locations—the temple just north of Tokyo where they had met last time, on a fireworks-viewing platform above Lake Yamanaka, high in the Japan Alps—but nothing matched the natural beauty of the island. Snowbird gazed with appreciation on the sheer cliffs that rose so suddenly from the dimpled surface of the sea, the lushness of the forest, the gulls wheeling in the clear blue sky. He would have enjoyed a few hours of solitude in the forest—just enough time to scramble up to the peak and attempt a few lines of poetry that might capture the simple perfection of the sea and the sky and the forest. But of course there was no time for that, nor would Snowbird have been able to achieve the right frame of mind. Not after the phone conversation in the car.

Snowbird got off the cart, and the senior disciple led him into the main building. At the door of the elevator that would take him up to Ono's private rooms, the disciple stopped and pointed at Sato, who was following them down the corridor. "He must stay here," said the disciple.

"Sato comes up with me," said Snowbird flatly.

"That is the will of the sensei."

"And this is my will. Either he comes with me or I return to Tokyo immediately."

The disciple was a head taller than Snowbird. He looked down, the muscles of his neck tensing. It wasn't hard for Snowbird to imagine what he was thinking.

"Do you defy the orders of the sensei?" hissed the disciple.

"Shut up and get out of my way," said Snowbird quietly. "It is thanks to the ineptitude of your security people that the whole project is at risk."

He slid his sunglasses a couple of inches down his nose and stared the disciple straight in the eye. The disciple looked away immediately. Not many people cared to hold Snowbird's gaze for long.

Sato arrived at the elevator and glanced quizzically at the disciple. "Is there some kind of problem?" he said, turning to Snowbird.

"Nothing serious," said Snowbird. "This man is waiting to guide us both up to the sensei's rooms." Though, of course, it was serious that Ono's senior disciples were showing such an elementary lack of common sense. The disease was obviously catching.

Snowbird left Sato and the disciple at the door of Ono's study. Inside, the sensei was sitting in the lotus position on a perfumed cushion. His eyes were closed. A cushion had been prepared for Snowbird, and on the floor next to it a glass of milk, some crackers, and a hot towel. Snowbird closed the door behind him, sat down, and waited.

The sensei remained silent. There was no point in hurrying him. Snowbird took a sip of the milk and nibbled at a cracker. He examined the disturbing mandala pattern on the wall—staring at it for too long made him feel nauseous—and the bookshelves of ancient esoteric works. How anyone could plow their way through that turgid stuff, he did not know. For that matter, he had no idea how anyone could get through any of Ono's own works either. The only time that he had tried, he had been unable to get past the second page.

"Has someone angered you?" said Ono suddenly, still without opening his eyes. "I feel that your *ki* waves are badly distorted."

Despite himself, Snowbird was impressed. The sensei had somehow sensed his displeasure with the ill-mannered senior disciple. "A trivial dispute, sensei, completely unworthy of your attention. However, there are more important matters which trouble me. Serious questions have been raised about the overall security of the project."

"Raised by whom?" The sensei's eyes were open now, and they were staring straight at Snowbird's sunglasses.

"By those at the highest levels. They say that they are dissatisfied with procedures."

"What! Just because of this single intrusion? That's absurd!"

Snowbird took another sip of the milk, then touched his mouth with the hand towel on the plate. "Our sponsors don't think so. As they understand the situation, this man you have captured is no casual intruder but a well-trained spy. Furthermore, this is not the only security breach. At almost the same time, we have problems at the financial end."

"What happens to the money-gatherers is no concern of mine," said Ono angrily.

"It concerns us all, sensei. If the security of the project has been seriously compromised, everything will have to be canceled."

Ono sat up straight on his cushion. "Canceled! That is impossible. We are almost ready to establish mass-production facilities. Kawasaki is here today finalizing the details. We cannot stop now!"

"I share your feelings, sensei. It would be a serious embarrassment for me to pull out of distribution contracts that took much time and effort to negotiate. Still, security is security. We have to recognize the risks."

"The project must go on," Ono boomed. "It has been ordained!"

Snowbird sucked air between his teeth. Ordained by whom? By Ono himself, of course—probably in close consultation with Jesus, Buddha, and Lao-tzu. That was the problem with relying on Ono. He didn't understand that the project was basically a business, and decisions had to be made in a businesslike way.

"That remains to be seen," said Snowbird carefully. "I have been asked to examine these security breaches and estimate the extent of the damage that has been done. The case for cancellation or delay will then be considered by our sponsors. It is certain that procedures must be changed and the personnel responsible for these failures removed. I will identify the culprits, and deal with them accordingly. I hope that I can count on your cooperation."

"Of course—but my disciples are my responsibility. We have our own methods of punishment and reward here."

"Snowbird smiled as he sipped the milk. "Security is my job, sensei. Leave everything to me."

"And what will you do about the intruder? He is untouched, as you instructed."

"I will interrogate him later. First, I must know all the circumstances surrounding his capture. Also, there is the question of the foreigner. From what I understand, he is not connected with this other man."

"Your understanding is correct. He has been questioned, first by Yazawa, then second by some of my senior men. It appears that he knows little of our activities."

"Questioned? And his answers are reliable?"

"We used some medical techniques which have proven their worth. Yazawa was insistent that we use the minimum amount of force."

Snowbird gave a little cough that communicated a mixture of surprise and irritation. "And since when has Yazawa assumed responsibility for security matters?"

Ono tugged gently at his beard. "If you have dissatisfaction on this matter," he said, "you should mention it to him directly."

"I do have dissatisfaction," said Snowbird. "A great deal. Where is Yazawa now?"

"Downstairs waiting for you. He is preparing to return to Tokyo this afternoon."

"Yazawa is not going anywhere today," said Snowbird crisply.

A few minutes later, he left the sensei's study and rejoined Sato, who had been waiting outside. Without a glance at the glowering disciple, he strode toward the elevator.

As far as Snowbird was concerned, Yazawa had been treading on thin ice for some time. The man was a prima donna, unreliable and indiscreet. That had been obvious from the first time they met, almost ten years ago now. At that time, Yazawa had been living a hand-to-mouth existence, running speculative money for a group of pachinko parlor operators. Word of his investment performance had spread, first to the people behind the pachinko parlor operators, and then to the people behind them. Impressed with what they heard, some of Snowbird's associates decided that the man's talents deserved better. An investment advisory company was set up, and Yazawa given progressively larger sums of money to manage. When the bubble economy took off in the late 1980s, there was suddenly a huge demand for stock manipulation, greenmailing, and money-laundering services. Yazawa was in his element. On some days, he was single-handedly moving the stock market as much as were huge institutions like Mitsutomo Life and Maruhaci Securities. His existence, however, remained unknown to all except a small group of backers.

Snowbird had been early to recognize Yazawa's talents, but he also saw the man's weaknesses. That was why he had been opposed to handing him exclusive control of the financial side of the project. It was at Snowbird's insistence that the alternative-funding channel—the CBJ connection—had been developed. How right that decision had been! Yazawa's lack of self-discipline had led to a serious problem in the area under his control. If the CBJ connection hadn't existed, the funding of the project would now be on the brink of collapse. Fortunately, however, it was possible to terminate Yazawa's involvement in the project without lasting damage. The credit lines from CBJ could simply be doubled.

Terminating Yazawa's involvement—that was a heavy responsibility, but Snowbird believed it was now the logical course of action. The man had failed, and would have to bear the consequences. In view of the need to preserve confidentiality, these would necessarily be severe. Yazawa would not be leaving the island that afternoon, nor the next day, nor at any time thereafter.

Yazawa was waiting in one of the small meeting rooms. When he saw Snowbird he smiled and made a banal remark about the weather. That was an interesting sign, indicating an unusual level of nervousness. Yazawa was an intelligent man. He probably suspected what was going to happen. Snowbird didn't mind that. Suspecting that something was going to happen and preventing it were different things entirely. Out here Yazawa was helpless.

Snowbird began by explaining how concerned he was about the information leakage on the securities side. Yazawa apologized. There could be no excuses, he said. The responsibility was all his. Snowbird then called his attention to the resources that had gone into the project, the necessity for firm management control at all times, the unavoidability of certain unpleasant decisions.

"I understand your meaning," said Yazawa. "You think that my work in the securities markets is no longer of value."

"Your work has been excellent, but we need to reassess all our options."

"You think you can replace the financing structure that I have built up? Using that CBJ official, perhaps?"

"Perhaps."

Yazawa shook his head. "Impossible. I spent several years working among bank officials. I know how slow their thinking is. It will not be possible to obtain the capital we need efficiently and quickly. For that, direct operations in the securities markets are absolutely necessary. There is no other way."

"Your opinion is useful," said Snowbird. "As I said, all options will be considered. Later this afternoon, I will be talking to our sponsors. I will inform you of their final decision."

"I was hoping to leave the island this afternoon. There are some meetings relating to the bond issue."

"That is impossible," said Snowbird. "You must stay here and wait."

Yazawa smiled. "I understand you well," he said. "But waiting is hard in such circumstances, isn't it?"

Snowbird was impressed. The man knew what fate had in store for him, and now he was hiding his nervous tension superbly.

"The foreigner has caused many problems," said Snowbird. "The whole business is most regrettable."

"Let me speak honestly. I am responsible for this foreigner. He knows nothing of our plans except for the question of the bond issue. If the decision is taken to shift to bank financing, he can no longer be a threat to us at all."

"And so?"

"And so in that case he might as well be released."

Snowbird was puzzled. Yazawa was again showing a strange lack of judgment. "That would be impossible," he said, getting to his feet.

"I am responsible. He relied on my judgment."

"We all relied on your judgment," snapped Snowbird, turning to the door.

Why am I laughing, you ask? What exactly is so funny? Everything, of course! The whole of creation, starting with you. Your head on a stalk that jerks around when you move; your face with the little black holes in the middle and the big red hole at the bottom. Your blinking eyes, your sprouting ears, that stupid squawking voice, those fingers which are all different sizes, like a bunch of bananas. If only you knew how funny it all is, how ridiculously, outrageously funny! The surface of the earth is infested with human beings—that makes me laugh. The sea and the sky are sometimes the same color—that also makes me laugh. And the questions that you ask—they make me laugh most of all. You cannot stop me laughing.

Mitchell laughed at the questions, and laughed at the answers that he heard himself giving. He laughed until his lungs ached, then he laughed at the pain. He giggled, chortled, hooted, whooped, cackled, guffawed, sniveled, sobbed, and wheezed until his muscles turned to water and his brain to jelly. He laughed himself asleep, then laughed himself awake, then laughed himself asleep again.

And while he was asleep, the laughter gradually evaporated.

When Mitchell woke, his head was throbbing, his throat sore, and he felt intense physical exhaustion in every part of his body. Nothing was funny anymore. Instead, old feelings of fear and confusion were closing in. Mitchell didn't want to open his eyes, but he knew that he had to because he was awake now, not asleep, and people who were awake had to have their eyes open.

He eased open his eyelids and stared at an unfamiliar ceiling. The memories were coming back—Eiko's giggle, Yazawa's fluent English, being tied to a chair so tightly that his hands hurt. As a matter of fact, his hands still hurt. That was because his wrists were still tied together behind his back. Of course—now he remembered why he was so scared! Yazawa and Eiko had lured him into a trap. He had been drugged, tied up, bundled into a car. His boss had kidnapped him! That was nothing to laugh about at all!

He wriggled into a sitting position and examined his surroundings.

He was lying on a filthy bedroll on the floor of some sort of storeroom. And he wasn't alone. There was a man sitting with his back to the wall at the other end of the room. He was a tough-looking individual, square-shouldered, with stubbled cheeks. His deep-set eyes were observing Mitchell with a half-curious, half-contemptuous stare that was hard to meet.

"Who are you?" croaked Mitchell in Japanese.

"Mori" was the laconic answer.

"What are you doing here?"

"I'm a tourist. I came to do some bird-watching, and this is what happened."

"Bird-watching? What kind of birds are you looking for?"

"Stupid ones, mostly. The kind that shit on your head just for fun."

Mitchell digested this information in silence. The man spoke quickly, in a flat, gravelly voice. Nobody in the Pearson office spoke like that, nor did any of Mitchell's Japanese friends. He tried to imagine the man called Mori sitting with a pair of binoculars slung around his neck and a sketch-pad on his lap. He failed. Mori couldn't be a bird-watcher. The birds would sense him coming and get the hell out.

"You're on their side, aren't you?" said Mitchell finally.

"Their side? I'm on my own side, nobody else's."

"So you're not a yakuza?"

"A yakuza? Do I look like one?"

"Well, yes, you do a bit."

"Is that so?" Mori snapped. "And how many yakuza have you met?"

"Not many," admitted Mitchell cautiously. "There was one in a pink salon in Kawasaki. He tried to attack me for no reason at all. And of course I've seen plenty in TV shows and films."

"Let me explain something," said Mori, his gaze trained on Mitchell like a gun barrel. "There are big differences between real-life yakuza and the ones on the screen. The first difference is that real yakuza have got ugly faces. It doesn't matter how much money they've got their hands on, it just makes them look even uglier. Now, do I have an ugly face?"

"Ugly?" said Mitchell uncomfortably. "Of course not."

"I'm glad to hear that. And the second thing is this. Five percent of yakuza are smart, but you'd never see them in a pink salon or any place like that. The smart ones don't even look like yakuza. Now, the other ninety percent, the ones you meet on the street who do look like yakuza, have got subnormal intelligence. When you talk to them, you soon find that out. Next time you drop in that pink salon, ask the guy what he thinks about Heidegger. The response should be interesting."

"Thanks for the hint," said Mitchell. Mori was a difficult man to read. He might have been joking, but there was no sign of it in his voice or his eyes.

"No problem. I just wanted you to grasp the main yakuza characteristics, which are ugliness and stupidity. Then you might learn how to distinguish one from an ordinary guy like me."

Mitchell finally got it: Mori was offended. Being mistaken for a yakuza had annoyed him. That was reassuring. It suggested that he really wasn't part of Yazawa's schemes.

"Look," said Mitchell apologetically. "I'm sorry for the misunderstanding. There are people out to get me, and I don't know why or even who they are. In fact, I've got no idea what's going on here at all. I don't even know where I am."

"In that case you've got a problem," said Mori. "The same sort of problem as me." He twisted around, showing Mitchell his hands tied behind his back, then clambered awkwardly to his feet. Mitchell noted the swelling over his left eye and the cut on the forehead. This Mori didn't seem to be in good shape at all.

"What happened?" he ventured, as Mori walked toward him. "Did you have some kind of accident when you were out bird-watching?"

"You believed that?"

"For a moment," admitted Mitchell.

The man called Mori smiled for the first time, and the smile changed the map of his face. Mitchell read a sense of humor that mocked everything, including its owner. "A bird-watching yakuza? Nobody called me that before."

Mitchell smiled as well. He had a feeling that before too long he might be needing his strange new acquaintance's help.

Mori leaned up against a stack of cardboard boxes and listened to the foreigner's story. The guy was called Richard Mitchell, and he worked in some American company involved in the big-money game. From what Mori understood, he was a kind of financial detective, snooping through companies' books and product lists to uncover information. Except that he obviously dressed better, ate better, and was paid better than a real detective ever could be. Mitchell's Japanese wasn't bad for a foreigner. Occasionally he got a word completely mixed up, and Mori would have to ask him to repeat himself, but most of what he said was pretty clear.

The story was complicated, and at first Mori had difficulty in fitting it with what he knew about Ono and what he had seen on the island. There was a man called Yazawa who seemed to be working some financial scam through a company called Otaman. There was strong yakuza influence on the company and a secret project that even the staff members didn't know about. This Mitchell was supposed to write a research report on the company, which would apparently allow a large bond issue.

"How big is this bond, did you say?"

"One hundred million dollars. Pretty big for a company like Otaman that hardly anyone has heard of overseas."

"One hundred million dollars! That's ten billion yen, isn't it?"

"Right," said Mitchell, apparently unperturbed by what was to Mori a mind-boggling sum. Mori had been involved in quite a few fraud cases in his time. He had come across bank clerks who embezzled twenty or thirty million yen; a prefectural governor who had gone down for accepting fifty million yen—delivered to his home in the dead of night in a giant sake barrel—from a construction company; a guy who had made over one hundred million from a pyramid sales outfit specializing in bogus health foods. But ten billion yen—that was on a different scale entirely. None of the conmen and bribe-takers whom Mori knew would have been able to generate that kind of money in a thousand years. Even if they could, they wouldn't know what to do with it. And yet the young foreigner spoke as if the ability to conjure ten billion yen out of thin air was quite normal.

"So what are these Euromarkets, and who put the money there in the first place?"

"Institutions," said Mitchell casually. "Insurance companies, banks, mutual funds, and so on."

"And where do they get it from?"

"They get it from everybody. For example, they get it from you, through your pension fund."

"Pension fund? I haven't got any pension fund."

"Well, your savings must go somewhere. Into an insurance policy or investment trust or something. The Japanese have the highest savings rate in the world, don't they!"

"I don't know anything about these Japanese," said Mori. "I only know about me."

Meaning that no matter what the condition of the economy, the money he earned just seemed to disappear like smoke rings into a ventilator. Savings didn't come into it. When the good times came—as they did once every six or seven years—Mori would drink single-malt scotch instead of Suntory White, eat good sushi instead of yakitori, frequent higher-class pink salons and soaplands, make heavier bets on the bicycle track. Then when business slowed down again, it would be back to normal.

"So tell me this," probed Mori. "Can any company just issue one of these bonds whenever it wants and collect billions of yen?"

Mitchell shook his head. "It's not quite as simple as that. The market conditions have got to be favorable. And you need a securities company with the right kind of placing power."

"Like your company, I suppose. But still the borrowing company, like Otaman in this case, has got to pay some interest on the money, doesn't it? I mean, no one is going to give them the money for free."

The foreigner smiled at that. "You might think so, but there's been a great deal of financial innovation over the years. This isn't a plain vanilla bond, you see."

"Vanilla?"

"Yes—like the ice cream. There used to be only one flavor, which was vanilla. Now if you go to Hobsons, there are hundreds and hundreds of variations, aren't there? Well, it's the same thing with bonds."

Hundreds and hundreds of variations of ice cream? That was hard to believe. Mori hadn't eaten the stuff since he was a kid. Even then he had preferred the crushed ice with sweet milk hawked around by an old guy with a hand-cart and a trained monkey. In fact the thought of ice cream—any flavor—made him want to spit on the ground and wash his mouth out with Suntory White.

"Anyway," Mitchell continued, "this Otaman bond comes with warrants, which give investors the right to buy the company's shares at a fixed price, which is close to the current price in the market. So the more the share price goes up from now on, the more valuable those warrants will get. In return for this benefit, the bond holders accept an extremely low interest rate, just one percent."

Mori reflected on what he had just been told. It didn't make a lot of sense, but that wasn't a surprise. This kind of thing rarely did. "So what if the share price goes down, not up?"

"Then the warrants would be worthless. Of course, that's a purely theoretical question. The life of the warrant is eight years. The stock is bound to be higher by then, even if it just goes along at the growth rate of the overall economy."

"And what if the company goes bankrupt in the meantime? What guarantees are there for the guys who buy this ice-cream bond of yours?"

"None. There's no collateral on a warrant bond. From the investment point of view, it's what we call a high-risk, high-reward strategy. The purchasers have got to accept some risk in return for the potential of capital gain."

Mori looked at the young foreigner, so keen to convince, so confident that others would believe whatever he did. "There isn't going to be any capital gain. You know that, don't you?"

"Why not?" said Mitchell. "Our corporate finance department have been involved in plenty of warrant issues this year. They're back in fashion again.

"I may not know much about financial markets," said Mori, "but I know plenty about yakuza. They take money away from people, and they don't give it back."

"Wait a minute—that would be theft!"

385

"They call it business. Putting it in your language, investing money in a yakuza-controlled company is a high-risk, zero-reward strategy. Zero reward because they keep the money. High risk, because if you try and stop them, you probably get killed."

"Killed?" said Mitchell with a gulp. "They wouldn't go that far, would they?"

The foreigner looked scared. Mori felt sorry, but there was no point in deluding him. "Think about it. Can they just let you go back to your company and tell the world everything you know? Are they going to let ten billion yen slip out of their hands and years and years of planning go to waste? No chance!"

"Tell me more," said the foreigner quietly. "Tell how you got caught up in all this."

"Unauthorized bird-watching," said Mori laconically. "It's better you don't know more than that."

"Wait a minute," said Mitchell angrily. "I thought you Japanese believed in cooperation and teamwork! I've told you what I know, everything. Now it's your turn to talk."

"I told you before," said Mori with a smile. "I don't know anything about the Japanese. I only know about me."

But he told him anyway. Not everything he knew, but most of it. After all, there was always a chance—not a large one, of course—that the foreigner might get out alive and be able to pass on the truth about Yuriko, Ono, and what was happening on the island.

As he talked, he thought about how his own story fitted with what he had heard from Mitchell. At first sight, there was no logical connection, but take a step back and a larger pattern slowly emerged from the jumble of events. A trading company called Otaman had been hijacked by some yakuza group, who were using it as a vehicle for large-scale financial fraud. Meanwhile, Ono had set up an operation on a remote island where hallucinogenic drugs were being developed by teams of high-powered scientists. A girl had been killed after trying to escape, and somehow they had made it look like a drowning accident. As soon as Mori had started his investigation, yakuza hitmen had tried to kill him. Yakuza—Ono—drugs—murder—ten billion yen being vacuum-pumped out of the world financial system at the flick of a switch. At the moment, Mori couldn't see how all the pieces would finally fit together, but he knew they were the right shape and size.

It took a while for Mitchell to get used to Mori's style of speaking. It took even longer for him to absorb the full meaning of what Mori said.

Mitchell had spent the past few weeks writing a research report—to be headed, according to Yazawa's specific instructions, "Top-Class Restructuring Play—Buy for the Long-Term"—on a company that was engaged in illegal activities. The special product whose existence Mitchell had been relying on, the focus of the secret Kawasaki project, was a narcotic. And not only were yakuza involved, but also some crazy religious cult. This was the stock that Mitchell had recommended to Henry Lazarus, which Pearson's trading desk in New York had bought in great size. In all probability, Otaman was going to be a debacle to rank with Maxwell or BCCI. Mitchell's career as a financial analyst was over before it had really started.

But wait—he had to stop trying to fool himself. It was worse than that, much worse. A woman had been killed already. According to Mori, these people—Yazawa's associates—wouldn't hesitate to kill again. This Mori was a strange character for sure—spiky as a bramble, tough as a lump of overboiled beef at the bottom of a noodle pot—but for some reason Mitchell trusted him. There was something in the voice, in the set of the mouth, that meant no bullshit. And what he said was that

Mitchell's life was in danger—all because of the research he had been doing into Otaman. It was a bizarre idea—so bizarre, in fact, that it couldn't be dismissed.

"So what's the solution?" said Mitchell, pulling himself to his feet. There was only one door, and the window was much too small to get through.

"What's the problem, first?"

"The problem's obvious, isn't it? How are we going to get out of here?"

Mori gave a noncommittal shrug.

"Come on," said Mitchell. "Cooperation and teamwork. That's the Japanese way, isn't it?"

"I don't know anything about the Japanese way," said Mori.

"You only know about your way, I suppose."

"Right."

"And what exactly is your way in these circumstances?"

"It's like karate. Unsettle your opponent. Keep him guessing. People who are unsettled tend to make bad decisions. And then when the opening comes, you move like lightning."

Mori walked over to the other side of the room and sat down on his bedroll. Mitchell went over to the door and maneuvered himself into a position in which he could grasp and twist the door handle. It was locked.

"They're not fools, you know," said Mori, staring up at him.

Mitchell went back to his bedroll and sat down again. Suddenly, he felt assailed by a deep and numbing despair. It wasn't fair. Things like this weren't supposed to happen. Japan was supposed to be the safest place in the world, but his life was under threat because he had tried to get a little extra information about a listed company. The whole thing was outrageous. He should have stayed in Britain. He should have stuck to what he knew.

All this was Yazawa's doing. He had taken Mitchell for a patsy, tricked him into promoting a worthless stock for the benefit of drug-dealing bandits, even used his own sister or half-sister or whatever she was as a decoy. The man was cowardly, unscrupulous, totally untrustworthy; Mitchell hated him with a vengeful ferocity. That would be the worst thing of all—if Yazawa actually got away with it. Mitchell would give anything to be able to stop that from happening!

There was the sound of footsteps in the corridor outside, then a key turned in the lock. Mitchell and Mori both glanced up as the door swung open. Two disciples walked into the room, staves at the ready. A third man followed, sleeves rolled up, jacket slung over his shoulder. He gave a slight bow in Mori's direction, then looked across at Mitchell and gestured around at the room.

"This is much different from the Pearson office, I think," he said in English.

"Yazawa," gasped Mitchell, unable to conceal his astonishment. "What on earth do you want?"

"I wish to explain some matters to you, Mitchell-kun. I wish to explain my point of view."

"To hell with your point of view. I don't want to hear it."

"But you must," said Yazawa with a laugh. "In this place, you simply have no choice."

The disciple with the swollen mouth walked across to Mori and prodded him in the chest with his stave. "It's time for you," he said with a leering grin. "The specialist is waiting."

Both disciples came forward, grabbed him by the shoulders, and hauled him off his bedroll. Mori turned to Mitchell as they shoved him toward the door. "Remember," he said. "Unsettle them. Keep them guessing."

"Silence," said the disciple with the split lip, and jabbed him in the small of the back with his stave.

"You do the same," called out Mitchell as Mori disappeared into the corridor. The door slammed shut, and he was left alone with Yazawa.

But how to unsettle the enemy when your hands are tied behind your back and four of them, well muscled and well trained, are dragging you down a corridor, pausing only to rap you on the arms and legs with their staves? There was no easy answer to that. Mori didn't resist. There was no point. He let them haul him up a flight of stairs, along another corridor, and into a small room at the end. The door banged shut and they swung him face first against the wall, his forehead crunched against the plaster. Mori remained in that position for several seconds, listening to the sounds of the disciples' breathing.

After a while, there was the sound of footsteps outside, and the disciples tensed. Someone else entered the room.

"Untie his hands, and then leave!"

The voice was icily authoritative. One of the disciples grabbed Mori's wrists and jerked them upward. In a second, his hands were free.

"Will you not require someone to stay to assist you?" said one of the disciples.

"That is unnecessary."

Mori heard the disciples step out into the corridor again, and the door closed.

"Turn around, please. Let me look at you."

Mori slowly turned. The man was several yards away, but the sight of him made Mori flinch. The colorless hair, the skin like rice paper, the dark sunglasses big enough to cover half his face—Mori had heard of only one man whose appearance matched that description, and what he had heard was unforgettable. Expressionless, he gestured Mori toward a wooden chair in the middle of the room. Mori obeyed.

"Perhaps you know me."

"Perhaps I do," said Mori.

"Good. That should make things simpler—both for you and for me. I am not a cruel man. Despite what people say, I take no pleasure in inflicting pain. Do you believe that?"

"I'll take your word for it," said Mori.

"But I do not shrink from inflicting pain either. In my experience, physical pain is the most efficient tool for influencing the human will. Very few are capable of withstanding its influence when it is expertly administered. Are you one of those rare individuals?"

"I doubt it," said Mori.

The man in the sunglasses nodded. "I doubt it too. It is one of my theories that the people who are most sensitive to pleasure are also the most sensitive to pain—especially when it comes from the same parts of the body, those which are most abundant in nerve endings. In your case, it would be an unendurable experience. It would shatter the core of your physical being. But, fortunately, there is no need for matters to go that far. Provide me with the details of your mission, then the matter will be at an end."

"At an end? You mean I can take the next boat home, maybe catch the Giants game on TV?"

The man in the sunglasses shook his head. "I will not insult you by making a childish pretense. Let's just say that if I were you, that is the course that I would choose."

Mori scratched his stubbly chin. He was feeling better now. His head

389

had cleared, and only about one third of his muscles and joints were causing him pain. "What makes you think I'm on a mission of any sort?"

The albino frowned. "You are certainly a stubborn sort of man! You broke into a high-security area, eliminated a guard, then spied around in the guise of a technician. If you expect me to believe that you did all this for amusement, then I must conclude that you are not showing me respect. And that would be a serious mistake on your part."

He stood with arms crossed, the blubbery lips twisted into a contemptuous pout. Mori remembered some of the stories that had circulated about the man—the failed assassin ripped apart by Tosa dogs while junior gang members cheered and placed bets; the police informant who had received his lover's head by parcel delivery; the sulfuric-acid facial for the uncooperative hostess. No doubt much of it was exaggeration, but Mori had no intention of testing the man out.

"Hold on," said Mori. "Don't get the wrong impression. I'll tell you what I know."

"Start with the names of your contacts. Explain exactly how they recruited you and why."

"But the problem is, I don't have any contacts. Just a guy who used to own a yakitori shop in the back of Shibuya."

"A yakitori-shop owner? That is impossible. I'm afraid you are showing me insufficient respect!" The man in the sunglasses stepped forward and put his long white fingers on Mori's shoulder.

"It's true," protested Mori, uncomfortably aware of the weight of the hand. "He's an old friend of mine. You can check it out with him if you like."

"And this yakitori man instructed you to conduct an undercover surveillance of this operation? You expect me to believe that?"

"I decided that myself. You see, he asked me to do him a special favor. It was about his daughter, who—"

"Silence," snarled the man in the sunglasses. Before Mori had time to react, the hand was jammed to the side of his neck and the thumb was digging into his throat. Instantly, his breath was blocked and the blood pressure was rising inside his head. The hand gave a sudden sharp twist, and everything went black. Mori could hear nothing but the pounding of his pulse loud in his ears. After what seemed like an eternity, the grip was released and Mori slid off the chair, his head cracking against the concrete floor. The impact brought back his vision, but he could hardly move. He lay on his side, blinking at the man in sunglasses. When he tried to speak, all that emerged was a gasp.

"I tried to treat you with some respect," said the man in the sunglasses. "Evidently that was a mistake."

He went to the door, opened it, and called down the corridor. "Get Sato. I want him here immediately."

Mori tried to rise from the floor, but his muscles were still refusing to obey the instructions of his brain. He lay there sucking in air in long gulps.

"This room is well designed for our purposes," the man said, pointing into a corner. "These drains in the floor will be convenient for washing out the mess that is left."

Words formed in Mori's mind, but he couldn't get them past the obstruction in his throat. The door opened and someone came inside.

"We are ready, Sato," said the man in the sunglasses. "This stubborn man insists that everything should be done in the most difficult way."

Using the side of the chair as support, Mori finally managed to drag himself up into a kneeling position. The man called Sato was a morose-looking yakuza, roughly the same age as Mori, with a big flat nose and thick eyebrows like a couple of hairy caterpillars crawling across his forehead. He was carrying an aluminum case of the sort that an amateur photographer might carry. He placed it on a small table under the window and clicked open the catch. The man in the sunglasses peered inside, as if unable to make up his mind which lens and filter to use. But what he carefully lifted out was something that would not normally be found in a photographic equipment shop. It was a strange-looking pistol, shaped more like a drill than a conventional gun.

"Shoot him," said the man in the sunglasses.

"You mean straight away?" said Sato doubtfully.

The man in the sunglasses nodded curtly and turned his attention back to the contents of the case. Sato stepped forward and pointed the stubby barrel at Mori's shoulder. Mori felt a twinge of pain in his bicep, then a shock hit him that caused the muscles of his arms and legs to spasm simultaneously. He ground his teeth and rode the sensation out, but when it passed he found himself unable to move an inch.

"Put him back in the chair. You might as well tie his hands too."

Sato grabbed Mori by the shoulders, heaved him onto the chair, and tied his hands behind his back. The man in the sunglasses walked toward him. Mori noticed that he was now wearing rubber gloves. He lifted something light and shiny toward Mori's face. It took Mori a few seconds to recognize it as a surgeon's scalpel.

"This is where we begin," he said softly. "Nose, lips, tongue. All very sensitive. Also certain areas of the ear and neck. You will be surprised, I think."

Sato was staring at Mori, his face as hard and still as stone. The man with the sunglasses grabbed him by the side of the neck again. Mori tried to pull away, but he was still numb with the jolt from the stun gun. "Wait," he wanted to shout out, but his mouth couldn't make the sound, and his eyes were swimming. He could just make out the blade of the scalpel hovering at the side of his cheek. Mori closed his eyes and gritted his teeth.

"Wait!"

He opened them again. Sato was pointing a finger at Mori's face. The man in the sunglasses turned.

"It's him! I'm sure of it! The detective I told you about. The one who's been snooping around after the girl."

"The girl? What girl?" said the man in the sunglasses impatiently.

"The girl at the Black Tulip."

The grip on Mori's neck relaxed, but the scalpel was still flashing an inch from his eye.

"Ah, yes!" breathed the man in the sunglasses. "That girl! A very attractive girl, wasn't she! But I thought the detective was taken care of."

"There was a problem. He managed to get away."

"Again?"

"The men we hired were ambushed. One of them was beaten quite badly."

"But are you sure it's him?"

"It's me, all right," rasped Mori.

The scalpel disappeared from sight. "Well," said the man in the sunglasses, bending down to peer into Mori's face. "Perhaps I was too hasty. Perhaps I owe you an apology."

"No problem," whispered Mori, and took a deep breath.

"So what is his name?" said the man in the sunglasses.

"Mori. He's based in Shinjuku, pretty well known there, by all accounts."

"Is he, now! That's interesting to know. Perhaps you could give me your autograph, Mori-san!"

"I'd be delighted," said Mori, his voice a little easier now.

"But first you must explain many things to us, many things." The man in the sunglasses walked over to the little table and returned the scalpel to its place in the aluminum case. He put a long white hand on the lid, as if to close it, then apparently changed his mind and left it open. "It's possible that I may still need this," he said thoughtfully. "I hope not, but I cannot be sure."

Mori hoped not as well.

Snowbird sat on a wooden chair and listened to Mori's story. If the whole thing weren't so serious, it would have been amusing. One man—with no equipment, no backup, no preparation at all—had succeeded in penetrating the center of Ono's operation and outwitting his entire staff of so-called disciples. And all in the cause of a ridiculous investigation. Snowbird's first reaction was of overwhelming relief. On the basis of what he had heard so far, it wasn't going to be necessary to close down the project, or even postpone it. True, procedures would have to be tightened considerably. The disciples responsible for these security lapses—such as the tall, arrogant one—would have to be removed and the others would have to come under the supervision of Snowbird's own chosen men. And Yazawa's side of the project might indeed have to be restructured.

As for the detective—Snowbird didn't know quite what to make of him. His story matched Sato's information. There was no reason to disbelieve him when he said he was working alone. By Snowbird's terms it didn't make sense. The man had risked so much for so little. Snowbird had risked much several times in his life, but the potential rewards had always been commensurate. Mori had risked and lost, but even if he had won—so what? His life would not have changed for the better. In this world, Snowbird reflected, there was nothing so incomprehensible as the mentality of another human being. That was something that he would never capture in a haiku, no matter how many tens of thousands he wrote.

"So do I get to go home now?" Mori was saying. "I wouldn't want to miss that Giants game. I haven't missed the first one of the season for years."

"So you're a Giants fan, Mori-san."

"The opposite, actually. That's what makes it interesting."

It made sense. Mori didn't look or talk like a Giants fan. Snowbird had little interest in any sport other than powerboat racing, but he could always recognize a Giants fan. Sato, for example, was a typical Giants fan—obedient, reliable, and totally unimaginative. He visited the dome to watch home games as often as he could, and he had the annoying habit of listening to live commentaries on an earphone radio.

"There's no point in deceiving yourself," said Snowbird. "You won't be watching any baseball this season."

"I thought you might say that."

"You're an intriguing character, Mori-san. It's unfortunate that all your talents have come to such a waste. And all for a girl you barely knew. Isn't that a strange thought?"

"For her father, actually. He's a good guy and a good cook too. Almost as good a cook as you are a killer."

Snowbird smiled at that. "That's quite a recommendation. Perhaps you should give us the address."

Mori shook his head vigorously. "You'd have to get it out of me with that knife of yours. I wouldn't want my friend to serve food to the men who killed his daughter."

"That's enough," snapped Snowbird. "Sato, call the disciples in. Remember this, Mori-san—how they dispose of you depends on my judgment."

Not that Snowbird was really offended. The girl was dead. It had been necessary, and that was all that could be said. If Snowbird hadn't taken advantage of the situation, the girl would have remained on the island, to be abused by the disciples and no doubt killed in the end anyway. Snowbird had spared her months, perhaps years of misery. And from her death he had created something extremely valuable. The father, of course, could not be expected to see things the same way.

NINETEEN

Mitchell had come to think like this:

Everything in Japan is back to front, upside down, and inside out. Everything is the opposite of what you expect. If you change your expectations, it doesn't matter. Somehow, everything is still the opposite. So the answer is always to expect your expectations to be wrong. Don't be surprised at being surprised. Not being surprised—for people actually to be what they seem and mean what they say—would be more genuinely surprising.

Mitchell expected to be surprised the most by one particular Japanese— the blues guitar–playing financial fraudster who had drugged and kidnapped him and brought him to the island. By Yazawa, he expected to be lied to, set up, tricked, and baffled in the most brazen way. That was all normal. So Mitchell wasn't really surprised that the man had the temerity to breeze into the room where he was being held and clap him on the shoulder. He wasn't really surprised that

Yazawa still addressed him as "Mitchell-kun" and spoke the same screwed-up English as in the office. And the fact that Mitchell wasn't surprised should have told him that his expectations were about to be completely reversed.

It didn't take long. Yazawa sat down next to him on the futon and apologized. At first, Mitchell couldn't believe what he was hearing. A contrite Yazawa—it was a contradiction in terms.

"There have been mistakes, Mitchell-kun. Misjudgments for which I am sincerely sorry."

"Mistakes—you're not joking! Your people are going to kill me, aren't they?"

"Not my people," said Yazawa gravely. "I have no control on their activities."

So he didn't deny it! Mitchell's stomach iced over. Mori's suspicions had been correct. "Why did you do this to me!" he blurted out in a burst of anger and mortification. "All I did was follow through your stock recommendation."

"I feel shame," said Yazawa, staring at the floor. "When I was instructed to bring you here, I obeyed. It was my belief that when your foolishness and naivete were openly displayed, it would be apparent that you have no capacity to inflict damage."

That stung. "Foolishness and naivete! Wait a minute—if you've got such a low opinion of my abilities, how come you entrusted me with this Otaman project in the first place?"

"The reason for this thinking is simple. I wanted someone who knew little of Japan and little of the financial markets. You were the ideal person available."

"So that's what you thought of me!" said Mitchell with lacerating bitterness. "Nothing more than a useful idiot. I believed in you, Yazawa-san! That's why I was happy to work with you on Otaman."

Yazawa made a slight bow. "Thank you," he said quietly. "Your evaluation is a kind one."

"Not any more, it's not! Once a crook, always a crook! I should have known what to expect from that embezzlement in L.A."

Yazawa stared at him, taken aback. "You have done more research than necessary, I think!" he breathed. "Still, you should understand the situation. In that bank no man of my young age was allowed to run money in the markets. All was done by men over forty who had no talent nor any desire to take risks. They were just bureaucrats. I saw opportunities and I borrowed money that was not being used for good purposes. This should not be called embezzlement, I think."

"I don't know whether to believe you or not. What I do know is that people are planning to kill me because of your crazy schemes."

"For this I apologize from my heart. It is a big mistake of mine, I think. Will you please tell me that you accept these sincere regrets?"

That was typical Yazawa. Here was Mitchell in fear of his life, and Yazawa was casually apologizing as if he had just spilled some coffee on his trousers. The man took insensitivity to the point of genius.

"Sincere regrets for being the direct cause of my death? Is that what you're asking me to accept?"

Yazawa put an arm around Mitchell's shoulder. "I will make big efforts," he whispered, his breath hot on Mitchell's ear. "There will be something for you this evening, I think. Take your chance, then do with all the strength of your spirit!"

At that point he suddenly stood up. "Farewell, Mitchell-kun," he said in a loud voice. "You are a nice person in my understanding. In the next life, you may be reborn as a giraffe or some other harmless creature. Now let us shake hands like good British gentlemen."

Before Mitchell had time to absorb what Yazawa had said, his bound hands were seized in a crushing grip and pumped up and down. Something tonight? What was the man going on about? And why in heaven's name a giraffe?

Yazawa dropped Mitchell's hands as suddenly as he had grabbed them, turned to the door, and rapped on it with his knuckles. "The interview is concluded," he barked. "Open the door immediately. I will not stay another minute in the company of this smelly footed foreigner!"

"Understood!" The door opened, and Yazawa marched out without a backward glance.

After he had finished with Mori, Snowbird sat in silence for several minutes, reflecting on what he had learned and the course of action he would now have to follow. As he had told Yazawa, he would have to contact the sponsor who would make the final decision about the securities side. But there was little doubt what that decision would be. Snowbird's advice on such a question would not be ignored. Mori, the foreigner, Yazawa himself—all would have to be eliminated. Then the next task would be to increase the pressure on the CBJ man. Yazawa had been correct about the difficulties of dealing with bank officials. They were slow and clumsy. They could not be relied on to act promptly unless they were squeezed very hard indeed.

"Much remains to be done," he sighed to Sato. "I'm afraid we will have to stay here tonight too."

"Really?" said Sato. "I thought you wanted to reconvene the meeting with the Chinese tomorrow."

"That will have to wait. Please arrange for rooms to be made available. I would like one that faces east."

A room that faced east had two attractions. First, he would be able to view the spectacular sunrise from its window. Second, it was on the opposite side of the building from Ono's quarters. The last thing that Snowbird wanted was to be woken up in the middle of the night, as he had been once before, by the sensei's insane cackling.

"I'll take care of it." Sato left the room, taking the aluminum box with him. Snowbird had an idea that he would be needing the contents again before very long.

Mori was bundled down the corridor by the same two disciples who had dragged him from the storeroom. They were disappointed. Mori could tell that from the way they stamped on his feet, thumped him in the kidneys with their staves, and banged his head against the wall of the corridor.

"I can walk on my own," complained Mori as an elbow jabbed into his ribs.

"For the moment you can," snarled one of the disciples. "But not for long!"

"I wouldn't sound so happy if I were you," growled Mori as they flattened him up against the storeroom door.

"What are you saying?" said the big disciple, his fingers twisted around the collar of Mori's overalls.

"There have been serious flaws in the security system here. That's what your friend in the sunglasses said."

"Silence! Your words are nonsensical." The big disciple drove his fist into Mori's stomach. Mori saw it coming and tensed his muscles just in time, but the disciple had put all his strength into the blow. Mori grunted with the impact and sank to his knees, sucking in air. One of the others unlocked the door, and Mori was picked up and thrown inside.

"I will beg to be allowed to dispose of you!" shouted the big disciple. "I will ask the sensei to grant this as a special privilege!"

The door slammed shut. Mori rolled over on the concrete floor. "Welcome back," said the foreigner, who was sitting with his back against a stack of cardboard boxes. "It looks as if you were successful."

"Successful in what?" said Mori, nursing his bruised stomach muscles.

"In unsettling the enemy. They didn't look at all settled to me."

"They're not," said Mori, struggling to his feet. "And neither am I. But I'm still alive, and that's a major achievement under the circumstances."

He walked over to his futon and sat down. The sun had tracked another few feet along the floor, meaning that it was late afternoon already. If Mori had read the man in the sunglasses correctly, it wouldn't be long before the disciples came for him again. What could he do to stall them? How could he talk them into keeping him alive? Mori sat slumped against the wall and racked his brains in vain.

After a few minutes, the foreigner got up and began pacing up and down the room. "Stop that!" growled Mori. "Can't you see I'm trying to think!"

"I've got a feeling something's going to happen," murmured the foreigner as he approached Mori's futon. "The opening that you talked about. We need to be ready for it all the time—just like in karate. We're going to have to move like lightning."

Mori gave a sigh of irritation. "You believed that stuff? I just made it up on the spur of the moment, you know."

"That doesn't matter," said the foreigner crisply. "Let's be ready. I have a pretty strong gut feeling about this."

"A feeling in your stomach?"

"That's right."

"And you believe your stomach instead of your brain? That's very Japanese."

The foreigner smiled enigmatically and continued pacing up and down the room. Mori decided to ignore him.

Terumasa Yazawa was a man who never made decisions. A course of action would occur to him, and immediately he would know that he was going to take it. There was no question of weighing the advantages and disadvantages. He would simply know that his destiny lay in a certain direction. It was the same with his reading of the financial markets. A certain pattern of events would occur to him, a confluence of forces that led to one inescapable conclusion. All that remained was to act—to buy or sell—in accordance with those forces. The course of action in which he was now engaged had occurred to him in the usual way. The possibility of failure, the dangers—these were merely abstract facts that had no bearing on his behavior at all.

After the meeting with Snowbird, Yazawa informed one of the disciples that he would be staying the night on the island. A small room was prepared for him on the top floor of the main building, and he spent an hour there resting on the bed. Looking out the window, he happened to glimpse Kawasaki being led by a group of disciples to the second laboratory building. No doubt the Otaman department chief would be shown the latest experimental data there and be given the usual encouraging reports. Kawasaki believed that the project would be in gear in a matter of months and that the profits generated would stay in the company, enabling it to return to past glories. Yazawa had never believed that. He had no desire to inform Kawasaki of his suspicions because they were just suspicions. He had followed instructions, just as Kawasaki had done. The two of them were just minor players who had not been informed about the grand design.

Now delays were certain. Even if the CBJ man were able to provide all the capital required, it would take him months to thread his way through the bank's internal procedures. That was the way banks operated, a fact that Snowbird and the others seemed unable to appreciate. Without the capital, the overseas manufacturing bases could not be set up, the political protection could not be secured, and Otaman, its financial resources already close to exhaustion, would be in danger of collapse. Kawasaki would not be told that, and, like the loyal, straight-thinking salaryman he was, he would not suspect it for a moment.

Yazawa genuinely liked Kawasaki. The man was good-humored, totally reliable, and fiercely diligent. Without men like Kawasaki, Japan would never have become what it was today. And like the others of his type, he deserved so much better. He deserved to taste the good things in life. In their brief friendship, Yazawa had tried to show him some of that. But their friendship, like Yazawa's involvement in the project, was now over. That was a cause of regret, but to Yazawa regret also was an abstract fact, a by-product of the confluence of forces that swept him through life.

When he had finished his short interview with Mitchell, he went down to the ground floor and asked one of the disciples to provide a telephone link for him. There were, he said, some important financial transactions that he needed to confirm. He was led to the communication center at the back of the main building and given a booth. Obviously the disciples would be listening in, but Yazawa didn't mind that much. Most of what he was going to say would be beyond their ability to comprehend.

First of all, he called Eiko. It was the time of day when she would be lazing around the apartment, just starting to get ready for the evening. She answered the phone in her sleepy daytime voice.

"Some complexities have arisen," said Yazawa. "I will have to stay here tonight. That means I will be unable to meet you at the club as I promised."

Of course, he hadn't made any such promise, but there wasn't even a tinge of doubt in Eiko's reply. "Really? I was looking forward to seeing you. Are you sure you can't make it?"

"Absolutely impossible, I'm afraid. And with your trip to Europe so close, we may not be able to meet for quite a while."

"Ah! That's a pity."

"It can't be helped," said Yazawa breezily. "Anyway, I hope you have a pleasant holiday. Don't take too much luggage with you. It will only get in the way."

He cut the connection. Eiko was a bright girl. She had gotten the message straight away. She would be on the train to Narita airport within an hour.

Yazawa made four other calls—one to Osaka, one to Geneva, one to Hong Kong, and one to Bermuda. He spoke in rapid English, replete with technical jargon. Any disciple capable of following the conversations would have heard a stream of verbiage about financial transactions—index futures, hedges, strips, and puts—and some casual references to alterations in nominee accounts and authorization procedures.

When that was done, Yazawa went back to the main building. Sato, he noticed, was leaning against a wall halfway down the corridor, a cigarette clamped between his lips. At his feet was an aluminum box. Yazawa had never looked inside that box, but he had heard about its contents.

Sato was gazing at him lugubriously. Yazawa gave a wave of the hand and approached him with a friendly smile. "I would like to speak to your boss," he said.

"He's not available. He's up talking with the sensei." Sato's eyes rose to the ceiling.

"I see. When will he be finished?"

"That's hard to say. Anything involving the sensei might take hours, or it could be over in a few minutes."

"So I may not be able to see him this evening?"

"You'll be seeing him sometime this evening, all right. You needn't worry about that." The ghost of a smile twitched across Sato's usually stony features.

Yazawa nodded. "Excellent," he said sharply, and sounded as if he meant it.

Sato stubbed out his cigarette and walked down the corridor, swinging the aluminum box like a schoolboy swinging his gym bag. Yazawa watched him disappear into a room at the end of the corridor, then took the staircase up to his room.

By the time he had taken a shower and drunk a cup of coffee, the sun had set. That meant it was time to act. The confluence of forces was starting to accelerate. There was a bulky glass ashtray on the table next to the window.

Yazawa picked it up and weighed it in his hands. It was heavy enough. He rolled it up in a towel, thrust it under his arm, and went back downstairs.

The ground floor was almost deserted now, with just a few disciples sweeping the lobby area, as they had to do every night, whether there was any dust there or not. Yazawa guessed that the others would already have returned to their living quarters for the evening meal of rice gruel and fish stew. He marched down the corridor and stopped at the door of the room that Sato had entered. The only sound was a faint crackle of static. He rapped at the door.

"What is it?" Sato called out impatiently.

Yazawa stepped inside and closed the door behind him. Sato was alone, sitting in an armchair.

"You again!" said Sato, his brows creasing. There was a pocket TV on his lap. Yazawa could just make out a figure in a baseball uniform winding up to pitch. The aluminum box was on the floor at Sato's feet.

"The reception's pretty poor here, isn't it?" said Yazawa pleasantly, stooping forward to peer at the screen.

Sato stared up at him in bemusement. "What have you got there?" he said, pointing to the bundle under Yazawa's arm.

Yazawa unwrapped the towel and dropped it onto the floor. "An ashtray," he said. "I thought it might come in handy."

"Useful? Useful for what?" said Sato, getting to his feet.

"For this," said Yazawa. He took a step to one side and brought the ashtray down on Sato's rising head. There was a crunch, and a piece of glass flew to the ground. Sato gave a surprised grunt and fell back in the chair. He looked up at Yazawa, eyes blinking in confusion. A trickle of blood was visible at the top of his brow.

"What?" he mumbled.

Yazawa looked down at the ashtray. There was a large crack running down the middle. The man's skull was as hard as a cannonball. Yazawa raised the ashtray higher this time and brought it down with a full swing of the arm. It shattered immediately, but the force of the blow was sufficient to knock Sato sideways onto the floor. He rolled over once and lay motionless. Yazawa dug his toe into the man's neck, but there was no response. Swiftly, he lifted the aluminum box and banged it down on the chair. It was locked. Yazawa squatted down next to Sato's prone body and went through his pockets, finally extracting a bunch of keys. The smallest one fitted the lock. He took out a scalpel and the stun gun, then closed the box again. Then he wrapped up the stun gun in the towel, bent down to switch off the crackling TV, and walked out of the room.

The rush of events was enjoyable. It gave him a bull market feeling.

Mitchell sat on his bedroll and patiently waited. What exactly he was waiting for he didn't know, but he was ready for anything. "Do, do, do!"—Yazawa's words echoed in his mind, and for the first time they seemed to make a kind of sense. He was prepared to take a chance, any chance, except that he wouldn't think of it as a chance at all.

There was no alternative, for this might be his last night alive. Yes, that was a strange idea, one that he had never had to contemplate before. On a plane plunging through a patch of turbulence, on a motorbike skidding out of control on an icy curve, sitting in a restaurant with his lips stinging with blowfish poison—those had been brief moments of physical panic, over before the full meaning could sink in. This, though, was different. There was plenty of time to reflect on the possibility that everything he had known and done was about to come to a sudden full stop.

Could it really happen like that—with so little justice, so little reason? He was just starting to find his feet in Japan, just starting to come alive.

He had slaved for two years to learn Chinese characters. He had worked hard at his job. Now everything was clicking into place. Serious money was there to be made. Women—attractive ones—plentiful and available. Was his life going to end at this crucial point, just as it was getting into full swing? Would he never be what he had planned to be—a brilliantly successful thirty-year-old, a dynamic forty-year-old, then a suave super-wealthy fifty-year-old? Would he never see the turn of the century, never see the turn of the year? All over, final whistle, end of the reel! The crashing finality of the idea was hard to grasp.

He glanced across the room at Mori, who was sitting with his back to the wall staring at the floor. "You'd better be ready," he said.

"Ready for what?"

"For whatever happens."

"Nothing's going to happen," said Mori flatly.

Then his eyes immediately flicked to the door, as did Mitchell's. Both had heard the sound of voices in the corridor outside. There were two people speaking. One was the disciple who had been keeping guard outside the door. The other, Mitchell felt sure, was Yazawa. They appeared to be arguing about something, Yazawa's voice harsh and hectoring, the disciple's weakly remonstrative. Then there was the sound of the key turning in the lock, and the door opened. Yazawa walked into the room, followed by the disciple. Mitchell noticed that he was carrying a towel rolled up under his arm.

"Mitchell-kun," he said cheerily. "I have come to say a definite good-bye this time."

"Remember what I said," muttered the disciple suspiciously. "Three minutes is the maximum."

"That will be enough for my purpose," said Yazawa in his brusque Japanese. He approached Mitchell's bedroll, the disciple one step behind. Suddenly, he dropped the towel to the ground and there was a gun in his hand, pointing straight at Mitchell's face. Mitchell dived flat on the futon.

"What are you doing?" yelled the disciple.

Yazawa wheeled around and thrust the gun into the disciple's chest. There was a muffled buzz, and the disciple leapt backward and fell to the ground, arms and legs flailing. Then Yazawa took a blade from his pocket, bent over Mitchell, and cut the cord that was binding his wrists.

"No time to lose, Mitchell-kun!" he hissed. "Help me tie this man."

Mitchell picked up the stave from the ground and turned to Mori, who was still sitting on his futon. "Come on," he said. "This is the opening you've been waiting for. I thought you were ready to move like lightning!"

Mori scrambled to his feet and hurried across the room to Yazawa, who sliced through the cords around his wrists. They dragged the disciple onto the bedroll and tied his twitching feet and hands with the cords. Yazawa cut the towel into strips, which they used to gag him. Mitchell took the disciple's stave.

"All right, Yazawa-san," said Mitchell as they made for the door. "What's the plan now?"

"The plan?" said Yazawa joyously. "There's no plan. We must do, that's all."

"That's what I thought," said Mitchell.

The three men stepped out into the empty corridor, locked the door, and crept along the corridor, Yazawa leading the way.

"What now?" whispered Mitchell when they reached the staircase. "We can't just walk out through the front door, can we!"

Yazawa pointed to the elevator. "We go up to the first floor," he said. "Then we can jump down from a window at the back."

That didn't strike Mitchell as a particularly good idea, but he didn't have a better one. Yazawa pressed the call button, and they stood there waiting. Mitchell glanced nervously up and down the corridor, cold sweat on the back of his neck. The few seconds that it took the elevator to arrive seemed like hours.

When it did, the doors hummed open and suddenly Mitchell found himself standing face to face with the gap-toothed disciple. Instinctively, he took a step back. The disciple stared bulge-eyed at Mitchell, then at the other two at his side. His finger jabbed at the control panel and before Mitchell had time to react, the doors were humming shut in front of his eyes.

Mori reacted. He snatched the stave out of Mitchell's hand, and slammed it into the tiny gap between the doors. All that was visible inside the elevator was the disciple's nose and the gap-toothed center of his agitated grimace. Mori worked the stave in a few inches more, then levered it sideways. To Mitchell's surprise, the stave didn't break. Instead, the doors sprang open again.

"You!" the disciple hissed, and made a swing with his own stave. Mori stepped forward, taking the blow on his arm, and thrust hard for the disciple's belly. The disciple caught the end of Mori's stave in his hand and pulled Mori into the elevator. What happened next was almost too fast for Mitchell to catch. Both staves clattered to the ground and there was a blur of fists, jabbing knees, stamping feet. The two men reeled from one side of the elevator to the other, and the doors started to close again.

"Quick," yelled Yazawa, who was waving the stun gun around wildly. "Stop them."

Mitchell punched the call button, but to no effect. Just as the elevator doors were on the point of sliding shut, he jammed his foot inside. The doors squealed to a stop, but it was impossible to force them open again, impossible to make out what was happening on the other side. Mitchell stood there helplessly, his foot wedged in the gap. If he removed it, the doors would slam shut and the elevator would go up to the next floor. If he didn't, he would have to stay rooted to the spot and wait for the door to be opened from the inside.

In a matter of seconds, it was. There was a grunt, a whoosh of breath rapidly exhaled, then a dull thud. The doors opened and Mori was standing there, his face screwed up in a wince of pain. Behind him the disciple lay slumped in the corner, legs splayed, head lolling on his chest. A stream of blood was dripping from his lower face onto the linoleum floor.

"Are you all right?" said Mitchell.

"It's those teeth," said Mori, holding up his blood-streaked knuckles for view. "Metal fillings shouldn't be allowed on a guy like that."

They took the elevator up to the first floor. Yazawa stepped out into the corridor and made sure that there was no one around, then they dragged the unconscious disciple through the nearest door. The room that they found themselves in was a large one containing an oblong table of polished wood with a dozen chairs around it and a blackboard covered in figures. It had obviously been used recently for some kind of meeting. There was an ashtray heaped with cigarette butts in the center of the table, and in front of each chair a folder of documents. Mitchell picked up one and examined it.

"Medium-term Outlook," said the embossed characters on the outside. Mitchell quickly rustled through the sheaf of papers inside. Many of them seemed to be covered with charts, tables of figures, and flow diagrams. In the dim light, Mitchell was able to make out only the headings of the sections of text—"Demand Elasticity under Scenario A," "Competitive Strategy," "Total Quality Control in the Manufacturing Process." They meant nothing to him, so he tossed the folder back on the table. To his surprise Mori, who had been standing beside him, immediately

picked it up and started stuffing the contents into the pockets of his overalls.

"What are you doing?" said Mitchell.

"Just a souvenir," said Mori, patting down his bulging pockets.

"Let's move," hissed Yazawa. "We only have minutes before they find
out what's happened."

Hurriedly, they hauled the disciple onto a chair and tied him in place
with the sash of his robe. He was still bleeding freely from the mouth,
and dark bubbles were forming around his squashed nose. Mori grabbed
a plastic wastepaper bin, tossed out the contents, and slid it down over
the disciple's head. "Nice fit," he remarked, and gave it a slap, then hurried to the window.

Mitchell looked out the window. There was a narrow ledge on the
outside and a drop of about fifteen feet onto a patch of uneven ground.
"How do we get down?" he whispered to Yazawa.

"No problem," said Yazawa. "We jump. Like this."

Yazawa pushed the window open, climbed out, and lowered himself
until he was hanging from the ledge. Then he disappeared from view and
there was a thump as he hit the ground. Mitchell peered into the darkness below. He could just make out Yazawa rolling over, then getting to
his feet and gesturing for Mitchell to follow. Mitchell turned around and
looked at Mori.

"It's a long way down," he said.

"Roll with the momentum," said Mori. "Use your shoulder, just like
in judo."

"But I've never tried judo!"

"Shut up and jump!"

Mitchell gingerly stepped out onto the ledge. Roll! That was easier
said than done. What if he rolled forward and landed on his head? What
if he broke his ankle? He wouldn't be able to move. The other two
would leave him to the mercies of these thugs with their staves. Looking
down nervously, Mitchell noticed that there was a dark patch of heavily
overgrown ground a couple of yards to his left. That looked like a much
more comfortable place to land than the hard ground where Yazawa had
dropped. If he could manage to work his way down to the end of the
window ledge, he would be directly above it.

Hands stretched out on either side for balance, Mitchell edged his
way along until he was standing above the dark patch. Yazawa was
nowhere to be seen, but Mori, he noticed, was glaring at him in appar-

ent comprehension. He lowered himself backward from the ledge, hung there for a moment, turned and glanced down to reassure himself of his position, then leapt.

It wasn't such a soft landing as he had hoped, the jarring impact rising through his ankles to his knees, then pitching him face first into the undergrowth. For a moment, Mitchell lay there motionless, the breath knocked out of his body. Then he shot to his feet, just managing to stifle a yelp of panic, and dashed out of the undergrowth. There was a fiery sensation spreading over his cheeks and neck and hands. Looking down, aghast, he realized what had happened. He had plunged straight into a bed of nettles and been stung on every exposed part of his body. His ears stung, his lips stung, his eyelids stung, the places between his fingers stung. And all stung with a ferocity that he had never experienced before. These, Mitchell realized, were Japanese nettles.

Mori watched the foreigner jump up and rush frantically to the side of the building. He looked like a man who had just swallowed a dumpling-sized plug of horseradish. Why hadn't he done what Mori had said? Why did foreigners always think they knew better? Mori shook his head in perplexity.

There was a small scraping sound behind him. Turning around, Mori saw that the disciple tied to the chair was slumping to the left now, not to the right. The wastepaper bin was still firmly jammed over his lolling head, but he was beginning to stir. It wouldn't be long before he returned to consciousness. Mori climbed out the window, hung away from the ledge, and jumped lithely to the ground. Rolling and rising in one movement, he sprinted to where Mitchell and Yazawa were waiting in the shadows.

It wasn't as cloudy as it had been the night before. They were at the side of the main building, shielded by the generator from the gaze of anyone entering or leaving the laboratories and living quarters at the back of the compound. But the fence was thirty yards away, across a patch of open ground bisected by the golf-cart track. There was no choice but to try and scale it in full view of the windows in the main building, many of which were lit. If it had to be done, it might as well be done quickly. Mori signaled to the other two to follow and, stooping low, scuttled for the fence. His brain registered as abstract facts the shooting pains in his knees and thighs and the bruise on his upper arm caused by the gap-toothed disciple.

Reaching the fence, he bent down and made a stoop for Mitchell, who then climbed onto Yazawa's shoulders and carefully picked his way over the barbed wire at the top. He hit the ground with a thump. Yazawa was next. Mori straightened to allow him to stand on his shoulders and he pulled himself up, leaving a foot hanging down for Mori to grab. The fence was made of thick wire netting. Even with Yazawa's foot to help him, it took Mori a good minute to scrabble his way up to the top. Yazawa leapt down on the other side and disappeared behind a clump of bamboo. Mori slid one leg over the barbed wire and eased himself into a straddling position. As he was turning to slide the other leg over, something made him glance at the facing wall of the building. Someone had just switched on a light on the top floor. Mori froze, half-fascinated, as a silhouetted figure passed in front of the window, then stopped and turned. Mori couldn't make out the features, but the profile was unmistakable. The man with the skin like rice paper was looking out the window, staring straight at him. Then, in the blink of an eye, he was gone and the room was dark again.

Mori jerked into action, vaulting over the barbed wire so fast that a spike ripped through his trouser leg and into the flesh of his calf. There was a flash of pain. His brain registered it as another abstract fact, and then his shoulder thumped into the ground. He rolled, sprang to his feet, and raced into the bamboo grove, where Mitchell and Yazawa were waiting.

"Run," he gasped. "We've been seen!"

"Run where?" said Mitchell.

"Straight ahead! Don't stop till you reach the cliff! There's an elevator down to sea level!" said Yazawa.

He stabbed a finger in the direction of the blockhouse. The three of them pounded through the fringes of the forest.

Mitchell had once been a useful track athlete—school champion, in fact, of the eight hundred and fifteen hundred meters—but now he was running faster than he had ever run in his life. Under the covering of the forest, visibility was poor. The ground was stony and slippery. There were fallen branches to leap over, strands of creeper to crash through, sudden dips and divots to make him stagger. But the obstacles meant nothing. He flew through the night, heart banging, air rushing past his cheeks. His legs were a machine, driven by his pumping arms and heaving chest. The others were racing through the undergrowth somewhere behind. And somewhere in the compound a siren was wailing. Mitchell plunged onward down a steepening slope. He couldn't feel the stinging on his face and hands anymore. He couldn't feel anything.

Time lost its meaning. He could have been running for five minutes or fifteen when the forest ended and his feet were thudding down on scrubby ground that caused his knees to buckle and his ankles to twist. He stopped and looked around. The other two were not in sight yet. In front of him was a towerlike building set on a cliff. That must be what Mori had been referring to. So now what? Should he wait for them? Mori had said not to stop for anything. Mitchell could still hear the siren wailing back at the main building, also a loudspeaker booming. That meant there were probably just a few minutes left to make a getaway.

Mitchell heard a noise a few hundred yards behind him. Someone was running toward him, tearing through the bushes and brambles. "Faster," he called out urgently. "They'll be here any minute."

The noise was getting closer. It was just one man, he felt sure. Would it be Yazawa or Mori? And what had happened to the other? He could glimpse a figure now, moving quickly between the trees. It wasn't in white, which meant that it couldn't be Mori.

But it wasn't Yazawa either. Mitchell gazed horror-struck as a disciple came bounding out of the forest, his stave at shoulder height. The logical response was to turn and run. Mitchell turned—and found that there was nowhere to go. To his left was the fence, to his right the slope falling away into a rocky gorge. Behind was the cliff's edge and a sheer drop to the glinting sea. There was no choice. He would have to fight.

The disciple was young, no more than twenty-two or -three.

"Hommm!" he bellowed as he charged toward Mitchell, his face distended into a mask of rage. What was that? A cry that they were trained to make in order to strike fear into the enemy? If so, it definitely worked. Mitchell had never before heard a human voice produce such a blood-chillingly savage sound. It told him that this wasn't going to be an Oriental version of a pub brawl. It was going to be a battle to the death. What had Mori said? Be unpredictable; keep the enemy guessing; don't let him settle. And how had Mori disposed of the disciple in the elevator? He had taken the first blow on his hip, then moved in close with knee and fist. That's what Mitchell would do too. It was the only way to neutralize the advantage of the stave.

"Hommm!" Eyes bulging and mouth stretched in a shrieking O of murderous rage, the disciple came rushing toward him. Mitchell turned sideways and dipped into a crouch. He felt like a club batsman adjusting his guard as a top West Indian paceman prepared to deliver his fastest ball. He had to stay cool. He had to keep the enemy guessing.

Without breaking stride, the disciple swished the stave at Mitchell's knees. That was what Mitchell had been expecting. It must be in the training manual, he thought as he stepped forward and swiveled to take the blow on his hip, just as Mori had done. But Mitchell timed the movement a little too early, giving the disciple time to alter the trajectory of the stave. And what he hadn't been expecting was the force of the blow. The stave smashed into his leg six inches above the knee, and the impact sent him staggering sideways, the whole of his upper leg numb with the shock. The disciple swung again, this time for his head, and Mitchell just managed to deflect the blow with his forearm. There was a stabbing pain from his elbow to his wrist.

411

The disciple feinted another blow to Mitchell's head, switched his grip with lightning speed, and made a vicious jab for the groin. Mitchell saw it just in time and leapt in the air, scissoring his legs to avoid the stave. The disciple followed forward with the momentum of his thrust, his head thumping into Mitchell's chest. Somehow Mitchell got a hand to the stave and wrenched sideways and then the two of them were falling to the ground, rolling over in a tangle of limbs, the disciple's face close enough for Mitchell to smell the pickle on his breath.

"Hommm," he roared. *"Hommm, Hommm!"*

The sound had been fearsome from a distance. At a range of six inches from his ear, it was maddeningly piercing. "Shut up, for God's sake," snarled Mitchell, and lashed with his fist, catching the disciple square on the nose. There was a crunch of cartilage, and the shaven head bobbed backward.

"Hommm!"

"Shut up!"

The two of them rose to their feet at the same time and came together in a clinch. The disciple stamped with his heel, catching Mitchell on the side of the foot. Mitchell kept punching with his free hand, but he was too close to get any force into the blows. The disciple pulled away, then raked for Mitchell's eyes with a claw hand. Mitchell saw the hand coming, twisted sideways, and sank his teeth into the tender area between forefinger and thumb.

"*Hommm!*"

Mitchell got it. The disciple was scared too. That ferocious scream was intended to hide his panic.

They staggered around like drunken lovers, locked together as they pounded with their fists, kicked, stamped, and butted. Finally, the disciple hooked an ankle behind Mitchell's knee and he fell backward, the disciple's weight doubling the impact as he hit the ground. Clutched in a hug, they rolled several yards down the stony slope, then came to a halt with the disciple on top. Mitchell struggled to move, but the disciple was pinning him and his hands were like a steel ring around Mitchell's throat. He fought for breath, arms and legs thrashing. The disciple's face was hovering inches above, his mouth twisted into a grimace of concentration as he focused all his strength into his hands. He was breathing in and out in long hisses, like a weight lifter.

"Keep them guessing, be unpredictable." Mori's words resounded in Mitchell's head as a red mist formed in front of his swimming eyes. Suddenly, he closed his eyes, threw out his arms and legs on either side, let his body go completely slack. He held the posture for several seconds, keeping his jaws clamped shut and holding his breath. The disciple finally slackened his grip, then removed a hand from Mitchell's throat and grabbed him by the hair and gave his head a violent shake. Mitchell didn't respond. His outstretched right hand had already located a smooth stone of the right shape and size. As soon as his fingers had closed around it, his eyes popped open again.

"Do!" he yelled. "Do! Do! Do!"

The disciple stared down at him in amazement. Mitchell swung the stone in a swift arc that ended with the side of the disciple's head. There was a *chock* and the disciple slumped forward, covering Mitchell's head with his body. Mitchell braced himself for the impact of fist, knee, or elbow, but there was nothing. The disciple was still. Mitchell grabbed him under the armpits and shoved him aside. The side of his head was wet with blood, which had soaked into Mitchell's shirt.

"Mitchell-kun! You are a very excellent man!"

Mitchell looked up to see Mori and Yazawa sprinting toward him. He staggered to his feet and bent down with his hands on his knees.

"No time to rest," said Mori. "We must move immediately!"

Yazawa stopped and pointed at the disciple, who was lying motion-less on his side. There was a faint bleeping sound coming from the area of his stomach. Mori reached down and pulled a walkie-talkie from in-side the disciple's robe. A small red light was flashing. Mori pushed the switch, and a voice came crackling through a wall of static.

"What happened, Fujita-kun? Did you intercept the intruders?"

"Not yet," said Mori, trying to muffle his voice with his hand.

"Where are you? Describe your position at once!"

"I'm at the back of the living quarters."

Someone else cut in. "What's going on? That isn't Fujita-kun's voice! Where's Fujita-kun!"

"Please wait a moment, honored customer," cooed Mori. "I'll con-nect you straight away."

He ran a few steps forward and hurled the walkie-talkie high into the air. Mitchell watched it spin against the sky, then disappear over the edge of the cliff. Yazawa grabbed him by the shoulder and the three of them scampered for the tower.

413

When they reached the fence, Mori bent down for Mitchell to climb on his back. The foreigner looked a mess. The collar of his shirt had been torn off. He had a swollen lip, scratch marks on both cheeks, and his hair was full of soil and leaves. He was obviously tougher than he looked. Af-ter all, he had just disposed of a fit, well-trained disciple single-handed. That wasn't bad going for an investigator of a purely financial type.

As before, Mitchell was first over the fence, followed by Yazawa. Mori yelled at them to go and check the elevator, then levered himself up over the barbed wire. There were other voices in the air now. Glancing in the direction of the main building, he could make out a golf cart bumping down the slope toward the tower. It was at least five hundred yards away, but closing fast. The disciples must have seen them climbing the fence. Mori watched Yazawa and the foreigner sprint for the tower and wrench open the door. If the elevator were waiting at the top, they should have time to get away. If it had to be called from the bottom, they would be in trouble.

There was no time to lose. Mori leapt to the ground, rolled once, and flipped to his feet. There was a zinging sound from the fence just above his head. One of the disciples had a gun! He hit the ground, rose in a crouch and zigzagged toward the tower. Without turning his head to look, he knew that the golf cart was closer now. He could hear the excited voices of the disciples.

"He is heading for the tower!"

"Aim low! Aim for his legs!"

Bullets were fizzing through the grass on all sides. Mori kept swerving and ducking. Glancing ahead, he saw that the main door of the tower was half-open. He could hear the squeal of the machinery from inside. That was a bad sign. It meant that the other two had had to call the elevator up from the quay below. How long did it take? Three minutes, five, eight? Mori couldn't remember. All he knew was that the disciples were getting closer all the time. It was going to be tight, desperately tight.

Thirty seconds later, he had reached the tower and was diving headlong through the doorway, as bullets rapped into the concrete all around him. He slammed the heavy door shut. Yazawa and the foreigner were at the other end of the room, peering down at the space where the elevator should be.

"What's happening?" snapped Mori

"It's coming," said Mitchell. "It should be here in another few minutes."

"We don't have another few minutes."

Mori dashed back to the door and opened it a few inches. The golf cart was just a hundred yards away now. It was being driven by the senior disciple, the one who had talked of the snake and the mongoose. Next to him was a younger disciple who was waving a pistol and shouting. Much farther behind, about five hundred yards away, a line of golf carts was appearing out of the gloom. Mori counted half a dozen of them before a bullet thwacked into the door inches from his head and he closed it again.

"Another hundred yards to go," reported Mitchell, gazing down at the elevator.

"That's no good. They'll be coming through the door any second now."

The machinery whined and clanked as if in protest. "Give me the stun gun," said Mori. "I'm going outside. If I'm not back when the elevator gets here, go without me."

"You're crazy," said the foreigner. "Step out of that door and you'll get shot."

"I'm not going through the door," said Mori, tucking the stun gun into his belt.

He grabbed the ladder that was leaning against the wall, set it into the open panel in the ceiling, and climbed up. In a matter of seconds, he had pulled himself up onto the roof. Lying flat on his belly, he wriggled along until he reached the edge. Peering down, he watched the golf cart come to a halt a dozen yards from the door. In the distance, the phalanx of golf carts was drawing closer. Mori judged that they would arrive in another five minutes at the latest. This looked like the last throw of the dice.

The two disciples left the golf cart and approached the door. The senior one put his forefinger to his lips. The younger one raised his pistol in acknowledgment. There was something about the way he was carrying it that suggested to Mori that he had never used one before. They paused at the door, gathering themselves for the rush inside. Silently, Mori raised himself onto his hands and knees. He would have to judge it exactly right. The senior disciple placed his hand flat on the door. He turned to the other, and his head bobbed as he gave the count. Mori counted as well. One, two—and jump. *Three,* he counted in midair, a split second before crashing down on the two disciples.

His aim was good. He caught the senior disciple with a knee on the back of the head, driving his face into the door with a loud smack. The other knee landed squarely on the younger disciple's shoulder, knocking the gun from his hand. He gave a squawk of surprise and went sprawling to the ground. Mori fell with him, hitting the ground in a heap. The impact crunched the breath out of him, and for a moment he lay there looking up at two moons in the sky. Then he blinked, and became aware that the young disciple had wriggled away from him and was scrabbling for the gun. Mori made a grab for his legs but missed. He rolled over once, fumbling at his belt. The young disciple got his fingers to the gun, rose to his knees, and swiveled around to face Mori. And Mori was waiting, with the stun gun aimed straight at his groin. Mori pulled the trigger. The disciple squawked again, louder than before, threw his hands in the air, and dived backward. The gun landed on the ground a few feet from Mori. He lunged toward it, stretched out his hands, when suddenly the breath left his body in a mighty rush.

It was a kick so powerful that it lifted his whole body off the ground. Mori went with the momentum, rolling over on his back and gasping for air. He looked up into the frowning face of the senior disciple.

"Come on! The elevator's here!"

That was Yazawa, suddenly sounding so far away. The senior disciple raised a finger at Mori and shook his head. Behind him Mori could make out the line of golf carts, now much closer.

"Go," croaked Mori. "I told you not to wait."

Would they be able to hear him? His voice sounded weak and pathetic. But they had to go now, before all the other disciples arrived. This would be the last chance for any of them to leave the island.

The disciple bestrode him, a foot on either side of Mori's hips. Mori wriggled a few inches backward on his elbows, but the disciple just followed him, never lifting his gaze from Mori's face. This was a dangerous enemy, thought Mori once more. He knew how to concentrate. He couldn't be unsettled or caught off-guard.

Until, that is, the foreigner's voice bellowed from the door of the elevator room. In English.

"Move it, Mori-san! We're fed up with waiting!"

It must have been the sound of an unfamiliar language. The disciple's head flicked around, his attention broken. Mori used the instant he had been given. He jackknifed upward, grabbed at the disciple's groin, squeezed and twisted. The disciple gave a roar of pain and doubled up. Mori released his grip, danced to his feet. He was amazed to see that the foreigner had actually come out of the tower and was jogging toward them.

"Go back," Mori yelled. "There's no time left!"

The disciple straightened, gave his injured groin a last rub, and went into his fighting stance. The man's physical control was incredible. It was as if nothing at all had happened. He glided forward on the balls of his feet and jabbed stiff-fingered for Mori's eyes. Mori saw the blow coming, but it was much faster than he had expected. He managed to jerk his head away just in time. The disciple backed away again. Mori shuffled sideways, feinted a kick to the knee, then aimed a fist at the disciple's throat. The disciple's huge hand plucked it out of the air like a tennis ball. Before Mori had time to react, his knuckles were being crushed in the disciple's iron grip and he was being twisted off-balance. Looking up, he saw the disciple's face, utterly calm, and his other hand rising for a hammer fist to the top of Mori's head.

That was the exact moment when the foreigner charged, catching the disciple in a rugby tackle that knocked him a yard forward. The disciple released Mori's hand, turned, and smashed his right elbow into the foreigner's face, knocking him to the ground. But once again his most powerful weapon—his concentration—had been disturbed. Mori didn't wait for it to recover. He swayed backward, took a deep breath, then put his whole body and whole mind into the production of a perfect reverse kick.

He wanted it to be the smoothest, fastest, most accurate kick that he had ever executed, and it was. Mori's scything heel caught the disciple full on the jaw. He went down like a sack of rice tossed from a delivery truck. But you could never be sure with a man of that power and resilience. Mori followed in, giving a little skip into the air before smashing his foot down on the disciple's lower face. There was no response. It would be a good time before he stood up again.

Mori looked up at the line of advancing golf carts. "Come on," he roared at the foreigner, who was rising groggily to his feet, one hand wrapped around his bleeding mouth. "What are you waiting for?"

He grabbed him by the wrist and they raced toward the tower. Mori crashed through the door, shoulder first. Yazawa was already inside the elevator, his finger hovering on the button. "Push," yelled Mori, as he sprinted for the elevator, jerking the dazed foreigner along.

Yazawa pushed the button. The elevator doors squealed as they slid together. Mori hurled himself through the gap, dragging the foreigner behind him. The doors banged shut. There was an agonizingly long moment of silence, then at last the elevator mechanism began to clank into life and they were slowly, steadily descending toward sea level.

Mori slumped to the floor, sucking in air in big, greedy gulps. He felt like a man who had been holding his breath underwater for the past fifteen minutes.

Sitting in the elevator, shaking his head and blinking, Mitchell remembered doing something foolhardy, but not the reason, if there had been one. It was as if it had happened to someone else. He remembered watching the disciple struggling with Mori. He remembered rushing forward and diving. And that was all. Now he found himself sitting on the floor of an elevator, with a nauseous feeling in his stomach and a mouthful of blood. Mori, who was sitting in the other corner of the elevator, looked across at him and smiled. Mitchell hadn't seen Mori smile like that before.

"That was pretty good," said Mori. "It looks as if you've got quite a talent."

"I am not surprised," said Yazawa, speaking to Mitchell in Japanese for once. "From the first time I met you, I knew that your sincerity was strong. Not so much intelligence, not so much knowledge, but super-sincerity! Well done, Mitchell-san. You have done good work."

Mitchell didn't say anything because he had no idea what to say. Mori had smiled a genuine friendly smile, and told him that he had a talent for fighting. Yazawa had told him that he was super-sincere, and even called him "Mitchell-san." It obviously meant that he was suffering from concussion.

The elevator cage bumped and swayed as it descended. There were mesh doors at both the front and the back. On one side was the rocky cliff face, on the other the sea. After a few minutes, the shape of the harbor became visible from where Mitchell was sitting. Peering straight down, he could see several boats lined up at the quayside.

"That is the one I used to come here," said Yazawa, pointing down. "Unfortunately, it is not such a good boat. The one next to it is much faster."

The other boat was smaller and narrower, with a jutting prow that seemed to curve up out of the water. Even to Mitchell's inexpert eye, it looked shaped for formidable speed.

"And whose boat is that?" he asked.

"It belongs to the killer," said Yazawa informatively. "It is one of his prized possessions."

"So won't he catch us?" said Mitchell nervously.

"In that boat, he could catch us in ten minutes. Fortunately, though, he will not be able to use it!"

Yazawa's face was wreathed with the kind of gleeful expression Mitchell was used to seeing when a stock price was collapsing or soaring in accordance with his predictions. He took a bunch of keys out of his pocket and rattled them triumphantly.

"Wait a moment!" said Mori, holding up a hand. "Can't you hear something?"

Mitchell listened carefully, but couldn't hear anything other than the noise of the elevator machinery. Then he realized what Mori meant. The clanking and squeaking was getting louder and more distinct. The elevator was slowing down!

"They must be in the control room," said Mori grimly. "They'll probably try and bring us back up again."

As if to prove his words, the elevator lurched to a halt. For a moment, it swayed to and fro in silence. Mitchell glanced at Mori and Yazawa.

None of them said anything. Then there was an oily squeal and the machinery started up again. There could be no doubt about what had happened. This time they were rising!

"I thought that might happen," said Mori in a low voice. He stood up, grabbed the mesh doors, and wrenched them open.

"What are you doing?" Mitchell said, wriggling back a few feet. He was uncomfortably aware that there was no longer anything protecting him from the drop of thirty or forty feet.

"This is the only choice," said Mori. He retreated to the cliff-side door, took a deep breath and a few bounding steps, then launched himself into space. Mitchell watched in astonishment as he disappeared from view.

"That's crazy," he said, peering gingerly over the edge. The surface of the sea was black and smooth. There was no sign of Mori. He turned to say something else to Yazawa, but Yazawa was already bracing himself against the other door.

"Do!" he roared, and then he too was leaping into space. Mitchell watched him tumble through the air, then land with a splash in the harbor. The elevator was picking up speed now. Mitchell considered the harbor below—would the impact knock him unconscious? Would he drown? Then he considered what was waiting for him above, and he realized that drowning might not be such a bad option.

In his school days, Mitchell had been quite a good exponent of the triple jump as well. Here was a chance to try out his memory. How did it go again? Long, measured steps, plenty of bounce in the knees—then go! Mitchell sailed into space, black sky above, black sea below. Then the sea was above and the sky was below and the wind was tearing at his clothes as he rolled over and over and the water was rushing up to meet him.

The shock tore at him. He wanted to shout, but kept his lips shut as he plummeted into cold, dark depths. The water dragged at him, slowed him, stopped him. He twisted over, fighting to hold his breath, his ears popping, his chest bursting. The pressure was a gloved hand squashing his face. He kicked his feet and saw bubbles in front of his eyes, rushing water, a glimmer of light, more light, and then finally, as his head punched through the surface, the moon and the stars.

Mitchell splashed wildly with his arms, rolling his head back as his lungs sucked in air. After a few seconds, he blinked the water out of his eyes and looked around. Mori was standing on the quayside, holding out his hand.

"What are you doing?" he bawled. "This is no time for a midnight swim!"

"Where's Yazawa?" shouted Mitchell.

The answer was a throaty roar from the powerboat farther down the quay. Mori pulled him out of the water, and they dashed along the quay. Yazawa was already sitting in the little cockpit at the front of the boat. "This is a unique opportunity for me," he grinned to Mitchell. "I have always wanted to steer a boat of such excellent capability."

"Wait a minute—do you know how the controls work?"

"I am studying quickly, Mitchell-san. There is no cause for worry!"

Mitchell clambered inside and took a seat at the back. He glanced up at the elevator, which had risen nearly two-thirds of the way to the top. Mori rapidly untied the mooring rope and jumped into the boat.

"Hold tight," yelled Yazawa.

Mitchell recalled how Yazawa drove the Isuzu. He locked his seatbelt and grabbed the handrails on both sides. That proved to be a good move. An instant later, the roar of the engine rose to a deafening scream. There was a jolt, and suddenly they were bucking and shuddering and careering at breakneck speed toward the gap at the mouth of the bay, leaving behind them a fat trail of churned-up water.

TWENTY

Snowbird stood on the edge of the cliff watching his precious boat disappear into the darkness. The three men would be on the mainland in a few hours. Between them they knew everything there was to know about the project. Snowbird understood what that meant. Operations would have to be suspended at once. If he moved quickly enough, all might not be lost. There might still be a chance to salvage the key elements and rebuild in an entirely different form. Of course the project would have to be taken out of the hands of the sensei and his band of religious lunatics. Their arrogance and lack of professionalism was the cause of all the problems.

"Prepare the boats!" he shouted at the group of disciples behind him. "Those men must be stopped!"

There was no boat on the island—indeed, probably not one in the whole of Japan—capable of catching Snowbird's boat when it was moving at top speed. He was well aware of that, but for the next few hours it would be useful to have as many of the disciples as possible off the island.

The elevator rose to the top of the cliff and the disciples streamed inside. After the door closed, Snowbird walked over to where the prone figure of the senior disciple lay on the grass. He was just conscious, making little grunting sounds as he tried to breathe through the crushed remains of his nose. When Snowbird knelt down beside him, his eyelids flickered open and he tried to say something.

"Stay quiet," said Snowbird soothingly. "There is no point in making exertions."

He put his hand on the disciple's throat and squeezed. It didn't take long. When the legs had stopped kicking, Snowbird stood up and wiped the smears of blood from his hand. Now it was time for what was likely to prove an extremely difficult conversation with the sensei. Snowbird picked up his attaché case and walked over to the cluster of golf carts. He sat down in one and opened the case on the seat beside him. He chose a stiletto, which he taped to the inside of his arm, and a custommade pistol with a built-in silencer that he had designed himself. It was a weapon that had proven its worth many times before.

Snowbird drove back to the main building and went straight to the top floor. His way was barred by a disciple standing at the door of the sensei's private suite.

"I must speak to the sensei urgently."

"No one may enter now. The sensei is conducting a group meditation session."

Snowbird stared at the disciple. He was young, probably twenty-two or -three.

"Let me explain something," said Snowbird. "If you do not get out of my way, I will kill you immediately."

It wasn't a threat, but a statement of fact. The disciple understood that from Snowbird's tone of voice. He nodded and moved aside. Snowbird pushed the door open and stepped inside.

The room was lit by a single, flickering candle. Snowbird took off his sunglasses, and even then it took him several seconds to make out the figure of Ono sprawling on a cushion in the center of the room, his limbs interlocked with those of two naked girls.

"You have come at an inappropriate time," he said in his rich, sonorous voice. "We are in the midst of a difficult tantric exercise. The minds of these disciples are like lotus buds on the point of opening."

"Please ask them to go," said Snowbird. "There have been developments of an extremely serious nature."

The two girls' bodies were covered in a gleaming lotion. Apparently oblivious to Snowbird's presence, they continued to twist and flex slowly in the candlelight.

"Sensei—the girls . . ."

Ono put a hand on each of their foreheads and muttered something in a language that Snowbird had never heard before. Then he slowly disengaged his limbs from theirs and led them to the door on the other side of the room. On his return he sat down on the cushion again.

"You should drink some tea," he said, indicating the tray of cups on the floor beside him.

Snowbird shook his head. He had seen what that tea could do. He took a seat on the cushion in front of Ono.

"Give me your hand," said Ono.

Without thinking, Snowbird stretched out his hand. Ono lifted it to his mouth and kissed it. "You have come to kill me," he said.

"What gives you such strange thoughts, sensei? I am here to discuss these serious problems that have arisen."

"Discuss? Why discuss when you have already decided? Already tonight you have killed one man, but still your spirit cannot rest."

Had someone observed what had happened at the cliff and reported to Ono already? It scarcely seemed possible. Snowbird ran his tongue over his dry lips. Even in the dim light Ono's luminous eyes were holding him fast.

"In view of what has happened, the project will need drastic restructuring. This should be obvious to both of us, sensei." Snowbird's voice sounded strange to himself, feeble and remote.

"You people have no understanding of the potential of this project," said Ono softly. "You are like monkeys playing with a diamond necklace that you have stolen."

Snowbird's hand slid under his jacket and felt for his favorite weapon. The touch of the cool metal was reassuring. "You are wrong. I fully understand the magnitude of your achievements here."

"No, you cannot understand. What we have created is not a mere narcotic to be peddled in the ghettoes by greedy criminals. It is the key."

"The key, sensei? The key to what?"

"The key to the door of enlightenment. We are in the process of developing new versions, infinitely stronger, irreversible in their effects.

Think of it—our miracle substance could be delivered simultaneously in major cities all over the world."

"Delivered simultaneously? But we haven't the right distribution network for that."

"No distribution network is necessary! With the potencies we have achieved, the possibilities are enormous. It can be introduced into the water supply, formulated as a gas and sprayed from the air, released in crowded places . . ."

Ono was euphoric. Snowbird had never heard him talk like that before. His hand closed around the gun. "And how would you achieve payback on that kind of operation, sensei?"

"The payback that you speak of is the permanent transformation of human consciousness. No price is too high for that!"

What would Ambrose Ho and the other overseas contacts say if they could hear this conversation? It was too disturbing a prospect to contemplate. Drug abuse must have scrambled Ono's mind completely. As Snowbird had suspected, there would be no room for any compromise. He lifted the gun out from under his jacket.

"It's time to dissolve the partnership," he said.

Ono smiled a gentle, weary smile. "Put that down," he said. "You do not need it."

"I'm afraid I do," said Snowbird, aiming the barrel at the center of Ono's forehead. Those eyes were boring into him again, seeming to pulse with a strange inner light. What was stopping him from pulling the trigger? Why was the metal suddenly so hot in his hand?

"You do not need the gun because you have already killed your last man. A wave of force is rushing toward you. In a few seconds, it will knock you flat on your face and end your life. Can you feel it? It is almost here."

Ono sat motionless. His voice was warm and comforting. It reminded Snowbird of the way his mother used to speak to him as a child. But what was he actually saying? Where was this lethal force coming from? Snowbird shook his head to clear it. Ono was talking nonsense again. The man was clearly insane.

"Here it comes."

Ono closed his eyes. Snowbird had just steeled himself to squeeze the trigger when suddenly there was a rumble rising from deep below and the whole room began to jerk like a doll's house being shaken by an angry child. Snowbird pitched forward onto the floor, the gun skidding from his grasp. He twisted, rolled, jumped to his feet with the stiletto blade ready in his hand. Ono was still sitting in the same position on the cushion, but now he was holding Snowbird's gun in his hand.

"You will die with a scream on your lips," he said, shaking his head sadly.

Snowbird measured the distance between them. It was too far. "Don't kill me, sensei," he said, edging a little closer.

"You were dead already," said Ono, raising the gun.

Snowbird leapt. Ono's finger squeezed the trigger. The yakuza's head jerked back and his mouth opened wide. From the depths of his being rose the shriek of a mortally wounded bird plummeting to the frozen earth.

Mitchell, Yazawa, and Mori arrived at the Tokyo waterfront in the darkest hours of the night, and on Mori's advice they parted company immediately. Mitchell had an urgent desire to get back to his apartment as soon as possible, but it was a dozen miles away and he didn't have a single yen on him. His first idea was to bilk a ride in a taxi, but not one would stop for him. It was hard to blame the drivers. With his face covered in blood and dirt and nettle rash and his shirt hanging off him in tatters, he didn't look like the ideal fare. So there was no choice but to cover the distance on foot. He walked briskly, keeping to the back streets where possible. After a while it started to rain—not the usual spring drizzle, but a heavy shower that soaked his hair and ran in rivulets down his neck.

It was shortly after dawn when Mitchell pushed open the door of his apartment and stumbled inside. His feet were soaking wet and numb, his knees and thighs aching with a deep ache that he knew would last for hours, maybe days. He wanted to strip off all his sopping clothes and plunge into his tiny box of a bathtub, but he didn't even glance in that direction. Instead, he went straight to his desk and picked up the phone.

"Midas Investments? Get me Murray Feinman, please."

Mitchell counted six rings. The voice that answered managed to communicate smoothness, cunning, and barely controlled aggression in just a single word. "Pawolski!"

"Good afternoon," said Mitchell carefully. "This is Richard Mitchell in Tokyo. I need to get in touch with Murray Feinman rather urgently."

There was a brief pause before the answer. "That's going to be something of a problem. The guy was just terminated this morning."

"What—at such short notice? That doesn't make sense!"

"It makes perfect sense," said Pawolski breezily. "Henry just got a printout of last month's numbers. Murray's performance sucked real bad, third month in a row."

"But what about Otaman? What decision has been made?"

"That Jap bond deal? Hmmm—I guess now that Murray's ass is grass, it's all down to Henry himself."

The phone turned to rubber in Mitchell's hand. "In that case I need to speak to Mr. Lazarus right away," he said tightly.

Pawolski's chuckle mixed incredulity and sarcasm in equal parts.

"You want to speak to Henry? Give me a break, pal! Henry's not big on calls out of the blue from brokerage phone jockeys."

Mitchell let that pass. He took a deep breath. "Mr. Pawolski, please listen carefully. The information that I have is big enough to have a material impact on your career and mine and even Henry's. We're sitting on a financial time bomb."

Mitchell's deadly serious tone had the desired effect. Pawolski stopped to think, and it didn't take him long to decide. "Okay—put like that I got no choice. But turns out you've been jerking my chain, you're gonna fry for it. It's your cock on the block, Jock!"

The line went dead for thirty seconds before Mitchell heard the distinctive Transylvania-on-Thames accent of Henry Lazarus.

"Ah, Mr. Mitchell! I understand that you have some information to impart."

"It's about Otaman," said Mitchell, the words sticking in his throat. "I want to tell you that something very bad is happening to this company."

"Bad . . ." repeated Lazarus, stretching the word out as if he were hearing it for the first time. "Please explain to me the exact nature of this—ah—badness."

Which is what Mitchell did. He started falteringly, but with the relief of finally being able to spill out everything, he soon found himself speaking with surprising articulateness. He described all his discoveries and suspicions—that Otaman was at the center of a web of fraud and criminal activity; that the company's financial affairs were under the control of yakuza; that the only new investments it was undertaking were for the manufacture and distribution of narcotics. When he had finished, he braced himself for the explosion of wrath. It didn't come. Instead, Lazarus sounded as urbane and relaxed as ever.

"A very interesting story," he purred. "It raises several questions in my mind. Would you say that there is any chance that the company might be rescued? That, for example, the bureaucrats would organize a secret bailout by a syndicate of banks? Such a phenomenon is hardly unknown in Japan, I believe."

"Not this time," said Mitchell. "Not with yakuza and drugs involved. Also, my research shows that the big financial institutions have been quietly dumping the stock for years. Otaman has no friends left at all."

"Really! Then how in your judgment are events likely to develop?"

"The company goes bust," said Mitchell grimly. "Probably the public will never be given the real reason. The newspapers will be fed a story about failed property speculation or something of that sort."

"Fascinating!" said Lazarus, as if the subject were of no more than theoretical interest to him. "So in that case the company's shares would be worthless. And the unsecured bond too."

"That's the only possible outcome."

"And therefore, I suppose, you are recommending that we should sell them short?"

At first, Mitchell was too confused to say anything. It hadn't been his intention to make any recommendation at all. He had only wanted to explain himself, to demonstrate that he too was a victim of this huge deceit, not one of its perpetrators. But then Lazarus's words sunk in, and a door sprang open in his mind. Of course! It would be a certain winner! Selling Otaman stock that you did not own at twelve hundred yen would be a surefire way to make twelve hundred yen. Selling Otaman warrants priced at one thousand dollars would be a surefire way to make one thousand dollars. There would be no risk at all!

"That's exactly what I'm recommending," said Mitchell, his pulse racing with excitement.

"It's certainly an intriguing idea," said Lazarus reflectively. "You make it sound like a no-lose proposition."

Mitchell remembered a phrase that Yazawa had used on more than one occasion. "That's exactly what it is! If you don't take this opportunity, you will regret it forever. When you get up in the morning, you will hate the sight of your own face in the mirror."

Lazarus laughed the warm and pleasant laugh of someone who has left all possibility of danger and damage far behind. "I very much doubt that! To my mind, there are no such things as mistaken choices. Indeed, without the periodic invalidation of theoretical constructs there could be no human progress at all. Farewell, Mr. Mitchell. Try to steer clear of the errors of positivism!"

The line went dead. Mitchell put the receiver back in place and limped across to the sofa, exhaustion and exhilaration mixed in equal parts. Game over, he thought to himself. Player plays again.

Mori spent the night in a capsule hotel in Shimbashi. It was comfortable enough. You couldn't stand up, of course, but Mori didn't want to stand up. He was happy to lie there in the peace and security of his plastic womb, with a small bottle of One Cup sake next to his pillow and a Mild Seven fuming in the ashtray. On the ledge next to his head was a radio that apparently had several hundred different channels. What were you supposed to do with that? It would take hours to go through them all and work out which one you wanted! Mori finally managed to locate some good jazz music. He stubbed out his cigarette, switched off the light, and gave way to Cannonball Adderley, Dexter Gordon, Lee Morgan.

He slept until seven in the morning, then went for a "morning set" at a nearby coffee shop. There was a pay phone in the corner, from which he made a number of calls. One was to Togo, another to a detective at the Marunouchi police station, another to a journalist on one of the weekly scandal sheets. The last call was to a midranking bureaucrat at the Ministry of Justice whom he had helped out a few years back. It was thanks to Mori that photos of the guy dressed in nothing but a bra and garter belt had never reached his wife or, still worse, his department chief.

Next to the coffee shop was a photocopy shop. Mori went inside and made six copies of the documents that he had stuffed into his pockets on the island. Then he bought some envelopes and posted them in the nearest mailbox. What would happen next? He couldn't be sure, but the recipients were all people who knew how to make a noise. And if they chose not to, Mori could find plenty of others who would.

There were still plenty of questions in Mori's mind. According to what Yazawa had told him in the boat, there was a kind of scheme to blackmail a top guy in the Commercial Bank of Japan. Then Mori recalled the two yakuza talking about something called the Black Tulip. That sounded like the name of a soapland or an SM club. If so, it wouldn't be registered as a business name. Without any assistance, tracking it down might take days. Assistance—that gave him an idea. He would call Sachiko at New Japan Research. This was just the kind of task that they were equipped to perform. He returned to the coffee shop, got himself another coffee, and went over to the pay phone.

Sachiko answered the phone herself. "Where have you been these last few days?" she said, almost angrily.

"How do you know I've been anywhere?"

"How do I know? I must have called your office twenty times yesterday. I spent the whole evening waiting outside your apartment!"

Strange idea of the detective business, thought Mori. He explained what he was looking for, then waited while Sachiko's fingers pattered over the keyboard. It didn't take her long to come up with the answer.

"Here it is," she said proudly. "The Black Tulip—a love hotel in Nakano. Thirty rooms, an underground parking lot, and two concealed entrances to the street."

"That's amazing," said Mori. "Next you'll be telling me what the room rates are!"

"If you want," said Sachiko. "It's three thousand yen for a two-hour stay, eight thousand for a full night."

"Very reasonable. Maybe I'll try it out one day."

"I wouldn't if I were you. At least, not unless you have exhibitionist tendencies. According to the note here, the management has recently installed concealed video apparatus in all rooms. Every move you made would be automatically recorded—though I can't imagine that anyone would want to watch!"

"Why not?" said Mori. "It might be quite educational."

She laughed. "You've got a dirty mind, Mori-san."

"You don't like that in a man?"

"On the contrary, I insist on it!"

Mori thanked her for her help.

"Wait a minute, Mori-san! Have you had a chance to think over that business proposition? You know, the agreement of cooperation with our company."

"Yes, I did," said Mori, frowning at the memory. "Generally I'm a cooperative kind of guy, but this one I'm going to have to turn down."

"That's a shame. But perhaps we can cooperate on a less formal basis. You know, just you and me."

Her tone had an underlay of meaning that no man could mistake. A girl like her interested in a man like him? Was she crazy? The idea should have flattered him. Instead he felt faintly disappointed.

"I'm certain we can," he said, and put down the phone. He went back to his seat in the window and swallowed the rest of his coffee. Just outside the window, the first few tips of blossom were appearing on a stunted cherry tree that had somehow survived the swirling carbon monoxide of the street. So the cherry blossom season had finally arrived. Mori had never cared for it much. Frankly, he couldn't see why the cherry trees bothered.

TWENTY-ONE

Mitchell spent the next couple of weeks in north Japan, traveling around the fishing villages, living in cheap inns, talking to older people about nothing much in particular. His resignation from Pearson Darney was communicated by a postcard sent from Sado Island on the Japan Sea coast. The photo on the front was of an idiotically leering mask used in comic dances of exorcism.

He read the newspapers closely. Finally, in early June, the Otaman stock price started to fall, first of all crumbling a few percent a day, then plummeting dramatically. Finally, it was suspended from trading. Then came the stories, at first just a few column inches topped with dull, matter-of-fact headlines. "Banks in discussion with midranking trading house." "Restructuring moves make little progress." Ten days after the process had begun, there appeared the headline that Mitchell had been waiting for—"One hundred years of glory are over—Otaman Corporation declared bank-rupt."

Once back in Tokyo, Mitchell returned to his apartment for what he thought would be the last time. Now that he had no job, a single four-and-a-half mat room with no bath or air-conditioning would be all that he could afford. He would live off cup noodles, tofu sandwiches. No more discos and designer shirts. He would trade in his Fairlady Z for a secondhand bicycle, one of the cheap models with a pannier on the front. An apple would be a luxury item, so would a taxi ride. Still, that was the choice that he had made. He was going to stay. He was going to start from scratch, whatever it might take.

At least, that was what he thought until he listened to the messages on his answering machine. There hadn't been many phone calls in his absence—a couple from his mother, three successive streams of abuse from Dan Rollings, the level of obscenity starting high and rising. Mitchell ignored it. He was past all that now. He went into the kitchen to empty the drawers when he heard the familiar Central European accent coming from his bedroom. He rushed back and listened, hardly believing the evidence of his ears. Henry Lazarus was expressing gratitude. Henry Lazarus wanted him to call back as soon as possible.

He did. The conversation was short. There was a position open at Midas Investments—director of Asian research. It could only be filled by a person with specialist, hands-on experience, someone who could understand not just the numbers but the cultural context. For without the cultural context, as Mitchell had demonstrated so brilliantly, the numbers were totally meaningless, was it not so? Mitchell readily assented. Richard Mitchell—Asian research director of Midas Investments. Asia! He tasted the word in his mouth as if it were a new and exotic fruit. Asia was big. Asia was booming. Asia was full of girls. It was made for him, he was sure.

A few days later, Mitchell went to look at Eiko's apartment, just on the off chance that she might be around. He didn't have anything to say to her, except that he was still alive and he wished her half-brother luck. The marble-lined lobby of the building was as cool and quiet as a tomb. Eiko's mailbox was sealed up with tape, and when Mitchell punched the number of her apartment into the security console there was no reply.

On the way back, he stopped at a little stand and bought a couple of flour-dusted doughnuts. He leaned against a wall and took one from the paper bag the old woman had wrapped them in. It looked good—glistening and spongy fresh. He bit deeply and chewed. Then his mouth stopped moving, and his mind boggled at the signals it was receiving from his taste buds. The doughnut had been spiked with some kind of fiery liquid. He ran to the trash can and spat—once, twice, three times—but still the tingling sensation remained. He walked back to the stall and glared ferociously at the old woman.

"These doughnuts," he growled, pointing down at the tray in front of her. "They are unfit for consumption. They are—"

Something caught his eye. He stopped and stared at the hand-written labels. "Bacon Cheese Doughnut," "Frankfurter Onion Doughnut," and, yes, there it was, "Curry Doughnut." He looked up at the old woman. She was smiling at him gently.

"Would you like to try a different type, honored customer?"

Mitchell shook his head and hurried down to the platform, where he sat down and took the other doughnut from the bag. He put it closer to his nose and sniffed. It wasn't bad, actually. Mitchell liked curry, and he liked doughnuts too. So why had he retched when he put the thing in his mouth? Because he had been expecting a sweet taste, of course. Because the doughnut had so thoroughly demolished his preconceptions. But now he knew. The fact that the doughnut contained curry was no longer a surprise—the doughnut contained curry because it was a curry doughnut. Mitchell took a tentative bite, then began to chew with gathering confidence. He needed to finish the thing before the train arrived.

433

Mori never did get his hands on the videotape, but he did talk to someone who had seen it—a former private investigator who was now loosely affiliated with a gang of low-grade yakuza. His job was to collect the tapes from the Black Tulip once a week, scan through them all, and weed out the promising sections, to be sold to petty blackmailers and porno dealers. Mori remembered him from the days when his arm wasn't as full of holes as a pin cushion and he didn't drink half a bottle of Chinese vodka for breakfast every morning. He owed Mori a favor, but all the same it took a powerful amount of alcohol before he would hint at what he had seen. The subsequent hangover had Mori gray in the face for days.

His fling with Sachiko was fun while it lasted, which wasn't long. After all, how could it be? Somehow Mori didn't feel comfortable sitting in fashionable bars drinking cocktails, or watching her try on clothes in boutiques. It made him feel like he was in a movie of someone else's life.

And as for the idea of taking it further, going to meet her parents, putting on a tuxedo one day and getting married, going shopping, pushing a carriage around a park—that could never have happened, not so long as Mori was Mori.

In the end, though, he did find out about acid jazz. Sachiko gave him a couple of cassettes as a sayonara present. It wasn't bad, actually—a little repetitive, but with a beat that kept on driving ahead. He played it on his Walkman while doing his karate workout in the grounds of the local shrine. The pounding beat was the right memory of Sachiko. It made him feel she was urging him on, telling him that he had to stay fit and youthful. But of course you couldn't stay fit and youthful forever, not when nature was saying the opposite. Time passed, and every summer felt a little bit shorter than the one before. Muscles stiffened up, reactions slowed, memories faded.

Mori heard about what happened to the Peace Technologists from a source in the anti-terrorist unit. A week after his escape, a surprise helicopter raid was mounted on the island. There was little resistance. Some of the disciples fled into the forest, but most gave themselves up immediately, as did all the scientists. The Sisters of Light were rounded up, most of them weeping hysterically, and taken back to Tokyo, where they underwent a long course of deprogramming. In the days immediately after, follow-up raids were made on all the cult's other branch offices and temples. Documents and assets were seized. The weekly magazines began to attack Ono openly, charging him with a litany of abuses and crimes. The only problem was that nobody knew where he was. According to Mori's information, he had left the island just a few hours before the police helicopters came buzzing over the horizon. His timing suggested to Mori that the anti-terrorist unit's much-prized secrecy was not all it was supposed to be.

The hardest part was going to see Sano and explaining what had happened to Yuriko. There was no nice way to put it. She'd been drugged, drowned, tossed onto a bed, and photographed in the arms of a naked stranger. Worse still, there was no hard proof. The verdict would stay accidental death. Sano took it all reasonably well. It was the uncertainty that had been grinding him down, including the suspicion that Yuriko's death might actually have been a suicide. He had spent many nights lying awake, wondering if he had been too harsh or too cold.

Afterward they had some drinks together, and Sano talked of his plans to open a chain of noodle shops in fashionable areas. "This is a new concept in noodles, Mori-san," he said. "I hired a market research company to do the background work. What we're trying to do is attract a new type of customer—younger, slightly higher income than before."

"And how is this new concept going to be different from your old place?"

"How? Everything will be different, of course. There'll be plain white walls, candlelit tables in alcoves, all different kinds of wine and mineral water—"

"Different kinds of water!" exploded Mori. "What do you need that for?"

"Women are a big part of the target here," explained Sano patiently. "Groups of office girls, dating couples, and so on. According to the market research, there is a huge group of people who want to have the experience of eating in a high-class, sophisticated environment that looks and feels like a French restaurant. Except that they don't want to eat French food. They want to eat noodles."

"And what about these noodles?" said Mori suspiciously. "What are you going to do to them?"

"Nothing," said Sano. "I'm using my special formula, the same as before. The first shop opens next month. I'm hoping you'll be there for the opening party."

Mori looked into Sano's smiling face. Making food for people, thought Mori, is this man's destiny. You don't fight your destiny, no matter how much money you make on a real estate deal. If you want to be content, you embrace it.

"I'll be there," he said.

It was about a week later that Mori ran into Miki. A contact in the police department had told him that she was working in a trinket shop in Harajuku, not far from where they had first met. They went out and got a coffee, and Mori introduced himself for the first time.

"So you're not really searching for a new direction in your life at all?"

"No, I'm not. The direction I've already got is basically okay with me."

Miki nodded and sipped her coffee. She didn't seem too surprised. She was looking much better—the color back in her cheeks, and her eyes sharp and lively. For the last week on the island, she had done exactly as Mori said, avoiding the tea and bean jelly, imitating the other girls as much as possible. As a result, she had managed to hang on until the police arrived. Many of the other Sisters of Light were still undergoing deprogramming, such was the strength of their attachment to Ono. Miki had been returned to her family in Hokkaido after less than two weeks. She had soon quarelled with them, though, and made her way back to Tokyo.

"I want to thank you for what you did," she said as he finished his coffee. "If you hadn't appeared that night, I would never have survived. And I remember what you tried to tell me on the day you took the test. The warning that you gave about the sensei was absolutely right. He is not a true leader, just a trickster who exploits people's weaknesses."

She was smiling radiantly again, just as she had that day in the Ochanomizu branch. Looking a little more closely, Mori noticed that she was wearing an unusual lapel pin, a silver disc emblazoned with a zigzag mark like a bolt of lightning.

"You like my pin?"

"It's certainly distinctive. Does it have any special meaning?"

"It signifies light," said Miki. "This is the light which breaks through the darkness of ordinary human consciousness."

"Breaks through the darkness," said Mori, puzzled. "Who says so?"

"Noda sensei. He is a man who has many beautiful and profound ideas about life. I have just joined a group of special people who live together, studying his words and trying to follow his principles."

She was looking across the table, smiling in that way that no one who knew anything about life would ever smile.

"Special people," said Mori, his heart sinking. "What kind of people?"

"People looking for new directions. I don't think you would understand."

"You're right about that," said Mori, getting to his feet. "I don't think I would."

He paid the bill and left the coffee shop without looking back. The rainy season was dragging on. The sky was the gray of a liquid-crystal screen, the pavements packed with umbrellas. Mori pushed through them, suddenly keen to get back to Shinjuku. People don't really change, he thought as he straddled his motorbike. The way they dress, the way they talk, the products they use, what they choose to believe in—those things may change. But how they feel when they wake up in the morning—that doesn't change at all. And the city doesn't change either. The ads get pasted over, buildings come and go, everything gets given a different name. But underneath, the patterns stay the same. There are some things that not even an earthquake can shift.

Mori slid the battered helmet over his head and turned the key in the ignition. The Honda started the first time, as it always did. Revving the engine to a whine, he went slicing through the rain-slick streets.

In a remote and tiny village deep in the Japan Alps, the rain patters continuously on the roof of the old temple. Eaves, gutters, the birds in the trees, dogs' faces, hunters' rifles, schoolchildren's satchels, the priest's battered old umbrella—everything is running or dripping with water. Several of the mountain paths have turned into mud slides, and the stream that divides the village has become a gushing torrent. Day after day, the world dissolves in the hazy rain.

One night, the priest waits up until the little street is deserted and all the lights are out in the village, then hurries back to the temple, where he enters a little-used back room. When he emerges an hour later, there is another man with him, shaven-headed and also dressed in a dark kimono. Together they are carrying a large box on their shoulders. It is not heavy, but cumbersome, and several times they slip in the mud as they make their way along the path that leads up the mountain from the back of the temple. The two men do not speak. The only sounds are the brushing of their arms against the wet branches of the trees and the sucking of their boots in the mud.

It takes them over an hour to trudge up the mountainside to the clearing and the little shed. There is no moon, and the priest fumbles at the lock for several minutes before he pushes open the door and goes inside and lights a candle. The other man, who follows him in, looks gaunt, with sunken cheeks and bony arms sticking out of his kimono sleeves. There is, however, a burning intensity in his eyes. Around his neck he is wearing a rosary of ancient wooden beads and he gives off a strong smell of incense.

The two men lay the box down on the floor of the shed, then open the canvas bag that lies on a dusty table. It contains shovels, picks, and other tools. They take two each, then walk out into the drizzle. The priest has in his hand a little instrument of polished wood and glass. The other man watches as he raises it to his eyes. In the dark it is hard for him to use it with any accuracy, but still he goes through the motions, squinting in the direction of the peak, then adjusting the angle of the joint to the calibrations notched into the wood. After some minutes of pacing around the clearing, the priest stops and scratches some lines on the ground with a pointed bamboo stick. Then the two men start digging.

The soil is soft and receptive to the blade of the shovel and the point of the pick. They work continuously, their kimonos soaked, their backs running with water. When the hole is deep enough, they take turns standing inside and shoveling. Gradually, the pile of soil at the side grows larger, and the hole grows deeper. When completed it is about six feet square and six feet deep. They return to the shed, bring out the box, and place it carefully into the hole. Then the man wearing the rosary looks at the priest and smiles.

"I am humbly grateful," he says and gives a deep bow.

The priest says nothing, but there is a sudden twitch of his Adam's apple. The man wearing the rosary climbs into the box and sits in the lotus position. His fingers entwined in a mystical sign, he begins to chant in a deep clear voice. The priest carefully lays the lid of the box in place and uses a hammer with a head of stone to bang in the nails. Then, picking up the shovel again, he begins to throw the soil down onto the lid of the box.

He works quickly, but he is alone now and his back and shoulders are aching. By the time he has finished the gray light of dawn is already seeping over the horizon. Still the droning voice can be heard through the covering of soil. The priest returns the tools to the shed and locks it up. Then, just as the first birds are cheep-cheeping a welcome to the new day, he walks back to the patch of freshly dug earth, takes the conch shell that hangs from his sash and lifts it to his lips. He gives a single blast that echoes across the rain-swept valley, loud enough to wake every living creature. Then he turns and starts to pick his way down the slippery path.

A week later the rains have lifted. The sky is the intense blue of copper-sulfate crystals, and the heavy sun is baking the mountainside. Shortly before noon, a ten-year-old girl runs screaming through the drowsy village, causing the dogs to bark and the chickens to squawk. She tears into the yard where her father is kneeling over a block of wood that he is carving into a mask for the village festival.

"Hide me somewhere," she shrieks, seizing her father's shoulder. "Don't let him get me, please!"

Her father lays his knife down on the ground and puts his arm around her waist. "Get you? Who's trying to get you?"

"The long-nosed monster of the mountains. I know it's him! I heard him screaming out for blood."

The father smiles and picks up the knife again. "That's nothing but a children's story," he says, shaking his head. "Aren't you old enough not to worry about such things?"

"It's not a story," shouts the child. "It's true. I was up there picking berries and I heard him screaming and screaming."

She stamps her feet, furious at not being believed, and erupts into a wail of absolute despair. The father looks at her thoughtfully. It is a long time since he has seen her cry like this. She is red in the face, and tears are streaming down her cheeks. He stands up, lifts her off her feet, and holds her to his shoulder.

"It's all right," he says soothingly. "You don't need to worry. Don't you know—the long-nosed monster never comes down from the mountain! He has to stay there all the time, to protect his den from monkeys and bears."

439

"Really?" she says.

"Really," says the father. "All you have to do is stay away and he will never bother you again."

"That's good," says the girl, her sobs dying down a little. "I promise to stay away. I promise I will never go to that path again for the rest of my life."

Her father nods and lets her gently down again. He is wondering how long she will keep that promise. He doesn't know that she will keep it forever.

Kinoshita-kun's run from the edge of the penalty box was superbly timed. He met the corner kick on the half-volley, and the ball rocketed into the top left-hand corner of the net. Mika Tamura watched her father jump to his feet, waving his noise-maker and bellowing his appreciation through a plastic bullhorn.

"*Goal,*" he roared. "*Kinoshita,* you're a *genius!*"

Mika still hadn't worked out the reason for the transformation in her father's behavior, but she approved wholeheartedly. Maybe there wasn't a reason. Maybe it was just his time of life. His working habits had changed completely—coming home at six-thirty every evening, giving up golf and mah-jong. Then there were all these new interests. He went to soccer games every weekend, sometimes with Mika and her boyfriend, sometimes on his own. On Sunday nights he took her mother to a dance club. He quizzed Mika regularly about her school work, which wasn't quite so welcome. He even talked of sending her to Europe this winter to learn French or Italian. Once she would have dismissed that as a typical empty promise. Not any longer. Just last week, he had given her mother a surprise birthday present—three plane tickets for a vacation in Brazil.

"Go, Kinoshita, *go*. Let's have *number two!*"

Mika Tamura watched her father bellow through the bullhorn again. She was resigned to the fact that he would probably keep on bellowing right through to the final whistle.

One steamy day in August, an unsigned, undated postcard arrived in the mailbox outside Richard Mitchell's apartment. The photo on the front was of the King Charles Bridge in Prague, but the postmark was from Vancouver. There were just a few lines of neat handwriting.

> *Dear Mitchell-san,*
> *We are different, you and I. You were born to this world in a building of stone. You learned how to live in a city of bricks and mortar. I was born in a building of wood and paper. I learned how to live in a city of signs.*
> *Stone is solid. Bricks make a good wall. Paper burns and crumples. Signs have many readings.*
> *Remember the only two investment principles that matter—*
> > *What is isn't.*
> > *What isn't is.*
> *Master this knowledge and no market can defeat you.*
> *Listen to the cry of the reptile deep within you!*
> *Do, Mitchell-san, do as if it is your last moment on earth!*

But by that time, Mitchell had already moved to a six-room luxury apartment in Akasaka, having failed to notify the post office of his change of address.